Claire Gingras

D1360289

THIRTY
PIECES

CHAPTER 1

Letňany Exhibition Center, Prague, Czech Republic,
April 7, 2012

Tomas scanned the crowd at the International Trade Fair.
This was his third time working the booth for Antiquanova, a
privately owned mint specializing in replicas of rare, historic
coins. Although the pieces Tomas made weren't authentic, he
earned a reasonable living helping the owner of the medal-
making business produce hand-engraved and stamped collect-
ables. But today he'd earn more with one transaction than he'd
earn in ten years working at the mint, and his employers
didn't have a clue.

He checked his watch. One more hour until he'd meet
his contact outside in the parking lot. Imagine, a member of

the Vatican commissioning him to create replicas of Roman coins. And they were paying him well to do it, too.

Thomas shuddered with excitement, putting one hand in each of his pant's pockets as crowds of people passed from booth to booth. He disregarded them, solely focused on the objects resting in his pockets, his meal ticket to a better future. In his left pocket, he palmed the authentic Roman coin that Everett Cardinal Jusipini, the Vatican archivist, had given him several weeks before. And in his right pocket, he fingered a bag of thirty coins, each an exact replica, perfectly aged and minted reproductions, if he did say so himself.

Unlike the owners of the shop where he worked, Tomas hadn't devoted his life to numismatics and history. He didn't follow archeology. He also wasn't a religious man. He was an artist, a laborer, someone with skilled hands. And soon, he and his wife would pack up the kids and move to a prestigious part of town where he would open his own shop, or maybe take up sculpting again. Now that he had connections in Rome, perhaps the Vatican would commission a sculpture for one of its churches. He could become famous.

"Prominte," he said, pardoning himself for ignoring an attendee standing on the other side of a glass case in front of his booth. The man was interested in the metal work and craftsmanship of one of the historic coins on display. Tomas then recited the details with little enthusiasm, his mind focused on the coins in his pockets instead.

As patiently as he could manage, he attended to the visitors and collectors who approached the booth. He had persuaded his two associates to take the early lunch shift so the booth wouldn't be unattended when he left for his covert meeting outside with the cardinal.

At exactly five minutes to the hour, Tomas slipped from the booth, hastily abandoning the exhibition patrons and his coworkers with the ruse of being incredibly hungry. It wouldn't do to keep the cardinal waiting.

He found it easy to disappear into the large crowd of trade fair goers. With his head down and his hands in his pockets, he passed discreetly through the aisles of booths, moving purposefully toward Entrance Four and the rear parking area.

Once outside in the cool air and free of the crowds, Tomas pulled his cell phone from the clip on his belt and checked again for a text message. Nothing. He was on time. Why had he received no message about where to go from here as they had discussed?

He paced restlessly back and forth in the VIP parking lot, cell phone in hand. He searched his memory, worried he had misremembered his instructions, when a black sedan rounded the corner, pulled up, and stopped several feet from him. The midday sun reflected sharply off the highly polished roof. Then the front passenger window rolled partway down, and Everett Cardinal Jusipini peered out at Tomas. "Get in," the cardinal said, sounding more like a Czech Republic officer than the soft-spoken man of God Tomas had met weeks earlier.

Whatever. As long as he got paid, Tomas would play any top-secret Vatican game they wanted.

He opened the back door and slipped in.

The heat in the car was set too high, and Tomas immediately started sweating. It was April and these guys were toasting up the car's cabin as though it were winter outside. He didn't dare complain. No use angering his benefactor.

"Your eminence," Tomas began, not sure what to say, wondering how this was going to play out.

The driver slowly maneuvered the car around the perimeter of the parking lot. Tomas wondered how much the driver knew about the coins or the deal he'd made with the cardinal. Was the man an assigned driver for Vatican emissaries, or just some local hired hand? The man could have passed for either Italian or Russian, with dark hair curling below his driving cap and skin that was neither dark nor pale.

"You have the coins?" The cardinal's voice startled Tomas, even though His Holiness hadn't spoken loudly. Something about the tone, the manner in which the cardinal inquired without turning in his seat, made Tomas shiver despite the heat.

"I do." He patted his pockets.

"You understand that discretion and secrecy are of the utmost importance regarding this exchange?" The cardinal's head turned ever so slightly toward the back seat, his chin lifting as he posed the question.

"I understand," Tomas replied.

The chin dipped in acknowledgement. "I have your payment, in cash, as we discussed, secured in this lunch pail. Please don't open it in front of anyone."

Tomas peered at the ordinary aluminum lunch pail the cardinal held, noticing the official signature gold ring flashing in the sunlight. The piece was extraordinarily crafted.

The car pulled up to Exit Four, having gone full circle.

"The coins?" the cardinal said, reaching over his shoulder,

again rudely not turning in his seat, as if looking at Tomas would be beneath him.

Tomas removed the coins from his pocket and placed them in the outstretched hand, the tips of his fingers connecting with the other man's palm. The cardinal's skin was burning hot, and although it might have been a trick of the light, Tomas swore he saw blood beneath the holy man's shirt cuffs. He felt burned by the contact, almost electrocuted by a strange energy passing through the cardinal's palm, and pulled away.

"Leave quickly and do not speak of this to anyone," the cardinal said, passing Tomas the lunch pail. At the same time, the door of the car unlocked, and Tomas understood that he was being dismissed.

No sooner had he exited the car than it pulled away and vanished around the corner of the building. Tomas felt lightheaded after emerging from the heat, the tension, and the uncomfortable exchange. His heart was thumping madly in his chest, so wildly, it almost hurt to breathe. Sweat oozed from all his pores, even though he was no longer hot, making his grip on the lunch pail slippery. He felt disorientated and flu-like, achy and shivering all of a sudden.

Tomas took only a few dozen steps into the building when, without any warning, he fell to the exhibition hall floor, the pail hitting the cement with a crack. The last thing he saw before he died of a unexplained seizure were several plastic-wrapped sandwiches scattered on the showroom floor spilling from the lunch pail where his money should have been.

Grand Cayman Island, Western Caribbean, May 24, 2031

As Celia ventured from the boat dock toward the maze of streets extending from the port, the lining of her sundress stuck to her in the mid-morning heat. She wanted to rip it off and yearned to return to the creature comforts of the cruise ship, the dark refuge of their cabin below deck, and the blessed distraction of a fruity cocktail. But she had agreed to go ashore with Sadie, her best friend, who insisted they take this trip in the first place.

This was a cruise into uncharted waters, out from a time of grief, with Celia fairly new to widowhood, venturing into life as a single woman again. She wasn't really ready to jump into those waters, but she'd agreed to stick in her toe. She was willing to try to move forward, never having been one to dwell too heavily on loss. In fact, she often preached to her friends the benefits of living in the moment, and it was during one of those very emails to Sadie that her words were thrown right back in her face. "We need to do something fun!" Sadie had insisted. And here they were in the Cayman Islands.

"I need some sunglasses," Sadie said. "Christ, it's hot!" Her sweat dripped on the map, and she flicked it off with a sweaty hand. "We're here, I think." She pointed to an intersection on the map.

On the hunt for souvenir shops, the women took the street leading them to several Cayman banks, and more jewelry stores than any civilization should require. They slipped quickly from the shade of one storefront to the next, finally stopping at the Cayman Treasure Coins Company.

The very moment they entered there, the two were sucked in and held by the variety of interesting, exotic ornaments, jewelry, and trinkets, and by the blast of a very effective AC unit. "This is a pirate store," Sadie said, holding out a mini-brochure. "It sells treasures and antique nautical stuff." She hovered over some antique ship parts while Celia browsed through the unusual furniture, also nautical in origin.

Toward the back of the shop was a case full of coins in an array of gold, silver, and bronze, some with the traditional skull and crossbones. Dozens of the coins were polished bright and shiny, while others were worn in places and tarnished.

Two salespeople appeared, and the younger one started to show Sadie some coins at her request. The older woman, with unusual greenish-gold eyes, stepped in front of Celia. A long pause took place, full of uncomfortable expectation. Celia wasn't sure what to do with herself, but finally felt obliged to speak. "Are these all from pirate ships?" she asked.

"No, but many have been recovered from the sea." the salesperson answered. "Some we trade or purchase from collectors. They're arranged by date. The oldest on the left and the most recent on the right."

"Are they more expensive the older they are?" Celia supposed so.

"Not necessarily. The rarest coins cost more than the common ones, even if they're more recent in date. We have papers of authenticity for all our coins."

A tiny brownish coin with unusual markings caught Celia's attention, and the salesperson seemed to notice so with her keen and watchful cat-colored eyes. She removed the piece from the case and placed it on a small velvet cloth. "This is a widow's mite, also known as a lepton," she explained. "Dating from before the time of Christ, it was worth less than a quadran—the smallest Roman coin at the time."

Celia recoiled slightly. She hated the word, "widow." It brought to mind hunched-back old women with walkers. The definition of the word bothered her, too, especially since she was one. She'd looked it up once, and the definition was of a woman whose husband is dead and who hasn't remarried. Did that mean that if you remarried, you overrode the fact that your previous husband had died because you were no longer a widow?

"What are these markings?" she asked. "Is this a ship's wheel?"

"That's the star of eight rays," the salesperson explained. "And the other side has the blooming lotus scepter of ancient Egypt. In the Synoptic gospels, Jesus was teaching at the temple in Jerusalem and he professed that the poor widow had given all she owned, which made her offering worth more than that of the others, who had plenty. That's why they call it a widow's mite."

The saleswoman showed Celia a few other samples. "We sell them for thirty-five dollars, US currency. They're really very common coins, but make for interesting conversation pieces. People like what they represent—generosity and sacrifice."

But Celia wasn't interested in buying a coin, especially one associated with the word, "widow." Sadie, at the far end of the case, was listening to the entire history of pirates in the Caribbean. Celia's stomach was growling.

The woman said, "Of course, even more valuable is the coin of betrayal."

When Celia's head came up, the salesperson apparently

caught her reaction. Her golden eyes held fast as she continued to say, "Silver coins, like the ones Judas was paid for betraying Christ."

Removing a darkened silver coin with strange, purple edging along the right side, the salesperson placed it in front of Celia. "People of faith understand that Judas's mission was to play the role of betrayer in order for us all to have eternal salvation. Heaven, if you may. If he hadn't betrayed Christ, how would He have been able to fulfill His destiny and God's will? Judas made the ultimate sacrifice. And in so doing, he lost the person he loved most in the whole world."

Her words crossed the space between the two of them and struck a resonant chord with Celia. She thought about her college love, Ryan, and his calling to the priesthood, a choice that had haunted her for many years. She'd often wondered if losing her been a sacrifice, or did Ryan find her love easily replaced by the Church?

To her, Ryan's choosing God had been a betrayal. It had broken her heart and she'd resented God and the Church for a long time because of it. That break with faith became more poignant when she lost a child, and then, more recently, her husband had died. God had stolen those she loved in one way or another.

The coin was warm and solid when Celia picked it up and turned it around, finding a head on one side and an eagle on the other. Many coins in the case were in better condition, but she like this flawed piece. To her, it represented the human condition.

Pointing to the head on the coin, she asked, "Is this Caesar?"

The salesperson laughed. "No, this is the face of the god

of the Phoenicians, named Melqarth, or Baal, who's related to Hercules." Celia raised her eyebrows in surprise.

"How does a shop in the Cayman Islands carry coins from ancient Rome?"

"We get them from everywhere. Roman coins have been unearthed all around the world. This one, I think, was from the ruins of Qumran."

"Yes," Celia said, pretending she had a clue as to what the saleswoman was talking about. She stared at the coin and said, "How far you have traveled," knowing she was speaking for herself, too, and wondering if she looked as worn.

The salesperson asked, "Shall I mount it for you on a chain?"

Celia hadn't agreed to buy the coin, but found herself saying, "Yes, that would be nice," not knowing why she wanted the thing except that the term "betrayal" struck something in her.

When the salesperson took the coin from her, Celia felt a sudden sense of loss. Her hand was light, and she missed the weight of the coin in her palm. She felt like weeping, and wondered if thinking about Ryan, being here after the loss of her husband, and considering the pain of Jesus and Judas was just too intense for a fun adventure in the Cayman Islands.

She shook off her emotion and turned to see Sadie paying for a mixed handful of coins. The other salesperson placed Sadie's purchase in a felt bag and then slipped that bag into a traditional shopping bag with a handle.

Ms. Cat-eyes returned with Celia's coin set in a delicate

gold harness of sorts, which crossed behind the coin and held it tenderly with little prongs on the front. She'd mounted it with the eagle facing outward—tails up, so to speak. A loop at the top wrapped around a pretty silver box chain.

"The eagle symbolizes strength, courage, farsightedness, and immortality. It's considered to be the king of the air and the messenger of the highest gods. The eagle is regarded as a holy bird, a protective spirit, and a guardian of heaven."

She placed the chain around Celia's neck, and when the coin settled above her heart, her pulse sped up. "The chain and setting are forty dollars," the saleswoman said, "so your total is ninety-five dollars."

"What'd you get?" Sadie asked.

"A silver coin," Celia said, but Sadie wasn't paying attention.

Sadie was, instead, looking through her bags, and saying to Celia, "Let's eat. I'm starved now. The store owner told me the best place for Cajun food isn't far from here. C'mon, before I forget how to get there."

Sadie grabbed Celia by the arm. "Besides, we only have three hours until we're due back on board, and you wanted to go to that turtle museum."

The heat hit as soon as they exited the shop, but Sadie directed them down side lanes, under the cover of trees, while she described the Cajun restaurant they were looking for. A few moments later, they were sitting at a square table in the center of the restaurant, directly under the air conditioning vent. For the first time all day they actually had a chill.

Maybe the air conditioning was messing with her body,

but Celia felt tingly all over, as if tiny electric currents were charging through her. She felt a little dizzy, too. Could she have heat stroke?

She took the coin between her finger and thumb and held it so she could see it without removing the chain from her neck. Her heart was pounding. What was wrong with her? She didn't feel sick. Actually, come to think of it, she felt great, better than she had felt in ages. She felt awake, wide awake, and more alive suddenly.

"Show me your coins," Celia said as they waited for the food to come.

Sadie poured her coins carefully from the velvet sack. Celia, knowing her so well from their decades of friendship, felt moved by Sadie's innocent interest in the pirate coins, her fantasies of adventure at sea, and her secret love of treasure hunting.

If Sadie hadn't been married, and she had more money to travel, she'd have hiked across the desert, wandered lost forests, and would have eaten her way across Italy - but she had done none of those things. Sadie existed in her quiet life, escaped through novels and movies, stayed home and got older, just like Celia.

The crab cakes arrived first, coated with Creole spices and served with a Cajun remoulade, followed by spicy chicken and corn chowder. This combination, with several helpings of the most delicious, sweet, tender, corn bread, was enough to make them stuffed.

"I don't know how I'll finish my pulled-pork when it comes," Sadie said.

"You'll manage somehow." Celia took a long drink of

water. "A cruise and vacation are nothing if not an opportunity to eat, eat, and eat. And we have eaten our share."

Sadie laughed.

Celia loved the aqua Caribbean décor of the restaurant, the funky artwork on the walls, and the eclectic dinnerware and serving plates. The smell of Gumbo was fresh and feisty, just like the lively banter of the wait staff.

Sadie's smile lit up her face. "Isn't this great?"

"It is," Celia agreed.

She felt different, transformed in some way from earlier in the day. It was odd, but she felt a little high. Could there be something in the food? She stuffed another piece of cornbread in her mouth. Her heart swelled with gratitude for her life-long friend, and for Sadie's intense loyalty and care through Celia's most difficult times. And even more, for her support and cheer when life was good and all was well.

Celia was grateful Sadie was here, despite her other obligations, and the enormous cost of the trip. She came because she knew Celia needed her to come, and that's true friendship. It's the kind of friendship that women write about in novels, and Oprah talked about on her show. It's the friendship of sisters, college roommates, or, in the case of Sadie and Celia, childhood pals.

The pain of Celia's loss eluded her for the first time in a long while. It made her so elated that she considered leaning over the table and planting a big kiss on Sadie, but she restrained herself and said, instead, "You're amazing, you know that? I love you so much and can't thank you enough for coming here with me. It's just what I needed." Then, she touched her heart for emphasis, and patted the warm silver coin nestled just under the fabric of her dress. She felt a peace so complete, so intense, that she didn't even realize she was weeping until a tear dropped onto her arm.

Sadie slid her chair next to Celia, thinking that she was sad - as she had been sad for so very long. But Celia wasn't sad, and didn't have the words to explain it to her friend. She just let the joy ride over her and swam in the love she felt for Sadie, as her best friend leaned over and held her, saying, "It's okay, Sweetie. Let it out."

Porta di S. Anna, Rome, Italy, May 24, 2031

Cardinal Jusipini fought to control his annoyance as he passed the ignorant, unenlightened masses along the street. Lost souls. It became increasingly frustrating, how powerless and misguided everyday mortals were, especially the rich ones who were so certain they had God's favor. Doomed, all of them, just like the pharaohs and hebrews in Egypt who perished in the Red Sea. These people, he sneered, have no insight, no true connection to God. Unlike himself. He was chosen.

Moses brought death, plague, drought, and other curses to those without faith. But unlike Moses who floundered and felt unworthy, the cardinal had no such doubts or misgivings. He would fulfill God's commands. There was no fiery bush to ignite him. The cardinal had read God's words in the Vatican archives, had experienced God's powers come through the coin, and he knew exactly what was expected of him. It had been foretold and now it was happening. He had healed with his will and the laying on of hands, and had killed with that same will, with as little as a touch, men who were weak and unworthy; greedy like the worthless soul who replicated the coins for him.

The cardinal ran his hand along the belt concealed under his robes. It had thirty small pockets sewn in, for thirty pieces of silver - the thirty pieces of silver, paid to Judas, another greedy weak soul, to betray God's only son. Three of the pockets were full. With each genuine coin he acquired, his power grew.

The first coin bestowed the power of healing and stigmata. The Cardinal had been exhalted in the church, given privileges, and had performed miracles.

The second coin's gift was leadership. By then, Cardinal Jusipini had poured over the Qumran documents with vigor. He knew the gifts associated with the coins varied. The documents listed healing, prophecy, tongues, discernment, ministry, leadership, teaching, and purification. Sometimes ministry was referred to as "service", and purification as "cleansing", or being able to perform exorcisms and heal damaged spirits.

As the Vatican Librarian, he had access to new coins that arrived and any documents relating to them. With his new leadership prowess, the Cardinal found himself suddenly very charismatic, his power of influence heightened. But even so, he could not persuade his Holiness the Pope to let him lead the initiative to reunite the coins. The Vatican wanted to control that initiative carefully, to hide away the coins in the library until such time that the prophecy would be fulfilled. They intended to keep him from his destiny.

He ducked beneath the archway and turned toward the archives, bumping head-first into Bishop Enzo who was supposed to be waiting further inside.

"Pardon me." He paused. "You caught me off guard,

Bishop Enzo. I understand you have a relic for me to cata-log."

The bishop's pale face was fleshy. He was one of several Vatican emissaries looking for coins. He was harmless. Bishop Enzo had not one drop of ambition or fear.

They walked toward the library.

Bishop Enzo handed a Roman shekel to Cardinal Jusi-pini. "We have word of a woman publishing propaganda about the church related to the coins. She claims to have stigmata, like yourself."

"Really," the Cardinal's pulse sped up as he deftly pock-eted the coin. He already knew about this woman, Renata, but the bishop did not need to know that. "Has anybody vali-dated her claims?"

"Not yet. They're sending someone. I'm surprised you're not going yourself."

The Cardinal paused, just outside the library entry, performing a ritual of security measures to enter. "Well," he swept his arm to indicate their surroundings. "I'm needed here, no doubt."

Once inside, he removed a replica from his other pocket. "Let's get this archived, shall we."

The bishop nodded, never noticing the switch had been made.

The third coin the Cardinal had acquired bestowed the gift of discernment. He now could read people with formida-ble accuracy. The combined gifts imbued him with a super-natural arsenal. However, there was great suspicion over the changes in him, and the Pontifical Commission had met several times to discuss the situation. They could not decide what steps to take and whether or not his growing influence was from God. He wondered what new power this fourth coin would reveal?

The lights flickered and the windows darkened. Within seconds, they could hear the crack of lightening and the boom of thunder outside the building.

"Sounds like a bad storm is brewing," the bishop said.

"Yes," Cardinal Jusipini agreed, feeling his powers surge from the addition of this latest coin to his collection. "I think you're right."

Grand Cayman Island, Western Caribbean, Carnival Cruise Ship, May 24, 2031

The cruise ship's dining hall was packed. Sadie and Celia sat at their assigned table with eight other passengers who were to be their companions at every meal for the duration of the trip. It was a good policy, if you liked the people in your group. Last evening, they spent the majority of the meal conversing with Alice and Andrew, an older couple who were frequent cruisers. Tonight, they welcomed the elderly couple with nods and smiles, before turning their attention back to their menus.

The two sets of honeymooners sat across from them, engaged in an animated conversation about a glass-bottomed boat ride they took earlier that day. The young, single guys, who got stuck at their table, ordered drinks and perused other tables for young ladies more their age.

After much deliberation, Celia ordered Chicken A La Grecque, described as grilled boneless chicken breast with herbs and garlic, served over linguini and topped with plum tomatoes, artichoke hearts and olives. When their server arrived, the meal smelled like heaven and looked delicious. She loved food presented like fine art - it tasted better. Go figure.

Despite the enormity of their lunch on the island, Celia was hungry again. All that walking, she supposed.

As old folks are prone to do, Andrew was well into his third story of a trip in his past, before the war. Niagara Falls was the destination and subject of this current tale, and Celia listened politely, enthralled more with his deep connection to his wife, and their years of marriage, than with the story.

After a few bites of his aged sirloin steak with three-peppercorn sauce, Andrew stood suddenly and grabbed for his throat. He turned from red to blue almost instantly.

"He's choking!" Alice yelled.

One of the single guys jumped behind Andrew and swiftly administered the Heimlich maneuver. A chunk of meat popped out, but Andrew's color did not restore itself. His hand flew to his chest, and he went down. Celia said, "I think he's having a heart attack."

All the trauma of Jeff's illness and heart problems came rushing back at her. She collapsed to the floor next to Andrew, stunned and panicked.

The single guy, whose name eluded her, started to administer CPR to Andrew. His companion said, "He's a fireman." This fact was immensely reassuring, but Celia stared at Andrew in horror, despite the good care he was receiving. She was remembering her husband, and she was losing him again.

Needing to do something, Celia took Andrew's hand in

hers. The coin around her neck pulsed, and she was filled with warmth. A hot flash enveloped her body, and all sound disappeared momentarily. The palms of her hands burned. She stopped breathing, and tried to stay in the present. This is not Jeff, she said to herself, while others got up from their chairs, and people pressed in to watch. "C'mon Andrew," she pleaded, then exhaled. "Don't leave me."

Nobody seemed to hear her comment, they were so focused on Andrew and administering care to him. The CPR continued and his wife, Alice, wept, standing over him shaking.

Celia looked up, and Sadie was not watching Andrew, or Alice, or the kid administering CPR. She didn't budge when the doctor pushed through the crowd and took over helping Andrew. Instead, Sadie was staring at Celia, her eyes full of concern – wide and watchful.

"You're bleeding," she said.

I am? Celia glanced at her body, but didn't see any blood. Perspiration fell into her eyes. It was the damned heat, she thought. She was on fire.

When she lifted her right arm to wipe away the sweat on her forehead, it came away red. She noticed her head was throbbing.

Suddenly, Andrew gasped and sat up. Celia was still clasping his hand in her left one, but the heat had abated, and her palms no longer hurt. She smiled, euphoric over Andrew's recovery, but people were looking at her strangely.

The doctor examined Andrew and praised the firefighter for his efforts. He asked Celia, "Are you okay, Miss?"

"Yeah," she answered.

"Did you hit your head?

"My head?"

He left Andrew and guided Celia to her chair. Taking a white linen napkin from the table, he pressed it against her forehead. "Hold this here," he said, and went back to Andrew, who was standing and objecting to the fuss.

"I'm fine," Andrew insisted. "Leave me be."

Andrew pulled away from the doctor and sat down in his place, as if nothing had happened. Everybody was still standing, except the two of them.

"I will not," the doctor responded. "You need to come and get some tests taken, right away!"

"When I finish my meal, I will," Andrew explained, as if that was the most logical thing to do. The staff tried to disperse the crowd and get everyone back to their seats.

Andrew looked at her, and said under his breath, "Thank you, Celia."

"I didn't do anything," she said back, embarrassed that she freaked out over his episode, and even worse, seemed to have hurt herself doing it. She held the napkin firmly on her head, feeling faint suddenly.

People were still hovering, and Andrew barked, "Go back to your meals!" He waved his hand at the passengers like he was shooing a stray mutt.

Stubborn old man, Celia thought, as the room started to swim in her vision.

The doctor left Andrew's side again to check her wound. She hadn't remembered banging her head, but she must have. She felt the doctor's cold fingers touching several spots. He looked around the table for a point of impact, but seemed befuddled.

"A utensil, maybe?" He lifted Celia's fork, and then a knife, looked at her head, and said, "No."

"Am I still bleeding?" she asked.

"The bleeding stopped," he told her. "If you have any dizziness, come see me."

"I will," she promised.

"No more alcohol," he warned her.

"Are you kidding?" she said. "If ever there was a time for alcohol, Doctor, this is it."

"Her husband died a year ago of heart failure," Sadie explained.

The doctor nodded in understanding. "Okay," he said. "But, take care."

"I will, I promise."

He touched her head a few more times, his mouth pursed, his blue eyes intent. Then, he looked around the table again, before reminding her to visit him in the morning, and ordered Andrew to come to his office directly from dining.

Sadie said, "Let's go clean you up, Sweetie." She took Celia's arm and lead her towards the restroom while, one-by-one, patrons sat down to resume dining.

The retro, fifties-style bathroom was decorated with giant horizontal mirrors. "Oh my God!" Celia said, catching sight of the trails of dried blood all down her face and on her collar. Her beautiful, pale yellow dress was ruined. Sadie continued to hold her elbow, like she was blind or something. She gently removed herself from Sadie's grip, and stumbled over to the sink.

The cool water was refreshing against her warm skin. After Celia toweled off her face, she made a lame attempt to clean the blood off her clothes, but it was useless. Her eyes looked tired, and her hands were shaky. Seeing her reflection, she understood why the doctor was so perplexed. Her forehead looked like one of those paper targets at a shooting gallery. Several puncture wounds defaced her scalp in an uneven pattern that would not be created by banging her head on the table.

She felt her scalp and found wounds underneath her hair, too. Her hair was matted with blood. "This doesn't make sense," she said to Sadie, who watched on, her face a mask of fear and concern.

Celia washed the blood out of her hair as best she could. She looked at her hands, expecting to find, well, something wrong with them. Earlier, her palms had been burning up and stinging. But now, there was nothing there – not a mark at all.

"You just started bleeding," Sadie said, her eyes so wide she looked like a caricature of herself. "When you took his hand. I was watching you."

"Sadie," Celia took a step towards her, but Sadie shook her head to stop her. She stood straight, still, with her arms flat against her body, unmoving except for her shaking head.

"I'm okay," Celia repeated. "Maybe this is some obscure reaction to the Cajun food. God, I hope I haven't caught a parasite, or something!"

"Maybe," Sadie said. "Do you feel sick?"

"No, I feel fine. Really."

"You always say that," she said.

"I know," Celia tried to assure her. "But this time, it's true."

Sadie softened her stance, but her eyes never left Celia's.

"Really. Scouts honor," Celia said, and made the girl-scout sign with her right hand. She looked at the mirror again. "I can't go back out there and eat like this," she touched the soiled fabric. "Damn, the chicken looked really good, too."

Sadie shoved her. "You scared the hell out of me."

"I know," Celia said. "I scare the hell out of myself."

Boston, Massachusetts, USA, March 18, 2032

It had been a year since the cruise and Celia had dreamed of calling Ryan several times. The stigmata she was experiencing gave her a legitimate excuse. If she were honest with herself, she had dreamed of calling before the cruise, before the stigmata, had dreamed of talking to him often in the twenty years since they parted in college, but this was not a dream and was not something she would have ever imagined needing him for. This felt more like a nightmare - a full-blown, shake in your sheets, sweaty, heart-stopping nightmare. Only, she was wide-awake.

"C'mon Celia, you can do this," she said out loud, holding her can of soda in a vise grip, and staring at the cell phone lying dormant on the table in front of her. She took one deep breath, then two.

When she picked up the phone and flipped it open, her hand was shaking. A picture of her late husband illuminated the LCD screen, making her heart lurch in her chest. Such loss.

After a moment, when she didn't touch any keys, the phone blacked out. She lowered it. The thumb on her left hand spun her wedding ring round and round, while she stared at nothing, lost in thought. There's no harm in calling. She needed help. It was as simple as that. Celia knew she couldn't manage this alone.

She looked at her wedding ring, and then she turned her left hand over and stared at the palm of her hand, at the life-line that ran from below her index finger to her wrist, then lifted her hand to touch the silver coin that hung around her neck. No more stalling. She dialed the phone.

"St. Joseph's Church, how may I help you?" A clear and all-too-cheerful voice said.

"Father Ryan Delaney, please," she heard herself respond, although she couldn't feel her body working or her mouth forming the words. Her voice would be different and surely older than he would remember.

"I'm sorry, Miss, Father Delaney no longer presides here."

"He doesn't?" she asked.

"No, I'm terribly sorry, not for several years now."

She had been certain he would be there. "No, I'm sorry," Celia said, her grip on the small phone becoming slack as she looked out her kitchen window to the woods in back of her house. She touched the coin again. "Do you know where I can reach him?"

"Yes. Father Ryan is a Professor of Religious Studies at Connecticut College."

"Really?" she replied, trying not to sound too disappointed. She never pictured Ryan in academia. "Thank you. I'll try calling him there."

"Okay, Dear. God bless you."

Indeed.

"Good-bye," Celia said, pushing the "end call" button, letting the shock and surprise numb her a moment.

She went into her home office and booted up the computer. Professor? Well, if she had known that before, she would have gone online months ago. The thought that he was on "LinkedIn" was absurd to her. He was supposed to be a priest. She had pictured him so often, imagining him traveling to third-world countries, helping the poor, or in his community counseling people, sharing God's word, and saving souls. That was why he had left her, after all, wasn't it?

The computer screen came alive and Celia Googled his name and the college to see what she'd find. Not "Father Ryan Delaney," but "Professor Ryan Delaney." Even more surprising to read, author and spokesman!

She scratched her forehead and continued reading about him. He'd left the church and preached spirituality outside of organized religion. He wrote a book about "Losing Faith and Finding Your True Spiritual Self."

The course of studies at his college, described online, included: Religious Phenomena, Mysticism, Millenarian Movements, Apocalypticism, and Esoteric spirituality.

Totally baffled, she said, "Who are you?" aloud. And she wondered, as she sat and stared at all the sites that mentioned him, what would he make of her after all this time? Here she was, this semi-spiritual lapsed Catholic who seemed to have run headfirst into God by accident. Would he recall how she once disregarded all he aspired to embrace? Does she now embrace all he desires to disregard?

And, what does she believe? That's really the underlying issue, isn't it? Did she believe in Christ? Or was she only delving into His life to better understand the bizarre events surrounding her now?

Celia stopped reading about Ryan. The irony was too overwhelming. After all these years wishing he had never entered the priesthood, she now found herself desperately wishing he were still a priest. She needed him to be. How would he react to what she had to share with him as Professor Delaney?

Connecticut College, New London, CT, April 26, 2032

Celia stood outside Fanning Hall at Connecticut College, in New London. It was warm and breezy for late April. Her coat zipper stuck, and she struggled with it for several minutes before freeing it, letting some air in.

She knew she should have called ahead, but she hadn't. And now, here she was waiting for Ryan to come out from his afternoon class. Her head was spinning with renditions of what she would say to him after all this time. How are you? Why aren't you a priest anymore? Why did you leave me for the priesthood when I loved you so much?

When she saw him emerge, surrounded by a group of students: mostly boys, she forgot all the words she had planned and rehearsed. Ryan was deep into an animated discussion, but Celia couldn't hear a thing. She was struck deaf as the sight of him threw her back in time, and her knees threatened to fold.

He was wearing khakis and a brown leather pilot's jacket over a light blue oxford shirt. His wavy brown hair blew in the breeze, and he laughed, head thrown back, at something one of his students had said.

She was in a vacuum of remembering. Although she was here, a few yards away, her heart had left her for the past, to her college days, on another campus where they had existed as a pair. The smell of him, his brilliant brown eyes, his kindness, his touch - and most of all, the sound of his laughter.

Eyes closed, she let the images of them sweep over her.

"Celia?"

When she opened her eyes, he was standing there, and Celia was forced back into the present and her purpose for coming. As the past slipped away, she felt dizzy and uncertain.

"Hello," she whispered.

Without hesitation, he leaned in and hugged her tight, like an old lost buddy. The eyes of a dozen students watched with interest. "What are you doing here?" he said, his tone friendly and welcoming. "You look wonderful."

"Thank you, so do you." And she meant every word.

He stood, waiting. She hadn't answered his question, and his momentary surprise at seeing her had passed. He was expectant, but she couldn't find her words. Didn't he notice her traitorous knees as she stepped back slightly to put a bit of space between them?

"I, I..." she stammered. "I need your help."

His smile offered reassurance, and he moved slightly closer, taking her arm at the elbow, and said, "Let's go get some coffee."

"Thanks. That would be great. Thank you."

The school's granite and limestone buildings glistened in the afternoon light while they walked to the North Campus to get coffee at Harris Dining Hall. She tried to look everywhere else but at Ryan as they walked, their bodies close together. Facing him again on a campus was more unnerving than if she had approached him living at the Vatican. It was too familiar to be at a school. He was so accessible here, so normal and human. Also, he was not the distant priest she had imagined, changed by his faith and untouchable and unavailable to her.

He said, "I see you're still married," pointedly glancing at her left hand, where she still wore her wedding ring.

"Actually, I'm a widow," she said. Then, she blurted out, "That's not why I'm here, though. I mean, I'm not here looking for anything, um, romantic from you." And, then, she truly wanted to die. She was an idiot.

"I didn't know—"

"Of course, you didn't," she interrupted. "I don't know what I'm saying. I thought you were still a priest until a few weeks ago. I'm not even sure you're the right person to help me, actually, but I was hoping you could tell me who to speak with. You know, with all your prior connections to the church."

"What is this about, Celia?"

"Ryan, this is a dozen-cups-of-coffee conversation. How much time do you have?"

"As long as you need," was his reply.

Harris Dining Hall was a buzz of activity, but when Ryan and Celia were seated at the oversized booth, the hubbub worked as camouflage. She felt invisible, and the students ignored them for the most part, except for an occasional greeting.

"Before I start," Celia said, unable to curb her curiosity. "What happened to you? How did you end up here?"

He laughed. "That's a seven-dozen-cups-of-coffee conversation."

"Do you still believe in God?"

"Yes," he said.

"Why'd you leave?"

He sighed and rubbed his face with open hands. "That's hard to answer."

After a moment he smiled and shrugged. "Let's just say, there seemed to me to be too many man-made rules that went against what I felt God was asking of me. I no longer wanted to be part of organized religion. I felt there was more, more about God I had to know."

He had always been yearning for something. She remembered that now. And her love had not been enough to satiate that thirst for, whatever. "What'd you do when you left?"

"I meditated, traveled on spiritual pilgrimages, and studied religions - a quest of sorts. I wrote a book about it. I wanted to find answers, a faith that encompassed all the beliefs I'd encountered. It was the acceptance of that possibility that I craved. Here on campus," he spread his arms wide, "I can practice spirituality and share the 'good news' if you will, without limiting it to what the men in the church proclaim is the 'right way.' The kids here are young and open-minded. They question and challenge. The discussions fulfill me and I feel like I am doing more good here, among them, than I ever did as a priest."

She nodded her head, but wasn't sure what to say.

"Are you disappointed?" he asked.

"No," she lied. "Just surprised." They sipped their coffee. "Are you happy, Ryan?"

"Yes," he said without hesitation. "It was the right choice for me."

Like all your choices? She wanted to ask, but didn't dare.

"What is this about?" He sipped his coffee, watching her cautiously over the brim.

"Ryan," she said. "What do you know about stigmata?"

His brows shot up into his hairline in surprise. "A little."

She saw a million questions in his brown eyes. "Have you ever met anyone who had them?"

"No," he admitted.

"Do you know any priests who have?"

"No. Celia, what's going on?"

She pulled her necklace out from under her jersey and said, "Do you know what this is?"

He gently took the coin from her hand and examined it. They were both leaning over the table since she had not removed the coin from the chain around her neck. His breath blew against her chest, and her heart pounded.

"It's a Roman coin," he said, releasing it and settling back into his seat.

"Yes, a Shekel," she explained. "Like the silver coins paid to Judas to betray Jesus."

"And?"

"And," she said, bracing herself and garnering her courage, "since I bought it, I have experienced stigmata. And," she continued before he could get a word in, "I have healed people. Most recently, I think I may have brought a child back from the dead."

The loud dining hall was in stark contrast to the intense silence that followed her confession. She was waiting for him to say, "C'mon Celia." But, he didn't. She started chewing her thumbnail like a maniac.

Ryan watched her face and looked systematically at her eyes and and then her hands with interest.

"Tell me," he said. "Tell me everything."

The dining hall was scheduled to close in half an hour. Ryan and Celia had been in their booth while the sun went down, students dined, and the air grew cold. He had listened without interruption as Celia described the Cruise, the coin purchase, and the event with Andrew.

"That was the first time I experienced a healing phenomenon or a stigmata event," Celia said, finishing off her third cup of coffee, and feeling her stomach starting to rot a little. They had not eaten, and she sensed she was not alone being unsettled by the caffeine and conversation.

"How do you know it was stigmata?" Ryan asked, as she

knew he would.

"I didn't, at first," she admitted. "But several other episodes occurred in sequence over the next ten months that culminated in the event that brought me to find you. I have bled from my wrists, my head, and my side. It doesn't happen every time I heal, and I can't predict when it will come. I'm worried because each episode is worse than the previous one. The pain is escalating, too. Each time it gets more severe and harder to recover from."

"What was the event that brought you here?" he asked.

"I told you already. When I brought someone back from the dead."

She could tell he was considering this, carefully weighing her tale in his mind. When she sensed he was about to speak, she held up her hand and said, "I need to eat. I can't talk anymore, and I know you have questions."

He smiled. "Well, you have given me a lot to think about."

"What?" she joked. "This doesn't happen to you every-day? I thought priests were accustomed to this stuff."

"Not really." He ran his hands through his hair and looked around, like he had just awakened. "Where shall we go for dinner?" he said, stretching and standing.

"Thanks, but I think I took enough of your time today." Purging her tale had left her spent. "If it's okay, I'm going to grab a bite on my own."

"Are you driving home to Massachusetts?" he asked.

"No. I'm staying at the Radisson here in town."

He seemed to think about that. "I need to make my morning classes, but I can get a substitute tomorrow afternoon. Will you meet me for lunch and tell me more?"

"Sure," she agreed.

"How long will you be here?"

"I took a six-month leave of absence from my job. It started two weeks ago. Honestly, I haven't planned much further than speaking to you. I need to get answers, and trying to retain a normal life in this state hasn't been easy. Plus, part of me worries I may be crazy."

His pity was evident. "Celia, you're not crazy."

She started to cry. "How would you know?"

"I know," he assured her. "I know."

"Then you'll help me?" she asked, composing herself.

"Of course I will. Did you doubt it?"

"No," she said, and realized that her words were true. She had doubted herself many times in the last twenty years, but never him.

CHAPTER 2

Raddison Hotel Restaurant, New London, CT,
April 27, 2032

Sitting with Celia again, Ryan couldn't help but remember all the lunches they had shared together twenty years earlier. Although their college café was a poor comparison to the hotel restaurant, the smell of French fries and cooking oil was the same. The small round table, so similar to the ones at school, allowed for comfortable conversation amid the kitchen noise and the sounds of other people eating and talking.

He couldn't believe she was here, back in his life after all this time. She had aged well, so beautiful and kind, so complicated and needy, too, just as she had always been. It hasn't been an easy choice, to join the church, to leave the church. His twenty-one-year-old self had been so sure that he could not have a true spiritual union with God and have Celia, too. That was what the church had preached, and he had believed it. He remembered now, though, as he observed the sparkle in her eye when she laughed, the way she carried herself, God, the way she smelled, how much he loved her, how many nights he lay awake in turmoil over his decision.

After leaving her yesterday, he was compelled by the need to help her, to learn more. He felt elated by her re-emergence into his life and bewildered by her claims of stigmata and her story.

"I've been doing some research about stigmata," he said, anxious to share his newly-found knowledge, to be useful to her, to prove his value so she would stay. They had a lot to sort out, and he knew she wasn't here for him, but she was here, and that was a start. "Although references in church documents mention stigmata, the church doesn't keep a running list of those who've experienced them. Or, if they do, I'm not aware of it. I put a call into someone I trust, Bishop Reilly. We go back a long way."

He stopped to consult his notes. "We've found some information in the books at campus as well as online."

"We?"

"I had some students help me check around regarding recent cases, and I was surprised to read that since the time of St. Francis, in 1224, several hundred cases of true stigmata have been reported. One source says over three hundred cases of stigmata have occurred in Christians. This source also states that there are perhaps twenty known stigmatics alive today. But here's the kicker: Most stigmatics are young, Celia, and they die before age 33, which is the age when we understand Christ died."

"I'm ten years late for that party," she joked.

"That's not funny," he continued to read from his notes, sharing things he learned from the book titled, Stigmata, by Michael Freze.

After a while, she interrupted, "You've learned a lot."

"I have a student, David, who's my research assistant. He did all the legwork," he admitted.

"What did he say when you told him about me?"

He shook his head. "I didn't. I told him I was writing an article. David's a computer whiz kid with a memory to put your average elephant to shame. We have a mutual interest in spiritual history and God through the ages."

"Did he find anything useful?" she asked, clearly hoping for an easy answer.

Ryan shrugged and said, "Monsignor Albert Farges termed the stigmata as a 'mark of favor' in his treatise, written in 1926. From what you've said, Celia, your condition is accompanied by the gift of healing. If that's not a mark of favor, I don't know what is."

"It doesn't feel much like a favor to me," she said. "Do you think you can get a copy of the Monsignor's writings or other documents about this that may not be published?"

"Are you searching for proof that this is real? Is that why you've come to me?"

"I don't need proof."

"So, you're sure this is what you're experiencing?"

"Yes," she picked at the salad she ordered, her eyes pleading with him to believe. She needn't worry. One thing he knew for certain, Celia wasn't a liar. She never was and never would be. She was not the type to manipulate.

She said, "The day after Andrew had his heart attack, I went to the doctor's office on the ship. The doctor examined my head, Ryan. There was no sign of the wounds everybody saw plainly the evening before. Not a scab or a mark at all."

She looked around the room, probably to see if anybody was paying them any attention. Ryan's eyes were glued to hers, and he had hardly touched his plate. She leaned in and said, "When the ship's doctor performed tests on Andrew that next morning, thirty years of heart disease were erased. And later, his primary doctor in the States said the same thing. A miracle."

"A miracle," he repeated.

"You know that my husband died of heart disease, right?"

"I didn't know that before," he answered, moving his food around his plate and avoiding eye contact. "But I know all about it now," he glanced at her. "I called Sadie last night —"

"You did?" Her green eyes widened with surprise then narrowed as though questioning him.

He looked away, embarrassed, worried he had crossed some sort of line. Who was he to snoop on her? But he wanted to hear from Sadie what had happened on that ship. "I hope that's okay," he said. He owed her the truth. "I haven't thought of Sadie in years. After your story last night, I wanted to hear her version, too. Not that I didn't believe you, Celia."

"I know," she said at last. "I mean, a scorned ex-girlfriend comes calling with this crazy story —"

"It's not like that," he dropped his fork and took her hands in his. "I was uncomfortable asking you the personal stuff."

"So you asked her?"

He nodded, embarrassed. Her appearance last night took him by surprise and he wanted to know what her life had been like after he entered the seminary. He should have just waited and asked her directly, but his desire to know outweighed patience and common sense. Now he had to own up to what he had learned. "She told me about your husband, Jeff." Ryan let go of her hands and started searching her face for a reaction, but he didn't know her well enough anymore to read her expression. He confessed, "Sadie told me about the miscarriages you had and the baby who lived a few hours."

She looked away and sighed. He couldn't imagine the pain and loss she'd suffered. He could see the shadow of that past pain pulling her shoulders down, draining her, just remembering. He said, "I don't think it's a coincidence that you healed someone with heart disease, and resurrected a dead baby, Celia," he said. "Those situations are ones that are intimately intertwined with who you are. You are predetermined to react intensely to those things."

He paused, and then asked, "Have you healed anyone intentionally? Anyone whose situation didn't resonate with you so deeply?"

He waited for her reply. She was still looking away, lost in thought. He prayed that she was not angry with him. "No," she said, so quietly he almost missed it. She faced him, tears coating her eyes, seemingly locked there by force of will. She breathed in and out, blinked, and the tears receded. "I seem to only be able to cure people when under extreme pressure or when highly empathetic to their situation. Like with my dad."

"Your dad?"

"He has Alzheimer's. I can't heal him, but whenever I visit, he improves. The nurses at the home tell me that the dementia returns when I leave."

He was sorry to hear that. Her father had been a kind, watchful, vital man back when they were a couple. Not knowing what else to say, he offered, "That must be hard for you."

"It's okay. He was in good form until just recently. If I could learn to control it—" she said, letting the thought hang in the air.

"What about the other times? What relation did those instances have to you?" he asked, feeling slightly guilty to be so fascinated by what she was telling him, but he couldn't help himself. Someone he knew, someone he had loved, had stigmata and healing, miraculous powers. It was astonishing, and incredibly compelling.

"None," she answered. "I've had several small episodes, like with my father, when I don't bleed. Then, I've come across accidents, accidentally." She laughed. "That didn't come out right."

He smiled. "I know what you're trying to say."

"It's like, well, not to sound dramatic, but I'm a magnet for disaster. I seem to keep arriving places where serious injuries or illnesses are happening, and I instinctually respond. Someone falls, or gets hit by a car – right in front of me. I cross the street and bump into a lady just diagnosed with cancer, leaving her OBGYN. Stuff like that."

Ryan exhaled and leaned back in his seat. "How do you

deal with it?"

She threw her hands up in the air, and then let them fall back to the table. "I hid in my house for a while, avoided crowds."

That broke him to hear. She was not someone to hide, she was strong, in his memory, unshakable. "I can't imagine what it must be like to wonder what may happen every time you walk out the door. And you've been all alone through this?"

She started to cry then, the strength draining from her, the brave face dissolving. "Yeah," her broken voice said.

He touched her hand across the table, a small gesture of comfort. He was glad she didn't pull away.

Celia admitted, "It feels good to talk about it. I haven't talked to anyone."

"Why not?"

She laughed then, but it was an angry sound. "You have no idea. This thing, it makes me, like, a freak. It's not something you talk to people about. Nobody wants to talk about it, nobody understands it, most people don't even believe it. They're afraid."

"Are you afraid?" he asked.

"Yes," she admitted.

He wanted to know more. Was she afraid of the pain? Or, maybe, where it will lead – perhaps to her own death? So he asked her and she laughed again. He looked around to see if they were drawing attention, this man and the wild-eyed woman crying and laughing at the same time, but their section of the restaurant was pretty empty.

"You must think I'm crazy," she said.

"I don't," he told her. "I think you're exceptional."

She shook her head, indicating that she wasn't. "I've wanted to die, Ryan, that's the thing. I lost you, I lost Jeff, and I lost my baby – what else was there?"

His regret was immense. He had caused her pain, he knew that. But at the time, it felt righteous, necessary. He thought that she had moved on. He knew she had married. It surprised him to hear that it hadn't been that simple, and he knew he had imagined otherwise so he could bear it himself. "You've suffered. And, now there's something positive that's come from that suffering. Healing. Rebirth. Stigmata. Do you know how I've dreamed of being touched by God? I've prayed for the connection to the Divine. I've felt it, fleetingly, like an elusive ghost, many times. When I became a priest, I thought that connection would magically materialize. But it didn't work that way. And even with fasting, prayer, meditation, and all else, the connection remained elusive and fleeting."

He faced the pain in her eyes, and said with all sincerity, "I'm sorry I made you suffer, Celia. I never meant to hurt you."

"I know," she said. " Thank you for saying that. I felt—" she hesitated. "I wasn't enough for you."

He did not know what to say.

She shrugged. "I knew you craved something that I couldn't offer. I've never been able to stay mad at you for that. And, I had Jeff." Her voice softened. "He filled the void your loss made. He saved me for a while."

And now she had come to him for help. "Celia," he said, "stigmata aren't something I know much about, or even have thought about before yesterday. My studies have focused on other areas of divinity and faith." He reached across the table and took her hand. Turning it over, he ran his thumb across her palm, fascinated by the thought of the bleeding, the symbolism, the power in her healing touch. He was in awe of it.

"What does it feel like?" he asked in a whisper.

She closed her eyes. He had no choice but to wait for her answer. The anticipation pumped through his body, mixed with feelings for her he had forgotten he was capable of feeling.

"They're overwhelming," she said after a few minutes. "At first, I felt just a simple, warm energy. I got feverish. When I bled on the cruise ship the first time, there was very little pain, but each significant act has been increasingly painful." She looked into his eyes for encouragement. "And the last time, the pain was so intense."

"When you saved the baby?"

"Yes." The tears came again, and she let them flow freely.

"What is it?" He asked. "You can tell me. I want to hear."

HealthAlliance Hospital, Leominster, Massachusetts, January 17, 2032

Celia dreaded hospitals. Nothing happy ever happened to her at a hospital. The brief shining moment of joy when she had a baby in the hospital years ago was overshadowed by the tragedy of losing that child. So many sad, dreadful moments had been experienced in a hospital. And since the stigmata had started, it was hard for her to bring herself to walk into one.

But she needed to be here for her best friend today as she brought her newest child into the world. This was no small thing for Celia, sidestepping the pain of not having a child herself, trying to let the love for her friends and their kids override all the other conflicting emotions. Even now, as she sat in the maternity ward playing with her friend Kim's daughter, Cloe, waiting for news of Kim's new baby, she was filled with sorrow and envy instead of hopeful anticipation.

And she missed Jeff. She felt alone. Jeff had been her family, had lived through her longing for a child, her disappointment, and had been her cheerleader. And now he was gone.

The stigmata, the healing, the strange occurrences, all added to her sense of isolation. Nobody understood what she was going through. How could they possibly?

As she sat and dressed a doll with Cloe, waiting for news of a new life in their precious circle, she tried to act "normal". She and Cloe had been playing with her doll set and carriage. Cloe practiced being a big sister, feeding, burping, and walking that doll around and around and around.

Kim's husband burst into the waiting room and announced, "It's a girl. Elaina Louise is eight pounds, two ounces, and Kim is doing fine."

They all clapped and congratulated him. Kim's husband hugged their daughter, Cloe, as she jumped up and down repeatedly and said, "I'm a sister. I'm a sister!" Then, he took her to Kim for some family time and to meet the baby.

An hour later, Celia and her closest friend, Sadie, stood outside the glass window in the neonatal care area together, watching as nurses tended to the newborns. All those beautiful babies, some sleeping, some crying, started off their lives in this strange place. Celia thought of her son, Dylan, who lived for such a brief time. His only impression would have been moments in her arms and then this room - this very room where things went so wrong.

Her hand automatically went to her womb, which still ached with loss. She loved and carried her children there and in her heart, but her arms were forever empty, except that one time, those glorious minutes when she held Dylan and marveled at the miracle of him. She remembered every second. She could feel his slippery skin and see his squinty eyes. She could smell him and remember every black hair on the top of his misshaped head. And she wished, for the millionth time, that she had had more minutes.

The next day, Kim's room was filled with flowers and the wonderful scent concealed the hospital smells nicely. Elaina, the new baby, was beautiful and smelled even better than the flowers. Her lovely, velvety, hairless head received Celia's kisses and rewarded her with the soft scent of powder and freshness. New life.

Perhaps Celia held the baby too reverently because Kim asked her if she was okay. Only a great friend would think to ask that when she was the one who had just pushed out an eight-pound baby the day before.

"I'm fine," Celia said. "She's perfect!"

"Thanks," Kim said, closing her eyes to rest. "And thanks for coming."

"You're welcome." Kim's husband had gone home with

Cloe to get some sleep, so Celia had stayed to keep Kim company

Elaina squirmed and started to cry as Celia held her. Reluctantly, she handed the baby back to Kim. Her arms felt empty as she sat and watched Kim nurse like a pro, something Celia never had the chance to do.

"Since I'm not much help here, I'm going to the café to get something to eat. Can I bring you anything?" she asked, looking for a reason to flee the tender mother-child moment.

"I'd die for some caffeine," Kim said, "but the baby would be up all night!"

"She may be anyway," Celia pointed out.

"Don't say that!"

She laughed. "I'll see if I can find a decaf soda for you. Maybe the sugar will give you a lift."

When Celia was in the elevator, it occurred to her, again, that being in the hospital may not be such a good idea. What if she stumbled upon some sick patient and that brought on a stigmatic episode? It was one thing to hang out in the maternity ward, but as she descended past the floors with cancer patients and Urgent Care, she started to panic. She knew she couldn't let fear keep her from leading her life, but she couldn't stay home or make herself unavailable to the people who needed her. Could she?

In line at the cafeteria, waiting to pay for her sandwich, she breathed a little easier. Her hand covered the silver coin around her neck, where the eagle stood proudly. She regularly took off the necklace, but the coin had already changed her, and the change existed whether she wore it or not. When she was without it, she felt even more the loss of all that mattered to her.

Celia was thinking of the coin when she headed back to Kim's room. As she opened the door, the chaos and noise stopped her short. Kim was crying. The baby, surrounded by nurses, had tubes coming out from all her little parts. Someone was squeezing a bag attached to the baby's mouth and was forcing air into her lungs. Several nurses were issuing orders and rushed around attending to monitors and beeping equipment. Kim noticed Celia from across the room and said, "She had a seizure."

Celia dropped her things on the table by Kim's bed as the panic hit. Kim looked desperate, her face twisted in anguish, and Celia wondered why Kim was just sitting there, holding her breath, while her daughter struggled for her own.

She felt the blood rushing through her veins with an intensity she'd never experienced before as she moved closer to the baby and the melee. One of the nurses noticed her and told her to leave the room, but Celia ignored her, and forced herself into the circle where a female doctor was examining Elaina. The monitor screamed in flat line.

She's dead.

She heard Kim wail, and a nurse apologized.

Celia's breasts ached; her milk long dried.

"Go to your friend," the doctor whispered as she began to remove the tubes and other obstructions from Elaina's tiny, unmoving form.

Celia brushed the doctor's hand aside and laid her head over the baby's body, while her tears fell onto the baby's soft, lovely skin. She knew it was happening when she felt the warmth. She lifted her head and placed her hands on

Elaina. Burning hot pain radiated through her, piercing her side. She screamed and cried as the energy surged. Like the painful shock of a bludgeoned funny bone, an agonizing sensation engulfed her, radiating like electricity from her head and extremities to her torso and then back out again. The room ceased to exist for a moment. And then, when she was aware again, the silence was loud. All eyes were on her as she shuddered and shook from pain.

In no time, Kim was standing next to her, holding her shoulders. Kim broke the silence by yelling at the doctor, "Help her!" And Celia didn't know if she meant her, or the baby.

And then the dead baby mewed; a small sound at first that grew a little louder after a second. Despite the mind-numbing pain, Celia moved her head to look at baby Elaina, now staring back at her, her little arms flailing in the air. The doctor was so shocked she jumped back. Celia was momentarily forgotten as the group, including Kim, gathered around Elaina and examined her once more.

Kim said, "Is she okay?"

Celia crouched on the floor, trying not to pass out.

The doctors didn't answer Kim, so she shouted, "Is my baby okay?" as she stood outside the protective and curious circle now surrounding her child.

"She seems fine," the doctor said, listening to the baby's heart and smiling.

One nurse turned to Celia with questioning eyes, and then noticed the blood staining Celia's shirt and jeans.

"You're bleeding," she said, and guided her to Kim's empty bed.

Celia called out in pain, while Kim took the baby into her arms, and then fell to her knees holding her healthy living daughter. She wept and wailed and, in between, thanked God, and then thanked Celia, and then thanked God again.

"I'm okay," Celia lied to the nurse, knowing there was nothing they could do for her. This needed to take its course. Gritting her teeth against the pain, she said, "I reopened an old wound."

The nurse lifted Celia's shirt and removed her jeans very deftly, then pressed a cloth against the flow of blood from her side. "You need stitches," she said.

Celia didn't have the energy to argue with her, so she left it alone. She couldn't stop shaking. The nurse told her, "It's the pain." The team eventually left the baby with Kim, and attended to Celia. A gurney arrived. They wheeled Celia away just in time for her to catch a glimpse of Kim's joyful tears before she blacked out.

Raddison Hotel, New London, CT, April 27, 2032

Celia sighed. Just the mere retelling of what happened at that hospital stressed her out. Celia's friend Kim had been elated and grateful when her daughter's life was saved, but that moment changed everything for Celia, and not in a good way. She was now a freak. Kim acted strange around her. Nobody seemed to want to admit the truth, herself included. She didn't want any publicity or investigation. So no one spoke of her involvement. Nobody in that room, besides Kim, had known of Celia's past and her healing powers. The nursing staff and the doctors were simply mystified. The incident was considered a fluke and her bleeding side wound an anomaly completely separate from the miraculous recovery of the dead baby. What happened was one of those rare things that no one could explain. Certainly not a miracle. Who believed in miracles these days?

"How long did the bleeding last?" Ryan asked.

The restaurant had grown cold, and the food was too. Celia hugged herself both for warmth and for comfort. "Several days that time. I received transfusions and was in the hospital for over a week while they performed tests and I regained my strength."

She had lost her appetite and Ryan had barely eaten more than a few bites himself. He moved his plate away, gave her a questioning glance and asked, "Why wasn't this in the news?"

She stretched, trying to work out the kinks from their long conversation. How could she answer him? How could she explain? "It's hard to believe even when you go through it first-hand," she said, eventually, trying not to sound as defensive as she felt. "Stick around long enough and you'll see for yourself."

He smirked, as if accepting her challenge.

"A few articles did end up in the tabloids," she said. "You wouldn't have taken notice, since my name wasn't mentioned. I think if I had been bleeding from the hands that time, it would never have been kept quiet. Bleeding hands are a more recognizable form of stigmata."

She looked at her watch. They'd been there for over two hours. "Let's walk for a while. I need to move."

He paid the bill, and they left a substantial tip since they had monopolized the table for so long.

The wind whipped around them as they left the parking lot and headed west down the street. Celia pulled her coat close, and said, "You haven't asked me the questions I thought you would."

"I haven't?" Ryan looked at her sideways while bending his head against the wind.

"Well, you haven't asked why this happened to me. I mean, why me, of all people? God knows I asked myself that a hundred times."

He laughed. It was a sound she loved in her past life, his laughter. She'd forgotten the deep warm timber of his laugh, but it came back to her now like an old friend. "Why not you, Celia?" he said. "Besides, those are questions that priests, even ex-priests, don't usually ask. Maybe this has happened to you because you've suffered. Maybe it's just His plan."

"What about the coin?" she said. "Don't you think it's strange that all this started when I bought it?"

"No, in fact, I don't. Many new age religions suggest that you bring to yourself the very thing you think about - the power of suggestion. You told me yourself that you were thinking about Christ's sacrifice and life when you bought the coin. Why couldn't your focus on Christ have manifested itself in you in this way?"

She shrugged and looked away from him. If she manifested this herself, then it didn't explain the other things.

Ryan must have noticed her discomfort because he asked, "What's bothering you, Celia?"

What's bothering her? What wasn't bothering her. They turned a corner and crossed the street.

She said, "I know the church frowns on worshipping

idols. I remember the story of Moses and the golden calf. I hope you don't think I've lost it, but, Ryan, I think the coin has power." She was so anxious around him, saying these things to him, her heart pounded, and her breath came in long, anxious pulls.

They kept walking a few minutes before he looked at her and said, "It's possible. Maybe the power is in you? Or it's from Him? There are those who believe it's in all of us."

She didn't respond. The wind stopped for a few moments as if it was listening to them.

"Besides," he said, "it's not like the church doesn't embrace symbolism, Celia. God knows, nobody gives any power to the crucifix, or rosary beads, or the papal ring." He looked at her. "That was sarcasm."

She elbowed him. "I know."

He nodded. "We kiss them. We perform rituals around them. What's the difference?"

"There is a difference," she insisted.

He asked, "What are you looking for me to say?"

"I don't know, but I think you are going too easy on me. You're not probing deep enough."

"What were you expecting? An interrogation?"

She faced him square on. "Yes, actually. That and…well, damn it! I thought you were still a priest. And I don't remember you being this open-minded."

"Celia," he said, "I was just a boy when you knew me."

"You were twenty-two," she shot back.

He laughed. "Well, it's been a long journey since then. I've done a lot of growing, a lot of spiritual and life exploration. I've seen and heard all sorts of things from wise and learned people of different religions, nationalities, and perspectives, not to mention my students. They're full of ideals, defiance, and questions. 'What does it all mean?' they want to know. And they want easy answers. Definite answers. Perhaps there aren't any."

"There have to be answers."

He sighed so loudly that she shied away from him, and then he said, "I don't know what you want from me."

She didn't know either. But what came out of her mouth was, "Help."

"Help how?"

She threw her hands up. "I don't know, Ryan. I need guidance. And shit, I need companionship." She moved her head left and right in small measure, shaking it back and forth as if doing so could erase her thoughts and the words she was about to say. But she knew there was no shaking off her feelings or fears. She blurted out, "I'm sick and tired of being alone, of looking down a future alone. I need protection."

He seemed to hesitate a fraction of a second before he asked, "Protection from what?"

"I wish I knew," she said, noticing he was the one who stepped back this time. After a pause, she told him, "There's this woman, Renata, in Italy. She's just like me."

"She has stigmata?"

"And she heals." She nodded and stepped closer to him, absorbing his warmth. "She has a coin, too, Ryan."

His hands were in his pockets. He was staring intently past her, at nothing, almost as if he was thinking so hard and fast that looking at her might slow him down. So, Celia kept talking before he thought himself right back to the safety of his campus.

"Her grandfather found the coin buried in a wall of an old building he was tearing down. Renata doesn't speak English well. It's hard to get the story straight. The coin has been in her family for years, but neither her grandfather nor her father had stigmata. They all touched the coin. As did her mother. But when Renata took the coin after her mother passed, she experienced the same things I did. Shortly afterwards, the stigmata and healing started. Ryan, Renata believes that her coin is one of the actual thirty pieces given to Judas. Judas coins, she calls them. And, one more thing, Renata's coin has the same purple markings on the right side."

She pulled out her coin and turned it to show him the front. "See the purple discoloration here on the right?"

He looked at her, his eyes deeply considering every feature on her face before they lowered to scrutinize the coin.

After several heart beats, she said, "Renata's coin is the same as mine. She scanned it and sent an image of it to me online. I don't think the data you read is accurate. I don't think there are twenty living stigmatics today. I think there are thirty."

"Thirty pieces," he responded, his eyes returning to hers.

"What concerns me is that Renata published things that were in opposition to the beliefs of the Catholic Church."

"It wouldn't be the first time someone did that," he said.

Celia turned around and started walking back.

Ryan followed, asking, "What did she publish?"

"A two-thousand-year-old manuscript," she said over her shoulder as he stepped up and fell back in beside her. "It was written by a Roman concerning the thirty pieces of silver. According to Renata, the ancient manuscript was buried with the coin her grandfather uncovered. On it was a message written by a descendant of the servant of the high priest whose ear was cut off by one of the Romans. In Luke, you know…"

"And one of them struck the servant of the high priest and cut off his right ear," Ryan said. "And He touched his ear and healed him. Christ healed him. His name was Malchus."

"Yes," she smiled, pleased. "That's right."

"You've been studying scripture?"

"Some," she admitted, feeling awkward. She was never the one interested in this stuff, Ryan was.

"Has the scroll been seen by clergy?" he asked.

"I don't know who's seen it." She stopped and cupped her hand around his forearm. "Renata received threats, Ryan. Angry emails and letters arrived from people calling her a freak, some saying she's a heretic. Catholics and non-Catholics stormed her house, wanting to hurt her, or be near her for one reason or another."

He nodded his head as if that was to be expected. "Is this why you kept quiet for so long?"

"I guess," she said, looking at her feet, unable to admit what a coward she'd been and how she disbelieved.

"Why go public now? Why did it take a year to contact me?"

She paused. There were so many reasons she had waited, but only one solid excuse for finally calling. "Renata's teenaged son was harassed at school. We spoke several times when her situation started to escalate. Once the press arrived, she couldn't manage the madness. Then, her house was ransacked one day while she was at work."

"Geez," Ryan says, shaking his head. "Does she know who did it?"

"No."

"Did they get anything?" he asked.

"I don't know. She's disappeared," Celia told him, crossing her arms over her chest while they resumed walking, and trying to look braver than she felt. "Renata was afraid for her own safety, and for her son's safety. I think she's in hiding."

"Why do you think that?"

"I tried to reach her several times after the break in. Then, I received a bizarre email claiming to be from Renata from an address I didn't know. The email implored me to come to the Vatican and to meet there. I have it back in my hotel room. I never replied, and I don't know if the email was legit or where she could be. Anyone could have sent it."

They stopped walking again and then stood, shivering, in the parking lot of the hotel. Ryan said, "Did she give you any indication of what she had planned?"

"Renata believes that we, and others like us, are meant to spread God's message. Because of that scroll - the message from the servant's son."

He looked perturbed. Ryan may have believed her all the way up until that point, but this seemed to have him doubting. Doubting her, she was sure. She guessed what he would ask before the words left his lips. And she knew she would give him the answer she had prepared – no matter the cost.

"What's in the message?"

"A prediction."

"Of what?"

"The end of the world. Or its rebirth," she said.

CHAPTER 3

Raddison Hotel Restaurant, New London, CT,
April 27, 2032

The hotel room was too warm. It had been an hour since their walk, and the heat that was so welcome at first was now stifling. Ryan sat at the desk reading several of the documents Celia had. He made his way through the email from Renata, and through the copy of the scroll Renata's grandfather found with the coin in Italy. Now, he was reading documents Celia had tracked down after Renata disappeared: photocopies of scrolls uncovered during an archeological dig.

Celia stood over his shoulder, her anxiety making it hard for him to focus on what he was reading. He yearned to take the papers back to campus and study them without an audi-

ence, but it was clear Celia needed him, and he was determined not to disappoint her again. She breathed on his neck
she was standing so close behind him.

He turned. "There's a lot here," he said in the most soothing tone he could manage. "I know you're desperate for
some sort of instant explanation, but I don't have one."

She looked deflated. With a gentle touch, he guided her
into the chair next to the desk. He put his elbows on his knees
and leaned in close to her, knowing that this body language
encouraged confidence, and safe intimacy. "I need you to be
patient. Take a deep breath, and let's talk through this one
step at a time."

She did as he asked, sitting up straight and inhaling
deeply, then letting her breath out in a rush. He took her
hands in his, feeling a connection, a longing, that he had
long ago dismissed as a young man's foolishness, but he
now recognized as something more. After all this time, and
only a few hours in her presence, it felt like only a blink, a
breath, a moment since they had departed from each other's
lives. It was incredible what he remembered, how familiar
she seemed, how right it felt to be together, talking, touching, even if the circumstances were so unusual. He tried to
stay focused on the topic. He had to tap into his vocation,
put aside boyish thoughts, and be the man she had sought to
guide her through this difficult time.

He picked up one of the documents. "This is signed
Antoninus."

"I know." She took the document. "Apparently, he was a
descendant of a Roman guard who was present when Judas
betrayed Jesus. The ancient writing is in Greek, but the notes
are in English, as you can see."

"Where did they come from? And whose notes are these in the margins?" He pointed to the page.

"A woman named Margaret wrote the notes. She was working as a researcher with an archeologist named Roland de Vaux in the 1940s when he discovered a hoard of five hundred and sixty-one silver coins at the ruins of Qumran."

"Qumran?" Ryan said. "The Dead Sea Scrolls were found there."

"That's right."

"So, you're telling me that significant religious documents, relating to Christ, were hidden with Renata's coin in Italy, and related documents were hidden with this 'hoard' of coins in Qumran?" He shuffled through the papers, scanning them again.

"That's what I'm saying."

He thought about that a bit, playing with his chin and plucking his lower lip. It was possible. "Well, at the time of the occupation of Qumran, Tyre was ruled by Rome. Roman coins could be found there."

"What I was told," she said, "is that the coins found at the ruins were divided in to three pots. This set of documents was found in the third pot."

He looked at the papers again. "Based on Margaret's notes here, Malchus was ordered to disperse the coins? Do you have a word-for-word translation?"

"I don't, not yet. I have software that translates Italian and Spanish. I bought it when I first started corresponding with Renata. I do not have one for Greek, and I'm not sure a modern translation software would work on this ancient Greek writing. All I have are Margaret's notes." She took another deep breath. "And from those I can conclude, and correct me if I'm wrong, these scrolls indicate that the coins are significant. There's so many references to them here. These documents mention the coins being cursed, being blessed, bestowing gifts, holding powers of healing, death, enlightenment, access to heaven, on and on."

Celia was focused on mention of the coins, for obvious reason, but these papers held words that made Ryan's mind spin. He kept returning to a section of Margaret's notes that sounded familiar, "The ability to see an eternal timeless reality, the eyes of your understanding being enlightened; that you may know the truth, the light." Ryan thought that he remembered these words from a Pope's speech, but he wasn't sure.

These familiar phrases of redemption, enlightenment, and eternity were in stark contrast to the other notes that Ryan recognized from Thessalonians, "This power will prevail because of a falling away from the truth." And another, "Exalts itself above God." And, "Will use signs and lying wonders." Written next to, "Will do unrighteously." These were eluding to the antichrist.

What did any of this have to do with the coins?

He said, "We'll need to get the Greek translated to be sure that Margaret's interpretation is accurate. Why hasn't this surfaced before?" he asked, leafing through the documents again, his fingers tracing some of the words in reverence.

She said, "They may have surfaced already. That's one of the things I was hoping you'd know: if the church is aware of the documents, and what their position is regarding them?"

"This is all news to me, but I've been out of the loop for

a few years now. I bet David could help me tap into the Vatican's records," Ryan said, still reviewing the papers while absently twisting a finger through his hair.

"Can he do that?"

"If anyone can, David can."

"What about your friend, the bishop? What did he say when you called him?"

Ryan shook his head. "That's the thing. I told him about your coin. If he knew about these scrolls, he would have said so, unless there's something the church is trying to conceal. He was evasive on the phone, insisting we meet face to face."

She sat next to him on the desk and said, "According to James..."

"Who's James again?"

"Margaret's son. I've been in contact with him several times since I started researching the coins. He's one of the reasons I've kept to myself so far."

"He advised you to be discreet?"

"Nobody knows his mother had copies made of these documents. When they were first found, the scrolls were photographed and catalogued. The Vatican was contacted and acquired the originals. Like you said, Ryan, the public knows about the Dead Sea Scrolls. Why is there no public record of these?"

"What does Margaret say? Wouldn't she know?"

"I'm sure she does, but she never lived to tell. She died in a car crash three weeks after the discovery. She left the documents, and her notes, for her infant son, James, who was raised by an aunt in England."

"How did you find James?" Ryan asked.

"Through Renata. He came to her. Right around the time she was publicly accusing the church of covering up the truth. That was several months after I first started corresponding with her. We are all trying to find answers."

She let out a big breath. "Here's the thing: three coins, one from each pot, were distinguished by purple markings, just like ours. James' aunt told him that several workers confiscated some coins. The theft was a big scandal at the work site."

"How many coins were stolen." Ryan asked.

"Guess," she tilted her head in challenge. He loved a challenge. She had no idea the thrill this whole situation presented.

"Three," he said

She nodded. "The three with the markings."

"Were the thieves caught?"

She reached up and touched the coin at her neck. "Two of the thieves disappeared after the coins went missing and were never found. The third was captured, but had some sort of breakdown and was institutionalized until he died in 1966. The thefts were in the papers, but mention of the scrolls was not."

Ryan shook his head back and forth, and then inhaled deeply. "I smell trouble," he said, letting his breath out in a whoosh.

He scanned the documents again. She watched him, no doubt knowing he was not capable of turning away from such a historical religious discovery and possible conspiracy, if the documents were authentic.

"So, what are we going to do now?" he asked.

"We?" She repeated hopefully.

"I'm in," he said, giving her a wide grin and a wink.

"Well, I was thinking —"

"I figured you might be."

She continued, "I was thinking we can hunt down other coins, trace any mention of stigmata in the news. Maybe make some calls to members of the church and see what we can find out – well, what you can find out. I hoped you would be my link to the church."

His eyes locked on hers. "Are you sure you want to pursue this with the church? The organization that is the Roman Catholic church has a lot of rules and restrictions. If what you say is true, there may already be a cover-up by the Vatican."

She sighed. "The power of thirty needs to be united in its purpose. That's what the documents say. Whether thirty coins or thirty people, I don't know. I do know that whatever is happening to me is tied to those coins. Whatever happened to Margaret was tied to those coins. Whatever happened to Renata was tied to those coins. And according to these documents, eternal life is tied to these coins. It also says the power in the wrong hands, in the hands of those who do unrighteously, means heaven will be lost."

"That's quite a prophecy," he said.

"Well, it's not mine," She told him. "It's Christ's, as related by Judas to Malchus himself."

Connecticut College, New London, CT, April 28, 2032

The classroom smelled like canned peas. David hated peas. What moron had brought stinky peas into class?

He looked around. The pea smuggler sat a few rows to his left, the kid with the freckles whose name he kept forgetting.

"Hey," David said. "Can't you take that to the café? What are you doing eating lunch at ten thirty in the morning?"

Freckles said, "I haven't slept yet, so technically this is dinner. You got a problem with that?"

David was about to tell him he did, when Professor Delaney walked in and stood at the front of the room. The room quieted, except for the scrape of chairs and the sound of Freckles chewing. He wanted to ask the professor about the lady friend who came to campus the other day, and why he cancelled his classes yesterday. It was unlike him, and David could tell something was up by the way his teacher was distracted, fidgeting and messing with his hair the way he did when you asked him a question he didn't want to answer.

"Please sit," the professor said, still standing there, shifting from foot to foot awkwardly. What was strange was that he was empty-handed: no notebook, textbook, or laptop. "I'm afraid I have some bad news. I met with the Dean this morning," he continued. "Something has come up, and I need to take a leave of absence. Professor Arnold will cover my classes until I return. I apologize for any inconvenience this may cause."

David couldn't think of anything that would pull Professor Delaney away from his students. So he asked, "Did someone die?" That was why most people's lives got derailed. It was with David's. And Professor Delaney didn't run from anything. So, if he was leaving, then somebody was probably dead.

"Nobody died, and I'd rather not discuss my reasons

with the class if that's okay. Please be assured that I'm fine and my family is fine," he said, looking directly at David. "Something has come up. It's personal. And, it needs my attention right away."

"Will you be back before the term's up?" David asked. Not for nothing, but Professor Arnold was a stiff and taught like a walking textbook. Professor Delaney was one of the guys. They all turned to him for advice, especially David after everything he went through the year before with his dad.

"I don't know," was the professor's answer.

"Well, that's just great." He hadn't meant to speak aloud, and he didn't really want to make this harder on the professor, but it just slipped out.

Professor Delaney stood there.

David felt like a jerk for putting him on the spot in front of everyone, but what the heck. "I hope she's worth it," David said, standing, and then marching out the door. It was a childish comment. It just made him so mad that the professor could just walk away so easily, just like every other fucking adult in David's life.

Subway Sandwich Shop, New London, CT, April 28, 2032

Freckles and his stinky peas had ruined David's appetite. So did the professor's announcement. But after the gym and a workout, he found himself famished. David wolfed down his turkey sandwich. There was hardly a soul in Subway, probably because it was three in the afternoon and every sane person had already eaten lunch. He began texting a friend when the bell over the door rang and Professor Delaney walked into Subway at full stride, stopping when he spotted David alone at the table.

"Hey, Professor," David said in acknowledgement, and then blew him off by finishing his text message.

"Can I join you?"

David shrugged.

"I'll take that as a yes," the professor said, going over to the counter to order.

The professor was a pretty solid guy. David looked up to him, probably relied on him more than he should now that his father died and he had no family. He could feel that something big was happening and, in David's experience, that usually meant he would be alone again. He should have never trusted a teacher, expected someone who was paid to mentor him, to really give a shit about his life, even if the guy was an ex-priest. It was just a job, and no matter how much David wished otherwise, Professor Delaney was not his friend.

The professor sat down, unwrapped his sandwich, and started eating. Ryan Delaney was the master of the pregnant pause, especially when he was trying to draw something out of you. David had experienced it first-hand many times over the past year. He knew he was being unreasonable. The guy had every right to leave if something, or someone, needed him. What was David but just some student the professor had helped through a hard time, right?

The dude must've been hungry because David had never seen him scarf food before. He waited him out, not wanting to be the first one to speak. It was not a coincidence that they were here. David ate here all the time. The professor wasn't a Subway guy, although you'd never know it by the way he was chomping down that sandwich. He came here to talk to David, and David knew it.

He got a text from his friend and the professor watched him read it without comment. This was how they started talking to each other in the first place. Professor Delaney would sit with David and his friends at lunch on campus, and he'd just listen while they all spouted bullshit and he'd say nothing. When he did speak, he was pretty cool, not preachy at all like David thought he'd be - just a regular guy. He didn't act like a priest, except like now when he was silent, patiently waiting for you to spill your guts like a confession. David wasn't falling for it. He was majoring in psychology and wasn't about to be mind-tricked into speaking first.

He waited.

"I need your help," the professor said at last. This was the last thing David had expected to hear.

"What's the deal?" he asked. "You can tell me, you know. It has to do with that girl, right?"

The professor kept eating, obviously considering what to say. David pick at his chips while he waited his teacher out. Two could play at this game.

The silence lasted until the last crumb was gone.

Finally, Professor Delaney said, "Remember all the research I had you do about Stigmata, David?"

Raddison Hotel, New London, CT, April 28, 2032

Where the hell was Ryan? He got out of class five hours ago and he wasn't here yet. Celia was sick of staring at the ugly wallpaper in her hotel room. The soles of her shoes were worn out from pacing, as was a good portion of the rug. What if he didn't come? What if he decided she was a nutcase and was arranging for her to be locked up at any minute?

She was terrified he was going to hand her over to some creepy Catholic purist who would performs tests on her or try to discredit her in some way. She knew that was not Ryan's style, but, really, what did she expect him to do?

Then she thought of Renata and started to panic. Please, Ryan, don't do anything stupid.

She resumed pacing, then wondered: what if something had happened to him? She was being paranoid. Just because Renata disappeared doesn't mean anything bad had happened, or that there was any kind of conspiracy to wipe out all stigmatics and their friends. Was there?

She called Ryan's cell and got his voicemail. "Ryan, you okay? I'm still here waiting. Call me, please."

Abandoning her pace marathon, she turned on the television to catch the news and see if any sweet ex-priests had been in car accidents in the last hour, but there was no news of accidents, or anything else for that matter, except for a hurricane looming off the coast.

She heard the scraping of a plastic key, and then Ryan came in with his hands full. Behind him stood a handsome young man, who she assumed was David. He hovered in the doorway and stared at her with piercing green eyes.

"Celia," Ryan said, "this is David. I brought some food." He deposited sandwiches and drinks on the desk.

When the kid didn't move from the door and kept watching them with interest, Celia stepped closer to Ryan and whispered, "What's going on?"

"Mrs. Alessandri," David said, striding over to her. "So nice to meet you." He put his hand out formally. His interest in Celia was obvious by the way he inspected her hands and face, so she assumed Ryan had explained her situation. She wasn't sure what to do with him here, so she faltered a moment.

When they shook, his hand was warm and dry. "Nice to meet you, David. I'm sorry," she stuttered, "I wasn't expecting you both, and so late."

"It's my fault," Ryan said from behind her. "David and I became involved with some research and lost track of time."

She had questions, but wasn't sure how much to say in front of the kid, who was now sitting casually on the couch like he was visiting a neighbor or something.

"Is he, uh, going to help us?" She managed, trying not to stare at David or look as uncomfortable as she felt.

Ryan nodded. "I filled him in. He's anxious to get a look at the documents. But, for starters, we have some leads on stigmata David found earlier. We delved into that further, plus matched it with stories of healings and coins to see what turned up."

"Good," she said, nodding her head. "It'll be great to have someone so skilled with research helping us."

David said, "Well, I can do more than that."

"I'm sure," she responded, not quite getting his meaning. "Ryan speaks very highly of you." He brought his research assistant? Well, she supposed that was better than the Catholic purist.

"Uh, Celia," Ryan said. "David's going to come with us."

"Huh? Ryan, I'm not sure we should be putting any other lives in jeopardy, here," she said, glancing at David who looked unconcerned.

"Mrs. Alessandri," David spoke.

"Please don't call me that," she interrupted. "Call me Celia. David, think about your education for a moment." She just could not understand his thinking. Why would Ryan involve his student?

"I am," David said, standing smugly, his hands on his hips. "This is an incredible opportunity, Celia," he said with a cocky familiarity that made her wish he would go back to calling her Mrs. Alessandri, even though hearing that always made her think of Jeff's mother.

He continued, "I'm a psychology major, with a minor in Religious history. You will not find a case study on this planet more appealing to me than this." He spread his hands wide and smiled.

"As appealing as it may be," she said, trying not to sound like a disapproving school marm, "Don't make any hasty decisions until you know everything. I mean, I don't know how much Ryan has told you, but —"

Ryan broke in, haltingly, "Uh, Celia, we just booked three flights to Texas."

"Texas?" Spinning on one heel, she faced Ryan. "What for?"

"There's something of interest there," Ryan answered.

"Yeah, a hurricane," she said.

Ryan was very still, his brown eyes calm and liquid.

"And a coin," David said from the couch. "Plus records of healings, like yours."

She turned, clasped her hands together and held them in front of her lips, tapping them a few times as if they would attract the right words. Lowering her hands, she said, "David. Are you sure you want to get mixed up in this?"

David answered, "What better religious education could I get? If I get to witness miracles, read secret historical religious documents and hunt treasure, I'm in."

"Kids," she huffed.

Celia resumed pacing, although it was harder now with two grown men in the small room. She bounced like a ping-pong ball between them and two pairs of eyes followed. She could see Ryan was waiting her out, knowing that eventually she'd calm down and accept his judgment, as she always had done.

David was less patient, "I can pay my own way. My family is loaded."

She laughed, unable to help herself. He was so eager. She was reminded of Ryan when he was young, only David was confident, bordering on presumptuous. Pushy was the word that jumped into her head. Clearly, he was used to getting his way.

She wrapped her arms around herself to hold in her protests. "I appreciate the sandwiches, but do you mind if I pass? I've been in this room all day and I need to get out of here."

"What do you feel like doing?" Ryan asked.

"Getting a martini," she said, surprising herself.

Kream Martini Bar, New London, CT, April 28, 2032

Kream Martini Bar and Lounge was not your average

college haunt. It used to be a coffee place. They still served great coffee, which is why David suggested it when Celia said she wanted a drink. Considering everything the professor had told him, Celia wasn't at all what David expected. After the first few awkward moments in the hotel, she turned off the deflector shield she had around herself and transformed into this funny, open, light-hearted person once they left the hotel. Now, at the bar, her long, wavy, caramel-colored hair surrounded her martini glass when she dipped her head to drink. Her make-up was minimal and her eyes had soft laugh lines. She acted young. You would think she would have been worn down and tattered after all she'd endured, but she wasn't.

David wasn't sure he believed all this hocus-pocus stigmata bullshit she was claiming to be experiencing. The professor was like a father to him. If Celia was trying to scam his mentor, David had every intention of exposing her. He just had to figure out what her angle was. Probably the only thing his father had ever taught him of worth was how to spot a con.

She was kinda hot though. David watched the professor interact with her. He imagined them at his age, and figured it must have been a pretty hard decision to have left a girl like Celia for the priesthood.

It was loud in here, so David had to strain to hear Celia when she asked, "Why are we going to Texas, and not the Vatican?"

"To meet a guy about some papers," David explained. This had been his idea. Why go to Rome when they don't even know if she's for real. He didn't say that to the professor, but when David suggested Texas, Professor Delaney didn't seem too anxious to go trotting off to mingle with his past life and agreed to go.

The professor sipped his beer. David had never seen him with a beer before. He was seeing a whole new side of his mentor: first the girl, now the booze. Interesting.

"What guy?" she wanted to know.

The professor said, "We're meeting a man who was a graduate student at Texas A&M when a ship was excavated in 1995."

"What ship?" she asked, leaning forward.

David tried not to look down her blouse, which had accidentally gaped open, as he answered, "The Texas State Historical Commission unearthed the wreckage of a ship called La Belle which sank in 1686 in Matagorda Bay. It's the oldest French shipwreck ever discovered on American soil. La Belle was part of a small fleet that embarked from LaRochelle and planned to establish a French colony on the Gulf."

She looked unimpressed as she sat up and asked, "What does a French ship have to do with Roman coins?" and then turned to order a second drink.

He was glad she asked that. "Exactly. That's the puzzle. Researchers have yet to understand how the treasures on the ship got there, including the Roman coin that was found."

Celia looked at him, and then at the professor. "Does the coin have purple markings?"

"I told you she would ask that," the professor said.

David answered, "No, and it was minted AD, but La Belle wasn't the only ship in the expedition. The Aimable, a store-ship carrying most of the supplies, ran aground while trying to enter Matagorda Bay. Documents from the Aimable were recovered from the ruins of LaBelle. Those documents are what we're going to see. A wooden crucifix was also part of the wreckage. I have a picture of it here."

He pulled a computer printout from his back pocket that showed the weathered cross. Words on the bottom of the page explained that the cross had brass components, including the body of Christ, with a banner that possibly was inscribed with "INRI," and a skull and crossed bones at the base. He showed it to Celia.

"Skull and crossbones?" She said. "Isn't that a pirate's symbol?"

Professor Delaney said, "The original image was used by the Knights Templar."

This is why he liked the professor. He was a 'did-you-know' freak, just like David, and he could spout useless facts at the drop of a hat, especially facts related to spiritual practice and Christianity - his expertise.

Professor Delaney said, "King Roger II of Sicily was a famed Templar. The pirate flag is called 'Jolly Roger' after him. The knights of the Temple were in conflict with the pope. After the Templars were disbanded by the Church, at least one Templar fleet dedicated themselves to pirating ships of any country sympathetic to Rome."

"Okay," Celia said, "but I still don't get why you think it's relevant."

"It may not be," the professor said, "but the guy who helped excavate the ship claims that he has information about healings that occurred on board the Aimable. Records indicate that other instances of healings were documented in that area of Texas, after the French colonists arrived. We can't dismiss the coincidence of one Roman coin paired with rumors of healing, even if the coin isn't one of the thirty."

Celia nodded. "Well, it's a place to start."

David raised his glass and said, "Yippee ki-yay, let's go to Texas."

Celia laughed and said, "Yee-haw." Then she lifted her glass to his.

CHAPTER 4

Boeing 737, cruising altitude 35,000 feet, April 29, 2032

The cabin of the plane was stuffy despite the stale cool air that blew from the grey spheres above David's head. The flight had been getting rough, and they were only half way there.

His nose was in the book Celia gave him to read about stigmata, but he struggled to absorb the material with her sitting so close. It was almost laughable that something this incredible had happened to her, if it was true, that is. She hardly seemed like a religious zealot or a con artist. In fact, she didn't seem like a zealot of any kind.

The plane lurched, and he put the book down. It was too bumpy to concentrate anyway. David turned to talk to the professor, but he was fast asleep across the aisle.

He asked Celia, "Do you think we can land with this hurricane?" The news reported that the storm was still off shore, and he hoped the airline would have delayed the flight if there was any danger.

"I don't know," Celia said. "I hope so."

The older woman in the window seat next to Celia was as white as the walls of the cabin and leaning precariously over a tiny blue barf bag. Great. If she managed to spew in that thing, it would be a miracle. Every time the plane dropped, she let out a whimpering noise and pulled the bag to her face.

"Don't like flying?" David asked.

The woman shook her head no, and started rocking back and forth in little manic motions. Oh, shit, she was freaking out. He was about to say something to her, trying to recall anything from his behavioral class, when Celia reached over and said, "Put your head down between your legs if you can."

The woman curled against the seat in front of her as best as possible considering the cramped space, and Celia placed her hands on the woman's back. Celia's face flushed and, after a few moments, she rubbed the woman's back a little. "Breathe in a few times," she said and removed her hands.

The woman complied and took a few breaths. Then, she sat up and looked at Celia. "Thank you," she said. "That worked wonders." Her color was healthy and she appeared calm. Resting her head against her seat back, the woman closed her eyes and lowered the barf bag to her lap. A few more deep breaths, and she seemed to be asleep, even though the plane was still bouncing around like an amusement park ride that wasn't amusing.

David looked at Celia's hands for signs of stigmata. There weren't any. "Shouldn't I have seen a lightening bolt or an aura when you did that?" he whispered, trying not to wake the lady.

She laughed. "That was nothing. Just a little calming."

The lady did seem healed. David would have suspected Celia of planting her there, but David had made the plane reservations himself only yesterday. "I didn't know you could summon up something like that. The professor said you could only perform in times of extreme stress."

She nodded. "Sometimes, I feel moved to help. If I'm not, it's like when you're a kid and you try to make the pencil roll across the table with telepathy. Nothing happens except you get a brain cramp."

He laughed, having done that not so long ago while in his 'power of the mind' phase. "You know," he said, "if you can relieve distress that easily, you can put the whole psychiatric industry out of business, not to mention a number of pharmaceutical companies."

"Well, that's a thought."

He snorted. "Easy for you to say. You practically walk on water, but I'll have no career if everybody cures their own mental issues."

"Wouldn't be the worst thing."

The plane lurched a few times. Immediately, the pilot reminded them that they should all be seated.

"You're not suggesting the world doesn't need psychiatrists?" he asked.

"No," she smiled. "I'm not saying that. I know that I could have used one when my husband died. Probably even before that, when he was sick."

"But you didn't go to one?"

"No." Celia looked out the window at the grey sky. "I didn't go to anyone."

He read a lot into that sentence. "What about your family?"

"My mother's passed. I was a late-in-life miracle, a menopause baby. My dad has Alzheimer's and is in a home. No siblings." She smiled. "But, I have two wonderful girl-friends. They've helped me so much."

"You came through it alright. Without a shrink, I mean."

"I had something else, too," she said. "Although I didn't realize it at the time."

"What's that?"

"God."

"The ultimate shrink. All-knowing and there to listen at all times, is that it?"

"Something like that," she said. "I take it you don't agree."

He shrugged and shook his head. "I don't know. I look at God and spirituality a little like a science experiment."

"So why are you studying religion if you don't believe in God?"

"To find the truth. It's not that I don't believe. It's just I don't quantify Him in the same way that some people do. I'm open to the idea of various realities of God, or the universe, or energy, or whatever created us, drives us, heals us, and fulfills us. All of that."

"Interesting. What does your father believe? How did he take the news about your leaving school to go with an ex-priest and a complete stranger on a mission of God?"

"I don't know," he paused. "He's dead."

Celia's face softened. Her eyes focused on him, and David was relieved not to see pity there. She's been through some shit herself, so David supposed she knew better.

"I'm sorry, I didn't know," she said. "Ryan told me you were estranged, but…"

"Yeah, well, what are you going to do?" he joked. "Life sucks, right?"

She put a hand tentatively on his arm, and then removed it. "Some circumstances do, but life as a whole doesn't."

He wanted to tell her to spare the sentiments, but he didn't. Just because her husband and baby died doesn't mean she understood his situation. Just because he'd read books about loss doesn't mean he understood anyone else's loss either.

"When did your father pass away?" she asked.

He didn't really want to talk about it, but wasn't sure how to change the subject. "Ask the professor," he said. "He knows all about it."

"I'm asking you," she said in a warm, motherly voice.

The plane jiggled slightly, and David wished they could have some drinks. He missed the distraction of the flight attendants, and was cornered here next to Celia's questioning hazel eyes. He looked to the professor for help, but, incredibly, he was still sleeping. Lucky Bastard.

David closed his eyes against Celia's stare and took a deep breath of resignation. "He died two years ago. Two weeks into my freshman year."

"How?

"Car crash," he said. "Drinking and speeding in one of his toys. Fucking stupid."

"That must've been hard for you," she commented. "Even if you weren't close. He was your only family. Trust me, I know how that feels."

The plane felt like it was doing cartwheels, and he opened his eyes and said, "We all die eventually, right? Although, if this plane crashes, God's going to be pissed, don't you think - what with his messenger on board? Isn't your being here some sort of insurance?"

"You're changing the subject," she said.

"It's a lousy subject," he said back.

"That's true."

She was too damned intuitive and reminded him of one of his nannies, Maria, who was one of the nice ones before his father slept with her and she left in tears a few months later. "I hardly knew him, my father," he said. "And what I did know, I didn't like."

She was quiet for a while, seeming to be pondering what he had said. "Was there anything nice you can say about your father?"

"Yah, he had a lot of money."

"But you didn't like that about him."

"I didn't," he admitted, not sure why he was telling her so much. "It was all he cared about."

She nodded. "What do you care about, David?"

He smiled. "Right now? I care about getting to Texas in one piece." On cue, the plane bounced and swayed in the turbulence.

As they descended toward the airport in Corpus Christi, the turbulence returned with a fury due, in part, to the hurricane lurking not far from their destination. The woman next to the window had been awake for over an hour, but her mania was gone despite the fact that now she may now actually have something to panic about. The barf bag lay unused in her lap.

In the front row, there was a man with his golden retriever service dog. David had never seen a large dog on a plane before and he was allergic. It always frustrated him when fellow passengers would cart their little pet pooches around in those fake-purse carrier things, but this was a full-sized fur ball. He had requested a seat away from the dog upon boarding, which is why their seats were separated now and the professor was across the aisle. The man with the dog had apologized, explaining that due to epilepsy, he needed the dog with him.

It was a beautiful dog and the animal had been still and quiet the whole trip, despite the rough nature of the flight. All of a sudden, the dog rose and started barking.

David didn't like the feel of the plane one bit. They were bouncing all over the place, and people looked panicked. Celia said, "This isn't good."

His body was tossed around as the plane fought the wind. He could see the ground out the window. The wing of the plane kept tipping down, and then up, and then down again.

The pilot advised to prepare for landing, and David broke into a cold sweat. As they bobbed like a kite on a string, his fellow passengers started to moan. The man with the dog shouted something about pills just as David saw a prescription bottle roll down the aisle. The oxygen masks dropped from the ceiling. This has never happened to him before, and his heart sped up as he grabbed for the mask. The ground was coming up fast, too fast.

Celia unsnapped her seatbelt and stepped over him, pushing the masks and tubes aside to squeeze by, then she rushed up the aisle to the front of the plane. Where was she going? It was then that David noticed the man with the dog was having a seizure in the aisle of the front row. The dog was next to him, moaning and barking.

Every face on the flight was watching the scene as, one by one, they put the oxygen masks on. David breathed in deeply and caught the concerned look on Professor Delaney's face.

Over the panic, he couldn't make out what Celia was saying.

He did hear the flight attendant ask Celia if she was a doctor, and when she shook her head no, she was asked to sit down and prepare for landing.

The flight attendant tried to establish calm. She stood firmly next to Celia, touching her arm and saying loud enough for everyone to hear, "Listen! Everyone needs to be seated. Are there any doctors or nurses on board?"

Celia said, "I can help."

David noticed the pill bottle rolling toward him in the center aisle. He reached over and grabbed it, then, against his better judgment, unbuckled his seatbelt, abandoned his oxygen mask, stood up to make his way to the front of the plane. He fell several times as the floor of the cabin dropped and rose beneath his feet. Professor Delaney stood too and followed him. He caught up to David during one particularly jolting bump. Frightened eyes peered above their masks in terror, parents clung to their children, and women wept.

A guy shouted, "Sit down, you idiots," as they passed.

Out the window, David could see they were about to hit the ground any minute and the plane wasn't under control.

Just then, the plane lurched up, his knees buckled, and he fell on his ass. His head hit something, and when he opened his eyes he saw Celia bent over the man having the seizure. Her body was very tense. Although David was several feet away, he could feel the energy surging from her.

Everything happened at rapid speed. The professor toppled over several passengers and then struggled to right himself. Several flight attendants sat with their heads between their knees bracing for impact. The two who were trying to get Celia back to her chair were on the floor, knocked down by turbulence. David grabbed hold of the arm of the closest seat.

As if entering a vacuum in space, all sound disappeared. Gone was the whoosh of forced air, the heavy panicked breathing of passengers, the sobs, and whispered prayers. As smooth as a feather on a calm day, the plane glided forward and down. When the landing gear made contact, the silence was disrupted only by the slightest hint of the skid of wheel against asphalt.

Adrenaline coursed through him as he watched, helpless. Celia toppled sideways while one of the flight attendants moved to help her. The flight attendant settled Celia on the floor, facing the passengers. Blood was flowing from Celia's forehead and wrists. This startled David out of his stupor, and he crawled over to join her. He heard the professor behind him, asking some passengers if they were all right.

"Get some towels," David said to the baffled flight

attendant.

The pilot announced their safe arrival at Corpus Christi International Airport, but he sounded far away, like a voice coming down a long tunnel. Whether his ears hadn't adjusted to the altitude, or they were still in the strange vacuum-like silence, he didn't know. Celia was pale.

"Get some towels!" he yelled.

The flight attendant nodded and lurched past him, while the second one picked up the intercom hand set. She ordered everybody to remain seated until further instructed and then she bent down over them.

"What happened?" she asked.

He wasn't sure what to say to her, so he shrugged and shook his head back and forth to imply that he had no idea.

Celia's skin was burning hot. The professor joined him and asked, "How is she?" in a calm voice, but David guessed he was as freaked out as everybody else.

"Did you see?" he asked the professor.

"Yes."

The first flight attendant returned with towels, and they applied them to Celia's head, and wrists. The second flight attendant sat and cradled the epileptic man's head in her lap. He had stopped seizing, but was unconscious. The dog whimpered and rested his head on his master's leg.

The plane taxied to the jetway where they could hear people outside the main exit door. In a matter of seconds, the cockpit door opened, and the pilot and copilot emerged. They paused when they saw Celia, the professor, two flight attendants, the epileptic man, the dog, and David on the floor in front of them.

"What's going on?" one of them asked.

The flight attendant said in a hysterical tone, "He had a seizure!"

The dog whimpered again. David looked down at the unopened bottle of medication grasped firmly in his left hand. He would have handed it to Celia, but she was bleeding, so he put the bottle on her lap when no one was looking.

Celia seemed to understand the unspoken gesture and said in a weak voice, "here's his medicine."

It was then that the pilot registered Celia's condition. He took the bottle from her lap, "You're hurt."

Celia nodded.

David said, "What the hell is wrong with you, landing in these conditions?" Hoping that if he put the pilot on the defensive, he'd drop the subject of Celia's mysterious injuries. "There's a God-damned hurricane out there, why weren't we redirected to another airport?"

Some passengers had unbuckled and were standing. The pilot ordered everyone to remain seated and asked them to stay calm and follow standard procedures to disembark as soon as they got the two injured passengers to safety.

David wasn't sure what to do next.

The main exit door nearest him opened, and one of the flight attendants told the men outside to get the paramedics. "Someone's been hurt."

A few people stirred in their seats, seeming anxious to get their bags.

Paramedics arrived and strapped Celia to a gurney.

"Where are you taking her?" the professor asked.

"Christus Spohn Hospital – Shoreline," the paramedic

said.

"My bags," Celia said, her voice weak and raspy.

"Shhh," David assured her. "It's going to be okay. We'll take care of everything and meet you there."

Christus Spohn Hospital, Corpus Christi, Texas, April 30, 2032

Every muscle in Celia's body ached. The hospital sheets bunched under her, an additional annoyance compounding her discomfort. She knew it was morning, but the dark severe-weather storm clouds obscured the sun outside her window, making everything feel more oppressive. It had been over fifteen hours and two transfusions since she arrived, but she had finally stopped bleeding.

Details were coming back to her slowly. She remembered David and Ryan leaving, taking the rental car to the hotel. David had two staples in his head from when he fell on the plane. The doctor had fixed him up and released him. The man with epilepsy had also been released, but Celia's mysterious injuries required further attention. Ryan had come back to stay with her once David was settled, the sound of his deep breathing coming from the chair next to her bed was extremely soothing and welcome. He had spent the night there and she couldn't have been more grateful for the company.

The hospital staff was attentive and caring, but she knew the onslaught of questions and tests were soon to come. She was like a circus side show, which reminded her they needed to get out of there - and fast.

"Ryan," she said. "Wake up."

He stirred.

"Ryan," she repeated.

"What?" He sat up. "You okay?"

She sighed, definitely not ok. She felt like she had been hit with a bolt of lightening. "I'll be all right. Listen, I want to make that meeting this afternoon."

"Celia, really, there's no need —"

"I can't stay here," she explained. "Trust me, I've been through this enough to know the curiosity that accompanies my stigmata episodes. We need to get out of here."

He rubbed his eyes. "Okay. What can I do?"

"I'll need a wheelchair and some bandages. Try a drug-store. Ask David to swap the rental car for a van. If you can pick up some Gatorade or fresh fruit, that'll help me regain my strength. Get some multi-vitamins with iron."

"Okay," Ryan said. "I'm on it."

"Thanks. And you may want to get yourself some coffee. You look like hell."

"Thanks."

He left and she hit the call button for the nurse.

After several minutes, a sweet young girl arrived. "You need something?" she asked with a heavy accent that confirmed they were in Texas.

"Yes. I'm feeling much better. Can you remove my IV?"

The young nurse looked skeptical. "Give me a minute," she said as she left. A few seconds later, the she returned and agreed that the IV could come out. Very gently, she removed the needle and then helped Celia into the bathroom. "Buzz me when you're ready, Darlin'." Her Texas twang was charming and annoying at the same time.

Celia stared helplessly into the mirror. She was dying for a shower, but her bandaged wrists were an issue. The pain in her wrists made bending her fingers excruciating, and she had no grip. She wiggled her fingers slightly and cringed. No use. Her head was wrapped with a thick band across her forehead. She looked like a casualty of war. Brushing her teeth was an Olympic event, and it took her a good fifteen minutes to accomplish, trying to lodge the toothbrush between her index finger and middle finger without actually grasping. Plus, she had to sit for spells when the dizziness and weakness overcame her. Somehow, she managed to carefully insert her hands into plastic bags. She dropped the face cloth several times, swearing, and sitting again to catch her breath. She wanted to clean herself up, so she wouldn't feel like such a bum, but it was impossible.

She should be used to this by now, but it's not something anyone can prepare for. She felt the tears coming, the self pity weighing heavy on her heart, when the nurse came back to check on her even though she hadn't yet hit the buzzer.

"You okay honey?" she asked.

Celia wondered how long she had been fumbling around in the god-forsaken bathroom. "I'm having some difficulty," she admitted, reluctantly, and she invited the nurse in to help her.

The entire washing and dressing process left her completely drained, and she needed to sleep again. At some point, breakfast was brought in, and Celia managed to get some food down. She felt revived after her nap and a glass of apple juice.

It had been two hours since Ryan left. Celia was relieved that, aside from the nurse who who helped her bathe, she had been left strikingly alone. Probably due to the storm. She had noticed the sounds of frantic activity in the hallway and news reports on the television confirmed the severity of the weather as the foremost story. Their little incident on the plane was not even mentioned.

Each time she closed her eyes, she relived the panic on the plane - the feeling of that man's life in her hands, and all the eyes on her while she summoned her healing, while the plane bounced around, hurling towards the runway. Even now, as she waited for Ryan, the storm that threatened their flight was wreaking havoc on the shore and at the very destination where they were headed next. If she thought about it too much, it made her want to vomit, so she turned off the television.

Where was Ryan?

Walgreens parking lot, Morgan Ave., Corpus Christi, Texas, April 30, 2032

The wheelchair they just bought slipped from David's hands onto the parking lot pavement in front of the drug store. The wind buffeted him around, and the door of the van nearly took his head off. Professor Delaney was screaming into the phone to be heard above the noise of the storm, and, even then, David couldn't make out what he was saying. This was insanity!

He struggled to rearrange their bags and purchases in the van to fit the collapsed wheelchair into a secured spot. The professor ended his call, and stepped over to help, his raincoat hood blowing off each time he pulled it back over his head.

"Is this the wrath of God?" David yelled, only half-joking.

"It's the wrath of nature!" the professor shouted back, shoving the wheelchair in place at last. "Hop in."

David scrambled to the passenger seat, grateful to be out of the wind and rain. He'd never been south during a hurricane. It was terrifying. Coming after the near plane crash, this was about as much excitement as he had ever had in his twenty-one years on the planet. Adrenaline and fear combined into an amazing elixir. He felt like he'd drunk several cases of coffee, or those super-powered caffeinated energy drinks, even though he hadn't had a thing all morning.

"Slight change in plans," the professor said when he started up the van. "Our contact in Matagorda Bay had to evacuate. I'm pretty sure the hospital will evacuate as well. From what I'm hearing, this hurricane is looking to be a menace. Our next stop would have been the Museum in Austin. Since Justin has family there, he and his wife and child are headed that way. We're going to meet them on the way."

They sped along the roadway, working their way back to the hospital.

"What about the documents from the Museum?"

"Justin has them. It's going to be interesting, we'll have to look at them in the car as we go." They took a left turn.

"I'm surprised the guy's willing to do that," David said.

"He's more anxious to meet us now after hearing about our plane ride." The professor drove with his chin over the wheel, as he struggled to keep the car in line, and to see through the pounding rain.

"Where are we meeting?" David asked, holding onto the dashboard, and eyeing the road for potential hazards.

"In Victoria, a few miles north of Corpus Christi. We need to get away from the shore where the storm will hit soon."

"It hasn't hit yet?"

The professor risked a brief glance at him, and then resumed driving. "No. It hasn't hit yet."

CHAPTER 5

Christus Spohn Hospital, Corpus Christi, Texas,
April 30, 2032

Ryan felt like someone poured a pool over his head. The pending storm was bearing down causing the hospital to implement emergency measures. The sound of commotion outside of Celia's hospital room competed with raging wind noises and occasional thunderclaps from outside the hospital.

"They're evacuating the hospital and have agreed to release you," he explained after bursting into the room. He glanced around, dripping everywhere as he moved. "Where are your things?"

David entered with the wheelchair.

Celia must have been sleeping. Her hair was sticking up everywhere and she looked confused. "They're letting me go?"

"Yeah." Ryan opened her hospital-room closet and took things out.

Celia sat up in bed. "I've been upstaged by the storm?"

"Pretty much," David said, as he leaned over and helped Celia get into the wheelchair. "And with good reason. The storm is hitting hard. We need to head north, away from the brunt of it."

They buzzed around her, swiftly gathering her things.

Ryan said, "Do you think you can travel?" He was worried about her, and feeling anxious about all the rapid activity. He had never been in the path of a hurricane like this, and Celia looked like she could be blown over by a summer breeze right now.

"I think so," she said.

"Then let's go. It's going to be one hell of a ride."

Route 77 runs parallel to the shore. Ryan was beginning to wonder if making this detour was a good idea. It took them an eternity to get Celia situated, to collapse the wheelchair, and to cram it into the rear of the van again. The rain was streaming sideways now, dumping so much water on the roads that they kept hydroplaning and risked stalling in flooded areas. They maneuvered around trees and debris that littered the roads.

"We should have taken the interstate straight north to San Antonio," David said from the passenger seat, gripping the seat cushion with both hands.

"Justin says the interstates are bumper-to-bumper," Ryan explained while swerving around several trash cans and a downed palm tree. "Everybody's trying to get ahead of the storm. We're lucky our rental has a full tank – the lines at the gas stations are impossible."

On a normal day, the drive to Austin would have taken three hours from Corpus Christi. At this rate, he worried they might not get there before nighttime. In any case, he wondered if this course of action was a smart one. Justin was part of a team who catalogued items from the recovered shipwreck and claimed there's some documentation about healing related to the coin. The coin doesn't match Celia's and it was found over thirty year's ago. Ryan was now second-guessing this whole plan.

Celia looked like she'd just been raised from the dead, and that made him nervous, too. He'd never seen skin that pale. She swooned in the back seat limply, strapped in tight, and looked like the weight of the world was on her shoulders. Which it was, he guessed.

He focused back to the road, barely able to see where they were going. Up ahead, the road vanished into water. He hit the brakes. The van skidded to a stop and threw them all forward. "Flood," he explained "We can't go this way. David, how do we get around this?"

David checked the GPS, and said, "I'm not sure, but I think we recently passed Fordyce Road. Turn back, and let's see. If so, we can take it to Timber Drive and meet back up with Route 77."

As he turned the van around, Celia was quiet and still. Aside from taking an occasional swig of Gatorade, she had hardly moved since they helped her into the van. She was weaker than she was letting on. He noticed a few spots of blood staining a portion of one of her bandaged wrists.

Something smacked the side of the van, making David twist around in the passenger seat, dropping his phone in surprise. "What the hell was that?"

Ryan ignored him, all his energy focused straight ahead.

Something flew by the windshield, followed by another item that banged against his window and slid back, stuck momentarily. It was a roof tile.

"Is this the turn?" he asked.

"What turn?" David said. "I can't see anything."

It was true. Visibility was terrible. That was scary enough, but where were the other travelers? Hardly anyone was on the road.

David shouted and pointed, "There. I think that's the parkway. The mall should be coming up."

They practically tipped onto two wheels for a second when Ryan yanked the steering wheel to the right. As the van pulled into the mall parking lot, it wasn't hard to find Justin, the man they were meeting to drive with them to Austin. The only car in sight was a Ford Taurus, a lonely silver bullet in the pounding rain. They pulled up alongside.

"It's a miracle," David said with sarcasm.

Ryan exhaled, and then shoved the gear-stick forward into park. Someone got out of the Taurus. He looked tall, even though it was hard to tell as he curled against the force of the wind to hobble over to the van, protecting his briefcase in the folds of a long coat. David scrambled to get the window down and yelled, "Hi, get in back."

Justin swung the side door open, and tossed in the briefcase before diving in and wrestling with the slippery door handle and pounding wind gusts. The door was only open a second, still the entire back seat, floor - and a good portion of the passenger chair up front where David was sitting - were soaked.

"77 straight north?" Ryan asked, before the newcomer was even buckled or was properly introduced. Ryan was usually one for making introductions, but he wanted to get out of there.

"Yup," Justin responded, repositioning his wet Stetson before he clicked his belt into place. "Hi, y'all."

"Hi, I'm David." David reached back to shake the man's hand.

"I'm Justin. Nice to meet you."

"Welcome Justin," Celia managed to say, although her voice was weak and trembling. "Thank you so much for joining us."

"My pleasure, Ma'am."

Except for the Texas accent, Justin looked a little like Harrison Ford in his sixties, or maybe Ryan was projecting that on him since Indiana Jones was the only archeologist he knew.

"I'm Ryan Delaney," he yelled from the front seat. "We spoke on the phone."

"I suppose you have a lot of questions?" Ryan said, steering them onto a main road and away from the storm. He had told Justin about Celia's healing and her stigmata.

Celia said. "Ask whatever you'd like, but bear with me. I'm pretty weak, and need to take breaks from time to time."

Justin didn't speak for a moment and then said, "Like the source of the sun pulsing through me, the heat consumes and restores and I'm left as weak as a sick and hungry child." He explained, "It's from the journal discovered in the shipwreck. The man who wrote it, we believe, was a crew member on the store ship, Aimable, even though the journal was found aboard La Belle. Apparently, he healed people and had visions. The passage I quoted described how he felt afterwards."

Celia nodded, almost imperceptibly. "Yes," she agreed. "Precisely."

Ryan asked, "Justin, were you involved during the entire nine-month excavation?"

"No, Sir," he replied. "I was a part of the team who catalogued artifacts at the Conservation Research Library at Texas A&M. It took us nine years. Now, I work for the Texas State Historical Commission and I'm writing a book about some of the discoveries, especially the particularly unusual ones."

"Like the coin?" David asked.

Justin nodded. It was clear Justin stood to make more money with his book sales if there was historical or mystical relevance to the artifacts he was writing about. Ryan now understood why he had been so eager to talk with them.

Justin said. "And the chest. There were over a million artifacts catalogued from the wreckage, many in good condition. For the first time, historians had access to an intact 17th-century French colonizing kit containing everything needed to establish a colony in the new world. That was big news. But I'm more interested in the items that were out of place on LaBelle. How did they get there? Why were they there? The journal is a key component to unraveling that mystery. The author of the journal refers to his coin as a source of power and here you are claiming the same."

"Also," he continued, a little hesitant, "there is mention of wounds, redemption, and the second coming of Christ. I looked you up, Professor Delaney, and I understand you're an ex-priest."

"I am," he confirmed, maneuvering around several lake-sized puddles. The wind and rain were lessoning. They had made the right decision to drive North.

Justin said, "I know for a fact the Vatican sent a representative here to review the journal and look at the coin back in 1998, and again in 2012. Any idea why?"

Celia asked, "Did the Vatican find any validity in the journal?"

"If they did," David said, "Justin wouldn't still have it, would he?"

"The Vatican decided the journal was not historically relevant," Justin tapped his briefcase. "Of course, when you read it, you may understand why the Vatican dismissed it. The author does not come across as somebody of sane mind."

"I know how he feels," Celia said with a weak smile. "But, you think there's some truth in his writing?"

"I do," he said. "But my opinion is the minority. That's why I am so interested in your story, and in learning what's in the documents you claim to have."

Celia filled him in a little about the story of Malchus and

Judas. She detailed Renata's disappearance and the references in the Qumran documents.

"According to the materials we have," she said, "the faithful of the church need to unite or heaven will be lost."

"Who are the faithful?"

"We don't know," Celia said. "The faithful could mean any number or combination of people. The documents suggest the faithful are related to those receiving the coin's gifts."

Justin asked, "Is there anything in your documents that mentions the antichrist or forces of evil?"

"Why do you ask?" Ryan accelerated slightly.

"Well, sailors are a suspicious lot. I've read many unusual entries in ship's logs and other various records. This journal, filled with some strange ranting, mentions demons and malevolent spirits."

Ryan admitted, "As a matter of fact, there is. The documents we have highlight passages from Thessalonian about falling away from the truth, exhalting oneself above God, using signs and lying wonders, and acting unrighteously. These elude to the antichrist. And in the Qumran documents they tie these behaviors to misuse of the coin's powers."

Nobody spoke for a moment, and then Justin continued, "In the journal, there's mention of visions, of craziness, despair, abuse of power, really bad stuff that this particular sailor attributes to the coins."

"Great," David said. "Wait, coins, plural?

Justin pulled a stack of photocopied sheets from his briefcase. "The coin recovered on LaBelle was not the only one. The journal mentions pirates in search of Roman coins, and the fact that the Belle had several coins on board," Justin explained. "Actually, the text refers to four coins on board the fleet with 'the powers of the almighty that carry the sign of His sacrifice.'"

"Stigmata?" Celia asked.

"I don't know," Justin said. "Can you tell me a little more about what happened to you? Not these last days, but in the beginning?"

As they drove north, Celia described for Justin the day she purchased her silver coin and the events that followed directly afterwards.

Justin nodded a lot and asked a few targeted questions. Ryan really wanted to pull over and take part in the discussion. It was difficult to follow along while driving.

"Is there anything in your documents or recovered from the Belle that you think will help us?" he asked.

"The journal that we recovered," he spotted Justin holding up a few photocopies when he glanced in the rearview mirror, "was wrapped and sealed in a wax pocket - kind of an ancient version of a Ziplock bag. This was stored in a small, flat, wooden box. The only problem is that over time water did penetrate to some degree, and a good portion of the journal was damaged - the ink had washed clean. Because of this, we have only been able to interpret and translate isolated sections of the journal. Without the missing content, it's hard to make out the context of individual passages."

Ryan heard the rustling of paper from the back seat.

Justin said, "There's mention of a new age. Here it is. It says, 'the people wondered and asked Christ when the time would come. The secret lost when Christ died on the cross.'"

"No shit," David said.

"David," Ryan warned.

"Sorry."

As the rain slowed to a drizzle, the he readjusted the wipers.

"May I see those?" David asked, gesturing toward his papers.

"Sure." Justin handed them over.

"Huh," David said, bending to read some of the journal. "The penmanship is disappointingly ordinary. Like you said, Justin, some areas are clear, while others are smudgy or faded. I can translate some of the Old French, but the context doesn't make sense. It may as well be in a language I don't know; this guy speaks in riddles.

"Wait, what was this?" There was a long pause before David said, "Redemption…a new age…heaven on earth…a vision of Eden in times to come…when, oh lord? Then, something about 'the chosen'." David looked at him. "The phrases are similar to those in the documents from Malchus."

David went back to reading. "You're wrong, Justin." He turned to look at Celia and Justin in the back seat. "You mistook the translation. This doesn't say the secret died with Christ on the cross. It says, 'The secret concealed by Christ on the Cross.'

"What about the cross recovered from La Belle?"

Ryan said, "Do you think..."

"Professor, watch the road," David ordered.

He turned back. "Sorry."

"Well?"

"First stop tomorrow," Justin said, "the Bob Bullock

Texas State History Museum. The cross is there."

Bob Bullock Texas State History Museum, Austin, Texas, May 1, 2032

They say everything's bigger in Texas, and the Bob Bullock Texas State History Museum is no exception. Sitting in a wheelchair only served to make Celia feel smaller as Ryan pushed her across the parking lot where she was dwarfed by a huge metal star, twice the height of her house, suspended over the main plaza of the museum. The star was so enormous that, from her position in the chair, it blocked the view of the giant rotunda in the center of the building and part of the dome at the top of the rotunda.

The wind whipped around them and the seven flags of Texas, atop fifty-foot flagpoles, waved ferociously as if signaling them to get inside. She could be paranoid. The storm hadn't reached Austin and by the time it got here it would be harmless, a nuisance at most. But she felt the pulse of the storm in her veins, the grey clouds reflected in her eyes, and the wind as it caught her breath when they entered the building.

Stopping in the entry, the big winding staircase posed a challenge for her in her new set of wheels. Ryan went off in search of an elevator, while she got some strange looks from visitors, her bandages and wheelchair drawing more than a few curious stares. It appalled her that people could be so rude.

To avoid any more looks from other patrons, she turned her wheelchair toward the directory, which described three floors of interactive exhibits. According to the sign: the first floor showcased the story of the land before it was Texas, the second floor visually told the story of how Texas became an independent nation, and the third floor showed how Texans had persevered on the land and how they approached everything from drilling oil to redefining world technology.

Justin explained, again, that over a million artifacts were recovered from La Belle. "They've been scattered among several of Texas' museums, including this one, and the Corpus Christi Museum of Science and History."

"What about the cross?" she asked.

"It's part of a traveling exhibit called 'Voyage To The New World' currently on display on the first floor."

"Let's go," David said.

Justin raised his hand to slow them. "I called ahead. The museum curator is a close friend of mine and a member of the Texas Historical Commission. He's arranged for a private showing of the coin and the cross in one of the offices upstairs."

"Cool," David responded.

In no time, the curator arrived and Justin introduced them. He didn't look like a museum curator to Celia, no stuffy suit or pretension whatsoever. With a surprising casualness, Jack, with his weathered skin and Texas ten-gallon hat, escorted them to the elevator and into a small room on the second floor. The center of the room had a wooden table, and on it was a piece of velvet. Placed on the velvet was the cross David had showed her a picture of that night at the bar, with the skull and crossbones engraved in it. Next to the cross lay the coin, although it was barely recognizable as one since it was so eroded by time and circumstance.

Ryan wheeled her to the table, and then parked her in front of the objects. He took the seat to her left, and Justin and David stood behind, watching with interest.

With two fingers of her bandaged right hand, she picked up one of the white fabric gloves. "I can't possibly manage."

The curator nodded. "You can touch them with your bare hands. I'll clean off the oils and dirt when you're through." He lifted the brim of his hat, tipping it like a gentleman, and explained, "If you need anything, Justin, you know where to find me."

Justin raised a hand as if in greeting. "We're fine, Jack. Thank you."

Once the curator left, Celia felt the coin with her fingertip. "It's very worn and tarnished," she commented. "Like some others I saw in Grand Cayman." She instinctively touched her necklace where her coin rested beneath her white t-shirt.

"Any purple markings?" Ryan asked.

"No. This coin is not one of the thirty." She lowered her bandaged hand and tried to pick up the cross as best she could. It was a large cross, the kind that would be hung in a home or church, almost as long as her forearm and half as wide. The wood was old and weathered - the inscription barely legible. It was heavy and ancient.

"Justin, is this one of the pieces you recovered from the excavation?" Ryan asked from beside her.

Celia couldn't keep her eyes off the cross. Her pulse sped up.

She heard Justin's voice from behind her. "No. The cross wasn't in the chest, or found in the same area of the ship as the journal."

Celia turned the cross over and looked very closely at the wood behind. "The secret concealed by Christ on the cross," she said. "Ryan, do you see it?"

Ryan took the cross from her, and peered at the very faint lines on the back. "It would be easy to miss them," he said. "Especially considering there were so many artifacts on board."

"Over a million," David repeated, and Celia tossed a glare at him over her shoulder for being a wiseass, but Justin didn't seem to register the barb.

"Interesting," Ryan ran a finger along the wood, "the lines form a circle at the cross's intersection and a rectangle below. Could be a compartment."

David said, "Anybody have a pocket knife?"

"Hold on." Justin grabbed David's shoulder, as if to anchor him in place. "Don't touch it! Let me get the tools I need." He walked to the door and exited swiftly, the sound of the latch loud in the silence of the room as the door clicked closed behind him.

David and Celia both leaned in to see the lines more clearly, while Ryan held the cross in two hands.

"Can I touch it?" David asked.

Ryan said, "No. You heard what Justin said."

"I won't do anything, I just want to see it." He held his hands out and Ryan tentatively passed the cross to David.

"Incredible," David said, tracing the faint lines with his finger. "Definitely a hidden compartment."

David returned the cross to Celia, and she noticed when the heavy crucifix rested on her bandages, her hands and wrist ceased to throb or ache.

"Ryan," she asked. "Would you remove one of my bandages?"

"You sure?"

She put the cross back on the table. "Please."

When he unraveled her right hand, she held her breath, certain that her suspicion was right. And sure enough, underneath the dried and bloodied cloth, her wounds were healed. She hastily removed the bandage from her other wrist, and found it equally recovered. "Amazing," she said, exhaling at last.

"Holy shit!" David shouted, reaching past her, grabbing the cross from the table and looking at it again.

Ryan took her hands and rubbed his thumbs over her wrists. She felt the excitement in his touch. "A miracle," he whispered.

"I know," she smirked in response to his astonished expression. "I've seen it before."

"Awesome," David exclaimed, nodding and smirking, holding the cross like a ten year old with a new video game.

Just then, Justin returned with his tools, spotting Celia's bloody bandages on the table. He threw them a questioning glance, and Celia worried that he would think she was a fake and wonder if they were trying to put one over on him. She considered explaining, but then decided to let him draw his own conclusions.

She carefully swept the bandages into the trash by the table and caught Justin looking at one of the security cameras in the corner of the room.

"You missed it," David said, oblivious to her inner turmoil. "C'mon, are we going to open the compartments, or what?"

Justin took the cross from David, all the while looking at Celia's hands and wrists with interest. "Ma'am, you're better?" He said.

"Yes."

"Completely?"

She held up both hands as if in prayer. "Healed from touching the cross."

David reached over and tapped the cross with his finger. "My mother had a cross with a compartment in the back for holy water when I was a kid," he said. "I'm surprised your guys didn't notice this."

Luckily, Justin ignored the comment. He sat down in Ryan's spot, taking out a thin, mounted razor with a long handle that looked like a dentist's tool. They watched as he ran it along the seam on the back of the cross very carefully, starting with the round outline. A thin powder formed around the sides of the razor. He rubbed a few particles between his fingers and smelled it. "Wax," he explained, and returned to the task. In moments, the circle of wood he had outlined began to spin slightly in the orbit of the recessed compartment. Justin maneuvered the fine blade and the circle of wood lifted from its resting place to reveal a single Roman Shekel, the same as the one Celia wore on her neck, with a slight purple tarnish.

Everybody stared, momentarily surprised.

"Well, that would explain the healing," Ryan said as he and David leaned over them, their breathing disturbing Celia's hair with each exhalation.

"What's in the rectangle?" David asked.

"Be patient, David," she said. "May I?" Celia held out her healed hands for the cross.

After a small pause, Justin passed it to her.

Taking the cross from him, she turned it over, face up, so the coin fell into her palm. Tears streamed down her face. Similar to a year ago, she experienced a kind of awakening, just like she felt when she first wore her coin. She could feel the rush of the air conditioner like a crisp arctic wind - the sound it made a melody of white noise mixed with breathing. She smelled the wax, the wood, and the dank scent of time. She held the coin out to Ryan and, tentatively, he reached out and took it from her.

He closed his eyes and rolled the coin around in his hand, testing it, feeling the weight of it in his palm, and touching it with his fingers. He also wept. "It's so warm," he said, and she realized he was feeling its power, too.

David said, "Can I see it?"

Ryan handed him the coin, and to Celia's surprise David tossed it about like a poker chip. "Relax," he said when he saw her face. "This thing has been through more than I can dish out." He stopped playing and inspected the coin more earnestly. She could tell that he was not feeling the same connection to the coin that Ryan did. It got passed to Justin, who stared at it as if it might bite him.

"Let's see what else we have," David said.

Justin nodded, put the new coin on the velvet cloth next to the other one, and began the same process on the rectangular seam. After several moments, the wood backing lifted, and they all leaned in to peer into the recess. A small roll of paper came out when Justin turned the cross over, much as Celia had done to remove the coin. When he started to unroll it, she was reminded of those miniature astrology scrolls they used to buy as kids in the grocery store to read their horoscope.

There was no mistaking it had the same penmanship as found in the recovered journal.

Justin translated the Old French and read, "Psalms 90:2 Before the mountains were brought forth, or ever thou hadst formed the earth and the world, even from everlasting to everlasting, thou art God."

"Psalms 90:4 A thousand years in your eyes are merely a yesterday.

"Psalms 90:12 Teach us to number our days aright, that we may gain wisdom.

"When the heavens below and the heavens above are aligned, marked with His suffering, the chosen will alight. When the circle completes, all will realize a new heaven and a new earth, for the first heaven and the first earth will have passed away...you will wipe away every tear, every fear, and death shall be no more, neither shall there be mourning, nor crying, nor pain anymore, for the former things have passed away."

Celia was stumped. This meant nothing to her. "Ryan, what do you know about the book of Psalms?"

He paused before he replied, "Strange, the last passage is familiar, but not a direct bible quote, I don't think. And definitely not from Psalms. I can't place it.

"Psalms is the longest book in the Bible, with one hundred and fifty individual psalms, which are a collection of prayers, poems, and hymns. It's also one of the most diverse. Psalms reflect upon God's creation, sin, evil, judgment, justice, and the coming of the messiah."

David says, "Psalms was written way before Christ."

"Yes," Ryan says. "But Christ is present in Psalms, and not only in the messianic psalms. Nearly half of all messianic references in the New Testament originate from the Psalms."

Just then, the curator returned, and Justin showed him the new discoveries. Although the man looked like Clint Eastwood, his voice sounded like Woody Woodpecker. Justin did not mention the miracle of Celia's healed hands and stood between the curator and the trash containing her soiled bandages. Coincidentally, he also blocked the view of the security camera. Celia reached over and casually slid the plastic trash can further under the table, and then kept her hands inconspicuously on her lap.

The curator left to document and photograph their findings, promising them a printout as a memento.

David, Ryan, and Justin stood awkwardly for a moment, while Celia sat in a wheelchair she no longer needed.

She whispered, "Justin, do the cameras in this room have audio?"

"No," he said, his back toward the camera, blocking her from view.

Her mind started to churn. How could they get their hands on that coin? She asked Ryan, "Do you think the bishop will help us once he hears about this?"

"I don't know," Ryan said. He started drumming the table with his fingertips in an annoying way.

"Which bishop?" Justin asked.

Ryan stopped drumming. "Bishop Reilly. We're meeting

him in Austin tomorrow." Ryan squeezed his forehead with his fingertips as if trying to ward off a headache. He breathed deeply.

Justin bit his lower lip. "Can you trust him?"

"With my life," Ryan answered.

"Justin," Celia said cautiously, "you understand our predicament. The documents we have indicate that the thirty coins need to be reunited. We don't know if the Vatican will agree, or disagree, with this information."

Justin said, "Ma'am, I'm an archeologist, not a tomb raider or treasure hunter. But I believe you." He started pacing. "I'll do what I can, but I can't guarantee I can get you the coin. There are procedures to follow—"

"Procedures?" David threw his hands up in the air. "Are you kidding me?"

"The coin is the property of the Texas Historical Commission. For now," Justin said. "Once news of this miracle reaches the Vatican, the museum and historical commission don't stand a chance of retaining ownership."

He stopped pacing. "What I'm saying is, once the Vatican is involved, I don't know if I'll be able to help you."

"But you're not sure you can get us the coin either way?" Ryan asked. "So the decision is, do we count on you, or involve the church and hope for the best?"

"Well," Justin mumbled under his breath, "We're the only ones who know about the miracle, for now. I can manipulate the video on the security cameras—"

"You can?" David gave him a skeptical look.

"I dabble in video editing for bands in the area. The system and tapes are often used to verify the validity of a find like this - nobody will question my taking them. Don't worry, no one has any reason to be suspicious, yet."

Threadgills Diner, North Austin, Texas, May 1, 2032

The diner was supposed to be some sort of historical music place, but David wasn't a fan of country music. Besides, the place was dead and he was so hungry he could have eaten the bar stools while they waited for the hostess to come and seat them.

It was a strange place decorated with neon lights, several of which were Texas stars. What was the big deal with the stars, anyway? They were everywhere!

Justin tried to be interesting and made small talk while they followed the waitress to their table. "This is where Janis Joplin developed her country and blues style. The food is excellent."

After they were seated, David browsed the menu. He'd never in his life eaten anywhere they served fried chicken livers with cream gravy, and he was sure his snob of a father would have been rolling in his grave if he could see him now.

The Texas Margarita sounded awesome, so he ordered one.

Once the drinks arrived, he read the scroll again, and then he said aloud, "When the heavens below and the heavens above are aligned."

The group ignored him for a moment while Justin expressed, for the eleventh time, how much he would like to come with them, to know more about Celia's gift and the power of the coins. But his family and new daughter were obstacles he couldn't get around, no matter how hard he tried.

"How old are you?" David asked rudely.

Celia nudged him with her elbow. "David!"

Justin laughed. "It's ok, Ma'am, I get that a lot. I'm fifty-eight, David. I have three kids from my first marriage, one older than you I suspect, and two from my second marriage. My first wife died of Cancer. Would have done anything to have been able to heal her. Truthfully, that's part of my interest in the journal and the coins."

"I'm so sorry," Celia said.

David returned his attention to the copy of the scroll, and read, again, "the first heaven and the first earth will have passed away."

This triggered something in him that he couldn't put his finger on.

He pulled out his mobile device and performed a few searches online, then began scribbling some notes on the back of the digital printout of the scroll. Engrossed, he completely forgot to drink his margarita until the meal came.

The food was absolutely amazing, the grilled tilapia perfectly cooked and seasoned, but David refused to give Justin the satisfaction of knowing he had made a good choice bringing them here. Something about the guy rubbed him the wrong way. Justin was too conventional, too formal. David was certain that Justin thought he was just some cocky kid with no regard for protocol. And he would be right. It probably galled Justin that David was the one to lead them to the hidden coin and message in the cross.

The discussion around the table was centered on Portugal, a place where they knew other coins had surfaced, but

David had missed most of the key points because he was glued to his mobile and the research he'd been doing online through the whole meal.

Finally, he spoke up. "I found the last passage. It's from Revelations, although the words aren't exact. Almost exact, though."

The conversation stopped and all eyes turned to him.

"And did you notice all the Psalms references relate to time or passage of time."

The professor said, "I did."

"Well," David continued, "I'm just thinking out loud here, trying to find some clue to what we're meant to learn from this. I mean, why go through the time to compose these thoughts or quotes if they're just random, right? There has to be some takeaway."

Celia said, "The last phrase is very, very similar to quotes from the scrolls found with the coins in Qumran. Especially the phrase 'new heaven'. I remember reading that and wondering what that may mean. Could there be an old heaven? It didn't make sense to me."

The professor said, "Pope Paul VI referenced something about a new world in the Gaudium et Spes." He started to search his own mobile and David scrambled to find the information faster than his mentor.

The professor beat him to the punch and said, "We do not know the time for the consummation of the earth and of humanity, nor do we know how all things will be transformed. As deformed by sin, the shape of this world will pass away; but we are taught that God is preparing a new dwelling place and a new earth where justice will abide, and whose blessedness will answer and surpass all the long-ings for peace which spring up in the human heart. Then, with death overcome, the sons of God will be raised up in Christ, and what was sown in weakness and corruption will be invested with incorruptibility."

"That's hopeful," Celia commented. "Interesting that he used the term 'sons' and not 'son'."

"My mother told me we're all God's children. I liked that. Jesus was cool and everything, but I preferred to pray to the big man directly," David said. "It always bugged me when people act like Christ is the be all, end all. God created the world long before Christ. Why do Christians always belittle that?"

Justin said, "What religion are you?"

David said, "All. And none. And science. I'm still figuring it out." He popped a bite of bread in his mouth.

"What are you doing here?" Justin asked, his brow furrowed as he leaned back in his seat dismissively.

David didn't have to explain himself to this redneck archeologist. He was about to say so when the professor said, "He's looking for answers, just like you."

Terrified that the professor might talk about David's parents, he blurted out. "About new heaven, Celia. The Vatican website says that Sacred Scripture calls this mysterious renewal, which will transform humanity and the world, 'new heaven and a new earth.' It also says the visible universe, then, is itself destined to be transformed. And that God is preparing a new dwelling and a new earth in which happiness will fill and surpass all the desires of peace arising in the hearts of men."

"What does any of this have to do with the coins?" Justin asked.

"Good question," the professor replied. "I've been wondering that myself."

David said, "When the professor first told me about Celia, I tried to find mention of coins or thirty coins in the Vatican archives online. I didn't find much, but I did find this." He scrolled through the notes on his mobile app and read aloud, "Pope Benedict XV wrote, 'we have got to meditate on the Law of God day and night so that, as expert money-changers, we may be able to detect false coin from true.'"

"That's just a turn of phrase," The professor retorted.

David leaned in, trying to be discreet now that a party had been seated next to them in the restaurant. "Maybe," he agreed. "But what if it isn't? What if the documents Celia has, or similar ones the Vatican has seen, mention the coins? What if there are others who suspect the power of the coins or predict what uniting them may mean to the world? What if others are looking for the true coins, actual Judas coins, just like us?"

Celia added, "They have to know. The church was notified in 1940 when the coins and scrolls were found. The scrolls clearly reference the coins. They mention the coins being cursed, being blessed, bestowing gifts, holding powers of healing, death, enlightenment, and access to heaven. Margaret was smart enough to take photos of the scrolls before turning the originals over to the Vatican. Ryan, you spoke to the bishop about the scrolls, but he wouldn't confirm or deny the church's position on them."

"I'll ask him directly when I meet with him tomorrow."

"What scares me is," Celia continued, leaning in as David had and speaking in a hushed voice, "Margaret died in a car crash shortly after their discovery of the coins and scrolls even though no one knew she had secretly photographed the documents. The three men who stole the coins from the discovery site, one from each pot, are all dead, two by mysterious causes. No one knows where those coins went. And Renata, the only other person we know of with powers achieved through a coin, is missing."

Ryan touched her arm. "We can trust the bishop. I'm confident he'll have answers."

David had very little faith in authority of any kind. He respected the professor, but he would rather solve this mystery himself than rely on the church, or Justin, or whoever else will know about this coin and message very shortly.

"You know," David said, "I always wondered, why thirty pieces? Why that amount? Why is that the mere number of coins offered to Judas. And why would uniting thirty pieces of silver mean anything in relation to heaven, or whatever it is we think is going to happen when we find them all, if we find them all?"

The professor said, "According to my studies at the seminary, thirty, being three times ten, denotes in a higher degree the perfection of divine order, as marking the right moment. A perfect example of this is that Jesus was thirty years old when he began His ministry."

"Well," David said, "I'm trying to figure out if the numbers on the scroll mean anything relevant. Don't you find it odd that the last quote has no scripture reference, but the first three do? Don't you also find it interesting that the three passages with numbers all reference time. 'Before the mountains were formed', 'everlasting to everlasting', 'a thousand years', 'yesterday', 'number our days aright'?

"The second part of the scroll reads, 'When the heavens below and the heavens above are aligned.' Have any of you heard about the planetary alignment with the Milky Way which occurred on December twenty-first in the year two-thousand and twelve?"

Justin leaned in, "You mean the apocalypse theory? Are you suggesting this relates to foolishness about the end of the world as predicted by the Mayan calendar? In case you missed it, the world didn't end y'all."

"I know," David replied. "I was born on that very day. But, to my knowledge, that is the astronomical moment when the heavens below and above were aligned. It is also the end of the Mayan Calendar. There's no ignoring the significance of that date. And not just because it's my birthday."

The professor spoke, "Apocalypse, in the terminology of early Jewish and Christian literature, is a revelation of hidden things revealed by God to a chosen prophet or apostle. It does not mean the end of the world, specifically."

Celia pushed away her untouched drink, "What about the planetary alignment?"

David stared at the trio of giant neon stars on the restaurant ceiling, one inside the other, and thought how appropriate it was that they had chosen to eat here. "A thousand years in your eyes are merely a yesterday," He repeated the passage from Psalms on the scroll. "The Mayan calendar was based on solar cycles.

"As you may know, our solar system is part of a huge disc-shaped collection of stars and planets called the Milky Way.

We were located somewhere on the edge of the disc, slightly on top. But on December twenty-first in the year two-thousand and twelve, the earth moved through the center of the Milky Way to the bottom of the disc."

Celia quoted, "When the heavens below and the heavens above are aligned."

And he concluded, "Marked with His suffering, the chosen will alight."

Celia asked, "What does that mean?"

David admitted, " I have no idea."

CHAPTER 6

The Vatican Library, Rome, Italy, May 1, 2032

Cardinal Jusipini was on the Internet investigating claims of Roman coins found in Turkey when he received an email about a hidden coin in a cross, discovered that morning at the Bob Bullock Texas State History Museum. He had inspected another coin found on that ship years ago when the wreck was first discovered, and then representatives from the church had gone back seventeen years later. Fools. How could they have missed this?

And according to his source, they were sending Bishop Reilly from Worcester, Massachusetts, to investigate. He knew of Bishop Reilly. The bishop had been the person sent to authenticate the validity of the Italian woman, Renata, and her claims of stigmata a year ago. Apparently, Bishop Reilly was acquainted with the ex-priest who was one of the three people at the Museum today. This would not do.

The Cardinal watched the digital footage of the discovery. After seeing the woman in the wheelchair with her wrapped head, he got to his feet and leaned closer, froze the screen, and zoomed in. There, around her neck, fuzzy due to the quality, but unmistakable: a shekel. Frantically, he fast forwarded. There was a blip in the timeline, made carelessly by some amateur. What had they cut out? He played the footage back and forth.

Picking up the phone, he quickly dialed the museum and reported the tampering. After waiting an eternity, the curator claimed he had no idea where the missing footage was, but clarified he would follow up with the coworker who had escorted the guests to the museum. The cardinal wrote down all the information he could get, then asked to see footage from any other security camera that had captured the visitors prior to entering the room. He was promised delivery in an hour.

Turning back to the computer screen, the cardinal watched the strangers open the secret compartments on the cross. He was not surprised or enlightened by the message found on the small scroll. He already knew the prophecy of reuniting the thirty pieces. He had but only six of the thirty now.

The fourth coin that Cardinal Everett Jusipini acquired had bestowed the gift of ministry. He soon found it difficult not to serve others, and the internal battle between his own ambitions and this newfound compulsion to serve made him sick at times. So sick, in fact, that he began blacking out, had suffered heart palpitations, and had been diagnosed in hospital once with unnatural levels of adrenaline. He tried to heal himself, but it didn't work. He was removed from his duties at the library. The church was at a loss with what to do with him. Whatever had been decided had been kept secret. Although he was allowed to continue to research coins, he was not allowed physical contact with them any longer.

The cumulative powers of the coins muddied his ability decipher the gifts of his fifth and sixth coins, but he knew they did not bestow prophesy or tongues, two gifts he longed for.

He needed to intercept the Bishop. Cardinal Jusipini was determined to prove to the Vatican that he was the chosen one, and keeping him from the grace of the coins was a big mistake.

How many coins did these strangers have? How much did they know already? Could they be the key to him finally, after all this time, fulfilling his destiny and Jesus's prophecy?

He started pacing, glancing over his shoulder at the computer screen as he played the altered video clip again and again. There is was, a flash of something at the corner of the screen, there one minute, gone the next. Bandages in the trash can.

He rewound and saw the ex-priest lovingly holding the woman's hands. Sinners. Fornicators. He focused on their hands, watching the priest gently rubbing his thumbs over the woman's wrists. He read the priest's lips, "miracle".

These people knew far too much. He memorized their faces, reviewed the email from his spies, locked their names in his mind, sat down and started to research whatever he could find about Professor Ryan Delaney, Celia Allessandri, Justin Miller, and David Caldwell.

Hilton Hotel, Austin Texas, May 2, 2032

"Well, maybe Justin can get the coin for us," Celia said, sitting down hard on the hotel-room couch, not believing for one minute that Justin could help them.

"Do you trust him?" David asked, leaning against the wall near the door to his adjoining room.

"She trusts everybody," Ryan replied, sitting next to her on the couch.

She elbowed him.

"It's true," he reiterated. "That's a compliment."

"Meaning, I'm gullible," she argued.

"Meaning, you see the good in everybody," Ryan said.

"Do you ever do the wrong thing, for the right reasons?" David asked.

Where was David going with this? He had a smug look on his face she didn't like. "Why do you ask?"

David stepped away from the wall. "If you could get your hands on that coin, would you do it?"

"I'm not breaking into the museum, David. We talked about that at the restaurant." She rested her elbows on her knees, staring him down, daring him to defy her.

"That was with Justin around. What if you could have the coin without anyone ever knowing, and —" he said before she could object, holding up a finger, "without breaking into the museum?"

"Then I'd be all for it," she agreed.

"Would you?" he took another step closer to the couch.

"Yes." She narrowed her eyes hoping her scrutiny would make him get to the point.

"Just checking," he said, flipping a coin into the air off his thumb, catching it, and then tossing it onto the bed.

She jumped up. "How did you —"

Ryan was quicker. He grabbed the coin and held it between his fingers, devouring it with his eyes. "It's the coin from the cross."

"That's impossible," she said. "I saw the curator take it."

"No, you didn't," David smiled, crossing his arms over his chest. "I palmed it. The coin the curator has is a decoy. I got the idea from Justin on the ride there."

She took the coin from Ryan. The warmth and power spread through her. How the hell?

She said, "But I saw the decoy. It had the same marks as mine."

David took a nickel and a match from his pocket. He lit the match and held it to the corner of the coin. "Heat turns the coin a purplish color that remains even after you wipe it with a cloth to remove the soot."

David was clever, but Celia wasn't amused by the deception. True, they needed the coin. She wasn't sure what was bothering her, except that David had been underhanded, and what was happening to her was no parlor trick.

"Where'd you get the substitute?" Ryan asked.

David shrugged, as if it was no big deal. "I bought several silver coins right after you told me Celia's story. Quite honestly, I was prepared to prove she was a fake until she pulled off that miracle on the plane. Once I recreated the mark, I guess I thought I would expose her eventually, and you and I could go back to class with an interesting story to tell."

"Unbelievable!" She shook her head in astonishment.

"Yeah, well, it kind of is, if you think about it," David commented.

"I meant you!" she snapped.

"Hey, look at the bright side. I know you're for real now, and I figured out how to manufacture a duplicate. The thing is: how will we know when we have a real Judas coin? If I can recreate the markings, somebody else can, too."

Celia picked up the coin, went to the bathroom for toilet paper, and then rubbed it clean. He was right, the mark did look a lot like the discoloration on her coin. She compared them under the bathroom light. The discoloration on the nickel and the silver coin were not identical, but it would be difficult to spot the fake, unless you were looking for it, and the metal composition of the nickel was not silver."

"Well, a fake coin wouldn't have any power," she walked back into the main room, answering David's earlier question.

"How can you tell? I've been carrying around that coin and you had no idea," David countered. "I can't sense anything special about it."

"You're wrong," Ryan said. "You can feel it – an energy. A deep warmth, like it's alive or something."

"That's right," she nodded her head in agreement.

"Bullshit. Let me see," David said, his hand outstretched.

Ryan tossed him the Roman coin. David palmed it, then shook his head. "I don't feel anything."

"Give it to me," she said. It was interesting that David couldn't feel the coin's power, but Ryan could. "Well, I say the marks aren't the same."

"They're close," David argued. "With the right heat source, the right metal composition, it could be possible to create an exact match."

"It may fool someone who hasn't seen or felt the real thing," she said. "Or perhaps only has had a quick view, like Justin, I'll give you that." She tossed the nickel back onto the bed and handed the real Roman coin to Ryan.

"Why thanks," David said, gesturing wide with his hands.

"I'll thank you as soon as I'm sure the authorities aren't after us for theft," she said.

"Okay, thank me later," he replied, and then left the room in a huff.

As Celia sat on the floor with Ryan, leaning against the bed in the hotel room, she felt the strongest déjà vu, and found herself reminiscing about the hundreds of afternoons with him in her dorm room, hanging out, talking, and later, making love. She wished that were the case now. She's rather be doing anything than sitting here with a computer trying to figure out their next move.

Ryan turned the coin from the cross over and over in his hand, deep in thought. He said, "I wonder what Christ would say about the world if He were to come back now?"

"I have no idea," she replied, continuing to read the article online, which explained about the earth's intersection with the 'Galactic Equator,' or center of the Milky Way.

"Why does the Vatican have an observatory?" she asked,

nudging Ryan when he doesn't seem to hear her.

"Ryan?" It was no use. He was lost in thought. Her brain started to hurt. She needed to stop reading this stuff and thinking so hard. It was odd that the Mayans had observatories and the Vatican had one too. Why would the Vatican need an observatory?

She looked outside. The view of Austin through the hotel window reflected a dismal weather pattern - the remaining wrath of hurricane Jessie. She'd become immune to the sound of the steady pounding rain, and after the torrent and winds of Corpus Christi, this level of storm paled in comparison. She worried, though, that the weather may delay the bishop's flight.

She commented about that to Ryan, who continued with his fixation on the coin. He said, "It's so hard to believe that this coin could be one of the actual coins given to Judas to betray Jesus."

"Ryan," she laughed, "have you heard anything I've said over the last five minutes?"

He jostled out of his trance. "No, I'm sorry."

"Look," she told him. "I appreciate all the sensations you're feeling right now. Trust me. I know how significant the coin is, and how intense this must be for you, of all people. Where do we go from here? What are we doing?" And more importantly, she thought, how do we control this and get our lives back? She was tired from all the drama, the miracles, the stress of it all. She didn't ask for this. Hell, it scared the crap out of her. It might be cool to Ryan, a real, honest-to-goodness spiritual mission, but it's not a path she would have chosen for herself.

"Ryan."

He straightened. "I'm sorry, what were you saying?"

She sighed. "It's not important."

What was she doing here, with a man she hardly knew anymore, yet felt she knew so intimately, so completely? She was ashamed to admit she felt like she was losing him again to God. But then again, perhaps he was never hers to lose.

She said, "I was thinking about the apocalypse theory, and about what Justin asked regarding evil when we were driving yesterday."

"Did you know," he said, twisting to face her. He looked almost eager, like a kid, but when he started talking, he was Professor Delaney all over. "Some modern theologians describe hell as the soul using its free will to reject the will of God. For the Eastern Orthodox, Heaven is not a place in the sky. Rather, it's being with God. The West, too, teaches that God doesn't cut off anyone from himself, and that hell is the self-exclusion we impose upon ourselves. Even Pope John Paul the second said that, while Scripture represents hell as a place, it is really a state of self-exclusion from God. What if the heaven described in the documents you have is, in actuality, people finally using their free will to embrace God in His true form, and if that's the Heaven on earth, or Eden, we expect will occur if we're successful?"

"So," she argued, "If we're unsuccessful, people will self-exclude or turn away from God?"

"I don't know. The scroll says, 'Heaven on earth will be realized.'"

"True. What if it's not realized?"

"Well," Ryan said, "There are many different opinions

on that. Revelations talks about the final judgment - the last test of mankind's sinful nature under ideal conditions by the loosing of Satan, with the judgment of fire coming down from Heaven."

"Fire from Heaven," she repeated, with visions of solar flares, comets with streaming tails, and unknown cosmic events.

"Revelations says, following the fire comes a destruction of the current heavens, and the earth to be recreated as a new Heaven, and a new earth."

"The loosing of Satan," Celia shivered. "I don't like the sound of that. I also don't like the thought that destruction precedes the new Heaven and earth."

"Well," he smiled reassuringly, "When Jesus said he would destroy the temple, his real meaning was misunderstood and taken literally, right? Maybe this is the same. Knowing history, we should expect resistance, even from the most unlikely places. The church regularly rejects groups that advocate what they call 'the falsification of the kingdom to come under the name of millenarianism'. There are many groups previously who have predicted the end of the world, or a new world order."

"Really, Ryan, we're not terrorists or extremists," she replied.

"I know, but you may relate more to other millenarian groups like Hinduism, Judaism, or even Nostradamus," he said.

"What's your point, Ryan?"

"My point is, Celia, that we have a long road ahead to convert people into believing us. I mean, look what it took to convince David. What would you think of you, or all of this, if you weren't you and hadn't experienced what you had over the past year? Roman coins claiming to be the actual Judas coins, Stigmata, hidden secret documents, and ancient prophecies?"

"I don't know," she said.

He nodded. "That's my point. History paints a very bleak picture for those who try to save the world in God's name, Celia. Not that I'm not ready to try."

She wanted to ask him where his faith went, but didn't. Instead, she said, "What choice do we have Ryan? It's not like I can just ignore what's happening and walk away."

He looked at her necklace, and then reached out and took it in his hand. "No, I don't suppose you can. In the dream recounted in Revelations, the eagle, representing the Roman Empire, is followed by the lion, which is the promised messiah, who is to deliver the chosen people and establish an everlasting kingdom."

His touch made her shiver, and the smell and nearness of him filled her senses. She was drawn to the sound of his voice now just as strongly as she was in her youth. Could he sense her desire? Or, is he oblivious after all this time? "What are you saying?" she asked, in a hoarse whisper. "That I'm a lamb, weak and vulnerable?"

"No, Jesus was the lamb. The sacrificial lamb," he said, letting her coin fall against her heart with a harsh thud. "Maybe you're the lion."

Just then, David walked through the door. "Am I interrupting something?" he said.

Celia's heart was pounding and her head was spinning

with thoughts she didn't want to be thinking. The lion? What was Run suggesting?

"What did you learn?" Ryan stood and stretched.

"Not much. How about you guys?"

Celia moved next to the window and stared blankly while rubbing her silver coin with her fingers. The motion jiggled the chain around her neck up and down, up and down. She said nothing, Ryan's words haunting her. She was getting in over her head with him and this whole thing. Why? Why would God chose her? What was she supposed to do with all this? She trembled. The enormity of their predicament shaking her to the core.

Ryan said, "Dead end. Can you help us translate some of this French journal?"

"Sure. What's up?"

"Just a lot to take in." Ryan answered for her, gathering up the copied sheets Justin left with them, handing everything to David, and sitting on the couch. "Your French is better than mine."

Celia walked over and sat on the other side of David, trying to calm herself.

David read a few passages aloud, omitting the sections that he claimed were unreadable or missing. "Here's something," he said. "The sailor writes about visions, healing, something about the coming of many, and it says, 'those who desire to thwart the word of God, bring evil, and hold tight the constraints of this current world.' I can't read sections, but it says something about 'fear of divine truth' and 'glory for all, not for one.' This portion is badly damaged."

Celia was leaning in, and pointed to a passage. "Is that a

swastika?" She stiffened. "Did this guy predict Hitler? What does it say here?"

The writing was faint and broken. "It says something about 'harmony,' which, actually, makes sense."

"How does that make sense?" Celia asked.

Ryan said, "In Hinduism, this symbol signifies harmony, but the Hindu symbol has four dots inside each of the four arms."

"That's right," David agreed. "Long before Hitler used the symbol to represent Nazi Germany, it was a symbol that represented good luck to ancient Indians. It was also the traditional symbol of Thor, the Norse god of thunder. Here's an interesting tidbit, too," he said. "The swastika symbol has been found in ancient Jewish synagogues."

Celia sat up, surprised. "I didn't know that."

"Even better, Mexicans, Aztecs, and Indian tribes of Central and South America have used it. And, it's an ancient Mayan symbol," he explained, reiterating that Mayan connection.

"No reason to believe this symbol represents the Mayan one," Ryan said. "It's also found in China, Tibet, and Japan where it's known as Manji. Did you know it was also a Roman pagan symbol, and was on ancient Roman coins? Early Christians carved it on their tombs as a symbol of everlasting life."

She leaned in and scanned the page. "So, what is the context of the symbol in the journal?"

David looked over the passage. "It's hard to say. This section is trashed. Either this guy was familiar with the symbol, or saw it in a vision.

"There's a lot of rambling here, 'pain, redemption, evil, healing, something about the old world, but I don't know the word or how it translates, of course, new heaven. A rambling about lost minds. He writes more scattered when he's referencing himself, but clearer when writing about 'visions'

"This is interesting," he said. "'Beneath the temple lies refuge for the chosen. Evil thwarted, the judgment shall pass, and the gathered will bear the truth of God.'"

"Riddles upon riddles," Celia said, straightening.

"Could they mean Temple Mount in Jerusalem?" Ryan asked.

"What if the temple isn't a real place?" Celia started pacing, trying to clear her mind. She said, "What if it's representational, like how Jesus spoke of his body as a temple? You were just saying that yourself, Ryan."

Ryan said, "That doesn't make sense in this case. First of all, the sailor doesn't speak in parables, like Jesus did. Secondly, the word 'beneath' and reference to 'the gathered' would suggest this temple is a structure."

She stopped pacing. All this talk of evil, sacrificial lambs and Nazis was making her crazy.

"Did you know," Ryan said, "that Hitler tried for many years to find the Holy Grail? He was obsessed with it, the power it represented, and the significance."

Celia groaned. "I need air," she grabbed her purse. "You guys should really get some sleep. It's a big day tomorrow. Lots to think about."

With that, she took off, leaving Ryan and David staring after her.

Celia's chest was tight, strained, and she couldn't breathe. She wandered down the hall of the hotel, her mind a whirlwind of thoughts and images from the Swastika and Hitler, to the Mayan calendar, to the Holy Wars, to fire scorching the earth, to visions of Jesus on the cross - each more daunting than the last. And, overlaying it all, the visceral pull of Ryan.

She ran down the stairs two at a time, nearly taking out a bellhop while rushing through the lobby, and then she burst through the front doors into the calming, warm Austin air. Seconds passed before a cab pulled up. She got in.

"Take me to the nearest Church."

The driver was a dark-haired man with close-set eyes. He smelled like cigarettes and so did the cab, but she didn't care.

Within moments, they parked in front of a lovely little stone church that had a tower on its left side which reminded her of the towers in fairy tales she imagined as a girl. The sign read 'Christo Rey Parish'.

She handed the driver a twenty-dollar bill and said, "Will you wait for ten minutes?"

He didn't respond, but took her money. She checked to make sure her cell phone was in her bag, and exited the cab.

The church was dark, so it was probably locked, but she ventured closer and tried the door. Sure enough, it didn't budge. Hiding in the shadows of the overhang, she squatted against the giant wooden doors and sobbed. The air was warm, and the sky was bright with stars that twinkled and blurred beyond her tears. She closed her eyes, struggling to find that place past sorrow and fear where God is. She sought to lose herself in meditation, to re-energize so she could face tomorrow.

She had hoped that finding Ryan would relieve her of some of her burden, but he seemed to prefer to entangle her in events with more importance than she warranted.

Maybe you're the lion.

Burying her face in her arms, she slipped further into her sorrow, and deeper into quiet contemplation. When Ryan was near her, she couldn't seem to get past his magnetic pull, which, ironically, was stronger since they found the coin in the old cross. Their connection, always so poignant to her before, had intensified. She knew he felt it, too. The question was, really, what was the point? So much was happening to her that there seemed to be no room to even contemplate a them.

She couldn't get to that place of quiet, even separated from him now. Her mind wouldn't let her. She banged her head a few times against the giant wooden door, and then the tears started again. They gained momentum until the sobs resounded in full force.

The cab driver tooted the horn, so she pulled herself together, and walked back. What if we're all wrong? What if we're all crazy, chasing after shadows, and believing in the ranting of a lunatic at sea and some old documents?

Her doubts were like water; they slipped through her fingers. She knew they weren't crazy, that was the problem. This was too real.

The driver asked, "Where to?"

She got an idea. "Take me to the hospital, please."

"Which one?"

"One with a chapel," she said.

He made several turns while she stared off, deep in thought. The hurricane in her head seemed more severe than the one they survived recently. She couldn't outrun the events in her life, her feelings for Ryan, and her fear of the path the coin made for her.

The cab pulled up in front of the North Austin Medical Center, and parked directly under an impressive reflective windowed rotunda. She paid the driver and got out.

"Thank you," she said.

He pulled away without reply. No doubt: he thought she was nuts. Heck, she thought she was nuts. Really, the last place she wanted to be was in a hospital right now, but she expected it was the only place she'd find a chapel or an open church at this hour. Her mood was almost manic at this point.

She walked into the entryway, and wandered about for some time, until a directory on the wall pointed the way to the chapel.

Once inside, and thankfully alone, she slumped into a pew. What was she doing?

Sitting with her head in her hands, she rocked back and forth trying to soothe herself and fight off the panic.

God. Oh, God. She chanted in her head over and over, like a mantra. God. Oh, God. And she rocked back and forth, back and forth - her mind going numb, her heartbeat slowing. She thought this was called self-stimming. Her autistic cousin did this when he was stressed. Celia did it now because she couldn't cry anymore, and didn't know any other way to relieve the tension.

After a while, her movements slowed. She lay down on the pew, staring at the wooden ceiling, breathing like a large Rottweiler. Throwing her arm over her eyes, she tried to slow her breath like she learned in yoga. It surprised her how frightened she was. This is not my life, she thought. I didn't ask for this.

Breathe.

Her mind showed her images that she recognized from news or ads on television. Mostly, the images were of victims, or suffering, and she knew she was trying to convince herself that there were others who had harder lives, and fewer choices. She envisioned starving children, war and rape victims, oppression and misery, and realized that she had an opportunity. Every person has an opportunity to help those less fortunate. Everybody has a chance to be a messiah – or liberator. Anybody could, if they only stepped outside their own lives and did something, well, Christ-like: helped the poor, taught forgiveness, cared for the sick, or fed the hungry.

She fell asleep briefly as the stress and exhaustion got the best of her. She awoke thinking about her ability to heal, and felt gratitude to Ryan and David for their help and care. "At least I'm not alone," she said aloud. And, even though she knew there was no voice, just her thoughts, she heard God say, "Of course, you aren't," before she fell back asleep.

Hilton Hotel, Austin Texas, May 3, 2032

The scent of coffee and bacon in the hotel lounge made Celia's mouth water. She was starving, and David and Ryan were late. She checked her watch for the fifth time, and groaned. Where are they?

The elevator dinged, and she glanced over expectantly, but the people who stepped out weren't David or Ryan.

Rushing to the courtesy desk, she dialed Ryan's room number. After three rings, David answered.

"Are you coming to breakfast? We're on a tight schedule today."

"I think you should come up here right away, Celia," David said. "Something's wrong with the professor."

"I'll be right there," she replied before hanging up.

The old elevator took forever to make its way up to their floor. It bumped and shimmied before finally grinding to a halt.

She sprinted down the hall.

When David opened the door, she spotted Ryan sitting on the floor next to the sofa with a washcloth pressed against his forehead. The morning sun streamed through the windows behind him blasting the far wall. Its brightness placed Ryan in stark silhouette.

"Are you sick?" she asked, as she stepped inside, and then crouched near him to feel his head.

"Maybe."

He felt warm and his color looked all wrong.

"I had the worst nightmare," he lowered the washcloth and stared at her with glossy eyes.

"That's pretty common when you're running a fever," she said.

He turned even paler, and then his eyes darted around nervously, panicked. "Awful. Bishop Reilly dead. He showed them secret papers: church documents. We're in danger."

"He's been babbling like that since I got here," David

interrupted, dropping onto the chair next to her. "He called me on the phone, hysterical, swearing that we had to leave right away, that our lives were in danger, and he wanted to save the bishop."

Ryan swayed and whispered, "I was too weak to leave the room."

"It's got to be the flu." Celia pressed the cloth against his face. He was clearly delirious. "Poor baby, I'm not so sure you should go anywhere today. Let's call room service and get some food. You can stay here, Ryan, and rest. David and I will meet the bishop at the airport and bring him back."

Ryan shook his head no. "I should come. He'll be expecting me."

"I'll check the weather," David stood, picked up the remote, and then switched on the television. "We don't want any more natural disasters messing up our plans."

Celia stood up, too. "I'll go online to see if the bishop's flight is on time."

On the way to the computer, David grabbed her arm as she passed him. "Celia," he said, staring at the television.

She turned to see what had caught his attention, when breaking news of Bishop Reilly's murder filled the screen. The reporter concluded with, "No response from the Vatican at this time."

She turned to Ryan, who was now a shade of brain-matter grey. In a rush, she asked, her voice coming out more shrill-like than she intended, "How was the bishop killed in your dream, Ryan?"

"Drive-by shooting," he said, barely moving his lips.

She grabbed the remote and flipped through the channels.

The reporter on channel four was talking about the murder: a drive-by shooting believed to be gang-related, with Bishop Reilly in the wrong place at the wrong time.

Again, panicked and shrill, she asked, "Ryan, in your dream, who was responsible for the Bishop's murder?"

"Don't know" he said, trying to stand. "But they're seeking us. For the coins. We need to get out of here. NOW."

David had never seen anyone move so fast. Like some cartoon character, Celia gathered the laptop, their documents, their research, and yelled, "Help Ryan, leave the rest – no time!"

He lifted the professor and slung him over his shoulder, fireman style. Professor Delaney weighed a ton and David was embarrassed to struggle with him in front of Celia. It wasn't as easy as it looked to carry a full-grown man.

"Anything valuable in your room?" she asked.

"No, just clothes and stuff. I have my wallet and passport."

She leaned towards them. "Ryan, I have our papers. Is there anything you need?"

"No, let's go," came the weak reply.

"Ok, we're leaving."

"To go where?" David followed her into the hall with the professor like a thousand pound bag of potatoes on his shoulder.

"I don't know!" she barked before banging on the elevator buttons. "I'll figure it out in the cab."

"The cab? What about the rental car?"

"Too easy to trace," she said.

"You've seen too many movies," he laughed, as he stumbled into the elevator with the professor.

She didn't miss a beat, and her seriousness freaked him out. She asked, "How much cash do you have?"

"About two hundred dollars."

The professor tapped him on the back. "Put me down, David, and support me under my arms."

He did, and the professor wobbled unsteadily, fished in his pocket, and then handed David his wallet. He opened it and counted out over three hundred bucks.

Celia said, "I only have eighty dollars. We need to be careful not to leave a trail of credit card purchases. And we probably shouldn't fly."

"Not using our own identification," David agreed.

"Oh, yeah," she commented, as the elevator doors opened to the lobby. "You know anyone who can give us new ones?"

"Actually," he said, smugly, "I do."

She gave him a wide grin, and then said, "I knew you'd come in handy."

Austin Public Library, Austin, Texas, May 3, 2032

Celia and the others sat on the front steps under three large archways, passing around the supplies they bought at the store moments ago, including some stale muffins and burnt coffee.

"Not the most nutritious way to get some sustenance into you, Ryan, but it'll have to do," she offered by way of apology when she handed Ryan his ration. "After we eat, let's find a private corner in the library where you can write down everything from your dream," she said. "No detail is irrelevant, Ryan. Write it all down."

"You think it was a vision?" He took a small bite from a blueberry muffin.

He knew the answer as well as she did, but she understood his disbelief. She remembered how long it took to accept how the coin had affected her. Celia had suspected, right away, that the coin from the cross belonged to Ryan. She could see it on his face when he first touched it - that look, like when a father holds his first child in his arms. "Of course it was a vision," she told him. "The coin gave you a gift, or a curse, maybe, just like mine."

"I don't have stigmata," he argued.

Now was not the time to go into this. They needed to pull it together and figure out their next steps. "Hey," she stood up. "I'm no expert, here, Ryan. You're the ex-priest. All I know is the previous owner of that coin had visions, and now you predicted the bishop's murder. You tell me what to make of it."

David snorted.

"What?" She turned toward him.

"I've never heard anyone tell off the professor before, that's all," he said, his face breaking into a wide grin. Nice that he could find humor at a time like this.

She tossed her trash into a nearby can. "I'm going inside to check the computer for news. No use risking anyone tracking my laptop and figuring out where we are."

David said, "Don't you think you're being a little paranoid?"

"Maybe," She looked up and down the street for signs of trouble. "But I remember some emails from Renata, right before her house was ransacked and most of her papers were stolen. Then she vanished. Not a word from her since. I thought she was being paranoid, too. Looks like she wasn't."

She brushed crumbs off her pants and stomped her feet to get better circulation in her legs. "Don't forget, the two other men who had coins from the ruins also disappeared. We don't know who, or what, is at work here."

"Renata and her son are fine," Ryan said. His eyes were clear now. The muffin seemed to have helped him regain some of his strength.

"How do you know?" she asked.

"It was part of my vision. She's safe. For now."

"Where is she?"

"I'm not sure," Ryan said, making a face. Clearly, he was still in pain. She empathized with him, but he needed to push through it.

"Could you draw it? Or draw what you remember?"

"I'll try."

Celia sat back down for a minute. "God, what a mess."

"It'll be okay," David told her.

"How?"

"I have money, connections, and ideas. I promise, everything will work out." His tone was assuring. He flashed her a charming grin, and then winked.

"I appreciate your connections and money, David, I do. And your optimism." She said. "But I'm guessing the Vatican has more connections and more money than you do. And more resources. If anyone in power wants to find us, they probably could."

"We don't know who's involved in this and who isn't," Ryan reminded them.

"Yeah, well, whoever they are, they don't have me, and they didn't learn how to be sneaky and underhanded when they were kids, like I did. I'm your ace in the hole," David said. "The pope's got nothing on me."

Ryan said with conviction, "The pope may be in danger, too. There are people who are hungry for power in the church, and they believe having the thirty coins will bring them glory, but the pope and the bishop know better. Glory for a few is not the way to heaven on earth."

Celia asked, "What do we do now?"

David said. "We need to solve one problem at a time. Let's write down the professor's dream before he forgets it."

"I won't forget it," Ryan rose to his feet unsteadily.

"Whatever," David stood, too. "Let's do it anyway. If you have another vision, there's no knowing what you'll retain from the first one, provided you survive another dream like that. No offense, Professor, you look like shit."

Ryan waved him off with a shaky hand. "I'm fine," he said.

"You will be," Celia said. "Not for nothing, though, I'm glad not to be the only freak in the room anymore."

CHAPTER 7

Roadside Motel, Dallas, Texas, May 4, 2032

The knock on the door was so quiet that Celia thought she was dreaming it. The clock next to her bed read 3:47 am. Then the soft knock repeated, and she heard Ryan's voice, "Celia?"

"Coming," She got out of bed to put on some pants, still wearing the shirt she had on her when they fled from the hotel in Austin yesterday. She pawed around in the twilight to find the door handle of her room.

When the door swung open, she found Ryan swaying like a drunk, holding onto the wall for dear life. Immediately, she recognized that he was sick again, so she grabbed him and dragged him into her room. He staggered along, trying his best to walk. Somehow, she managed to guide him to the bed, where he fell back onto the mess of blankets.

"Are you okay?" She sat and felt his head for fever.

He grabbed her hand and kissed it. She stared at him while he lay there with his eyes closed, working through the pain. Then, she spotted a tear trailing down his left cheek.

"What is it?" she asked.

He breathed deeply. "Thank you."

Huh? Thanks for what? For dragging him into this mess? What could he possibly be thanking her for?

She asked, and he replied in a soft, hushed voice, "For giving my faith back to me."

"It wasn't me," she was confused and trying to distract him, to ease him through whatever his body was experiencing as a result of his visions. "I'm just a passenger on this ride."

He struggled to sit up, but couldn't.

"Shhhh…" she whispered, and wiped the sweat from his brow. She continued to smooth his hair, like one might do for a sick child, and repeated, "Shhhh. Rest."

"I don't want to rest," he said. "I'm euphoric."

She laughed. "Could have fooled me. You look like you just donated a kidney or something." Then she bent over him and kissed his feverish forehead. She kissed each closed eye, tenderly, and then his lips, just briefly, innocently, but with great affection.

Next, she rested her head on his chest, and he brought his arms around her. She felt the intense warmth from his body next to hers. Or, was the warmth emanating from her?

Her heartbeat accelerated and she was dizzy from the nearness of him, his smell, and the security of his arms. Before she was even aware of it, the healing energy dispersed through her, passing between the two of them like breath. She took all his pain, his weariness, his anxiety, and she inhaled, absorbing it.

He opened his eyes and whispered, "What did you do?"

She didn't know how to explain what just happened, and was not ready to admit the intensity of the feelings that washed over her. All she knew was that, without any effort on her part, she healed him.

"You should write down your vision, before you forget it," she said, instead.

"I won't forget it," he adjusted his body to prop his head on his hand and stared at her. "You're not bleeding," he noticed. "But you just healed me?"

She started to feel drained. "I just calmed you a little. It's complicated." She tried not to respond to the closeness of him, or to acknowledge how well he knew her even though they had been apart for what seemed like centuries. To avoid his gaze, she rested her head on his chest again, listening to him breathe.

"You didn't need to 'heal' me, because my affliction is grace."

"I don't understand grace."

"Blessing from God. God's favor."

"I could do without this favor," she said.

After a while he recited, "Three times I begged the Lord about this, that it might leave me, but he said to me, 'My grace is sufficient for you, for power is made perfect in weakness. Most gladly therefore will I rather glory in my infirmities, that the power of Christ may rest upon me." He touched her face to lift up her chin so she was looking at him. "Corinthians."

"Yeah, well," she said. "I've only asked two times."

He smiled again. Then he said with an even voice, almost as if he was talking to himself, "The spirit helps us in our weakness; for we do not know how to pray as we ought, but that very Spirit intercedes with sighs too deep for words. And God, who searches the heart, knows what is the mind of the Spirit, because the Spirit interceded for the saints according to the will of God."

The passage moved her, so beautifully written. Sighs too deep for words...she had felt those. "What's that from?"

Ryan's gaze held her as firmly as his fingers did, still lingering on her chin, caressing. "Romans. Bishop Reilly quoted that to me when I asked his advice about leaving the church."

She nodded and he withdrew his touch.

"And this helped you make your decision? About leaving?"

"I prayed, and followed my heart, which I think is what he was trying to urge me to do."

Celia felt overwhelmed with guilt. The bishop had been just a figure to her, someone to help her find her way through this maze of events. But to Ryan, he was a friend. He was someone close and trusted. "Now he's dead," she said.

"Celia," Ryan rubbed her back absently, but in a way so intimate strictly because he did it familiarly and without thought. "The bishop's murder is not our fault.

"We should try to find Renata. In my vision, she was with people, not alone." He wrapped her tighter in his arms. "And you aren't alone either."

Ryan's closeness, his attention, even the deep soothing sound of his voice, was like a balm. The years vanished and she knew that he had always resided in her heart, even when she shared it with someone else.

He said, "You're connected to Renata through your correspondence. It probably won't take long for our enemies to track you to Texas and put two and two together."

The words, "our enemies," hung in the air between them. She wanted to put them back in his mouth, to forget everything that was happening and just explore what was going on between them. But the rest wouldn't go away. It remained.

"I suppose it's not safe to go home." She sighed, knowing nothing would ever be normal again, and wondering if she embraced that, or loathed it?

"Do you need anything from your house?" he asked.

"There's nothing there for me." The words so true they made her shiver. "I can have Sadie wire me some money."

He nodded.

"Should I involve her?"

He thought a while about this, his face softer now that the pain was gone. "I think that's up to you."

"You were right," she said, with a heavy heart. "You warned me we would face opposition."

"Well, being at odds with the church isn't new to me," he said. "Now sleep. I'll stay here with you, if that's okay?"

She looked at him. "Are you my protector now?"

He gently guided her head back to his chest and said,

"No. You're mine."

Roadside Motel, Dallas, Texas, May 4, 2032

The knock on the door interrupted David from his research. He didn't like to be disturbed, which is why he had hung the sign on the motel door. He couldn't just yell, "Come in!" He was the only bastard with the room key and the door was locked.

"This better not be housekeeping!"

"David, it's us," Celia said.

He got up from the desk, strode to the door, and then opened it. The professor and Celia waited outside. They looked pissed and anxious.

"I hope you at least brought me breakfast," he joked as he stood there.

"We ate hours ago, David." The professor said, stepping past him into the room. "We called twice. Where have you been?"

"Doing research on the computer," he explained, feeling like a naughty teenager who stayed out all night without calling home. "You know I don't like to stop when I'm in the middle of something."

Celia took stock of the room. He watched her look over the stacks of bags from Walmart, the boxes of electronics, the clothes and junk food. "What is all this stuff?"

"Supplies," he explained. "I bought them last night."

Celia moved to the far bed where he had piled everything.

"Untraceable purchases," he told her smugly.

"What?" She moved a package of tube socks out of the way.

"I have a bank account under a fake name. I bought this stuff with it."

She frowned, picking up a backpack and then putting it back down.

"It's legit money," He added. "Not stolen or anything."

"That's a relief," she said, not sounding relieved.

The professor asked, "David, what is all this and how is it untraceable?" He spread his hands wide.

"Stuff we need." He stepped back to the computer and sat down to save the document he had opened when they interrupted. "My friends and I started a bogus bank account when I was in high school. I needed a way to use my dad's money without him knowing. It was easy: a fake ID, a few checks to a phantom pool guy, fun money and a credit card - whola."

"So, it is stolen," Celia argued.

"Are you kidding?" David snorted. "Do you know how hard we worked cleaning that stupid pool?"

"Why didn't you just have your dad give you the money for cleaning the pool yourself?" the professor asked, moving over next to Celia to look at the stuff on the bed.

Baffled by their stupidity, he threw up his hands. "Because." They had no idea how rich people thought. His father would never have paid him anywhere near the bloated rates he paid the pool service. Anyway, then there would have been no deception, no payback for being ignored, and no credit card if he had earned the money honestly. What fun was that?

"Because is not an answer," Celia quipped.

The professor put a hand on her arm. "What's done is done." The professor knew David. He got it, even if Celia didn't. "Let's see it."

David showed them his fake ID and credit card.

"Gerald?" The professor laughed, seeing the name he had used.

"Yeah, well, what do you expect? I was sixteen, and that was the name my friend thought worked for an older guy who looked young. You know, geeky."

Celia looked over his shoulder at the picture ID. "Nice glasses and greasy comb-over. How'd you get an account without a social security number?

"It wasn't easy. My best friend's mom had started a small business and had a tax ID. We used the business name. She had a drinking problem and didn't pay good attention to her accountant. Two year's later, we were eighteen, my friend had her transfer the business name over to him. When my father died, I kept writing checks to him from my trust fund and inheritance for helping me out. I called him and gave him a heads up that I would be withdrawing from the joint account. Speaking of calls—" He rummaged through some boxes and handed her a Motorola. "Here's a pay-as-you-go phone to use so we can stay connected when I leave. Untraceable, of course."

"Of course." Celia accepted the phone. "Where are you going?"

"To New York to get your IDs."

She glanced at the bed. "Hence, the new digital camera?"

"Yup. I'll set you up in front of the blue screen." He motioned to a roll of blue seamless paper.

"Unbelievable," Celia said, with a trace of admiration.

He stood a little taller. "It pays to be sneaky and underhanded at times."

The professor picked up a crisp, white, button-down shirt. "For me?"

"If you like."

He sorted through some clothes and checked the size tag on a pair of jeans. "You've been busy."

Celia reached over and grabbed something from the pile. "You bought me panties?" She held up a black, lace pair. "How did you know my size?"

"I didn't. I described you to the sales girl."

The professor coughed to disguise a laugh.

David said, "If you don't like them…"

She sighed, rolled her eyes, inspected the matching bra, and then threw him an unreadable glance.

"You bought a computer, too," Professor Delaney said, nodding at the desk where he had been working.

"I have a plan."

"Do tell." The professor moved some things out of the way, and then sat on the edge of the bed, looking over at David with interest.

"No time now. My flight leaves in four hours, and I have to finish my research. I'll brief you at lunch in, say, an hour."

"What are you researching?" Celia stepped over to the computer and started to read from the screen.

"Temple references from the Bible. I'm trying to find some connection to the gathering at the temple mentioned in the pirate's journal. If we're meant to go there, we'll need a plan. Temple Mount is under Muslim control, and the eastern gate is closely guarded."

"Why Temple Mount?" Celia asked.

The professor said, "It's predicted that one day the Messiah will land on the Mount of Olives, with all His saints, and walk down to and right through the Eastern Gate and into the temple area."

"That's right," David agreed.

"Only," the professor continued, "the temple mentioned in the sailor's journal is not Temple Mount."

Get out! David had been online for over three hours, sure that they would need to travel to Jerusalem. "It's not?"

"No."

"How do you know?"

The professor pulled out his notebook and said, "Because I saw the temple in my vision last night. I've seen Temple Mount. This is not the same place." He flipped through several pages of notes and drawings, and then pointed to an illustration of a skull and a pyramid-like temple with five windows at the top. "I don't recognize it, but it's where Renata is."

Celia peered over. "Maybe this is an inner structure of Temple Mount or a building that no longer exists at this present time, but that stood in Jesus's time."

David was stunned and jacked at the same time. "No," he said. "It is an ancient building, but it still exists."

They both stared at him with anticipation. So, he explained, "That's the Temple of Inscriptions at Palenque." He knew it well, he had studied it in detail, spurred on by his mother's stories when he was little about the mystical day on which he was born and the culture that made that day significant.

"Where's Palenque?" Celia asked.

"Mexico."

"Mexico?" She looked between him and the professor.

"Mayan ruins," he announced with excitement.

Surprise was reflected on Celia's face. She fell to the bed, still holding the lace panties, and said, "Well, I'll be damned."

"Or saved," he said with a grin.

Arlington, Massachusetts, May 8, 2032

Cardinal Jussipini entered through the back door to Celia's house in plain clothes. He had taken public transportation and walked several miles on foot so there would be no trace of his journey here from the Logan Airport.

Breaking into her home had been easy since she didn't have pets or an alarm system. He needed to find out what she knew and what she had planned next. Was she seeking the coins, too? Had she already amassed some?

It was a small house, nice and tidy. He found the home office and sat down at her computer. It booted up without requiring a password. In the search history, he saw she had been researching Father Delaney, which he knew already. And, of course, multiple searches for Roman coins, stigmata and healing. So, she was a healer. How many coins did she have? He went to her email account and couldn't believe his luck. She had not logged off of her account.

His grip on her computer mouse intensified with his accelerating heart beat as he started to read her correspondence with Renata. The two most disturbing things were that she apparently had copies of relevant documents Renata had sent her, but the attachments were not to be found anywhere on her computer system. Also, it was evident that Celia has lost contact with Renata at some point and had no idea where she was hiding. That was a problem.

He made a thorough search of her desk and found a loose key that looked to be for one of those small fireproof safes people kept in their homes. Twenty minutes later, in the closet with her shoes, he found the little box, about the size of a toaster. No documents, but there was a portable drive and her social security card, plus the deed to her house and other titles and important papers.

Back at her desk, he loaded the drive and leafed through some bills and paperwork, taking her credit cart statement, her social security card, and a bill for a nursing home and pocketing them.

Then he printed out the documents stored on the drive and removed it from the computer. He had everything he needed. Not even bothering to turn anything off, he left the house out the back door and started his long trek to the subway.

Looks like his next stop would be the nursing home. Whoever lived there was very likely to know where Mrs. Alessandri was.

Boeing 737, cruising altitude 32,000 feet, May 8, 2032

Just his luck – the guy who sat next to him on the flight was a gabber. He'd been yapping at David for over half an hour. On the previous flights to and from New York that past week, David had also been stuck with old or chubby men as his seating companions. Couldn't a guy get a break?

David glanced past the gabby fellow to look across the aisle, and tried not to cringe as he caught sight of the professor, now bald and sporting a scruffy mustache. He'd never heard someone make such a fuss over his hair before. You'd have thought that he and Celia had been castrating him when they shaved his head with all the fuss he'd made. David had to admit, the professor was not a good-looking bald man.

Celia, on the other hand, was hot with her new blonde, short crop. She came back from the salon commenting that between the new do and the sexy panties, she felt like an entirely new person. Which, of course, was the whole point.

David interrupted his chatty neighbor, thinking that if he could out-talk him, maybe the guy would shut up. "Well, at least we're not flying in a hurricane. Recently, I had a flight that was a white-knuckle ride from hell. We almost crash landed-"

"Try escaping an erupting volcano or tsunami," the guy cut him off mid-sentence.

"Yeah," David agreed reluctantly. Crazy nutcase.

He tuned out again when the guy started in on a story about some boat ride he missed, until David heard him say, "You'd think this was the apocalypse or something."

"What?"

"I said, you'd think this was the apocalypse or something," the guy repeated.

"I know. I heard that part. Why would you say that?"

"Because of the tsunami heading toward the east coast."

"What?"

The guy looked at him like he was a moron, and slowly, as if speaking to someone hard of hearing, enunciating each syllable, he said, "The tsu-na-mi hea-ding to the east coast."

David looked around, desperate. They were on a smaller

plane without video or satellite service, totally shut off from the news, Internet, or phone. He grabbed the guy by the front of his grey oversized t-shirt. "How bad? When? Which part of the coast?"

"All of it, from Florida to Canada. Part of Cumbre Vieja, the volcano in the Canary Islands, fell into the sea around ten this morning. Scientists predicted this cataclysmic event in 2010. The waves are in motion. They'll take nine hours to make impact."

"So, around seven tonight?" David asked, calculating in his head.

"That's right," he confirmed, seeming not to care that David still had his hands wrapped in the fabric of the guy's clothes. "There's a major evacuation happening. I'm surprised you didn't hear. It was all the buzz at the airport, with the potential catastrophe disrupting flights.

"The good news," he kept talking after David let his hands fall from his shirt, and then stared off in dazed confusion, "they say the damage won't be as far-reaching as they first expected."

"How far?"

"Well, they're evacuating two to three miles from the shore, especially in low-lying areas, all along the east coast. But the tsunami may only reach a half-mile from the shore. Mexico is protected from the brunt of the wave by Florida and Cuba, which will be hit hardest. What's your destination?"

His mind processed what the guy just said.

"Not traveling to some vacation home or spring break on the shore, are ya?" the guy added.

"Excuse me," David said, getting to his feet, and waiting for the guy to stand so he could step past him to the aisle.

Mr. chatty, bearer of bad news, huffed a frustrated sigh and unlocked his seat belt. Rather than stepping into the aisle and giving David room, the guy half-stood, so David was forced to squeeze past him.

Celia spotted David and elbowed the professor, who was sleeping. Plane rides were clearly like sedatives to the professor. Once the wheels left the tarmac, he dozed off. It was amazing.

He nodded to the professor, now awake, hoping he would follow him to the bathroom, so they could talk. They did not sit together at the airport, nor did they board the plane together. Each of them took separate taxis from the hotel, checked in separately, and avoided conversation while at the gate. Celia's credit cards had been reported stolen. Whoever made the call knew her social security number and could access all her bank accounts. With all their preoccupation and precautions to travel without detection under their new false identities, it looked like they missed some critical news.

For the first time ever, David was glad to see a line at the restroom. He said to the flight attendant, "The gentleman next to me was mentioning the tsunami headed toward the States. Have you had any updates?"

He sensed the professor behind him by the smell of his over-applied aftershave.

"What tsunami?" Ryan asked, predictably.

The flight attendant gave them a debriefing of the situation, and assured them in a very professional manner that their destination in Mexico was clear of danger.

"How's the evacuation going?" David wanted to know.

"It's chaos," she said. "The military's done a good job, but the roads are gridlocked in areas, especially in the big cities. They're flying out as many as they can, and asking people to car pool. We learned a lot from Hurricane Katrina. The National Guard and local law enforcement are assisting as many people as they can. They're also permitting outward-bound cars to use both sides of the interstate."

She placed her hand on David's arm. "We'll be landing in fifteen minutes. Personnel at the airport have been updated if you need more specific information. If there's anyone you need to call?"

"No," he said. "Thank you for your help." He tried not to think about everyone at the school in New London. He'd never wanted to talk to the professor as badly as he did right now, and wished he could turn around and ask him what to do. But they had a plan. They were splitting up and meeting at a rendezvous spot where they'd a rental car to take them to Palenque. Until that time, in the off-chance that they were being followed, they couldn't interact. It was David's plan and they had to see it through.

After an elderly woman vacated the restroom, David sealed himself inside, and wondered what it all meant. Was this the beginning of the end of the world, like so many people had assumed over the years? Or, were natural disasters just that – a natural result of change, planetary evolution, and climate? Or, could they be acts of God?

CHAPTER 8

Rte. 199, Palenque, Mexico May 8, 2032

Ryan fought to calm his thoughts and pay attention to the road as he drove to the resort in Palenque. The rental jeep, paid for in cash and registered under his new fake name, veered as Ryan's thoughts churned and volleyed for his focus. The onslaught of visions, premonitions, and mental noise had spilled from his dreams into his waking hours, and he found himself struggling to stay of "right mind," a phrase that now had more relevance to him than he could have ever imagined. Was this prophesy? Is this what the bible prophets, and folks like Nostradamus, suffered? Ryan knew this was from God and he should trust it, but he was confused and overcome. There was no "off" button to stop and analyze what he was seeing, no "pause" button to freeze and properly record images or phrases, feelings and impressions.

Celia sat next to him in the passenger seat, conversing on the pay-as-you-go phone with the nurse at her father's long term care facility. Her voice wafted towards him soft and loud depending on the direction of the breeze and the speed of the Jeep. She was confirming that everyone was evacuating the facility in preparedness for the incoming tsunami.

Ryan tried to focus on her conversation, but his mind drifted to the revelations he'd been having as a result of his visions. Revelations, he dwelled on that word a moment, feeling altogether different about the meaning now. A whole book in the Bible stemming from John the Baptist's visions. So many interpretations had come from those words. How many interpretations would come from what Ryan was seeing now?

Celia was saying, "I'll call you later tonight to make sure you're ok, Dad. No, I'm not nearby, but I can't tell you where I am, even if you won't remember." She laughed. It was amazing how she could joke about his Alzheimer's. That alone spoke volumes about Celia's ability to cope. As they drove past trees and rocky shoreline, his fear for her safety grew with each premonition that came to mind. She was in danger, they all were.

He would have said, even two weeks ago, that he would have welcomed this mission from God, having searched his whole priestly life for a vocation like this. Today, however, he felt the weight of that burden, for the first time really understanding what it must have been like for the apostles, for all those with Christ when they knew what had to be sacrificed for redemption. The silver coin, tucked neatly in his pocket, reminded him of the cost Judas paid to fulfill Jesus's destiny. What was his destiny?

"We're almost there," David said from the back seat with child-like expectancy. After all, he was a child, pretty much. He sensed that this was just a game to David, a grand adventure, the chance to use his smarts and his money to play spy like in some movie or book. But this was real and Ryan wished now that he had not involved his favorite student.

The road curved and he caught his first view of La Aldea Halach Huinic, the villa where they were going to stay. The palapa-roofed cabanas looked like something from Gilligan's Island and he heard monkeys and other exotic animals calling to him.

"Oh my God," he said and braked the car.

Celia and David said, "What?" at the same time. Celia was still holding her phone, but giving him her attention. What could he tell her? That he had seen this very place in a vision with fire raining down from the heavens and burning it to the ground?

It all became clear suddenly as the visions lined up in his mind, making him grip the steering wheel and close his eyes in an attempt to hide the truth from Celia so she would not see. Air, water, earth, and then fire. He had seen it all.

They had been forced from the air by the hurricane on the way to Texas, chased down by its ferocious winds, evacuated from the hospital. The water was coming. A giant wall of water, right this minute, was on its way to the coast. So many were in danger. And recently, a vision about Celia, trapped in the earth, near death in a hospital bed, he and David at her side. Earth. When would that be?

That left only fire.

Celia said, "Oh, sorry, I'm still here," and returned to her phone call.

Ryan slowly accelerated again. When he pulled into a parking spot in front of the main building and shut off the car, he turned to face David, who was looking at the brochure for the villa, completely oblivious to the turmoil going on in Ryan's head right now.

David said, "I booked Celia in the deluxe accommodations. Supposed to be spacious and air-conditioned. Professor, we're bunking in the cabanas with mosquito nets, hammocks, and all the trimmings of indigenous-style décor. It'll be great."

David should be somewhere drinking with friends his own age instead of being here. He should not have involved him. Ryan now knew, with certainty, that David was in danger, too. He felt it in his bones.

He struggled to maintain his poker face, the pretend-you-are-not-surprised-by-this-confession face he had mastered in the seminary. Keeping his voice and expression neutral was a well-practiced art-form in the priesthood.

Then, Celia said, "who visited my father? What priest?"

Celia, on the other hand, projected every feeling in her expressions, and every emotion in her voice. Something had happened. Her body stiffened, as if she were about to be attacked. "If you didn't know him, why did you let him in to see my dad? No. I know you didn't mean any harm, Amanda. Just describe him to me."

She made eye contact with Ryan and he nodded once to her. He was listening.

She said, "About five feet ten, receding hairline, curly, salt and pepper hair. Square, black glasses. Brown eyes." Her frown deepened. "Big mole on his forehead."

Ryan stared at Celia as she continued, "I know he seems like a nice man, Amanda, but don't tell him anything about me. If he comes back, don't talk to him, you hear me. If he asks, pretend you don't know anything. I can't explain more."

A lone tear slid down her face. Ryan put a caring hand on hers.

She wrapped up her conversation, hung up, and said, "Some priest visited my dad out of the blue yesterday."

Ryan kept his silence again. How much should he reveal about what he'd seen?

David stood, resting his arms on the Jeep's roll bar. "Do you think they know anything?"

"No. My dad forgets everything and I never talked to him about the stigmata, the coin, or anything else cause, well, what's the point?"

"That's good." David said.

"God, what if it's the same person who murdered the bishop?" Celia asked.

Ryan recounted a vision he had the night after the bishop was killed. The vision revealed Vatican emissaries in an argument, one claiming that they had to be careful amassing coins. Someone else commenting on sociopaths and the antichrist, one Vatican member claiming that he knew how to keep the powers from cumulating and causing harm, his curly hair bouncing with emphasis when he made his point, and the mole on his forehead catching the light in the dim room.

The dining area opened to the outdoors, and their table was so close to the railing that you could view the entire compound. Ryan was glad it was the off-season. They were three of only ten patrons in the restaurant. The still air was deceiving with the pending tsunami. Although it would not affect them here, it was difficult to think about anything else. Three hours until the first waves would hit the U.S. shore, and they were told the evacuation of the east coast was only forty percent completed. Tens of millions was a huge number to disperse.

Celia said, "What's the plan?"

It was Ryan's drawing that had brought them here, but his visions revealed little else to aid them in finding Renata. She was below ground, he knew that much from the cavern-like environment he had seen in the same vision as the temple he drew. But where?

Ryan said, "David, you're the Mayan expert. What are your thoughts?"

"Beats me." David squirmed in his chair. "Let's keep track of the tsunami for now and figure out the rest later. I can only handle one major crisis at a time." He pulled out his mobile device and logged on to the free wireless, then put the news feed on with coverage of the tsunami.

"Tomorrow, we'll check out the ruins," David said. "Honestly, I don't know what else to do."

The professor nodded, but didn't speak. He was still struggling with how much to tell them about what he'd seen.

Celia ordered some tequila for herself and he ordered a coke. Alcohol was not going to clear his head, it would muddy it. David joined Celia and requested a shot. When in Mexico, drink tequila.

David asked, "What's up, Professor? You're acting strange"

He frowned. "Just trying to figure out some things, that's all." He rubbed his newly bald head, which he hated, and yearned for his hair back.

"What things?" Celia asked.

"Messages," he said, as the waitress brought their drinks.

She was a gorgeous, olive-skinned girl. When she gave David his tequila, Ryan noticed David's eyes followed her every step, every move.

"Messages? Like visions?" Celia asked, as she licked the salt, downed the shot, and popped the lime into her mouth. That was a move she must've learned after college. Celia had not been a drinker when they were together. Matter-of-fact, he had never seen her do a shot before.

"No, more like messages. I keep having these recurring impressions." He sipped his cola, deciding to open up and tell them what he was experiencing. "Not like the vivid dreams, but more like – well, I don't know how to explain them. It feels like thoughts are being forced into my mind. Things I can't forget. No, forget isn't the right word. It's like my mind's being invaded."

"Are you hearing voices?" David teased. "Do we need an exorcism?"

He didn't laugh at this. Instead, he just stared at the table.

"Are you?" David asked.

"No, not exactly. But thoughts and images keep coming to me, and it's disorienting."

Before Ryan could elaborate, the waitress returned and requested their order. Her liquid eyes focused on David. She waited. David just sat there, entranced.

"What do you want to eat?" Ryan asked.

When David didn't answer, Ryan nudged him under the table with his foot.

Celia snickered.

The girl waited patiently.

Finally, David broke out of his funk, inhaled, looked at the menu, and then ordered.

After she left, Ryan fired David's earlier question back at him, "What's with you?"

"Oh, c'mon. What do you think is with him?" Celia said with a smirk.

"It's not like that," David said. "The waitress is pretty, but something else I can't describe is going on with that girl. Back to the voices."

Ryan sunk down into his chair a little. He said, "I can't stop writing: phrases, Bible passages, nonsense, sketches, sometimes random numbers. This is the biggest struggle for me – trying to make sense of all the parables, symbolism, and gibberish. You know, I've spent my life chasing faith and studying religion, but with these new developments, I feel completely lost."

"Imagine how I feel!" Celia said. "I haven't studied any of it."

He nodded and opened the notebook where he had been writing down his visions and sketching. "Here's the most recent."

David leaned over and read from the Ryan's notebook, "And to the woman were given two wings of a great eagle, that she might fly into the wilderness, into her place, where she is nourished for a time, and times, and half a time, from the face of the serpent. And the serpent cast out of his mouth water as a flood after the woman, that he might cause her to be carried away of the flood...the earth helped the woman, and the earth opened her mouth, and swallowed up the flood, which the dragon cast out of his mouth. And the dragon was wroth with the woman, and went to make war with the remnant of her seed, which keep the commandments of God, and have the testimony of Jesus Christ."

Ryan rubbed his head again. "It keeps coming to me over and over. It's from the book of Revelations."

"Words from a seer," David said.

Ryan nodded.

"I don't understand. What do you mean, words from a seer?" Celia asked.

Ryan said, "The book of revelations is all about dreams and visions. I used to think it wasn't reliable, but now, I don't know. Notice the wording about time, repeated three times. Something so interesting about that since the scroll in the cross kept referencing time. Not feeling so good about the antichrist references."

Celia said, "Do you think the water refers to the tsunami?"

"I think so." He frowned. "It just keeps coming to me, like I said. More urgently since we arrived here." He shared his revelation about the hurricane and tsunami. He danced around telling Celia too much about seeing her buried alive and hurt. But he told them about the fire from heaven he saw burning down the building where they ate right now.

"So you think Celia is the woman?"

She glanced sideways at David when he said that, and then shook her head. "First of all, the tsunami is not going to be reaching us here where we are, so I will not be 'carried away' by the flood or anything like that. Also, I don't have any 'seed' and I'm too old for children." She held up a hand. "Before you argue that I'm not, you forgot one other thing. We both have coins now, Ryan. We both have gifts. And, Renata does, too. I am not the only one bearing the eagle."

Celia found it to be surreal being here in the rustic wilderness while at the same time watching footage on David's computer of the impending tsunami. Of course the fact that she had way too many tequila shots didn't help. They had left the restaurant as soon as they finished their meal to come to David and Ryan's funky villa. She wasn't one to get drunk, but right now she felt the occasion warranted it. The tequila had the desired effect of making her woozy and numb.

"Eighty percent of the potential victims evacuated and they call it a success?" David hollered from the other room.

She didn't want to think about it. She stood in the middle of the room, swaying, closing her eyes to stave off the dizziness, and hoping her father and the other nursing home residents were safe.

An onslaught of barking erupted from the woods and made her jump. "What was that?"

David walked in. "Those are howler monkeys. The loudest land animal."

"You never heard my late husband snore." She waved her finger at David and nearly toppled over.

"Okay, lightweight," David took her arm and led her to the table. "I think you need to sit down."

"Two minutes until contact," Ryan told them, pulling the computer closer to him and staring in sick fascination. "Look at that."

She leaned on him and watched the screen, rocking slightly to some internal rhythm inspired by alcohol.

The giant wave, filmed from a helicopter over Miami, moved steadily toward land. It looked as if everyone had been evacuated. There wasn't a car on the road nor a person in sight.

The view switched to another camera, one of the many strategically set up along the shore in specific cities all along the east coast from Mexico to Port a Prince in Canada. Some areas would be hit harder than others, but this was a cataclysmic event. They watched the ocean via a low mounted camera fixed to a dock on Jupiter Beach, Florida. From this perspective, the pure height and enormity of the wave was easier to see, and it was terrifying.

She leaned in further, her chin almost resting on the table, and watched with horror as the camera caught the wave in its approach. When it hit the lens with a pounding force, they abruptly lost the feed. The television station, broadcasting online, switched to a camera mounted atop the Empire State Building. The words on the screen informed them that the camera, secured over a thousand feet above sea level, should record the eighty-foot lead wave, and equally powerful secondary waves, as long as the building structure could withstand the force of the water.

Like some Hollywood special effects movie, water poured over the familiar New York streets and landmarks with a frothy vengeance.

"This is real," she said aloud, more to herself than to make any kind of point to the men in the room. "This is really happening."

Waves kept hitting and receding.

"My God," Ryan said.

Celia turned away, and then fell off the chair, to her knees. The bamboo mat was hard against bone and flesh. Ryan's strong arms grabbed her from behind and held onto her, sharing her grief and helplessness.

She felt acid rise in her throat and forced herself not to vomit, but she was unaccustomed to the strong liquor. Pulling away from Ryan's embrace, she crawled, with as much speed as possible, to the edge of the doorway leading outside and expelled the alcohol and her meal.

"That ought to keep the bugs and animals busy," David said.

"Shut up, David," she said, for once unappreciative of his humor. She knew it was his mechanism for coping, but was in no mood.

Ryan poured water on a napkin and pressed the cool cloth into her hand. She sat back against the doorframe and raised it to her face. "Thank you."

He returned to the computer to survey the damage to the coast and to hear news reports.

"Is it over?" she asked.

"Yes," Ryan said.

"Is it bad?"

Ryan replied, "It's bad."

Mayan Ruins, Palenque, Mexico, May 9, 2032

David stood next to their Jeep, looking out over the ruins of Palenque. The day was starting stifling hot, and the air was thick with moisture like the steam room at his father's old clubhouse. "Let's do this." He took the lead and stepped forward under the early morning sun, followed by Celia and the professor, with the hopes of finding Renata somewhere based on the professor's visions and sketches.

Unlike the ruins in Tulum, where there wasn't a molecule of shade to be found when David went there as a teenager, Palenque had a blanket of rich, green forest to keep people from sweating their asses off when they went exploring.

Being born on the very day the Mayan's had predicted the end of the world gives you a sense of having pulled something off. It also is why David was fascinated with the Mayan temples. That and the fact that his mother had spoken of the Maya, talked about the prediction of the world's end, sometimes hugging him when others were around, joking that life as she knew it certainly ended the day when he was born. He was seven when she died and he had held onto her words as treasures to unwrap and comprehend later. He studied the Mayan culture with fervor in high school, thinking that doing so would bring back the magic and joy of his mother's words, but it hadn't.

Because of his knowledge of most things Mayan, they

were letting him call the shots. That was probably a mistake. Totally making things up as he went, he said, "Let's start at the Temple of the Foliated Cross." He took a few purposeful steps, then turned to make sure they were following.

"You're the guide." Celia dragged behind the professor in a pitiful, hung-over state. She had deep-blue marks under her usually sparkling eyes, and looked even more wretched and tired than she did after her healing episode on the plane.

Once at the temple, they climbed the slippery stone stairs between the moss-covered hills, the temple seeming raw and tortured, much like Celia looked. The front wall of the temple, and the mansard roof, had long since collapsed, leaving the front structure exposed. The cutout shapes of doorways and openings reminded David of a carved jack-o-lantern. Stains streaked down the front of the building making it look like it was weeping.

He said, "As an ex-priest, you might find this interesting, Professor. The temple was constructed with two parallel galleries that intersect at right angles by another corbelled passage, creating a great chamber."

"Common to many church designs." The professor hitched his backpack higher.

David moved ahead, saying over his shoulder, "That's right. And each temple has an inner shrine at the rear of the building." He stepped inside where it was cooler, touching the stone surfaces with admiration. He wished he could have seen this place in its prime.

"Pib na," he said, admiring the shrine at the rear. "The underworld house within the sacred mountain."

The professor walked the length of the room. He circled

around and then settled next to David. "What's the significance of the symbolism?" He asked, gesturing toward the artwork ahead.

David pointed. "This commemorates the earthly realm."

The professor studied it, and shook his head. "This isn't the place."

"I came here first because of the line from the passage in your notebook you read yesterday, 'And the earth helped the woman, and the earth opened her mouth...yadda yadda' like I said," David felt along the wall. "This commemorates the earthly realm. I thought there might be a hidden passageway around here."

The professor inspected the artwork again. "What's this?"

"The Foliated Cross represents life rising from the waters. The maize plant depicted here was a source of life for the ancient Mayans."

"Life rising from the waters, huh?" Celia frowned. "Between Ryan's bible passages and the Mayan symbolism, I'm beginning to think nothing is random."

"You may be reading too much into the coincidence of the tsunami right now. Those who believe in evolution assume all life comes from the sea," David said. He knew Celia was freaked about the tsunami, but that was done, her father was ok, and they were here now. She needed to pull herself together. There was nothing they could do at this point except figure out a way to save all mankind, if you believed that's what would happen if they reunited the coins.

David was about say just that when the professor pulled out his notebook and said, "I wrote this last night, Celia. I hope you take comfort in it. 'And God shall wipe away all tears from their eyes; and there shall be no more death, neither sorrow, nor crying, neither shall there be any more pain: for the former things are passed away. And he that sat upon the throne said, Behold, I make all things new.'"

The professor took Celia's arm and said, "That's why we're here, right? A new beginning?"

David smirked. His teacher had stolen his thunder, again, making the point before he had the chance to.

"I also wrote this. The professor dropped Celia's arm and lifted his notebook. "And he said unto me, Write: for these words are true and faithful. And he said unto me, It is done. I am the Alpha and Omega, the beginning and the end. I will give unto him that is a thirst of the fountain of the water of life freely.'

"It's from Revelations. Again, the words kept coming to me."

"The voices," David said. "Tell Sybil I said 'Hi.'"

"Cute, David," Celia shook her head and rolled her eyes.

"Thanks, I thought so. Read all about her in my psych class." He took a swig of water.

The professor looked around. "Is there anything here that looks like a passageway?"

They spread out, each of them alternately pushing on stones, pulling on loose rocks, trying to find levers, or to lift stones with their bare hands. Clearly, they had all seen too many treasure hunting adventure movies. David hated to admit it, but if Justin were here, he'd probably know right where hidden passages could be found.

The professor scoped out the space again, and said, "I understand your logic, David, but I don't think this is the place. Let's explore the Temple of Inscriptions, since that's the one I saw in my dream."

"Okay." He led them out.

They walked around the Temple of the Sun, admiring the massive stairs and square columns. Several other tourists greeted them in passing. The howler monkeys were quiet at the moment. David smelled moss and other deep green earth scents he couldn't identify. Occasionally, a whiff of salt water was carried in the wind from the sea beyond.

He yearned to enter the palace and investigate, but knew the professor wouldn't want to.

Stopping at the base of the hill, David gazed toward the pyramid with its distinctive five windows at the summit.

"Impressive," the professor said. "Just as I saw it."

"You know," David took advantage of a moment's rest. "A tomb of the king was discovered at the base of the pyramid, just like in Egypt."

He unscrewed the cover of his bottled water and took a slow, appreciative drink. "Mayans have particular beliefs about death, sacrifice, resurrection, and the afterlife. Matter of fact, the imagery on the sarcophagus discovered here in the 1950s depicts a giant tree emerging from the bowl of sacrifice. The tree represents the Milky Way as it stretches across the sky from the southern horizon to the north."

"Of course it does," Celia said.

"Passing through the hole of the Milky Way," he ignored her, "or the White Road as the Mayans called it, symbolizes rebirth or new beginnings."

She smiled at him, some of the severity in her eyes fading with the widening of her lips.

"Let's move," the professor said.

Scaling the fifty-some-feet of stairs to the summit sucked in the heat, so they stopped several times to drink and rest. Low clouds had moved in and obliterated the sun, but the humidity was incredibly thick, and the air remained warm and oppressive. Sweat poured from every inch of David, soaking his clothes.

They no sooner reached the summit, before they started descending more stairs to the east into a small room.

The professor entered first, placing his hands on one wall, feeling around the tiny space before shaking his head. "This isn't the place."

"No visions or thoughts?" David asked.

"No," he said. "Nothing."

Celia said, "It's okay, Ryan."

The professor made no move to leave. He lowered his backpack to the floor and slid down the wall to sit next to it. David remained standing, as did Celia.

Two college-aged couples tread down the stairs and peered around. Seeing the confined space was full, they retreated back to the summit.

David whispered to Celia, "Is he meditating?"

"Be quiet, David," the professor said, eyes closed and head lowered, chin to chest.

They waited. The small space felt like it was shrinking and expanding with their breath. David heard the distant sounds of tourist's voices and footsteps. It wasn't much cooler here and sweat trickled down the front of his chest and the middle of his back, making his shirt even wetter than it was. He breathed dust and mold from the air. Celia looked poised and calm, the alcohol sweated out during their trek here no doubt.

He forced himself not to shift from foot to foot, trying to wait the professor out, even though staying still for long periods wasn't his strength. He attempted to use some techniques he had learned in psychology class for calming and relieving stress with little success. He was impatient to get out of there and investigate the other ruins.

Hold on. "Professor," he said.

"Patience, David."

He let that slide and took a step forward. "What did you say earlier?"

The professor opened his eyes and focused on David. "When?"

"At your first sighting of the temple. You said, 'Just as I saw it'." He gestured with his fingers. "Let me see your journal."

Footfalls sounded above them as more tourists came to explore.

"Let's go outside," he said. This place was too confining.

The professor got to his feet, scooped up his backpack, passed by David with a nod, and then started to climb the steps back to the summit. David followed with Celia lagging behind.

The stairs on the way back down from the summit were still damp from the dew and humidity, and David nearly slipped several times because they were rushing.

Almost to the base of the pyramid, the professor had his book out and was glancing between it and the temple summit. "I think over there somewhere," he said, pointing.

David nodded, happy that the professor had understood his revelation. They should look for their answers from the perspective of the drawing.

"I'm glad you're here, David, did I tell you that?" The professor clapped him on the back.

"No," he said. "Must have missed that earlier when you were telling me to 'be quiet.'"

"No one's perfect." The professor smiled under the Indiana Jones hat protecting his new baldness. Earlier that morning, David had argued with him about wearing it. He looked like a dork and it was embarrassing.

David reached out. "Let me see that sketch."

The drawing showed the temple at a slight angle with the left side facing them, which meant they should be standing somewhere northwest of it. Also, the professor sketched some rocks in the foreground that are clearly part of the palace structure. He motioned with his free hand toward another ruin, the Palace. "We need to get beyond that wall."

The palace is the largest ruin in the complex and, from what David had read, was built in sections. The rectangular building had a tower in the center with four main courtyards and a maze of corridors. The tower had been built to observe the sun falling directly onto the Temple Of Inscriptions during the winter solstice.

They end up in one of the courtyards to the east of the palace for the right perspective of the other temple.

"This is it, I think," the professor said.

David glanced at the drawing and agreed. They shifted left and forward a little until the drawing of the rock structure resembled what they saw.

"A perfect match," Celia said. "So, boys, what did you expect we'd find here?"

David looked around for a trap door, corridor, or some entry to a secret passageway, but he didn't see anything obvious. "No clue."

Celia and the professor looked around, too. Celia asked, "What was this rocky area?" She gestured to the ruined formation.

"I don't know." David wracked his memory. "Could be a courtyard, gallery, sanctuary, latrine, or steam bath."

"Lots of little nooks and crannies, but nothing that looks safe to explore," the professor said with a sigh.

Celia held out her hand. "Let me see the drawing."

The professor moved closer to Celia, and they looked at the notebook together.

"You wrote some things here. Maybe they're relevant," Celia said.

"What'd you write?" David asked.

The professor said, "Just some Bible quotes that came to me. I always imagined 'visions' and people hearing God's words so differently. I literally see these bible passages in my head, they pop out at me like flashbacks, as do the visions."

David said, "Maybe it is all in your head. Could these things be just memories or random thoughts? I know you predicted the bishop's death, but you haven't had an event like that since Texas, and you claim to still be seeing things and hearing things."

Celia and the professor exchanged a look.

"What?" David asked.

"After my second vision, I went to Celia's room and she

healed me. Now, I don't suffer afterwards."

David considered this. "How do you recognize a real vision as opposed to random thoughts?"

"There is a physical change within me, very distinct, a tingling, a heat, like an electric shock but no longer painful since Celia intervened. But I do still get a little tired afterwards."

Speaking of heat, David was melting, so he leaned against a large rock to steady himself. "What are the quotes you wrote down?"

The professor read, "Unless the Lord had shortened those days, no life would have been saved; but for the sake of the elect, whom He chose, He shortened the days - Mark 13:20. He that walketh with wise men shall be wise; but a companion of fools shall be destroyed. – Proverbs 13:20."

"Great," Celia said, "Which are we? The elect, the wise ones, or the fools?"

"Depends on how much tequila you drink," David said.

"Ha ha." She slapped at a mosquito. "Sorry, Ryan. Continue."

"Only one more," he said. "Judges 13:20 - Yahweh was the God that answereth by fire."

"Fire again," Celia said, wiping sweat from her brow. "Based on this heat, I'd say God already answereth."

The professor shut the journal, tucked it away, and looked around again.

David blurted out, "Each of those passages is the same!"

"They're related," Celia said, as she swatted at another bug. "The saved, the damned, death by fire - more morbid predictions-"

"No. I mean numerically: 13:20. You know, 13:20 - the science behind the Mayan definition of time." David moved to sit on a nearby stone, bouncing his leg with excitement.

Celia rolled her eyes, and sat next to him. "Here we go," she said. "Lay it on me."

"I read all sorts of material on this a while back," he explained. "The pre-Mayans defined cyclical time. Their whole culture revolved around it."

"Cyclical time?" she asked.

"Yes." David smiled. He loved this shit. "Everything that has ever happened will happen again. There are some highly complicated mathematical theories around this-"

"I'm sure," she held up a hand to stop him. "But can you put it in terms I'll understand?"

He shrugged. "I'll try."

The professor said, "The cyclical approach to time is also discussed in Hindu and Vedic traditions and cults that are still using the swastika to indicate cyclic evolution."

"Back to the swastika again, are we?" Celia rubbed her eyes. "Can we stick to 13:20, please?"

David said, "The current twelve month calendar – the Gregorian Calendar - is based on a sixty-minute hour, often called the artificial timing frequency, and denoted as 12:60. Scientists and mathematicians have defined a standard of measure and mathematics underlying the Mayan calendrics. Rather than the metric or decimal 10-count code, the Mayan calendar is based on a 20-count vigesimal code."

"David," Celia said. "Focus. How is it relevant to finding Renata?"

"I don't think it is, but I do think it may be relevant to

everything else. That is, if you believe in the science, spiri-tuality, and the theories around the laws of time defined by scholars."

She looked impatient. "Which are?"

"There is a theory that the 13:20 frequency correlates with fourth-dimensional mathematics," he said. "Have you heard of a fourth dimension? The possibility of spaces with dimensions higher than three was first studied by mathema-ticians in the nineteenth century. It's regarded as spatial, and not temporal, dimension."

"David," Celia sighed. "If you're going to tell me that Renata exists in some invisible sci-fi dimension in this very spot, I think I'll kill myself, or go back to the bar for more alcohol."

The professor laughed. "I don't think that's what David is saying. Actually, I think he's speaking about what some describe as God. Or higher power."

"The Professor's right," David leaned over and scratched at a bug bite on his shin as he talked. "The papers I've read about it refer to this dimension as the highest spiritual source, where scientific truth and spiritual revelation unite. The divine. Also, speculation exists that defines this dimen-sion as telepathy or the essence of prophecy.

"Think about it. If time is cyclical, then everything that ever happened has already happened. That would explain how prophecy works. A prophet would, in theory, already know what has happened, or what will happen, if existing in a cyclical time experience. The Bible describes cyclical time, which we interpret as heaven, and where we know every-thing there is to know past, present, and future. Think about the phrases 'world without end' and 'everlasting life.' You said it earlier, Professor. Revelations: says the Lord, 'I am the Alpha and Omega, the beginning and the end.' A circle. Cyclical time." He stood up, barely able to contain himself. They had something here. The passages they found in the cross related to time, too. What if time is the key somehow? It didn't make sense to him now, but it was interesting.

"This is different from reincarnation, right?" Celia asked.

"Yeah," the professor said, sitting in David's vacated spot on the rock. "If you do not live, or think, in a linear sense."

"I don't think I can think other than linearly. Is that a word?" she said.

David started pacing. "You're trained to think that way because it's what you know. Just like we all know the world is flat, right?" He held his hands out to emphasize his point.

"And consider the passages on the scroll we found. 'A thousand years in your eyes are merely a yesterday.' And, 'Teach us to number our days aright, that we may gain wisdom'-"

"Forever and ever, and from everlasting to everlasting," David added. "Cyclical. Jesus was a highly enlightened man, and understood the mysteries of the world, right? He would know if time was not linear. All that was, and ever was, will be, is, and always will be. What if Jesus knew that time was cyclical? What if he understood all dimensions of time and space? After all, wouldn't he? Wouldn't God?"

Celia interrupted. "David..."

"Think about it," he said. "If you understood everything about the universe, everything that would ever happen, or had happened, how evolved would you be?"

"I don't know," Celia said.

David resumed pacing. "Even Einstein wrote, when talking about the forth dimension, that there was nothing to represent "now" objectively, the concepts of happening and becoming are not completely suspended, but complicated. He said, It may be more natural to think of physical reality as a four dimensional existence, instead of the evolution of a three dimensional existence.'"

Celia said, "More natural to Einstein, maybe, but not to me. How do you know all this stuff, David?"

He shrugged. "I've read a lot about it."

Her stare softened. She asked. "Why?"

He knew she knew the answer, but wanted him to say it, to admit why he came along, what motivated his passion for religion, science, and all things supernatural. "I began wondering about God a long time ago. And life after death. And the possibility that a spirit or essence still exists even though a body no longer does."

Could it be possible?

He said, eager to get off the subject of him and his motivations, "We live in a three-dimensional world under the laws of linear time. Maybe the Mayans truly understood that the world has four dimensions – or more – and time is cyclical. This would explain their acceptance of death and the spirit world. Maybe that's what drew me to them in the first place! The Mayans were considered both primitive and advanced. What if they were, in fact, enlightened, and what if we could gain that enlightenment, too?

"We've already seen that the coins grant gifts, tap into abilities that were dormant within us, like healing and prophecy. What if reuniting the thirty pieces grants us ultimate enlightenment? What if we are able to see the world with all its hidden dimensions?"

CHAPTER 9

Mayan Ruins, Palenque, Mexico May 10, 2032

Celia stood in the same spot as the day before, staring toward the Temple of Inscriptions. The only difference was now they were standing there in the pouring rain. Ryan had drawn another picture of the temple from a vision he had last night, which brought them back to this spot a second time.

Celia contemplated being transported to a new dimension, trying to make sense of David's crazy hypothesis, but she couldn't. It was a hard thing for her to entertain, no matter how convincing David's scientific theories were, or how much Ryan believed David may be onto something.

The only good thing about yesterday's speculations was

that they seemed to have snapped Ryan out of the funk he was in.

"We've been standing here for an hour," she pointed out as the warm rain pelted her hair, dripped into her eyes, and pooled at her feet. She hadn't stood out in rain like this since she was a kid, braving a summer storm in her bathing suit to ward off boredom. It was fun to do back then, but today it just felt stupid. What are they doing out here?

"Can we find shelter so we don't drown?" she asked, trying not to sound whiney.

"Let's go inside the palace." David led the way. "I had hoped the rain would let up, but it's not."

They took shelter under the roof of the main building. Nobody, not a soul, was around. They shook off the wet as best they could, and then sat cross-legged on the floor. It was dark, and the rain was so loud Celia needed to shout to be heard. "Let me see the drawing again."

Ryan handed her his notebook, which he had stuffed into a plastic bag. She slipped it out, and then flipped between the first sketch and the latest one. Her flashlight beam and the flipping motion created a shifting, choppy, black-and-white, old-time movie effect, which reminded her of art school and her first rough attempts at animation. "The same perspective," she said. "The same details, too."

She flipped back and forth a few more times. There were no new quotes or passages to accompany this drawing. "Is this a mistake?" she asked, pointing the flashlight and a finger at a smudge on the page.

Ryan looked at it. "No, not a mistake. It's just a shadow I drew."

She looked at it again. It was a shadow of the tower atop this very building. "What was it you said yesterday, David? About the Mayans and the tower? Something about a shadow?"

He shrugged. "I didn't say anything about a shadow."

"Yes," she searched her memory. "You did! Remember? Winter solstice…"

"I said, the tower was built to observe the sun shining directly onto the Temple Of Inscriptions during the winter solstice."

"Look at this shadow." She pointed to the newest drawing in Ryan's notebook. "It may lead to something?"

"Possibly," David agreed. "But, we'll never find it in this rain."

Ryan said, "Let me look at that."

Celia handed him the notebook. He stared at the sketch, holding the flashlight and pointing it at the book. "I didn't think it was important before.

"Yesterday, we stood in this spot and the sun was here." Ryan placed the book in his lap and used the flashlight and his finger to cast a shadow on the page. "The shadow is on the wrong side. By afternoon - I'm guessing around three or four o'clock - the shadow should be in the proper position." He moved the flashlight to prove his point.

"If the rain breaks, we can come back this afternoon," David said. He smoothed his wet hair back from his face with his fingers. "If not, we'll try tomorrow or the next day. It's dangerous enough exploring these ruins in good weather. These tropical storms can be a bitch."

"No argument from me!" Celia stood. "I'm all for getting

out of this creepy temple, drying off and having a drink."

David shook his head. "I'm not letting you feed the bugs again."

"No worries," she said. "I was thinking of hot coffee and some dry clothes."

"Amen," Ryan said.

"Once a priest," David teased.

"Once a spoiled brat," Ryan said with a grin.

"Once a stigmatic," Celia said, and they all cracked up.

It was ten after two and the heat and sun had burned through the torrential rain to create an intense humidity so thick Celia could hardly breathe. She was trying to stay motivated, but was facing moments of doubt and confusion. Were they in the right place? Should they be doing something else? Were they in danger? Where the hell was Renata?

Definitely, not here.

Celia sighed for the hundredth time as they stood in the same spot, like morons, waiting for a miracle. They had tried to explore the forest earlier when the rain first stopped, thinking they could find a clue without the shadow guiding them. All they managed was to get eaten alive by the bugs. David had wandered into a giant spider web, complete with an enormous, hairy occupant. He screamed like a girl for about five minutes until Ryan got the thing off him. Hell, it scared the crap out of her, too.

She sighed another time. David threw her a dirty look. They were are all getting on each other's nerves.

Ryan said, "I think this is close," as he compared the present position of the tower's shadow with the sketch.

"Let's just walk out and look," Celia said. "I can't stand here another minute."

"We already searched down that path." David pointed to a break in the jungle ahead. "And the ones left and right of it."

"Let's try again," Celia said, and started walking along the shadow's edge. When she stopped abruptly, David walked into her.

"Look here." She stepped back a bit. "The shadow from the square window of the tower practically frames this square stone on the ground."

David squatted to get a closer look. "That's a piece of Mayan sculpture."

"I've seen this," the professor said. "This could be it."

In vain, they tried to lift the giant stone. People passing by stared at them in confusion, and an angry guard blew his whistle, yelling something in Spanish that she was sure translated to, "Don't do that!"

David held up his hands in surrender and then looked at the carving again. "This depicts a captive," he said.

"Really." Celia's patience was running thin with David and his useless facts. "Does it tell you where she's hiding?"

He frowned at her, then ran a finger over the carved stone slab. "See how the captive has one hand on the opposite shoulder. That's a sign of submission. And the captors have placed their bows and arrows on the ground. They would cover their right hand in saliva, press it to the ground, and then to the side of their heart as a sign of respect. They respect this captive."

"All the arrows point the same way," the professor said. "To the mountain behind the temple."

"Let's walk." Celia swatted at a bug.

The humidity made hiking unbearable, even in the shade of the forest. There was definitely a path, dead ahead, and it was not an obscure path. You could see the worn footprints from others who may have ventured back here in search of history, random scattered ruins, and outbuildings. They passed a group of Asian visitors with packs that look stuffed with enough gear for several days and nights. The hikers looked tired and wilted, with their cameras limp around their necks.

Twenty minutes into the forest, they come across a small stone outbuilding.

"Hey," David said, "a mini-temple!" He walked over to the base.

Ryan scrambled up the small, rocky incline and peered inside. "I've seen this, too."

David said, "There are dozens of unexplored temples in this forest."

Celia was not encouraged. From what she could gather, Ryan's visions were coming like a kaleidoscope of fragments. He had told her he was seeing words, symbols, images, clips of moments like little movies, sometimes with sound and sometimes not. How he was supposed to make sense of all that, she had no idea. His floundering around and saying that things looked familiar was starting to wear on her. This was not the help she envisioned him giving her when she sought him out. She followed Ryan and David and scaled the decomposing stone stairs.

The mini temple felt like something out of a made-for-TV movie. It was smaller than her walk-in closet at home and the three of them barely fit in it. "Cramped," she said, standing with her head lowered. "And built for people much shorter than me."

The walls were worn, and any art or markings had been obliterated by weather and time.

Celia looked down the steep decline to the base, which was three-sided - like a pyramid. When she looked up, she spotted a toucan in a tree. He watched her with wise eyes in a way that suggested she bored him. She had never seen a toucan that wasn't in captivity, and was surprised to find he wasn't spooked by humans.

David and Ryan dropped to their hands and knees, pressing stones.

"Solid," Ryan said.

"They built these things to last," David sat on the edge of the entrance, hanging his feet down.

Celia joined him, exhausted from the heat and needing to sit. She swatted at another bug, looked for the toucan, couldn't find him, and decided she didn't like the forest. The raw earth smelled like her grandmother's root cellar and the bugs were buzzing and zooming so loud it sounded like a gazillion fluorescent light bulbs acting up. She had the creeps. Everything felt like it was pressing in around her, including the small temple.

Ryan kept poking around, hunched over or on all fours. "This is the place; I'm fairly certain."

"You said that already." She sighed. "Do you really think we'll find Renata here?" No sooner had the sentence left her mouth, she saw the waitress from the restaurant walking out of the dense trees, followed by a cute teenaged boy. As surprised as she was to see her there, the waitress didn't look surprised to see them. The couple nodded to them. David said, "Hi."

They passed by without slowing and vanished in the deep growth on the other side of the path. Ryan poked his head out, and said, "Hi who?"

When they were out of earshot, David said, "Hi pretty waitress."

"Oh," Ryan said and sat down next to them. "There's nothing here. I don't see any clues or passages"

It didn't escape Celia that David was staring with longing at the place where the waitress had gone. "Don't worry, David, the kid with her looks like her brother, not her boyfriend."

He scrambled down the face of the temple, starting a small rockslide. "Who says I'm worried."

Celia called after him, "Where are you going?"

"Investigating." He walked up the path to the spot where the waitress had emerged with the boy. He disappeared into the growth for a few moments, then returned.

Celia slid on her bottom down the side of the temple and joined him.

"No path," he said.

"Wonder what they were doing in there?" She wiped sweat from her brow and scratched at bites on her skin.

"What do you think they were doing?" David said with sarcasm, placing his walking stick where the couple had emerged. He started back down the path they were originally following and she and Ryan followed.

After several hours without seeing anything but foliage, they turned back. When they passed the tomb again, the toucan was back on his perch, keenly watching them, mocking them, Celia thought, as they aimlessly made their way back to the hotel, famished and tired.

Celia's skin was raw from scratching, and she looked like she had chicken pox. "How come you guys haven't been eaten alive like I have?" she asked as they were escorted to a seat at the hotel restaurant.

"We're not as sweet as you," Ryan said, sitting at the very same table they had yesterday by the railing, open to the outdoors.

She was starving, the long day of random wandering had taken its toll. Celia frowned. "I'm seriously considering buying body netting. You know, like the bee-keepers wear."

"I have a whole other definition of body netting," David said.

"I bet you do." She put her napkin on her lap.

David's smile faltered when he saw their server. The pretty waitress greeted them with a warm, "Hola."

"Hola," they all said in return.

The waitress looked directly at Celia, and then glanced over her shoulder at a young boy busing tables. The boy fumbled with the plates a little, but recovered before setting a table by the bar. Something about him was familiar. Still, Celia was sure she'd never met him before.

"What's your name?" Celia asked the waitress after the boy retreated to the kitchen.

"Madeira," she said.

"And, your brother?" Celia asked.

David kicked her under the table.

"He's not my brother," the waitress said. "Cerveja." She shook her head. "May I take your order?"

They ordered, and the boy came back to pour water in their glasses. Again, Celia was struck by the feeling that she knew him.

The boy said, "Bueno."

When Ryan said, "Grazie," answering him in Italian rather than Spanish, Celia looked up and studied the boy's face. She recognized him now, from pictures sent to her almost a year before: Renata's son.

"Salvatore?" she asked, grabbing his arm.

He looked panicked.

"Where is she?" Celia whispered, letting go.

He shook his head. "Non qui," he mumbled under his breath, and walked away.

The waitress stepped up, placing their food on the table. When leaning over, she quickly allowed Celia a glimpse of the Roman coin around her neck before returning it to safety beneath her shirt.

"Is a messy meal," she said with intention, and then placed a pile of napkins directly in front of David.

David said, "Thank you."

The waitress glanced at the napkins again, and made a quick head-nod before leaving.

Celia couldn't believe they had located Renata's son. She

strained her neck to see Salvatore as he disappeared into the kitchen. She started to rise, but Ryan pushed her back into her seat by her shoulder. He said, "What a hot day it was!" and sipped his beer. "Feels good to be out of the sun, doesn't it, Gerald?"

David looked up at the sound of his fake name, and fell into character. "Yes, yes, it does, Pete."

They didn't need to knock Celia over the head with a hammer; she got it. She shouldn't have called Salvatore by his name out loud. She tried to calm her pounding heart.

David nudged her under the table, but she didn't know how to act normal. Or, rather, she don't know how to act like her fake character would, and not like she would.

Ryan said, "C'mere Hon," and pulled her to him. Before she knew what was happening, his mouth was on hers. She let his lips move in a familiar dance. The kiss did almost as much to disarm her as finding Salvatore.

Her mouth opened to Ryan's and her head swam.

David said, "Guys, you're ruining my appetite."

Ryan ended the kiss and returned to his beer. After a moment, Celia noticed the pile of napkins had been moved.

David said, "This salsa is messy." Then he grinned at her and nodded his head. "You better eat, Krista, before it gets cold."

She flashed him her best "disgusted" expression. David knew she hated that made-up name — a feminine play on "Christ" — mostly because he assigned it to her as a joke.

After rushing through their meals, they went to Celia's room. She shouldn't have inhaled her burrito like that, and was certain she'd pay dearly for it later.

She didn't waste any time. "Ryan, what was that?"

Looking innocent, he held up his hands. "I had to do something to distract you before you started asking more questions in front of strangers."

"Bullshit," David said. "Even I know you've been wanting to do that since she showed up at school."

He glanced at Celia and she felt the heat rising to her face.

"Besides," David said. "Who's going to notice some schmuck snatching a note out of a pile of napkins while you two make out? Nice moves, by the way, Baldie."

"That's Professor Baldie to you, Gerald."

Celia huffed, feigning false indifference. But she was still blushing and her knees were trembling a bit. How could Ryan still make her feel like this? She was not some wide-eyed virgin, but she was sure acting like one.

"We have a rendezvous," David said, handing her the note Madeira had concealed in the napkins.

Celia read aloud, "An hour past sunset. Find us where you marked the way." She looked at David and asked, "Does that mean?"

"It means:" he said, "she's one smart waitress. She's referring to the path I marked in the forest when we saw them earlier."

"If we're going out in the forest at night, we're going to need some supplies," Ryan said.

"Can I soak in a tub of bug repellant before we leave?" Celia dug at one of her many bites.

Ryan touched her face tenderly. "The bugs really do like you."

"Can't you just heal yourself?" David asked.

"It doesn't work that way."

"Why not?"

"Too self-serving, I guess."

"Have you tried it?"

She puffed up her chest in defiance. "Think about it, David. Why make myself sick healing myself?"

He said, "I just thought a little miracle, not a major one. How hard could it be to repel bugs as opposed to catching Malaria or Triple E?"

"Well, if I catch either of those things, I'll reconsider; How's that?"

"Knock yourself out." He handed her the bottle of repellant.

"Thank you."

An hour after dusk, the forest took on a new life. The howler monkeys' barking echoed over the treetops, while the buzz and hum of insects filled Celia's ears like incessant white noise. Each shadow presented a curious mystery: friend or foe. Each step they took more treacherous in the darkness and dew.

The danger of the forest, mixed with the anticipation of what they might discover here, filled Celia with adrenaline and jittery nerves. The most potent cup of coffee or energy drink held no comparison.

Was Renata here? What had happened to her? Why was Salvatore here and who was sheltering him?

She swatted the air, tripped over a tree root, and then jumped at some noise to her left. She imagined she looked like a skittish rabbit with a bad case of hives - some fearless leader. Ryan stepped closer to her and offered silent encouragement with a touch on her arm.

He had been leading the way, like a confident tour guide. Celia knew his past travels brought him to remote places, and she wondered, as she watched him now, if he had finally found the purpose he sought after all those years?

The further into the jungle they went, the darker it got. The wind rustled the trees, making Celia jump again, as the noise joined the other jungle sounds. Their flashlights danced along capturing plants and bugs and small creatures.

A chill gathered at the small of her back, then crept up her spine at the sight of a moonbeam piercing the canopy overhead and falling directly onto the pyramid-tomb.

"Here we are," David said.

"Do we go inside, or stay out here?" Celia asked. "Isn't it safer inside?"

Ryan stepped closer to her again. "If you discount scaling those crumbling stairs in the dark, it is."

Something fluttered overhead. She wondered if it was the toucan.

"I'm going up," Celia said, and started to turn toward the tomb.

Ryan put a hand on her shoulder. "Wait."

They all looked back to see bouncing lights flickering far in the distance.

"Turn off the flashlights," Celia said. She grabbed Ryan, and then guided him back behind the tomb where they waited.

She tried to calm her breathing.

The lights approached silently; no voices or heavy steps accompanied them.

The moon slipped behind a cloud, and the forest, already dark, became a black hole in space - the only pinpoints of light coming from their approaching guests.

Three figures stepped into the clearing.

"It's okay," a female voice said. "It's just us." Then Madeira's flashlight lit up her companion's faces.

"Renata." Celia slid past Ryan to join them, embracing Renata, rocking side-to-side holding her. She had never been so happy to see another person before. Renata was alive and well. Months of despair melted away with that embrace. She looked good, happy even. Whatever she was doing here suited her. The last time they had attempted to video chat, using translation software to bridge the language gap, Renata had looked wan and frazzled.

Celia introduced Ryan and David. Salvatore said something in Italian.

Ryan said, "He wants us to follow them."

"Where?" Celia asked.

Ryan said, "Dove?"

"Rifugio," Salvatore answered.

Ryan nodded. "Refuge."

Madeira led the way, followed by Salvatore. Celia took Renata's hand and squeezed it before nodding to indicate that Renata should go first. Renata stepped into line with Celia on her heels. Ryan and David took up the rear. The brush was thick - the path treacherous. They walked for what seemed like several minutes before they came across a small brook. Celia strained to hear the sound of it over the forest noises, the breathing of their squad, and their footsteps as they plodded ahead.

The bouncing dance of flashlight beams was hypnotic, making her dizzy. She tried to stay focused dead ahead, to keep up with the crew, and not to fall into the water. A small bird, or a gigantic bug (she didn't know which) darted at her head from the left and made her bob like a lunatic. She felt like a kid sneaking through the woods at Girl Scout camp to meet boys or drink beer; blindly following along without serious concern for repercussions. But unlike when she was a kid, there were very serious repercussions now, and it frightened her.

After several twists and turns, they separated from the brook on their right. She had no idea what landmarks, if any, Madeira was using. Ryan stumbled behind her. When she turned to see if he was okay, she accidentally blinded him with her light.

He held his hand in front of his face. "I'm fine, Celia, keep going."

She resumed, speeding up slightly to catch up. They were heading uphill again as the landscape became rocky.

"Watch your step," Celia said, as she scrambled over and through several large boulders.

She was so focused on her footing, she didn't notice the group had stopped, and she bump right into Salvatore. "Sorry."

He smiled. "Nessun problema."

Madeira said, "We're here."

"Where?" She asked, as she stepped up to the front. All she could see were trees and some boulders.

"Portale," Madeira said. "The city gate."

City? What city? Celia spun and focused her light beam all around, but there was nothing but more of the same: stones and trees.

"Come," Madeira stepped around a large stone and disappeared into some brush. Celia followed behind Renata in line, and realized that the brush covered an opening into the ground. One by one, they stepped through to descend down a stone passageway tunneling beneath the soft forest floor.

Celia had long since given up skepticism over the events following the purchase of her silver coin, yet the feeling that her life was a big hoax, or an enduring dream of some sort, had resurfaced as she stepped down the lengthy corridor, ever deeper into the earth, behind the ruins at Palenque.

In front of her, Renata moved deftly, clearly accustomed to the surroundings. How long had she been here? When did she go missing? Celia tried to calculate, but kept getting distracted by ancient carvings decorating the walls, the worn stairway, and the people with her as they descended further.

She saw a dim light far ahead, warm and flickering. David was babbling behind her, commenting on the Mayan artwork and craftsmanship. He said, "Too dark to tell. We should come back with a camera and photograph this."

This is a pivotal find for him, considering his obsession with the Maya. She turned to speak, but the flashlights of those following deterred her, so she focused on what was ahead and not behind.

Her pulse raced as the bottom step came into view, and when she breathed in deeply, the cool air smelled like minerals. Renata reached over, took her hand and led her forth into a giant cavern.

"Holy shit," David said.

It was hard to gauge the extent of the space. As she waved her flashlight around, Renata spoke in Italian. The beam threw light on ancient stone furnishings, doorways, and hallways leading out to places momentarily unknown to them. She jumped, surprised and startled, when her light revealed people stepping forth.

A man in a white shirt was flanked by a red-haired woman, an Asian man, a couple from India, several Mexicans, and others.

Ryan clearly wasn't surprised to see people here, either because he understands Italian or he had seen it in his visions. He quoted from the pirate journal, "Beneath the temple lies refuge for the chosen. Evil thwarted, the judgment shall pass, and the gathered will bear the truth of God."

CHAPTER 10

Underground cavern, Palenque, Mexico, May 10, 2032

Four times the size of the Palace at Palenque, the underground city Madeira calls Debiaxo - which she tells David is Portuguese for "beneath' - is as impressive, mysterious, and unfathomable as the Pyramids at Giza. The space is majestic and primitive all at once. David was hyperventilating with excitement as he moved from one facet to another, sure that if he didn't see it all immediately, it would vanish right before his eyes.

"You know," he said, navigating around a large column, "they found an underground temple, or a maze of caverns, in the Yucatan Peninsula years ago." He slid over to a wall of inter-fitted stones that looked like a New England fireplace, with no fire pit, and admired the surface, so ancient, firm, and textured.

"The Archeologists who found the caves believed they were constructed by the Mayans as a portal to the underworld, known as Xibalba." He moved further down the wall, maneuvering his hands reverently. "The Mayans had to swim underwater to excavate it. Really, they were amazing architects for their time."

A regal, grey-haired man said, "We believe this cavern is also a portal of sorts."

David nodded, but he was too engrossed in his surroundings to pay the man much mind. This was fucking amazing. Dotted along the outer chamber walls were stone benches and large, loose, table-like stones. Mayan symbols, in mint condition, were engraved all about.

The grey-haired man said, "Come here and join us, David."

How did the man know his name? Several conversations were going on in Spanish and Italian, but David only studied French, so he had no idea what was being said.

"Coming." He joined them, marveling at the largest Mayan enclosed space on record, to his knowledge. At the man's request, all eighteen of them gathered sparsely around a Fred-Flintstone-like table. There was easily room for a dozen more and, as he considered this, it was so obvious he said aloud, "Thirty seats."

Nobody commented, but he estimated again and decided that, yes, the table would sit thirty perfectly. Since he didn't have a coin himself, he refrained from commenting again, in case they decided to kick him out.

David's stomach lifted and fell like a yoyo. Their ménage a trois had become a gang, and he felt lost. He couldn't help worrying that his opinions may not be valued now that there was a think-tank here, so he sat between Celia and the professor, staking claim to them.

Renata sat across from them, with her son to her left, and Madeira on her right. The other twelve settled in. Nobody took a seat at either end of the table, putting everyone on equal terms - no leader. Interesting.

Celia was the first to speak. "What is this place? How did you get here?" She asked, directing her question to Renata. "Did you all come together?"

The grey-haired guy spoke in Italian to Renata. She said, "Bueno."

He said, "Renata and I came here together, with Salvatore, of course. We were the first. I will explain in a moment how I knew about this underground chamber, but I'm more curious about how you came to find us and what you're doing here." He looked American in his white polo shirt and jeans, although his accent was not American. He carried himself with an air of importance. His posture was tense, his smoky eyes alert and intelligent.

David said, "It's complicated."

The man replied, "I know about the scroll you found in Texas."

David froze, stunned.

He heard Celia ask, "How?"

Renata spoke in a slew of rapid-fire words, all Italian, and David understood none of it.

The professor leaned in, listening intently, and David waited, as patiently as possible, for someone to tell him what the hell they were saying. Several others, who clearly understood Italian, nodded their heads and listened, too. David heard the name Reilly, and the professor stiffened at the sound of the dead bishop's name.

The man translated, "When Renata went public with her story, the church came to see her to test her claims. Although they couldn't negate her healing power, or dismiss her stigmata, some were debating the validity of the documents she had copied. The church wanted the originals to perform tests, but Renata would not have it."

The professor said, "She hid the documents."

"Yes," the man said. "And when her house was ransacked, she fled with Salvatore."

"And came here?" David asked.

"No, she didn't know about this place at that time."

Madeira spoke up, "In an attempt to find others like her, Renata began tracking coins. She contacted me in Portugal, and we had planned to meet, but she never made it to our rendezvous. Bishop Reilly reached her first. He brought her to a safe house near the Vatican where he briefed her, and sheltered her for a while."

The grey-haired man said, "That's where I met Renata. My name is…"

"Jonathan Cardinal Margrave," the professor said. "I didn't recognize you at first, out of your robes. You were a dear friend to Bishop Reilly."

The cardinal nodded. "Yes."

The professor said. "We met in Rome, once, a long time

ago. I'm Father Delaney."

The cardinal said, "I remember. And the bishop spoke of you, and of Celia, before his death. We had been in contact with him. He was prepared to help you, to shelter you, much like he did with Renata. That's how we know about Texas and what you found there. The men who killed the Bishop have his coin now."

"He had a coin, too?" David was surprised.

"Who are the men who killed him?" Celia asked.

"They're led by the archivist, Everett Cardinal Jusipini, who had access to private Vatican documents," the cardinal said.

"The Vatican Librarian," the professor clarified.

"Access to Codices?" David asked, thinking of the Mayan texts at the Vatican.

"Yes," he answered.

"Then they can find us!" David stood. "This place would be documented…"

The cardinal said, "He cannot find us, I assure you."

"How do you know? We found you, didn't we?" He planted his palms firmly against the stone table.

Madeira captured him with her liquid eyes. "Sit," she said softly.

As he sat, Professor Delaney rubbed his scalp. "If you knew of this place, the Vatican knew, and we found it, others can find it, too. How many are are hunting coins? What's their purpose? Do you know how many coins they have?"

Cardinal Margrave's square jaw jutted forth under the frame of his graying hair. "We are not sure, exactly, about the coins. My best guess is Cardinal Jusipini has six, maybe more."

David was confused. "Why doesn't someone stop him? If they know he killed the bishop-"

"Nobody has proof of anything. The Vatican is watching him closely."

"Not too closely," Professor Delaney said. "We believe he was recently in Boston at Celia's father's nursing home."

"I'm sorry, I wasn't aware," Cardinal Margrave said. "The bishop was working on behalf of the Vatican, discretely keeping an eye on Cardinal Jusipini and following leads regarding the coins. I'm uninformed about what's happening now that he's dead.

"No one knows how Everett and his counterparts will behave once the effects escalate."

"Effects?" Celia asked. "What effects?"

"We found your hiding place," David said, unable to let go of this point. "If we found it, who's to say the others won't? Especially now that the bishop's dead."

Renata spoke in Italian, and Madeira nodded her head.

The cardinal nodded, too. "We have yet to hear how you managed to find us." He glanced between Madeira and the others, translating the conversation. The whole language barrier made simple conversation difficult. The Asian man and the Indian couple seemed to understand English, although none of them had spoken aloud yet. David wasn't sure if the Mexicans spoke English either.

A dark-haired man, who had not been introduced, said in a British accent, "I would like to hear how you found us, too."

Madeira gazed at David again. "You don't have a coin?"

she said, as a question and a statement all at once. From the very first time he laid eyes on her, he sensed she knew him intimately somehow; her eyes like some hypnotist's tool. How did she know he didn't have a coin? He felt exposed under her scrutiny, her gaze like an X-ray machine, looking at the secret, inner workings of him. Can she see the breaks? Under her examination, in front of all these people, he was sure his emotional ass was hanging out of the back of his johnny.

She removed her coin from around her neck and placed it on the table. Renata took off a bracelet with her coin mounted as a charm, and she put it in front of her on the table, too. The cardinal removed a loose coin from his pant pocket, and, around the table, others follow suit, ending with Celia and the professor. David was relieved to see four of them without coins, one being the male half of the Indian couple. Salvatore was one without, just like David, and one of the Mexicans, too.

The cardinal said, "When I touched a coin from the Vatican collection, I began to speak in tongues. Almost instantly, I was able to understand language, written or spoken, and speak fluently in return. To my knowledge, I'm the only one able to read ancient Mayan writing that has, to this date, been indecipherable. The Pope sent me off, by this time recognizing that he could not trust the Vatican archivist any longer."

He asked, "What gifts you have received?"

"I have none," David said.

Celia said, "Healer."

Renata said, "Healer."

Madeira said, "Discernment"

Salvatore said nothing.

The red-haired woman next to him said, "Evangelist."

Another said, "Ministry," and around the table they went, "healing, wisdom, teaching, faith…"

"I'm prophetic," the professor said when it was his turn. "Prophecy. That's how we found you, clues pieced together from visions and logic."

David appreciated the professor including his contribution by mentioning 'logic'.

The cardinal translated, and murmurs of appreciation followed. "We've been hoping for a prophet. And, as you'll learn, we're hoping for other gifts, too, in order to reclaim the coins stolen by Everett and his apostles."

David asked Madeira, "What's discernment?"

She said, "A kind of empathy."

Salvatore spoke a few words and the cardinal said, "Salvatore says Madeira can see your soul. He's right, in a way. It's only because of her abilities that we have safely gathered and that you were allowed to join us. Madeira can gauge good intentions from bad ones."

"A human lie detector," David said. "I knew it!

"Of sorts," the cardinal picked up his coin and held it between two fingers as he spoke. "Madeira knows when someone deserving lays claim to a coin."

"What happens when someone undeserving does?" Celia asked.

The cardinal looked down at his hands. "Negative effects. Mental degradation." He looked up. "We have reports of multiple personalities, Schizophrenia, Dementia, Phobias, Hypomania, other things of that sort. The church has been debating for some time the cause of the behaviors and mental changes. When one lays hands on a coin there is a bonding, or a rapture experienced the moment coin and person are united. There is a mental clarity, a euphoria. When you're separated from the coin, even though your gift remains, there's a sense of disconnect and loss. This creates a longing and an addiction in some people."

Celia said, "I always felt like the gift was a curse, not a blessing."

The cardinal nodded. "For those who experience stigmata, it can feel that way. But for those like Cardinal Jusipini, suffering like Christ is a fulfillment of a lifelong calling. The after-effects of some people's gifts can be challenging to overcome as well."

The professor put his hand on Celia's shoulder. "We figured out a way around that. Celia has aided me in recovering from the after-effects."

The cardinal alternated between speaking and translating in several languages. "Renata says that works for you, but there's nobody to heal the healer."

"That's true," Celia said.

The cardinal continued, "Most of us recognize how problematic bonding with one coin can be, imagine having several, each bestowing gifts that are disorientating, or in cases debilitating, yet euphoric and addictive all at once. Now imagine you crave that power, you feel chosen by God to wield it."

David said, "Is that why you mentioned Hypomania earlier?"

The cardinal nodded. "Yes. With the euphoria comes a

heightened sense of creativity and power. Delusions of grandeur."

Celia agreed. "The coins do that. I feel that way, sometimes, after I heal."

The cardinal said, "It's being able to discern between the delusions and reality that is critical. One needs to understand limitations, or else symptoms escalate to full mania, or the other illnesses I mentioned. I believe in Christ's time, these people would have been considered possessed."

"What's essential to us now," Madeira said, "is that we can tell the difference between an individual who's negatively effected by a coin, and may cause harm to himself or others, from someone who is just naturally euphoric or typically disturbed. That's where discernment comes in."

"Sounds like a reality show, 'Sort Through The Psychos." David joked.

The cardinal ignored him. "It's imperative that potentially destructive individuals are separated from their coins. Madeira can identify them, but we have not yet secured a way to sever the coin's powers from any dangerous individual who has one or more of the select coins, including Cardinal Jussipini."

The professor stood up. "Madeira's not able to tap into the other aspect of discernment?"

Madeira looked away and said, "No, I cannot."

"What?" David was confused. "What's the other aspect of discernment?"

"We need to disarm the men who are disillusioned," the cardinal said.

"You said that already." He still wasn't following.

"David," the professor leaned forward on his elbows. "The difference is between sensing someone's demons, weaknesses, or disabilities and eliminating them."

Everybody's eyes were on the professor now as the cardinal translated his words.

Madeira sank down in her seat a bit. "I can't fulfill the prophecy on my own. I can only identify evil and weakness, I cannot cleanse or purify. I need help."

"None of us is able to do this ourselves," the professor said. "That's the point and, I believe, why the documents mention gathering." He stood. "Madeira, I think your answer is here. I think David is the partner you seek"

The cardinal stopped translating and stared at the professor.

Huh? What is the professor talking about?

The professor continued. "I didn't understand my premonition before this moment, but I believe David will be the one to help you."

"Help her what?"

"Exorcise the demons," Madeira announced, as the cardinal echoed, "demonio."

David got to his feet, laughing. "You've got to be joking."

Celia steadied him with a cool hand. "I don't understand. Wouldn't a priest be better suited…"

The professor said, "I don't know, Celia, but a vision I had is becoming clearer to me now. When you think about it, it makes perfect sense. David's studying psychology—"

Exorcize Demons! What the hell? That was about all he wanted to hear. David stepped away from the table, his heart accelerating. "This is a far cry from psychology, Professor. I mean, c'mon." He thrust his hand into the air. "What do you expect me to do, charge a fee? Coerce a possessed maniac and his buddies to lie down in my subterranean Mayan office and tell me about their childhoods?"

"David," the professor said.

"No, really, I'm curious!" The walls of the giant cavern shrunk around him, as expectations built in the room. The darkest corners flickered in shadow. He shuddered all over, like someone just walked over his grave. This was crazy. The whole thought of it made him nauseous. He wanted nothing to do with demons of any kind and he started to shake a little, the thought was so surreal.

Madeira came around the table and planted herself in front of him. Vertigo consumed him, and the room swam. Perhaps it was the depth of the cavern, or the lack of clean air, but he was having trouble breathing. Shit, he was going to faint in front of this beautiful girl.

Madeira put her hands on his elbows to steady him. "It's okay," she said.

The hell it was. Movies about possession, the devil, and evil spirits ran through his brain, and they scared the shit out of him. He liked not having a coin, spinning hypothetical solutions, and using his knowledge to help, while Celia and the professor practiced their hocus-pocus.

"David," Madeira urged, her brown eyes attempting to reach out to him and secure him there.

I won't faint, he said to himself. I won't. Then, he threw up all over her.

One would think that being covered in puke would be a detriment, but as Madeira led David through the underground passages to a central stream, she could not have looked more poised or regal, and he could not have felt like a bigger loser.

"I'm so sorry," he said again, putting his lantern down next to hers on the rock ledge.

"Don't be." She stepped into the stream and kneeled down, splashing water on herself to wash off his humiliation.

He stepped in with her. "Cold!"

She laughed and flicked some water at him.

He had thought she was his age, but she acted like someone much older – showing great reserve and sophistication. But now, kneeling, wet, and covered with puke, she looked childlike as she flicked water at him again, and dared him with her captivating eyes to retaliate.

Naturally, he doused her with a spray worthy of an elephant.

She screeched and, more deftly than he expected, reached out, grabbed him by each calf, yanked firmly, and sent him sprawling on his ass in the water. He would have felt totally beaten if not for the incredible sound of her laughter, and the amazing view of two round breasts beneath her wet blouse.

She noticed his interest and flipped a handful of water in his face, laughed again, and then turned her back to him to finish cleaning off.

The view of her from this angle was just as erotic, but he kept quiet. They cleaned off in unison, and as the cold water worked its magic on his attraction, it also brought him back to reality. He took a moment to assess his surroundings, again overwhelmed by the magnificence of the Mayan craftsmanship and foresight.

He said, "It shouldn't surprise me to find the underground city built around a water source," then looked back, ashamed to see her having to rinse off her hair. He really nailed her good when he threw up.

"Let me help you," he stepped around her, and scooped water onto her hair and shoulders. He rubbed her soft cheeks with his moist hands, focusing on getting her clean and avoiding her gaze.

She ran her fingers through her hair and they brushed against his, making him shiver in the cold.

She said, "You weren't expecting to become involved in this way?"

His hands froze in the act of rubbing her upper arms. "Excuse me?"

She locked eyes with him. "With the coins and their gifts. You expected to stay clear of them."

"Do you read minds?" he asked, taking one step back from her, but maintaining contact with his hands on her body. He liked the way she felt, liked being alone with her.

"Kind of. Does it matter how I do what I do?"

"It does now," he said.

"Why?"

He didn't answer. Let her guess. He squeezed his eyes tightly shut, and she pushed him, saying, "Stop that," and laughing. "It's not telepathy. I can't hear what you're thinking."

"That's good." He moved around her, trying to get a little distance. "There's very little private from you, isn't there?"

She shrugged, and grinned a shy grin. The combination of her bashfulness and confidence was so appealing.

"Great." He shook his head at the futility of it all. "I have the professor predicting my actions, and you knowing my thoughts. I'm like a puppet."

"We all have free choice, David. That's lesson number one in every Catechism class on earth."

"Did you choose?"

She tilted her head like a curious puppy and said, "Of course."

"Aren't you afraid?"

"Fear is our enemy," she stated with authority, squeezing the water from her hair with deft fingers. "Choose the path of fear, and you choose wrongly."

Such a contradiction: these scholarly, wizened words coming from a girl who, with her damp hair framing her face, looked like she could be as young as fifteen. "How old are you?" he asked, while she stepped out of the water, and her clothes dripping onto the ancient rocks, the clinging fabric outlining her luscious curves.

"I'm twenty."

A year younger than him. He stepped out and stomped his sneakers to expel water. The sloshing vibrated under the bottoms of his feet. He said, under his breath, "That's legal." Then he asked, "There aren't any Mayan towels around, I suppose, or a giant blow-dryer?"

She laughed accordingly, and he pretended, for now, that her laugh was authentic, and she didn't already know what he was really thinking.

Every man faces a time when he's confronted head-on with his destiny, and he needs to step forth, take a new road, armed with enthusiasm, enthralled, and excited about where it might lead. This was not that time.

David wanted nothing to do with demons, or exorcisms, and had every intention of averting this disaster before it got started.

"How do you expect me to do this voodoo exactly?" He asked at the top of his voice, nearly hysterical, while seventeen people calmly stared back at him like he was the one being unreasonable. His drying clothes were itchy, making a very uncomfortable situation worse.

He said, "How can I expel a demon, to get a coin, when I don't have a coin? It's not like I can just walk up to someone, someone mentally unstable no less, and take a coin from him. Can I?"

"You can't," the Indian woman said. "The power remains with the person bonded to the coin. The only way to receive the coin's gifts and powers is if the coin is not bonded to anyone, or the person who was bonded with it is dead."

"I guess killing is out of the question." David laughed, a little out of his mind with incredulity. "I've held the professor's coin and nothing happened to me. Wouldn't its power have transferred to me since it wasn't bonded with anyone and I held it first?"

"We're not sure how the transfer of ownership works," the cardinal said.

"How can we find out?" Celia asked.

The cardinal leaned back and drove the palms of his hands into his eye sockets as if he was trying to ease a headache. "I don't know."

This was exasperating. David said, "With all due respect, anyone unworthy with a coin, or multiple coins, as you've said Cardinal, might be deranged, possessed, and most likely armed if you consider that the bishop was shot. I'm not seeking out coins in anyone's possession until I know we'll be successful acquiring them. I'm no coward," he said, making eye contact with Madeira. "But we've come a long way already, and we still have no idea what we're doing!"

The cardinal said, "I would never dream of jeopardizing any of the lives here. We have an immense task ahead of us. Not only do we want to ensure the prophecy is fulfilled, but we need to do so wisely, safely. That is why we have gone into hiding here, are working from this secure location, pooling our talents and knowledge."

"What have you learned, Cardinal?" The professor asked. "We've been running, full steam ahead, since Celia came to me a few weeks ago. It's been a marathon of events. Are we in agreement that the coins need to be reunited? What does this cavern have to do with the coins? We are really in the dark like David said."

"We believe this cavern is the place where the coins need to be reunited. This information has been kept secret from most at the Vatican until such a time the Holy See appoints." The cardinal and others nodded agreement. He stood and walked over to a wall on the far side of the room. "The codex and the writing here both proclaim a battle of sorts, a cataclysmic event ending with fire. In Vatican documents, there is a prophecy of the second coming, a person who will have all the gifts of Jesus, and will conquer evil. Cardinal Everett Jusipini believes he is this person and that in gathering the thirty coins himself he will fulfill the prophecy. But we believe, and the church believes, that it is through community, a gathering of thirty, rather than gathering the thirty, that will fulfill the prophecy. Only by sharing our gifts and working together will evil be eradicated and heaven on earth be realized."

He looked at David. "I don't know the answer to your question, young man. Except that we must have faith and no fear."

"Easy for you to say." David sat on a stone, putting his head in his hands, suddenly feeling very tired.

"Actually, it's not." The cardinal said, returning to the table and sitting down. "We have been trying to piece this together for a long time. Cardinal Jusipini has been hunting coins, to my knowledge, for eighteen years. As I said, I believe he has six or more, and that's six too many for one man. These recent acts of violence only prove that with each coin, he falls farther from God's grace and fulfilling the prophecy of returning Eden to Earth."

The professor stood. "What do you know about the fire? What does the fire from heaven have to do with this cavern?"

David couldn't listen to another word. "We need a plan. Someone needs to map out what we know, what you know, what we've learned from scrolls, documents, visions, and codices, and put it all together, analyze it, and then we can agree on a plan of action. All this supposition is bullshit. Sorry, but that's the way I see it."

"If our intel is confiscated by the wrong person, like Cardinal Jusipini, all is lost," the Indian man says. "That's why we have not done so yet. All Renata's information was stolen or destroyed by whoever broke into her home. Luckily, she had the foresight to make copies and back up everything."

"We have an ancient road map, right here," Cardinal Margrave said. "Charted out in the hieroglyphics in these caverns."

"And you're the only one who can read them," David said. "Hardly helpful. We need to put together what you know, and what we know, in a way that allows us each to analyze the data as needed."

The Asian man spoke up for the first time. "We can encrypt the data. This was an aspect of my job, before-"

"Now we're talking." David liked this idea. It offered him something concrete, some modicum of control. This could be his contribution. To hell with exorcism. He was a research assistant, a damn good one. He could find answers if everyone was willing to pool what they knew, he was certain of it.

The cardinal stretched his back. "The pope has given us unlimited resources. We also have the support and confidence of your president."

"The President of the United States?" Celia's asked, her eyes opening wide.

"Yes," Cardinal Margrave said. "The Bishop worked hard for that alliance."

"The question is," the professor said, "Who can we trust?"

"The president and the pope can be trusted. I've met them both," Madeira said, and David almost fell off his seat. She stood, looked right at David, and then walked around the table, explaining, "Once the Pope learned of my gift and validated it, he spoke to the President, an active and avid Catholic, and arranged a meeting. Having the president discerned created an alliance with the Vatican. Once the President was convinced that there was a threat to the world that he could help temper, he agreed to assist. He made it clear we could count on him privately, but not publicly."

Cardinal Margrave stood, too. "We want to avoid mass hysteria and doomsday panic. Many of the world leaders are supportive of the preparations underway."

"What preparations?" the professor asked.

The Cardinal said, "Constructing underground sanctuaries, in strategic areas, to house those who will be saved."

"There are many such areas being created in India, too," the Indian woman said. "We will need to be below ground when the coins are reunited. There are predictions of fire from heaven."

"Yeah, we heard about that." David said, feeling even more uncomfortable than he had earlier when they were talking about exorcism. Was this shit for real? He looked around him, taking stock of the fact that he was in a secret, ancient underground Mayan structure. Doesn't get any crazier or more real than this.

"The same precautions are being made in Europe," the British guy said. "Supposedly, there are hidden caverns like this already around the world."

"A tunnel was constructed in 1852 that linked the Ards estate in Co Kildare to St John's Church of Ireland, supposedly so Lady Isobella could travel to church in private," said the red-headed girl.

David argued, "That has nothing to do with this."

"Don't be so sure, David. Tunnels and underground

caverns are everywhere," the Cardinal said.

"Like this one," said one of the Mexicans. If David remembered right, he listed his gift as 'ministry'."

By now, David's head was spinning, and his stomach - empty from having expelled his earlier meal - let out an impressive growl.

Madeira said, "It's late and this is a lot to absorb." She winked at David. He liked her slight Portuguese accent. "Tomorrow we can start putting together what we know, and build a plan as David suggested. The hotel is secure and I screen all visitors," her tone was assertive, her body language full of confidence. God, he liked this girl.

"I own the hotel," the Mexican 'minister' said. "All the employees have been screened by Madeira and briefed on security, etiquette, and secrecy. There are too many of us to meet at once, but smaller groups can break out at the hotel, so we can transcribe notes, research, whatever we need to do."

La Aldea Halach Huinic, Palenque, Mexico, May 11, 2032

It had been a grueling day. Celia found herself nodding off slightly as Lang – their Palenque technology expert – and David worked through the best way to encrypt their data. Her room in the villa provided welcome comfort, modern electricity, and soft chairs. After almost eleven hours down in the cavern, she was eager to breathe fresh air and have a soft cushion under her body. But now, after three hours of transposing information, she was finding the soft surface all too welcoming, and the discussion much too technical.

Ryan rubbed her shoulders. "Why don't you lie down,

Celia?"

They were already sitting on the bed. She was afraid if she reclined, she may not get up again. "You all were up at dawn, just like me." She stifled a yawn.

Madeira stretched. "Well, I'm going to go. I have to work my shift tomorrow at the hotel, and we have several new guests arriving."

Madeira paused, stared at David a moment, then said, "Besides, I'm not needed for this."

David lifted his head. "Will I see you tomorrow?"

She nodded. "After closing."

He seemed placated, and went back to his work, while Madeira gathered her things to leave. Ryan caught Celia's eye and smiled. He must have noticed it, too. Something's going on between David and Madeira.

Madeira reached the door. "See you tomorrow."

"Good-night Madeira," Ryan and Celia said in unison.

That left four of them remaining, and since Celia really had little to contribute, she took Ryan's cue and laid back on the bed for a moment, her arms crossed behind her head, and rested her eyes.

Ryan stayed sitting next to her. She was glad, feeling safe from his proximity. She let her mind process what they'd learned today. It would be easy to become fearful and anxious in the face of their overwhelming obstacles, but Celia found comfort in the company she now kept. There was sanctuary in the cavern, combined with fellowship. Knowing that Madeira has, for lack of a better term, 'approved' everyone had allowed them all to speak frankly and move forward in unity without concern about deception or opposing interests.

She had never, in her forty-plus years, participated in any group or project where that was the case.

Breathing deeply, she contemplated what leaving this sanctuary would mean.

Ryan placed a hand on her leg, just above the knee. She peeked at him through her lashes as he watched David and Lang work. Even bald, she found him undeniably attractive. She closed her eyes again, trying not to focus on the heat from his hand resting on her thigh. Instead, she thought about the world they hoped to create, the destiny they sought, the awakening of a living heaven, or – as David would have them believe – the expanding of the conscious to new dimensions. What would heaven on Earth be like?

She imagined a world where love was unending, where kindness prevailed, and jealousy, greed, and animosity were distinguished forever. She tried to comprehend a reality where one could experience time in all its dimensions, without feelings of fear or loss for what was to come, or what had passed before. Could there be such a thing? Could there be a circumstance for humanity where fear was obsolete and each man (or woman) behaved unselfishly - where no one suffered, and each individual acted responsible for the whole?

She found the room slipping away as she sunk into her dreams where this place did emerge, and she helped it to be.

Debiaxo Cavern, Palenque, Mexico, May 12, 2032

Explaining encryption to those who have limited technical capabilities, not to mention those who can't speak

English, can be a challenging endeavor. Having to do that in an ancient cavern without electricity, would be nothing short of a miraculous – or maybe even ludicrous. Yet here David was, attempting just that.

Yesterday, as a group, they had established a plan and agreed to break up into five teams. Team one and two would venture out in search of unclaimed Roman coins: Team one following leads pertaining to stigmata, visions, or other related religious phenomena, and team two tracking coins through traditional collectors and news leads.

Team three would travel as ministers, helping churches, governments, and individuals plan for the anticipated environmental effects, particularly fire from heaven. They believed a massive underground chamber was being constructed beneath the Mindrolling Buddhist Monastery in Dehradun. After they visited India, they planned to go to the Hanging Temple at Xuan Kong Si, near Datong, China where they would confirm a secret sanctuary there, and then to the Shrine of Our Lady of Manaoag in the Philippines.

Team four would remain here at Palenque. The cardinal, who continued to assure them that their location was secure, would stay behind with Renata and Salvatore. Pablo and Hector would also remain, and would act as guardians to their home base at the hotel where Renata could use her healing powers if needed.

Madeira, Celia, the professor, and David composed team five. They would pursue leads through psychiatric avenues to try to recover coins already in the possession of, as the cardinal put it, "those who would misuse them". It seemed to David that this was the most dangerous of the assignments.

What they hadn't decided was what to do about the six

coins that Everett Cardinal Jusipini had. All they could think of to do for now was to find the coins currently unclaimed, if they could be found. Nobody wanted to risk exposure to Cardinal Jusipini or the power of the multiple coins he wielded. The Vatican was keeping tabs on him, so they claimed, until they could see a clear, safe way to contain the problem. It seemed to David that the Vatican was being predictably passive. Maybe they knew something he didn't.

David was equally excited and freaked out. If it weren't for Madeira's magic mind, the professor's friendship and visions, and his growing admiration for Celia, he didn't think he would've agreed to do this.

He concluded, "When the encrypted files must be accessed, the private key can easily be imported from the removable media." David demonstrated. "That's it. We're ready."

CHAPTER 11

La Aldea Halach Huinic, Palenque, Mexico, May 13, 2032

Ryan had never been in the military, had never even considered it. Having been in the seminary, he understood the self-discipline and the sense of brotherhood that was needed and valued in both instances.

This last week - as they met, day after long day in hotel rooms, and secret meeting places - he got a taste of commitment to something bigger than himself, bigger than his own calling to the church and his own relationship with God. Similar to his time in the seminary, he was experiencing the union of joining minds, hearts, and purpose with others. It excited him and filled him with purpose. But for the first time, he experienced the gut-wrenching anxiety that comes with dispersing from your home base, exposing your troops to danger, and hoping for a safe return.

That morning, they said good-bye to team one. And now, as it neared the lunch hour, he sat on the floor of their hotel room with David, Celia and Madeira deciding where they would head first when it was their turn to leave in three days.

David said, "Patient information is confidential. We can't just go online or to the library and look up psychiatric diagnosis."

Ryan agreed. "We won't have much luck getting information from the news, either. Mental disabilities aren't publicized."

"Unless there's a crime involved," Celia said. "We can search online for crimes in the news that involve suspects with mental illnesses."

"It's a start," David said, bending over as only a young person can, and typing search terms on the laptop.

Madeira asked, "Professor, tell us about the vision when you saw David exorcise the demon."

"Do you have to say it like that?" David moved to his right, putting a little distance between him and Madeira. "Geez, just hearing that phrase gives me the creeps."

Madeira snorted. "Well, what would you prefer I say?"

David's shoulders tensed and hunched as he sat cross-legged, like a toddler in preschool. "I don't know. Anything that doesn't conjure images of priests with holy water standing over people floating above their mattresses who look like resurrected corpses."

What could Ryan say? This was going to be something way out of David's comfort zone. And it was his fault that

David was here. He tried to joke with him. "How about we say, 'zap the virus' or some computer-related phrase? Sounds less sinister."

David smiled and leaned back on both arms. "I like that. Madeira's a human lie detector, and I'm anti-virus protection."

"SPAM man!" Madeira said.

David's smile faded. "How will I know what to do?"

"You'll know," Madeira closed the gap between her and David, nudging him with her shoulder. There was definitely a bond forming between them and, knowing David as well as he did, Ryan could imagine how scary it was for David to have any real feeling of any kind for anyone. Losing his mother at a young age and then having an estranged and awkward relationship with his philandering father did little to give David warm or loving social skills. Ryan knew David was best when hiding behind sarcasm and pretending not to care or need care.

"What about your vision, Professor?" Madeira asked, serious again. "How did you know what David was going to do?"

He said, "I saw him laying hands on people, saying, 'I cast you out.'"

"Please tell me you're joking." David turned pale.

"I'm sorry, David." Ryan said. "I'm not." It was not all he saw, but he did not understand the other images yet.

Madeira looked at him. "Professor, try to remember what surroundings you saw in these visions. Maybe there's something we can connect to a physical place."

He opened the journal and flipped through pages of notes

and sketches. Celia moved over to sit nearer to him. Her shampoo smelled flowery.

David said, "We really need to scan those drawings and include them in our documents."

Ryan wished he had been more artistic. "This room could be anywhere," he pointed to the rough drawings. "These windows could be in an institution."

"Or a hotel," Celia said.

"I'm sorry." Ryan felt terrible that the drawings were so nondescript.

"No, They're good, just unfinished. Maybe rushed?" Celia reached over and turned the page. "These passages from Matthew are part of the same vision, right?"

"Ah, yes, the demon passages," David said, rolling his eyes and sighing.

"No computer viruses in ancient times – Captain Vanquish." Madeira said, this time nudging him with her foot.

He lifted an eyebrow at her attempt at levity.

She surprised Ryan by taking the journal, standing, and saying with her slight Portuguese accent, "I interpret this as judgment, but not the judgment day one thinks about in a traditional way," she looked at David briefly, then returned to the notes. "This message relates to us right now – two armies dividing, separating good from bad, no? We are the good, and those misusing the coins are the bad." She read: "Every kingdom divided against itself is brought to desolation, every city or house divided against itself will not stand.

"And if I cast out demons by Beelzebub, by whom so your sons cast them out? Therefore they shall be your judges.

"But if I cast out demons by the Spirit of God, surely the kingdom of God has come upon you.

"Either make the tree good and its fruit good, or else make the tree bad and its fruit bad; for a tree is known by its fruit.

"A good man out of the good treasure of his heart brings forth good things, and an evil man out of the evil treasure brings forth evil things."

She looked at each of them in turn. "We have good in our hearts and will do good things with the coin's gifts. Others may not and may bring forth evil. Don't you think?"

Ryan was speechless. She was something, obviously relating to the discernment of good and evil, which is her gift.

"No offense, Professor," David said, "But I wish your visions were less like riddles and parables, and more direct. Go here. Get the bad guy. Do this. Kick ass!" He motioned wildly with his hands.

The doorbell rang and Madeira said, "There's lunch."

Ryan got up to answer the door and found Hector on the other side with a tray of food.

"How's it going?" Hector asked, stepping inside, and putting the tray on the counter.

"Slow," David answered.

"He's always impatient," Ryan told Hector, who shook his head when he attempted to pay for the meal.

"Ah, well, chasing insanity is not an easy thing," Hector said. "I had a cousin who was as loco as can be. His poor mother, it just broke her heart. Still, she loved him and was proud when he painted the iglesia, the great church, I forget its name, in Mexico City. I was thinking about it the other day, when we were talking about the monasteries. The monks put my cousin's paintings up in the residence - they were so beautiful. My aunt, his mother, used to say, 'sometimes the insane are closer to God than we are.'" Hector nodded. "She believed it, too."

He clapped his hands together and rubbed them briskly. "Well, let me know if you need anything else, eh?"

"We will, Hector, thanks," Ryan said, closing the door behind him. He uncovered the large tray of assorted sandwiches, chips, and salsa, "Hector's right. There is a religious connection between psychosis, spirituality, and artwork. And, often, the works of art are published."

"Or mentioned in a dissertation, or an academic paper," David said, putting his laptop on the counter, grabbing a Southwest Chicken Sandwich, and then bending down to query the search engine again. "If we're lucky, we may find something on artwork and coins or stigmata."

Ryan put some guacamole on his plate, but suddenly wasn't very hungry. "What if none of the people we seek have been institutionalized?"

"Then there'd be no record," David said. "But, if we're chasing the coins, and they're chasing the coins, maybe they would follow the same clues we would?"

"What do you mean?" he put his plate down, untouched, and opened a soda can instead.

"Think about it. We were chasing signs of stigmata and searching the news and web for traces of newfound coins. So are the bad guys, and in many cases, we know they've arrived first, like with the Bishop." David typed away on his keyboard. "I'll enter the keywords: mental, institution, apocalypse, crime, religion, psychosis, and art; to see what comes up."

Madeira said, "What you're saying makes sense, David. Someone possessed by a coin may not hesitate to steal or kill from another, especially if they think it'll bring them more power."

"Yes!" David said, and dramatically swiveled his laptop around to face everyone.

Ryan scanned the article on the screen, "Respected professor Killed In Institution," the headline said. "Ayci Ibrahim, former Associate professor at Gazi University, Turkey, was brutally killed when two men evaded security at the Mental Hospital of Elazýð, and stabbed Professor Ibrahim in his sleep. Authorities wouldn't confirm whether the crimes were connected to the professor's highly publicized and controversial theories on the galactic alignment and the end of the world."

"According to friends and family, Professor Ibrahim was subjected to a multitude of negative press and hate mail. 'There are many organizations who wanted him silenced,' says Professor Tansel Yilmaz (the University Dean). 'He was a hard worker when I hired him. Then, last year, he began frightening students, professing himself as God's messenger, and ranting about the apocalypse. Such a shame. I am sorry for the pain his family has suffered. Maybe this will provide closure for them.'"

From behind him, Ryan heard Celia sigh. "More death."

He said, "His son was a student at the College. He dropped out after his father was institutionalized."

"We should talk to him," David said.

"This article is only eight weeks old," Ryan said. "We'll never get near him. The authorities will still be investigating, and I'm sure the family won't speak to strangers."

"I can," Madeira said. "He'll speak with me."

Ryan turned to her. "How do you know?"

"Because of this," she moved him aside, reached over and manipulated the touch screen. She clicked on a small picture inset, which enlarged full-screen.

Ryan looked at it in utter amazement. "It's you," he said to Madeira, reading the caption, "Artwork created by Professor Ibrahim, formally hanging in the Faculty of Fine Arts Building, will be returned to the family after the investigation."

The painting of Madeira, rendered in oil, was almost an exact replica, with the exception of her eyes, which were on fire - tiny flames in place of irises.

"He must have seen you, in a vision. He knew you had gifts, too, by the looks of this." David said. "We can't go to Turkey, you'll be a sitting duck."

Ryan thought about that a moment. "Maybe not. Muslims believe Jesus was a prophet, as he preached for people to adopt the straight path in submission to God's will - to guide the Children of Israel. Muslims believe Christ was able to perform miracles, all by the permission of God. Depending on which authorities we contact, we may find the Turkish government will aide us.

"It certainly wouldn't hurt to tap into those who support us in Washington, or at the Vatican, and see if they can arrange a meeting - if the boy will agree. Remember, we don't know his opinion about his father's illness or murder. And, he may be in a deep state of grief."

Madeira said, "If my father was wrongly accused of being crazy, and then brutally murdered, I would grasp at anything I could to redeem him. The son will talk to me; I know it."

Everybody was silent for a while.

David said. "What are you going to say to the kid once we get there?"

"That depends," Madeira touched the image of her fiery eyes on the screen, "on whether he's good fruit or bad fruit."

Ankara, Turkey, May 16, 2032

Not far from the American Embassy in Ankara, Turkey, David and the others approached Anitkabir, strolling down Lion's Road with twenty-four statues of Hittite lions guiding the way: symbolizing serenity, power and protectiveness.

David felt high, in a sick-to-his-stomach way – probably because he was exhausted and hyper all at once. The fifteen-hour flight from Mexico was grueling, and he hadn't slept much before they left. He never dreamed of visiting Turkey. His only knowledge of the country came from an exchange student he spent a few hours drinking with once, almost a year ago.

The professor yawned widely, covering his mouth with his hand, but the sound carried. He was walking next to David, hand-in-hand with Celia. Madeira had taken the lead, accompanied by the American ambassador, and a Turkish officer wearing a navy blue uniform and cap.

The Mausoleum was designed as a temple, in Greek fashion, in honor of Atatürk, founder of the republic of Turkey. At the center of the steps, there was an inscription.

The professor said, "These are Atatürk's famous words. It reads, 'Sovereignty belongs unconditionally to the nation.' He was a great leader who professed peace at home and in the world."

David said, "Do you see the irony of meeting here, traveling halfway across the world to stand beneath the roof of yet another temple?"

"Most people don't realize how steeped Turkey is in ancient Christianity," the professor said, as they climbed numerous steps to the Mausoleum. "Turkey is home to all seven of the churches mentioned in the opening chapters of Revelations." He looked at David and said, "When John was in exile on the island of Patmos, not far from Turkey, he had a vision. In his vision, he was instructed to write what he saw and to send his visions to the seven churches."

They reached the top of the stairs. Madeira and the officer were speaking. The officer announced, "They'll be arriving soon."

David took in the scenery. The open square below was crowded, swarming with locals and a few tourists with cameras.

Celia engaged the American ambassador in conversation. As David turned to talk to the professor, he caught him staring off in space, his eyes glazed over.

"Are you okay?" David touched his arm, making the professor twitch and snap out of his trance.

"I was just remembering," the professor said, still staring, only this time looking directly at Madeira, "that when John had his vision, and the voice told him to record it, it is written that the voice belonged to a brilliant white figure with eyes blazing like fire."

David was beginning to wonder why he left college to join this crazy quest, when the ambassador said, "Here they come." This just got weirder and weirder.

A dark-haired, dark-skinned young man ascended the steps surrounded by four Turkish police officers. He must be Melik, the dead guy's son. He was wearing a red and white striped polo shirt and jeans over an athletic build, and he scanned the area nervously while approaching, carefully avoiding looking directly at them.

Madeira stepped forward. David moved to her side, stepping around the professor.

The kid reached the top step, hardly out of breath, and finally made eye contact with Madeira.

"Thank you for coming," she said in English, and smiled at him.

Melik was spellbound, and David couldn't blame him. He felt the same way the first time he laid eyes on her, even without the haunting painting and a father's murder to spook him. Her gaze was electric, hypnotic, and alluring, no ordinary scrutiny.

Melik said, "I was compelled to come."

"I know," she replied.

"The authorities tell me that you may know why my father was killed?" His eyes never left hers, not even for a second.

David wanted to introduce himself, but felt breaking her trance would be a mistake. It was unnerving meeting in such a public place, especially after having been so reclusive and secretive in Mexico, but Melik insisted on it. David could only imagine why – maybe for fear of being trapped, or maybe in hopes of exposing them somehow.

Madeira said, "Did your father have one of these?" and she lifted her necklace into Melik's view to show him the Roman shekel.

It took him a moment to glance at it, and then he nodded, returning to Madeira and reconnecting with her. "Why did my father paint you?"

"I don't know," she said. "Do you?"

He paused, biting his lip. "Is it true? Is the end of the world coming?"

"Maybe," Madeira said in a low tone. "But it won't be the way your father predicted – not if we can help it."

The professor said, "There are two different possibilities, Melik. We believe rather than an end, like your father proclaimed, there could be a new beginning, a heaven on earth. That's why we're here."

"Was my father killed for that coin?" Melik asked, still locking eyes with Madeira. Had he even heard the professor speaking?

"I believe so." Madeira said.

Melik looked away, taking some time to digest her words. David could tell he was on the edge – balancing in that space between fear and curiosity. His tense posture mimicked theirs as they all held their breath, waiting to see what the kid would decide.

"What is it you want from me?" He asked, his eyes full of caution. He clenched his jaw several times while opening and closing his hands.

David wondered what Madeira could see in this kid.

Celia stepped forward, put her hand on Melik's shoulder.

"We want to help you to understand that what happened to your father wasn't his fault. And we want to help the authorities capture the men who killed him."

"What's in it for you?" He stepped back from her touch. If she was trying to calm him with her gift, it wasn't working.

"The fate of the world," she said, straight out, without hesitation.

Melik's eyes darted nervously between Madeira, Celia, and David. "How do you plan to catch his killers?"

David sure wasn't going to tell him that. He would think they were as crazy as his father. He said, "We'd like to see the artwork your father painted and to look through his things at the institution. And we need your permission to speak to his doctors."

"You're wasting your time," he said, turning his back on them and shouting over his shoulder. "I know who killed him." He started down the stairs.

Madeira chased him, and David stumbled after her. She grabbed Melik's arm and spun him. "Who are they?"

He rolled his eyes and pulled away from her. "The men who were with my father when he found the coins at the Citadel."

Celia caught up. "Coins? He found more than one?"

"What's the Citadel?" David said at the same time.

Melik huffed, and threw his left hand out. "The Citadel at Ankara - right over there. My father was fascinated with ancient civilizations and Turkish history. He spent years of his life following the work of Frank Calvert who claimed that Anatolia is the location of the lost city of Troy. He loved to explore ancient, primitive locations like Hattusas. He even went to the Pergamon Museum in Berlin to see the sphinx they found. He was always eccentric…"

Melik's voice cracked, and he was clearly struggling to compose himself. He swallowed several times, and then said, "He and some associates involved with the Istanbul Prehistoric Research Project found several dozen coins when excavating areas of the citadel. I remember when my father brought them home. I don't know why anyone would kill him for those coins. We had them assessed and they weren't worth much."

"How many men?" Madeira asked. "How did they distribute the coins?"

Melik swiped at his eyes with the back of his hand. "Three men. They split the coins between them. Right afterward, my father began to act strangely. He became paranoid. He started to talk about the end of the world. There were days when I didn't even recognize him - he was so crazed. I had him institutionalized," he said with emphasis. "I did this!"

His shoulders shook, no longer able to hold back his grief.

"You did the right thing," David said, trying to comfort him.

"What do you know?" He screamed at them. "You know nothing!"

David said, "I know what it's like to look at a parent and recognize that they aren't who you thought they were anymore."

Melik covered his face and sobbed. "I did not even recognize his voice at the end. He was not the man I lived with." He lifted his red eyes to look at David. "Why?"

"We can tell you," David assured him. "But not here. Not

like this."

Melik composed himself, nodded, and dried his face with his hands. "You can see his artwork. Come to my home and we'll talk some more."

"Thank you," Madeira said.

"Don't thank me yet," he said, and stormed down the stairs.

Melik and his family lived in a white corner villa on a private lot with a semi-covered patio less than two miles from the mausoleum. The thick exterior walls were cracked in places, but the building looked sturdy. The rounded front entry had a large mahogany door polished and gleaming in the afternoon sun.

"No one is home now," Melik explained, as he unlocked the front door and ushered them down a long hall into the main living area. His place was really cool, exotic. There were tiles on every surface: bright blue on the walls and archways, deep brown on the floor, some in disrepair and others covered by decorative rugs in similar colors.

"My family doesn't know I'm speaking to you. Ever since my father was institutionalized, my mother has been staying at her sister's house in Istanbul. Neighbors shun us. My sister goes out drinking with friends and often doesn't come home." Melik shrugged and shook his head. "This is our life now."

"And the police?" David asked. "Are they here for us, or have they been guarding your house since your father's murder?"

When David said the word, "murder," Melik closed his eyes as if in pain.

"After my father's…" he was unable to finish the sentence, and opened his eyes. David saw disdain reflected in Melik's stare. "The police have been here, expecting the killers might return, protecting me and my family from the press and other fanatics."

He implored them to continue further into the house with a wave of his arm. David stepped by him into a small room, followed by Celia, the professor, Madeira, and lastly the American ambassador.

Melik inhaled and said, his voice still very small and laced with grief, "Before my father's episodes, he was a respected citizen. We all were." Then he gestured towards a sofa and several orange chairs. "Please sit."

Celia took one chair and the professor took the other. Madeira and David sat together on the couch. The American ambassador remained standing in the corner by the entrance. He was under strict orders from the U.S. President to help them in any way possible.

Melik said, "I'd offer you a drink, but I haven't been to the store. All I have is water. I apologize. My mother is better at these things."

"How well did you know the men who were with your father at the Citadel?" Celia asked.

"Not very well."

David leaned in, his elbows on the edge of his knees, as he said, "Did you see them after they found the coins? Did they visit with your father at the institution?"

Melik had not taken a seat. He stood, as if on trial, nervously wringing his hands and watching them with caution. "No."

"Melik," Celia said in a very motherly tone, "tell me about your father's illness."

"I already did," he said. "And I prefer not to speak of it."

"I studied psychology back home," David scooted forward to the edge of the couch, physically reaching for closeness with Melik. "We have reason to believe, for some, contact with these coins can cause mania, multiple personalities, and other psychological disorders."

"Well, then," Melik stepped away from them the tiniest bit, "how do I know that you don't suffer from the same symptoms?"

"I have had symptoms that some would consider problematic," Celia said, most likely in an effort to gain a fraction of his trust. David was impressed by her fast thinking. "Have you ever heard of stigmata, Melik?"

"Yes, I've heard of it."

"Well, after I got my coin, I had stigmata. I was worried for a while that I was crazy. I avoided the media and my family and friends. It was very scary."

The professor put his hand on her back.

She asked, "Do you know if the men you suspect of murdering your father had any reactions to the coins like that?"

Melik breathed deeply several times, then said, "Excuse me a moment," before stepping out of the room.

"I think we lost him."

"Don't be so sure, David," Madeira said. "His heart is in

the right place, but he's very wary."

A few tense moments passed. David wondered what the heck Melik was doing when he suddenly returned, dragging a box behind him containing several canvases. "Here are my father's paintings." He picked one up and turned it to face them. It was a rendering of a hand, holding a chain with a silver coin dangling; Red blood dripped from the palm.

"Geez," David said.

Celia covered her mouth with her hand and the professor rubbed her back.

"I don't want to be a part of this," Melik said. "My family has been hurt enough. But you're free to look over his work and drawings." He handed David a folder. "Here are some notes he took, prior to his hospitalization. You'll find the names of the men you seek there, as well as other information that may help you. I called the hospital and gave my permission for his doctors to share my father's files with you."

David stood and extended his hand, which Melik gave a tentative, little shake. "Good luck," he said, clearly dismissing them.

Celia stood. "Good luck to you, Melik. I am so terribly sorry for your pain."

Mental Hospital of Elazýð, Ankara, Turkey, May 17, 2032

Dr. Aydin Sadock was not as guarded as Melik. In fact, for a licensed psychiatrist, he was very gabby. So much so, David felt more uncomfortable with every fact the doctor shared. He realized how easily this might have been his life, tending to the mentally disturbed in a sterile office that smelled like disinfectant. It didn't seem quite so noble anymore now that supernatural, spiritual, and life-threatening events surrounded them.

David and Madeira sat, while the professor and Celia stood in the cramped space. The American ambassador waited outside the room.

"They cut his stomach open," the doctor said. "They emptied him out."

"Why would they do that?" Celia wrapped her arms protectively around her middle.

"Ayci had a habit of swallowing his coin to keep it safe," Dr. Sadock explained. "They blinded two orderlies on the way out, slashing at their faces with their knives and yelling, 'you were blind to His greatness, now let blindness be your other weakness!' That was a big topic for Ayci."

"What was?" David was confused.

"Weakness." The doctor sat back. "He recognized it in himself and developed his alter egos to compensate for his own shortcomings."

"How so?" the professor asked.

"Well," Doctor Sadock said, stretching his arms out and placing them on the desk on either side of his notebook. "I had only started documenting the changes, but once, under hypnosis, he presented as a child he called Lynik. In theory, he recreated himself before he had sinned, when he was, as he said to me once, 'pure'. He frequently talked about purity, and when he harmed himself physically, he claimed it was punishment for impurity."

"He was punishing himself? Inflicting wounds on himself?" David was fascinated.

"Yes," the doctor said. "Didn't you see the painting of the hand, bleeding, holding the coin? He cut his hands often."

David turned to Celia, who had gone pale. She said, "Was Ayci's coin on a chain?"

The doctor settled in his chair, his brows knitting together. "No. He could not have swallowed it so easily if it had been. He refused to be separated from the coin so we allowed him to keep it, at the time feeling it could do no harm."

"Did Ayci self-inflict wounds anywhere else? I mean, aside from his hands?" the professor asked.

"Yes."

"Where?"

"He stabbed himself here once," the doctor said, indicating his side.

"What about his head?" Celia asked. "Did he hurt himself there?"

"Well, after the first two incidents, we rarely allowed him anything that he could use to harm himself. There was a time," he said, scratching at his beard, "that we found him poking at his head with the blunt end of a paintbrush. We stopped art therapy shortly afterwards which was very frustrating to him since art was a big part of his life and therapy."

"He was recreating Christ's wounds," the professor said.

"Or faking stigmata?" Celia's voice was low, contemplative.

"I don't think so," Madeira said. "It wasn't deception. I also don't believe it was punishment."

"Then what was it?" David looked at her, waiting.

"Envy," she said, nodding her head in affirmation.

"Well, that was a waste of time," David said as they left the building and headed back to the rental car. The sun was setting, and the warm rays managed to paint the homely parking lot an inviting, warm, orange color. Turkey was unlike anywhere David had been before. It felt intensely foreign.

His neck was stiff and achy from sitting in the cramped office for over two hours. He bent his ear to his shoulder in an attempt to crack the kinks out, when something buzzed by his neck, zinged the roof of the car next to him, and shattered the window of the car beyond.

"What the fuck?" he said, grabbing Madeira and throwing her to the asphalt.

Like lightening, another crack and flash hit the van next to Celia as the ambassador dove into her, dragging her and the professor down in one quick motion.

Someone was shooting at them. David felt a rush of adrenaline powered by fear.

The ambassador motioned for them to follow, then crawled around some cars to lead them closer to the street. He had his cell phone out, and, almost instantly, they heard a siren.

David felt a sharp pain as he crawled forward. He lifted his palm to find he had cut himself on some glass. Wiping his hand on his jeans, he turned and said, "Watch out!" to Celia when the tire nearest him exploded. A piece of rubber skimmed his cheek and hit Celia in the face. The car dropped several inches with a whoosh, then another shot echoed out in front of the ambassador who stopped crawling, pivoted onto his backside, and pressed himself against a blue car covered with rust and grime. They were all panting heavily. Madeira, still on all fours behind him, froze in her spot.

"Are you okay?" he asked, and the ambassador, Celia, and Madeira all answered at the same time.

The professor crawled up to Celia from his position in the rear and said, "Where are they shooting from?"

The ambassador hooked a thumb over his shoulder. "The parking garage is my best guess."

David started to get up to peer over the top of the car, but Madeira pulled him back by his shirt collar. "Stay down!" she said.

He jumped a mile when the car alarm started honking right in his ear. They all scrambled forward at the same moment the windows of the blaring car burst out and scattered on the ground they had just vacated.

The police sirens stopped. David thought he heard shouts coming from the direction of the snipers over the sound of the incessant car alarm. His hand throbbed, and his pant leg was soiled with blood and dirt.

They all huddled next to an old grey service truck.

"You're wounded," the ambassador said, tearing off a piece of his dress shirt using his teeth and some effort. He shuffled over on his knees, keeping his head down, and then wrapped David's hand with a few deft motions, eyes darting left, right, and then left again.

He whipped around at the sound of footsteps, his hand still throbbing, and Madeira yelped as a uniformed police officer rushed out and took aim right for them. The ambassador yelled a few phrases in Turkish, putting his hands up in the air and pointing to the parking garage. David was frozen in his spot, trying to swallow down his heart, which had leapt into his throat.

The officer said something and the ambassador stood and translated, "It's okay. They apprehended the shooters."

"Are you sure?" Madeira asked, still crouched next to the professor and Celia between two cars. Her lips were trembling, and her eyes were huge, pupils dilated. She was in shock. David scooted forward to take her gently by her arms and help her up. They stood together while the professor and Celia rose on unsteady legs.

He tried to think of something funny to say, but his mind was blank. Being shot at was more terrifying than it seemed in the movies. He rubbed at Madeira's arms, trying to get her blood moving, his bandaged hand making the gesture clumsy and ineffective. She wasn't breathing, so he pulled her close and said, "It's okay," while he held her as tight as he could.

Feeling her exhale, he turned toward the officer and ambassador, "Where are they taking the shooters?"

The ambassador exchanged words with the officer, and said, "One man is dead. The other will be taken to Akay Hospital for treatment."

Madeira started to tremble in his arms. He looked the ambassador in the eye, and insisted, "I want to speak with him. I want to see him! Do you understand?"

Akay was one of the largest hospitals in Turkey, with an enormous, angled, glass facade and a terrace offering a view over Ankara. It took several hours of negotiation to be allowed access to the prisoner. And only two of them could go in at a time, with an armed escort.

Standing in the waiting area, next to the nurse's station, the ambassador briefed them. "He was grazed by a bullet to the right side of his head. His left side is paralyzed, but the doctor doesn't think it will be permanent. He'll live and, most likely, regain use of his body again."

"Oh, great," David paced. "Soon he'll be out chasing us again."

"No." The ambassador held a hand up, shaking his head for emphasis. "He'll be detained. He didn't just shoot at you, he shot and injured a police officer as well."

David hadn't meant to insinuate inefficiency on behalf of the Turkish law enforcement. "Don't mind me. I talk nonsense when I'm angry."

Celia said, "Or nervous, or happy, or concerned, or…"

"Yeah, yeah," he said. "Very funny."

The ambassador nodded, the corner of his mouth turning up. "Apology accepted. Let's go." He turned and led the way down the west corridor to the room where the prisoner was being held. Two armed policemen guarded the door: one tall and lean, the other short and squat, but powerfully built.

The tall one stood as they approached and greeted the ambassador. "Who is going first?" the officer asked, squaring his shoulders and breathing evenly.

David exchanged glances with Celia and the professor, who said, "You go, David, and take Madeira."

He looked to Madeira for confirmation. She swallowed hard, and then nodded assent, seeming to have recovered from the shooting, although she wasn't the confident, brave, undeterred girl she was five days earlier in Mexico. Flying bullets and raving lunatics have that effect on some people.

For someone who recently tried to kill them, the shooter looked helpless and confused, as he laid there, half broken, on his hospital bed.

"Does he speak English?" David asked the officer who showed them in.

"Yes," the officer moved over to the window and leaned on the ledge. His casual stance wasn't fooling anyone. David could see his intense eyes watching every move they made.

Madeira was also watching the prisoner with a calculating glare. She said, "Bad fruit." She frowned. "If he has a coin, he hasn't bonded with it."

Drool ran from the left corner of the prisoner's mouth. He avoided her eyes, and refused to acknowledge her - staring blankly at a spot on the ceiling. The prisoner could not have looked more pitiful and less menacing if he tried.

"He can't hear you," David said. The guy's body was there, but his mind was out to lunch.

"He can hear me," she said with conviction, walking to the prisoner's right side and placing her hand on the bandage over his head. He blinked several times and his fingers twitched very close to where she was standing, but he didn't look at her or speak.

"He's fucking with you, then," David said, to see if this got a reaction. Sure enough, the prisoner's eyes flashed before returning to the ceiling.

"Let's see of he has a coin anywhere around here that doesn't belong to him." David snooped around the room and rummaged through the belongings in the little hospital closet. The officer watched on, probably wondering who was more dangerous: the shooter or David.

The shooter didn't flinch.

Madeira checked for a chain around his neck just as a nurse entered. She stepped away from the prisoner while the nurse checked his medication and replaced the saline bag on his IV drip. When the nurse started to close the privacy curtain, the officer stopped her with some curt words. She closed it halfway giving the man privacy from everyone except the officer.

By now, Madeira was standing next to David, and hooked her hand around his elbow. She leaned over and rose on tiptoes to whisper, "He's nervous - ever since the nurse arrived."

The nurse talked to the patient, but of course they couldn't understand a word she was saying.

When she opened the curtain, the man's eyes darted back and forth across the ceiling and he was clearly agitated. He started babbling, but the nurse didn't seem to be listening to him. She was adjusting the sheets and blankets.

Madeira said, "Let's go," and tightened her grip on David's arm, drawing him out the door to follow the nurse as she left.

The ambassador, Celia, and the professor stood anxiously in the hall outside.

Madeira said, "Stop," and touched the nurse on the back of her shoulder. "I need to find out what he said to her."

The nurse gave all of them a look of exasperation. She and the ambassador began a conversation, which David interrupted when he saw what the nurse was holding.

"Give me the bedpan," he said, and the ambassador looked at him like he just grew a second head.

"Of course." Celia agreed, following his logic. According to the psychiatrist they met that very morning, Ayci, Melik's father, used to swallow his coin. "We need to inspect the bedpan."

Although clearly uncomfortable and uncertain, the ambassador translated the request to the nurse, who shook her head in the negative and spoke a few words in response.

David said, again, "We need to see-"

"Not here," the ambassador interrupted. "It's not sanitary. There's a room where they clean out the bedpans, with gloves and proper equipment."

"Let's go," David looked up and down the hall. "Which way?"

The stout officer shouted some orders to his lanky partner, and then followed as the nurse lead them down several hallways.

Garbed in protective gear and a surgical mask, David found himself standing over an oversized utility sink with a pair of metal thongs to dig through the nastiness that came out of the prisoner. Sure enough, he withdrew an ancient roman coin from the waste and held it up for Madeira.

"Well, shit," she said, stealing his line, smiling widely and nudging him with her elbow.

He looked past her at Celia and said, "Tell the officer we need an autopsy of the other shooter."

CHAPTER 12

Ankara, Turkey, May 18, 2032

The ambassador drove the four of them in a van back to Akay Hospital where an autopsy of shooter number two was scheduled in less than an hour. David was surprised by how accommodating the authorities in Turkey had been. The US president's personal relationship with the Prime Minister was a huge advantage.

The coin from yesterday's shit-digging, now disinfected and shiny clean, resided in David's pocket. He finally understood the seductive power of the coin, and how, in the wrong hands, it could corrupt both mind and spirit. As soon as he had touched it, he experienced what Cardinal Montgrave had called "bonding". It was intense, more intense than anything physical that had ever happened to him in his short life. More exhilarating than orgasm, or the thrill of a roller-coaster ride, more heart-stopping than being frightened at a horror film, more adrenaline-producing than a near car crash, the transformation could only be described as "spiritual". It was like being keenly aware, in an instant, of a part of you that you didn't know existed.

David recalled seeing a show on television where people who had been born deaf and never heard sound were given implants. He remembered being intrigued by how the introduction of sound to a previously soundless existence had been so traumatic, disturbing, in some cases impossible to tolerate. He now understood. This was like discovering a new sense, while at the same time your other senses grew stronger. Only these were not physical senses he was experiencing. This was a spiritual experience beyond his physical existence. He understood that, but could not have explained it to anyone in words, not even to himself.

One thing was for certain-he didn't feel worthy. David had not been the poster-child for goodness, nor had he been its advocate during his lifetime. As he sat next to Madeira, and felt the goodness in her, he wondered if he would ever measure up? Could he fulfill the destiny that the professor had predicted for him? Would he be strong enough, pure enough, to keep sanity within reach?

The hospital came into view. David took a deep breath, drawing strength from the coin, and knowing that if he invited doubt, or got too high from the power, he would be no better than the other shooter whose body was about to be dismantled in the morgue.

At least in the morgue there was little chance of someone ill bringing on an episode of stigmata. As Celia stood in the cold room, as far from the body as possible, she tried not to think of her dead loved-ones, but it was hard. These rooms brought out images of tragedy, sickness, and death like none other. And the smell was nauseating even though she had a mask over her mouth and nose.

Madeira leaned in to her and said, "Remember, we have the ability to change the way the world sees death, and life. That's why we're here."

Celia shivered from the cold and the stench, but also in response to Madeira's eerie acuteness.

She'd never seen an autopsy, and was no scientist. The dispassionate inspection of this man's body was difficult for her to watch. She closed her eyes, trying to remember Jeff as he lived, not as he died. She hoped that this man being dissected now was with those who loved him in spirit. She prayed for his soul, seeking out the part of her that was forgiving, and gave herself over to it. She ignored the sight of the man's body, the physical vessel, although the coin it might protect was essential to a new beginning for all of them.

"There it is," Ryan said.

The medical examiner dropped a coin into a small metal dish of disinfectant and continued his work.

"Two down, several more coins to find," David said. "Hopefully the others will be easier to get at."

The floor shifted below Celia. She swayed a little, feeling

unsteady, and then she heard a faint rumbling.

The examiner stopped abruptly, bracing his hands on either side of the body.

A door opened behind them at the same time Celia noticed the tools on the table vibrating, and the body jiggling left and right. The ambassador's voice called out sharply, "Earthquake!"

The vibration lasted only a few seconds, and then the power cut out. Celia heard yelling and commotion from the hall. She stepped forward, heedless of infection or morgue etiquette, grabbed the slimy coin from the metal tray, and enclosed it protectively in her fist while the medical examiner was distracted by the excitement.

"We should exit the building," the ambassador said. "Quickly. Now!"

"C'mon Celia," Ryan took her arm and lead her to the door.

She pocketed the coin before they arrived at the closest stairwell and pulled off her face mask, the threat of yet another natural disaster making her tremble. She started sweating.

In contrast to the panic that raged in Celia, the hospital seemed prepared for this kind of event. An organized and calm procession marked the evacuation of rooms and hallways, most on foot, but others in wheelchairs and in beds on wheels.

Out in the street, however, there was chaos. People were wandering aimlessly, patients arriving were being turned away, and those who had been evacuated stood unsure of where to go next. It was difficult to follow the conversations since she didn't speak the language. Most seem confused and frightened as they searched for a safe spot, a loved-one, a doctor, or a sign of where to be.

The ambassador closed his cell phone and said, "It's bad. Early reports indicate this quake to be larger than the 7.4 that hit the North Anatolian fault in 1999. We lost power for three days after that one, with over 30,000 killed. Luckily, we're on the outskirts of it here, but be prepared for aftershocks."

Celia helped a nurse wheel out a patient. The nurse smiled her thanks, and then turned back to go in for the next patient. Just then, the ground rocked, and a section of the entryway collapsed all around the nurse. Celia ran over, and several people automatically began digging through the debris. The glass façade rained down, making the dangerous situation ever more hazardous. Celia uncovered the nurse's hand and detected a pulse there. "She's alive!" she yelled in English, hoping someone would understand.

The ambassador, David, Ryan, and Madeira stepped forward to help, but the shattered glass plates made a menacing landscape. Each precarious move had to be made with caution, not only for themselves, but for the welfare of those already hurt and covered with debris. David's bandaged hand gave her an idea. She ran back to some of the patients in the street and began pulling blankets off the beds and laps of many. Ignoring their protests, she hurried back to David, and yelled, "Rip these up! Have everybody wrap their hands to protect against the glass!"

He nodded, and tossed a few blankets to the ambassador. "Tell them," David said, before biting a corner of one blanket and tearing a nice, wide, strip.

She headed back for more, finding patients offering the

blankets to her now.

Ryan wrapped her hands and, side-by-side, they continued to dig out the nurse and others harmed by the falling shards. People trying to get out the main door decided to exit through the large exterior lobby windows, now barren without the panes in place.

"Be careful," she said, forgetting she wasn't in America. She didn't know how many understood, but her actions, and the actions of those around her, seemed to speak for them. Even with covered hands, progress was slow due to all the glass. The nurse was badly cut, but Celia thought she'd be okay. She tried to calm her while the nurse stood unsteadily, speaking rapidly to her, and refusing to leave the rubble and go out to the street to safety.

"I don't understand you," she said.

A man behind her shouted, "She's trying to tell you her daughter is in there. Her daughter works here, too."

"Okay," Celia said, nodding her head. "Can you tell her we're clearing the pathway as fast as we can?"

He translated for her, but the nurse was too worked-up to listen, started scrambling over the debris, seemingly careless of other people or herself. Celia yelled, "STOP!" But she wouldn't heed.

With extreme caution, Celia followed her, stepping where the nurse stepped. The nurse faltered several times, further injuring her left leg on broken glass. Celia grabbed the woman's hand to slow her when the earth started to move again and they went down, landing just inside the entry where people were standing, waiting to get out.

Celia covered her head with her free hand, as pieces of

plaster and tile broke off from the lobby ceiling. She pulled the nurse over to a sturdy column. The building moaned. She watched in horror as the structure tipped and roared as it fell on top of them.

When the front of the hospital split in three, Ryan watched in slow motion as the structure crumbled, swallowing Celia with its maw of plaster, steel and glass. He and David barely made it clear, dragging Madeira with them.

The ambassador went down, knocked off his feet by steel brackets, which had been supporting the front overhang.

Ryan wanted to move, to go and try to help Celia, but he was overcome with a strange paralysis as visions assaulted him. He saw, again, Celia buried underground. It seemed to him a different scenario, one with explosions. A sob came from his left, and when he turned his head, he found Madeira on her knees with tears streaming down her face. Past her, David was trembling, his hands covering his mouth in surprise. If he could breathe, he would have offered them comfort, but he couldn't inhale. He was frozen solid by the shock of seeing Celia swallowed up by the collapsing building and by the onslaught of visions invading his mind.

The noise from distraught people overwhelmed the alarms and emergency rescue sounds. He realized that many of the sirens were from ambulances that had arrived to bring people to the hospital, rather than emergency vehicles to help people out of the hospital.

This was not the epicenter of the quake. As terrible as this was, this was not the worst of it. Even if the ambassador had not confirmed this earlier, he could see it in the terrified eyes of all those around him. Their fear snapped Ryan out of his paralysis.

"Oh, God," Madeira said.

"Let's go." Ryan wasn't sure what to do, and he was pretty sure nobody else here knew what to do either, but they had to do something. The earth trembled again. Everybody around him groaned and braced their feet, but it was nothing: just a hiccup.

"C'mon, Madeira. Let's get her out of there."

"You're bleeding," David said, helping the ambassador to his feet.

"I'll be okay," the ambassador dabbed at a deep cut above his temple with a handkerchief.

It took only moments for everyone to regroup and begin the tedious process of trying to find survivors under the rubble.

The ambassador said, "Don't expect much. Based on what I remember from the last earthquake, rescue operations will be hampered by blocked roads and downed power lines. We'll be lucky if we get equipment here before tomorrow."

"Let's just focus on the area where Celia is for now," Ryan said, looking around, finding nobody in control of the rescue effort. "Ambassador, we need to get everybody organized. If we don't handle this right, we'll never be able to tell which areas have been searched. Can you go around and assign places where we can pile the debris? If we move everything around, we might accidentally cover up something that someone else just uncovered."

"Yes," he said. "And we need to mark off search areas in sections, noting places that are unstable. I'm on it."

A man with a red baseball cap stepped up. "We take from here," he said, swaying both hands in the direction of the rubble, "and we put here." He swung his hands toward a bare portion of the parking lot.

"Yes," Ryan took his hand and pumped it.

The man nodded a few times, breaking Ryan's grip, and started to bellow orders to a group behind him.

Piece by piece, they united in the process of moving the ruined building off of the people trapped underneath.

After three hours of labor, the situation seemed as hopeless as it did when they first started. You could hardly see where they dug for survivors. If it weren't for the cut and bleeding fingers, the sore backs, and the piles of rubble, you'd never know they'd labored at all.

EMT's stood by with oxygen, ready to help any survivors, but so far they hadn't found any. The pieces covering Celia were too big to move. They needed heavy equipment. It was the most backbreaking and frustrating futility Ryan had ever experienced.

A vending machine delivery truck had pulled up right before the building fell. Sadi, the driver, distributed water, soda, and vitamin drinks from his truck to those working, then he pitched in to help with the recovery efforts. Ryan was so grateful for the water, he could have cried.

"I know she's alive," Madeira said again, most likely

misreading Ryan's anguish as lost hope. "You have to have faith."

"I do." He drank down the entire bottle. "I just wish I knew where she was." The whole building looked like some child just dumped his Legos all over the place. Celia could be anywhere.

David said, "We know she's somewhere in this area." He gestured with his filthy, torn, bleeding, bandaged hands.

Ryan disagreed. "I think she's to the left of the pile," he said, shaking his head. "I really do." He had started trembling. The physical and mental anguish was taking it's toll. They were not getting anywhere and they were running out of time. How long could Celia survive under there?

Just then, a group of emergency vehicles arrived with heavy equipment for digging. They passed out gloves and hard hats, and then set up floodlights and connected to generators, while others set up tents for the injured.

"It looks like a war zone." He was overwhelmed by the extent of the damage.

All at once, his phone started vibrating, ringing a tune, and chirping. Ryan found a text from Renata, asking if they were okay. This gave him an idea. He tapped the numbers, and hit send, moving around the pile, listening.

"Do you hear anything?" He asked Madeira as she followed him.

He dropped to the ground and crawled over some concrete blocks, pressing his ear as close to the surface as he dared.

Madeira called out, "Here!"

He heard it, so feint and weak, but it was there: Celia's phone was ringing. She was closer to the center than he'd guessed.

If her phone wasn't crushed, maybe she wasn't either. "Celia!" He yelled. "Celia, can you hear me? We're coming! Hang in there!"

There's no reply. They started digging again, but the concrete pieces were enormous.

David was bracing himself against one block and pushing with his legs to dislodge another. His efforts had little effect. "We need help!" he yelled.

"I'm on it." The ambassador headed toward the machines. As he passed Ryan, he said. "I'll get the machines over here."

Ryan and Madeira joined David, all three of them pushing with all their might against the immovable stone.

"She's alive," Madeira said again through gritted teeth, and Ryan hoped and prayed she was right.

Running on little food and no sleep, they had slaved for over twenty hours total before hearing the first voice call for help. When the building had split, the two side sections broke off and collapsed left and right, away from the center. The center section crumpled backwards, which meant that the area above Celia was closer to the surface than all the areas surrounding it.

The whole scene was a gruesome mess. Down on the street below, to the right of where they were digging now, bodies lay strewn about, toppled from the progression of earth, steel, and stone when the hill split open and pulled the right side of the building with it. A pile of broken bodies and body pieces accumulated behind them, soon to be a health hazard. The bugs and buzzards arrived before the rescue workers came, and would probably be here long after they left.

A team of experts catalogued the dead and the remains. This is a job Ryan never imagined, nor cared to imagine. In all his travels as a priest, he had never witnessed anything like this. How ironic that he was exposed to this now only after having left the priesthood. He kept swallowing down the bile that rose to his throat again and again as they dug, hauled, and prayed. It was a humbling experience. He wished he had seen a vision of this. Or rather, he wished the vision he had seen of this had been clearer. When they found her, would she survive? He had no vision of that. Heck, he couldn't even tell if she was alive now.

Finally, they were asked to move aside so the heavy machinery could do its job. It had taken forever, or so it seemed, to get the equipment in place. Ryan didn't know if it was the exhaustion, or the relief that help was here, but he was so overwhelmed he fell to his knees. Somebody handed him a cup of water. He thanked them before taking a long, shaky draw, and then sat on the ground while the machines and the professionals took over the search and rescue.

David sat down next to him while Madeira wandered off to the tents to offer her help there.

David's head was coated with soot. Small cuts covered his face and scalp. He ran a bloodied, bandaged hand over his head, and said, "What do we do now?

He had a broken look on his face as he stared out over the building, flies swarming around. David hardly knows Celia. Look at how lost he seemed after having known her for only a short time. That's how amazing Celia was. She draws you in with her love and acceptance. It had been that way for him in the beginning.

"I lost her once. I moved out of her love for God's love. But, even so, she was with me. I never told her that. I should have." He breathed deeply, not even blinking, his mind far set away, swimming in memories of his youth.

"Can you see anything? Do you have any visions?" David asked.

"I can't tell if she's alive." He held back tears. He would not lose hope until there was none left. "Whatever happens, we move on, and finish this. For the world, but for Celia especially." He peered into the night at the mayhem around him, at the equipment moving the shattered building, at the lights from the empty medic tents, at the dirty, fear-filled expressions of those around him, and said, "These natural disasters are escalating, David. If we don't reunite the coins soon, there may not be anyone alive to save."

Ryan forgot to breathe as he sat in hopeful anticipation that yet another miracle might happen for Celia today.

The first survivor to be pulled from the wreckage was a teenage girl. Although she was a sobbing, filthy, scraped and bloody mess, she was alive, and her tears gave Ryan hope, each breath and sob bringing encouragement that others would be found. Almost like a floodgate opening, the rescue team began to unearth survivors from beneath the jumbled mass of concrete and glass. The tents, so long empty, filled up with people needing care.

Through strained lungs, Ryan forced the breath to come evenly again. Hope, like oxygen, began to sustain him.

They contributed however they could, bringing water to the survivors, and helping the medical team clean wounds and bandage superficial cuts or scrapes. Where, at first, dead bodies and body parts accumulated along the periphery near the debris, now living people, recovered from the building's center, walked the tents and surrounding areas, most with minor injuries. Ryan counted over fifty.

"We need more water," he said to one of the rescue workers. The man's name was Iliam and he spoke English. Disaster unites strangers in unusual ways, and that bond is strengthened by blood, sweat, and kindness.

Iliam said, "They're sending in more supplies." He looked around at all the people and shook his head several times. "Unbelievable."

"I know." Ryan scanned the crowd, taking in the wreckage and mayhem.

"I've never seen anything like it," Iliam said.

"It's awful," Ryan said in agreement.

Iliam looked at him crossly. "No," he said. "It's a miracle - the likelihood of recovering all these people, unharmed, from this wreckage!" He threw his hand out toward the crumbled building. "The quake pulled the building apart in such a way that the center area sheltered those on the first floor. Hamit tells me they may recover as many as two hundred! Also, a large percentage of the upper levels made it out, or made it to the first floor, before the crash."

"We still have not found our companion," Ryan said, by way of explanation. He did not dismiss the man's use of the word, "miracle," though. He embraced it and held it tight.

"I'm sorry," Iliam placed a dirty, calloused hand on Ryan's shoulder. "Don't give up hope, though."

"I won't," Ryan said right before he heard David's frantic voice shouting for him.

Turning, he spotted David in the adjacent tent, surrounded by a shaken, frightened mass of people. A woman was there with him, holding tightly to another woman seated next to her on a cot. They were both grabbing at David's clothes and talking rapidly in Turkish.

David said, "Get the ambassador. I need an interpreter!"

He spun around in a futile attempt, having lost track of the ambassador and Madeira several hours ago when they first started to pull people from the wreckage who needed help. Now, as more and more people congested the tented area, it was hard to find anyone. Besides, it had been dark for over an hour and that meant Ryan had been awake for almost two days. His twenty-minute power nap earlier that day had long since served its purpose. His brain was mush and his legs unsteady.

So, he relied on a technique known to every five-year-old child. He cupped his hands around his mouth and yelled at the top of his lungs, "Ambassador!" Listening for a response, he took a few steps, and tried again. "Ambassador!"

"Over here," the ambassador called back eventually, waving a hand high in the air for him to see. Ryan motioned for him to follow, and they met up at the tent where the women were still pawing at David with hysterics.

"What are they saying?" Ryan asked.

The ambassador's tired face renewed. "This is the nurse,

and her daughter. Celia saved them. They were with her in the building. Do you remember? Right before it crashed."

Madeira appeared out of nowhere. "I remember."

The ambassador and the women exchanged words, and then he said, "She pulled them over to a column, but they couldn't see anything while they were buried under the structure."

"Were they together?" David asked. "When the building collapsed, were they together?"

The ambassador nodded, "Yes."

As the ambassador spoke to several nurses and searched the tent, Ryan focused on staying upright. He was so fatigued from the lack of sleep and emotional turmoil, that he was on the verge of collapse.

The ambassador reached out, took Madeira's hand, and then said, "come," before leading them to the farthest tent. Ryan moved with leaden feet.

There, on the edge of the madness, was Celia's crumpled, bloody body. He felt his knees wobble. Under the dim work-lights, it was hard to tell if she was breathing. When Madeira reached out to take Celia's pulse, Ryan noticed the distinct placement of her bleeding wounds: head, side, and wrists.

CHAPTER 13

The American ambassador's house, Ankara Turkey,
May 24, 2032

As one inflicted with a fiery fever, her mind screamed with delirium. Behind Celia's closed eyelids, heat melted, irises on fire. Her arms and legs, like bricks in an oven, lay heavy and immobile next to her burning body. The pain was intolerable, but she lacked the ability to scream. MAKE IT STOP, she thought, again and again. Oh, please, God, make it stop.

Set up as a temporary care unit for Celia, and in order to keep her condition a secret, the American ambassador recruited the nurse, Ayla, and her daughter, Ceyda, to stay around the clock at his home, providing care as Celia recovered from her ordeal.

The room was fully-equipped with all the supplies to keep her comfortable, although Ryan felt the intricate wooden headboard, embroidered tapestries, and antique furniture were more suited to royalty than to any kind of care unit you'd expect. The ambassador's wife had excellent taste in decor, and since they had practically lived here for a week now, they had all come to appreciate her cooking, too. Due, in part, to boredom and inactivity and, in part, to the delicious food, Ryan could hardly button the waist of his pants now.

Celia, on the other hand, was wasting away on the bed, pale, lifeless, and feverish. An intravenous drip provided nourishment, while regular transfusions kept up her blood levels, and her pulse remained steady.

Renata had come and gone. They recruited her from Mexico and sent her back when it became obvious her healing was useless for helping Celia in this instance. They were more hopeful for a quick recovery prior to Renata's visit.

Thinking that the coins' powers might heal her, they all placed theirs on her person - including the random coin recovered from the dead man, which Celia had in her pocket when the building collapsed. They surmised that the combination of the two coins Celia had in her possession during the earthquake helped her to perform her greatest miracle to date: protecting an entire floor of the hospital from the wreckage. Every single person with a foothold on that level of the building had been recovered, relatively unscathed. That is, every person except Celia. Celia remained comatose.

David said, "Shouldn't we be doing something? It's been a week. I don't think Celia would want us all sitting around like this."

David was right, they were wasting time and nothing they were doing was helping Celia in the least. They needed to keep going, to pursue the coins, but Ryan wasn't sure where to go next and David hadn't found any more leads.

Ryan stood and went over to Celia, putting his hand on hers. "We need a plan. Thousands were killed in the earthquake. If my theory is right, the joining of these coins has something to do with the earth's and atmosphere's instability. I'm confused about how to proceed. It concerns me that nobody has bonded with this new coin. The ambassador and his wife have touched it, Ayla and Ceyda, too. Could it be bonded to someone else already?"

Madeira sighed. "Where do we go from here? We don't have any other leads. Team two found a coin in Scotland three days ago, and since so many of the discoveries have been widespread, geographically speaking, I don't think we'll find more coins in Turkey."

That made Ryan think. "We can go to the island of Patmos where John wrote Revelations, and take a pilgrimage to the seven churches. It may be a waste of time, but maybe we can gain some greater understanding of what's happening. Who knows, maybe I'll have better visions by visiting these holy places."

"It's a good idea," Madeira said. "You're right. We're

not helping Celia by hanging around here. And maybe we should stay in Turkey until she's well, or until it's clear that she won't get well."

The words "she won't" echoed in Ryan's ears. Without thinking, he said, "She will," and prayed it was true.

"You're the prophet," David said.

Ferry, Aegean Sea, approaching Patmos, Greece, May 25, 2032

They weren't the only ones who had been traversing Turkey like zombies, carrying their worries on hunched backs, and viewing their surroundings through tired, fearful eyes. The trip to the airstrip, where the ambassador had arranged for a helicopter, was grim and fraught with detours as they skirted the damage from the earthquake, passing broken streets, wounded buildings, and hollow-eyed survivors. Even on the ferry to Patmos, despite the clear sky and calm seas, the unseen fog of the recent catastrophe hung heavily over everybody.

David didn't feel like talking. He stood at the railing, looking over to the island while it grew larger at their approach, his silence emptying him in a way he couldn't describe. He felt stripped of himself, and wanting. But, wanting for what?

Madeira said, "At least the ferry is running."

He nodded. From what they were told, the boat would have been jammed to overflowing this time of year. Today, only a handful of passengers littered the deck.

"I've often wanted to come here," the professor said. "I just never pictured being here under these circumstances."

David saw the Monastery of St. John, a castle-like structure standing proudly atop the hill that dominated the island. He didn't feel connected to this place like he did to the ruins at Palenque. But the professor stood fixated and intent, breathing deeply, his chest rising higher with each inhalation. He could feel the professor's anticipation as the wind picked up, carrying his breath, and hopes, to the sea.

They took the KTEL bus to the cave and monastery. The minute they exited the vehicle, David could smell flowers and incense, while the sounds of birds chirping lured him away from the bus and the exhaust. The professor took the lead as they navigated through the whitewashed, stone walls, past intricate wooden doorways. David had only seen tourist pictures of Greece and movies made in Greece. And although this looked very much like those movies and pictures, the air had a quality not captured in print. There was no way to describe it other than softness. Is there such a thing as soft air? He wouldn't have said so, until today.

From a distance, the building surrounding the cave looked like a chapel, its rounded dome topped with a small cross. But as you entered, the walls – sometimes rough and sometimes smooth – captured light and shadows like the watercolor paintings his mother used to admire in the countless small art galleries she brought him to on Nantucket island. Must be an island thing, or a by-the-sea thing.

The stone and brick steps were worn, so David held tight to the railing for support as he looked over the half walls to the sea beyond. The birds continued to make noise while the play of light hypnotized him around every corner. He felt the weight of concern lift and recede with each step closer to the grotto. Rich with texture, he couldn't help but touch everything as they passed: the unusual plants, the weathered metal gates, the rough stone surfaces, and the recessed window-sills, all the while fascinated with the shapes of the shadows as the sun moved through the architecture. This place was very cool.

It felt like a dream, like he'd stepped back in time. Someone was chanting up ahead, and the ghostly air lifted the sound to his ears, moving through him like mist.

Due to the earthquake, the cave, usually crowded with pilgrims, had only a handful of people today.

The professor ran a finger along the golden frame of an icon of St John the evangelist. They were all quiet, as the chanting from within seeped past the rounded corners of the doorway.

Just then, David heard a commotion from the stairs behind them. A small tour group approached, and the leader, narrating a script about the place and its history, had a deep scratchy voice that carried. He said, "You can still see the crack in the rock, where St. John heard the voice of God."

A person in the group asked a question David couldn't hear, and then the guide said, "Correct, the great fissure in the roof splits into three at the mouth of the cave in an echo of the trinity." David instantly thought of the hospital and how it split into three, and then his knees gave way. He went down at the same instant as the professor, and Madeira, struggling to grab onto something as they shrank to the floor. People noticed them as they slumped to the floor, but nobody came to their aid.

The surprise reflected in Madeira's eyes disarmed him. For once, she didn't seem to know what was going on. For that matter, neither did he.

Madeira leaned against him, her breast on his arm. "Are you all right?"

"I think so," he said, stunned, "You?"

She nodded.

What was happening? Everybody else seemed fine, except the three of them. Could this have something to do with the coins?

The professor started to crawl through the arched entry on his hands and knees. Madeira sucked in her breath as she watched him, both of them sitting just outside the doorway.

The crowd parted, and the professor crawled over to the corner where visitors could see the nightly resting place of St. John's head, fenced off and outlined in beaten silver.

David didn't know what was more messed up: his inability to move from this spot, the professor crawling across this sacred place, or the impartiality of the other tourists who stepped around them, unconcerned, probably thinking they were praying or sitting in adoration or something.

The professor reached the corner, wrapped his hands around the silver bars, and leaned his head against them. He closed his eyes.

"What's he doing?" Madeira asked.

"I don't know."

"Can you get up?"

"I feel weak," he said. He hadn't meant to use that word, especially not in front of her, but it just popped out. He tried to sound braver than he felt, "I just need a minute."

She nodded in agreement.

At any other time in his life, he would have been freaking out right now, but he felt surreally calm, like he just received an anesthetic and a good dose of Valium. He wondered if the weakness in his legs and the surreal calm were related.

The professor put his hand into the silver-rimmed circular recess of the wall. His eyes were still closed. The wind outside picked up. David was aware of the press of newcomers as the space became crowded, and he was embarrassed to have them step around them as he and Madeira sat in the entryway like lumps.

It took considerable effort to stand, almost as though the sacred ground had absorbed his strength. He practically scratched at the walls for a handhold, but it was futile. He didn't have the ability to get up, and slouched back to the ground slowly.

They weren't the only freaks here, though. Others took a knee, bent to kiss artifacts or paintings, and performed the sign of the cross. And, of course, there was the man chanting. Most seem moved by this place, but not crippled by it, like they were. Several waited in line behind the professor for their turn to place their hand in the sacred wall. How long would they wait?

Madeira said, "This is intense."

No shit, he wanted to say, but didn't. "I want to see the chamber. Let's crawl like the professor did."

He mustered his strength and made it a few feet inside, stopping to rest against a bench behind where the professor was still meditating. Nobody had spoken to him or approached him since he established his position.

If you avoided looking up at the roof of the cave - which was very cave-like, all rocky smooth mounds – you could almost imagine you were in a church or a religious museum.

Unlike the Aztec ruins, it was almost impossible for David to picture this place as it was before it was consecrated. He stared into the crevice where the professor's fingers disappeared, and tried imagining the space without the churchly embellishments.

John came here in exile and isolation. Moses went up the mountain alone. Maybe they shouldn't have come when there were tourists here?

He leaned into Madeira, sitting to his left against the bench. Their shoulders touched, and he extended his head toward hers until their temples met. "It's too crowded here," he said, with his hands firmly on either side of him, holding him up.

Just then, an old man moved to the front of the line that had formed behind the professor. The man reached out to touched the professor's shoulder, and on contact, the man fell to his knees between the professor and the next man in line, who instinctively grabbed the old man, and, like dominoes on a table, the line of seven people collapsed in a row.

Normally, David would have helped, but his legs wouldn't carry him. Freak show of all freak shows, the tourists lunged to help one another, and it was "ring-around-the-rosie" time: they all fell down, out cold, even the others sitting near him on benches and chairs. He and Madeira remained the only people conscious in the cave, their eyes open and shocked. His heart hammered his chest, and he said, "What the fuck?" Even though that is the most inappropriate thing to say in this holy place. It was all he could manage.

Madeira locked eyes with him for a moment, and then she looked past him to gaze at the professor, who remained in the same position he was in before the incident.

"Geez," he said, "They aren't dead, are they?"

Madeira shook her head "no," but he noticed she didn't touch anybody to check for a pulse.

Now that the chanting had stopped and the people were still, David could again hear the birds singing outside, their high chirps joined by the wind and the sound of his own heavy breathing.

The American ambassador's house, Ankara Turkey, same moment

In Celia's dream, his white robe trailed behind him, not a whisper of sound as he walked to her across the stone floor. Where was she, and why was Ryan wearing a white robe?

When she looked closer, she noticed he had no feet. The robe floated like a ghost attached to a familiar face. She focused on his brown eyes, warm and sweet. His hair had grown back. How long had she been sleeping?

When she tried to look around, she was unable. She must still be asleep, because she could neither move nor speak.

Floating Ryan moved nearer and passed through her. Were they dead? Was this cave a chamber of heaven, or hell? Wherever she was, connecting with Ryan, or the spirit of Ryan, was lifting her fever. Like water on a hot driveway, she cooled ever so slightly as he connected with her, again and again, until her body was merely the warm vessel of life it once was – before.

Cave of the Apocalypse, Patmos, Greece, same moment

David was reminded of a drunken frat party he had attended once, when all the students passed out in a heap.

In the morning, they woke up in a groggy mass, feeling nauseous, and suffering from one hell of a headache. This experience was not dissimilar to that one.

Several stunned moments after the occupants of St. John's cavern hit the ground, he began to regain some feeling and strength in his legs. His excitement grew as first one tourist awoke, and then another, and another.

"What happened?" A lady with white hair asked as she dusted off her khaki pants and looked around, bewildered.

"I don't know." He stood, squinting away the pounding in his temples. "Are you all right, Ma'am?"

She cupped her hands around her ears, deftly removed her hearing aids, and said, "Say that again?"

"I said, are you all right?"

She smiled at him, nodding her head, then turned to a man near her and said, "Frank."

The man stood and embraced her. He said, "It's amazing."

"I know," she said as they cried together, hugging, sharing some understanding that did not include David.

Others in the room began to exclaim with joy at some miraculous dispensation. Several stood, only to fall to their knees with thanks for some gift they had received during their mass fainting episode.

David was in awe that this happened, mostly because he was certain there was a correlation between their presence in this holy room and the grace of the coins. The hangover feeling lingered and the easy high he had earlier had passed, leaving him anxious and jittery.

Madeira stood and together they stepped toward the group of people now surrounding the professor, who was working the room, speaking in turn to as many people within reach who would listen. "Remember the grace of God, which exists in all of us the opportunity to help one another."

This is the first time David had ever heard him sound like a priest - a God's-honest priest. It was strange. "What happened to you?" he asked the professor as he pressed between two men, one touching the professor's arm and the other pumping his hand, like he was a diplomat or something.

The professor didn't answer.

Someone asked, "Did you heal me?"

"No," the professor. "It's your faith that has healed you."

David turned away, embarrassed to be embarrassed, and freaked-out by the professor's words.

It occurred to him that he had been walking around, completely clueless, but thinking he knew so much all his life. He'd heard the stories of Christ and listened in Catholic school with a dull ear, his mind numb to the awesome and unfathomable reality of what the apostles experienced, sacrificed, and overcame to follow Jesus. Whether man or son-of-God, it mattered little. These men witnessed things that no others could imagine or understand, and they gave up their lives to impress upon the world the magnitude of that gift. And now, the same was being asked of him.

Maybe he had been desensitized by television or by having seen magicians and read fantastical novels. Whatever just happened in this room involved him in some way. He was here to help it happen, and to witness it. And there was no pretending it was a hoax, or some show he was just along to watch. Something was expected of him.

Is this what the apostles felt? Were any as clueless as he was?

The crowd began to disperse, some with exuberance, others with reluctance. For some reason, David wanted to get out of there, too.

"What now?" he asked, and Madeira glowered at him, and then laughed. Nice that she could find him amusing. He hated that she knew the conflict he was feeling.

He turned away from her.

The professor said. "Let's continue to the monastery and see what we can learn there."

"How can you both be so calm?" David said through gritted teeth. He felt like the only one with a rhinoceros running around in his chest, and hoped he wouldn't puke on Madeira again.

"I'm not calm, David. I'm impassioned." Professor Delaney said, facing David, and forcing him to look right into his eyes. "I don't know how to explain what just happened. But I'll tell you, I can feel things like never before."

"This is messed up," David said, feeling a constriction in his chest as he tried to force the rhinoceros out.

"Yeah, well, it beats being shot at," Madeira said, turning to take one last look at the cave as they left.

This time, the professor was in no hurry, and they walked the rest of the way from the cave to the monastery in silence.

As the bells rang from above them at the top of the hill, a priest-like figure wearing black robes and a pillbox hat stepped out from a group standing below one of the many arched passageways of the Monastery. David recognized several people from the incident in the cavern, and guessed the news had now spread to the monks who resided here.

He felt like a celebrity of sorts. All eyes were on them as they moved closer to the group. Again, he found himself thinking of the apostles and wondering how they felt when news of Christ's miracles began to spread, too.

Professor Delaney stopped a few feet ahead of him and asked one of the priests, "Do you speak English?"

The priest answered in Greek, but David caught the word, "Francais".

David said in French, "Have you heard about what happened in the cavern?"

The priest nodded in affirmation, and said in French, "I'm Father Alexander, in charge of the archival library. Let us talk together. My office is right through here."

He indicated some doors across the patio, under yet even more archways. There was a cistern containing holy water to David's left, and a balcony with three more arches above on the second floor. It was a beautiful building, less intimidating inside than it appeared from down the hill.

The priest looked like a Jewish Rabbi with his full graying beard. His skin was tan, and his face was sculpted with wise and honored lines. His thick hooked nose supported wire-rimmed glasses, which sat delicately below black and grey, bushy eyebrows. He squinted in the sun as he turned to them and said, "Welcome to our monastery."

"Thank you," David said, before they entered a small room and the priest asked them to sit.

He said, "How can I help you?"

David shrugged. How the hell should he know? Turning to Madeira and the professor, he translated to English, "He wants to know how he can help us?"

Madeira looked between the priest and the professor and then announced quietly, "He has a coin."

David looked, but could see none.

"You sure?" The professor asked.

She nodded. "On his person somewhere."

"Is he good fruit?" David wanted to know.

Madeira smiled and nodded. "Yes."

David looked to the professor for guidance, but he inclined his head and said, "Go ahead, David. You speak French. Talk to him."

"Father Alexander." He shifted from foot to foot, thinking over what he should say. "Do you know why we're here?"

The monk held his hands out as if in prayer, and asked, "Do you?"

"Quite frankly, I don't have a clue. But my friend tells me you have a Roman coin and that I can trust you. So, I'll tell you, we're here searching – derailed from our mission by the earthquake when one of our party was critically injured."

"You have not been derailed," the monk told him, and he interpreted for Madeira and the professor. "You are on the correct path. I've been waiting for others with coins to come. Now, you're here."

"You knew we were coming?" David was sitting so erect in his chair that his spine began to hurt. He couldn't relax. Unlike Professor Delaney, this guy was a priest with a capital P. He looked like one, he smelled like one, and he definitely talked like one. Honestly, it gave him the creeps a little. He felt like an alter boy serving mass for the first time. How can he help us? He can help us by giving us some answers.

"Yes, we've been expecting the gifted ones," the monk said. "Are you only three? I expected more."

"There are more of us. Why were you expecting us? What is your gift?" David asked him.

"I protect the monastery. I prepare the way. Our manuscripts have predicted your arrival. We've waited many years." He smiled at them and then held his hands, palms up, as if in prayer, and extended them to Madeira. "Corinthians says, 'There are varieties of gifts, but the same Spirit; and there are varieties of service, but the same Lord; and there are varieties of activities, but it is the same God who empowers them all in everyone.'"

"What does that mean?" David asked, and then translated at the professor's request.

Father Alexander said, "I find the truth and examine the spirit of those who would proclaim it."

Madeira was nodding. "I believe Father Alexander is like me. His gift is discernment."

Father Alexander asked, "Where are the others?"

Halfway through explaining about their home base in Mexico and the teams they had dispersed in search of coins, the priest said, "He will send His angels with a great sound of a trumpet, and they will gather together His elect from the four winds, from one end of heaven to the other."

"Are we the elect?" David asked.

He leaned in over his wide, spare desk and said, "Only you can answer that."

David stood. "What can you answer?" He'd already had enough of this guy – they'd encountered too many riddles. When would they find someone with answers?

The professor touched his sleeve. "Ask him if he thinks we should visit the seven churches of Revelations?"

We? The last thing he wanted to do was traipse around Turkey with this guy. Then he got a brainstorm, motivated by wanting to keep Madeira with him and put Father Alexander somewhere useful, so he suggested, "Should we send him to Mexico in Madeira's place?"

He knew Madeira would see right through him, but her small smile gave him some encouragement. "Hey, I know he's no waitress, but his skills are needed there."

The professor said, "Ask him what he thinks."

He made the suggestion to Father Alexander, and told him they planned to visit the seven churches.

The moments stretched while he waited for the monk's answer.

Father Alexander stood. "Come with me to the library." He gestured patiently with a slow wave of his hand, his eyes looking down at them from behind his spectacles.

The professor and Madeira stood, and they followed David and Father Alexander out through the atrium, past archways, doorways, down stairs, and through rooms decorated with faded frescos and religious art. They entered into a pillared library with columns of polished stone and a floor that was crisp and clean, despite the feet that had trod there. Dark, gleaming, pristine wooden tables were roped off cautiously. Ancient books sat on crimson velvet placeholders, next to which lay white gloves for handling fragile and precious documents. Candelabras hung from the ceiling and a blood red carpet lined the walkway on the far side. The full bookshelves along each wall were stained the same deep mahogany brown as the tables. The matching chairs were ornate, their carved tops stretched above the brown leather cushions and metal studs. David pulled Madeira to him and whispered, "I feel like I'm in Dracula's castle."

She said, "You've seen too many movies," and politely pulled away from him back into step with the monk and Professor Delaney.

He had seen too many movies, he decided. But this incredible room felt like it leapt out of Hollywood, for sure.

They stopped at a far shelf where Father Alexander removed a thin book. He said, "It's been an honor protecting the Monastery these many years, and it will be an honor to help those fulfilling God's will in Mexico." He stepped over to the professor and handed him the book. "This codex is mine. Observations about the seven churches. I do not know if it will help you. Your interpretation of these signs and notation will be different than mine." He straightened and touched his hands to his lips as in prayer.

David translated and Madeira said, "So, you think we should go there? To the churches?"

Father Alexander said, "Yes, I think you should follow John's footsteps to find the answers you seek. If you are the chosen, I believe all will be revealed by this pilgrimage."

On the ferry ride back to Turkey, the waves broke against

the boat almost as if they were trying to climb aboard. The water leapt up toward David in a spray of sea tears.

Madeira tugged on his sleeve, drawing his gaze from the water. "What?"

"Come sit with me. You're going to get seasick, staring over the edge that way. I don't feel like washing puke off my clothes again." She smiled and tugged at his sleeve one more time. "C'mon."

He followed her inside and they sat away from other passengers on two chairs in the corner.

"Let go of the dread, David." She cut right to the chase. He knew she couldn't help it: it was her style. "Ride with the waves, don't swim against them."

It was difficult when she saw his weaknesses, although at the same time there was something comforting about it, too.

They were facing each other and she leaned forward, pulling him close by the neck of his polo shirt. To his surprise, she parted her lips as their faces drew close. Like magnetic fields, their mouths come together in a rush, tongues intertwining, and the heat from her body repelled the sea breeze whipping around them through the open doorway. Her soft hair filled his hands as he pulled her into him, trying to absorb her strength, her goodness, and to let her passion work to his advantage.

Her cool hand caressed his cheek and wrapped itself around his neck. When the kiss ended, he buried his face in the soft space between her chin and shoulder and breathed her in.

They sat for a while like that, connected, comforting. He rarely allowed anyone to hold him this way. David wasn't one for snuggling. He had put most women at arm's length as long as he could remember. His mother's death had left him at a loss for knowing how to love and be loved. Madeira's small arms moved over his back in such a soothing way that, combined with the rocking of the ship, he recalled his mother's touch and the way she swayed with him in her arms when he was small. Startled by the memory, he pulled back, away from the coconut and cream shampoo smell, away from the heat of her need, and away from the love he knew was growing between them.

Her eyes darkened. She said, "It doesn't always end badly, you know?"

But it had for him - all his life. And she knew it.

His cell phone rang. It was the ambassador's number.

"Hello," he said, as Madeira stood and put some more space between them.

"Her fever broke," the ambassador said over the line. "Celia's still unconscious, but her fever broke."

"We're on the ferry," he said. "It'll be a few hours until we make it back, but I'll tell the professor." He snapped the phone shut. "Her fever broke."

Madeira nodded, spun on her heel, and walked briskly back out to the chill on deck.

The American ambassador's house, Ankara, Turkey, May 26, 2032

David was on his computer mapping out a plan for their visit to the seven churches, which he just learned are not actual churches. Of course, he had only looked up the one, the Basilica of St. John in Ephesus, which is now an ancient ruin.

"More ruins," he said, as the hum of Celia's machines and monitors harmonized with the click of his mouse and the tapping of his fingers on the keys. In reality, there are no clear "footsteps" of St. John to follow, and a whole lot of speculation when searching online for clarity. The book given to Professor Delaney by Father Alexander was in Greek. They were sending it to Mexico to be translated by Cardinal Margrave. They planned to use it as their guide through the churches.

One of the nurses replaced a bag on Celia's IV and stepped around Madeira who was on her mobile speaking to Cardinal Margrave, telling him about their experience at the cave and monastery. He interrupted, "Are you sure Father Alexander isn't sending us on a wild goose chase? You used your X-ray vision to scan him for the crazies, right Madeira?"

Just then, the door to Celia's room opened and the ambassador stepped in. Right behind him was a familiar face: Melik. David hadn't expected to ever see him again.

Madeira ended the call and paused. The nurse politely left the room.

Still guarded and cautious, Melik inched toward the bed - all the while fiddling with the car keys in his hand. He said, "I heard about the miracle. My cousin was in the hospital when the quake hit."

David waited him out. Professor Delaney had been sleeping upstairs for over twelve hours, exhausted from the episode in St. John's cave. He was going to be bummed that he missed this.

Melik said, "Is she okay?" He nodded in Celia's direction. "I mean, will she live?"

"We think so," David said.

Madeira stepped over to Melik and said, "Thank you for coming."

David found it amusing to notice that, try as he might, Melik could not avoid looking at Madeira's eyes, even though they surely frightened him. They never had the chance to explain her gift. The image Melik's father painted of Madeira with fiery eyes was disturbing when you didn't know the context.

Melik shied away from her and moved over to Celia's bedside. Better to stand next to the miracle-worker than the girl with the fiery eyes.

David watched him take stock of Celia's injuries as he timidly touched her bandaged hand and looked over her wrapped forehead and side. Then, he noticed the pile of coins they laid on her chest.

David said, "We were hoping they'd help cure her."

Melik's hand reached out towards the coins.

David stood. "Hold on a minute!"

Madeira said, "Let him."

Melik picked up the five coins and rolled them in his palm. He probed them with the pointer finger of his other hand, moving them, and turning some of them over. David watched the necklace of one coin dance between Melik's thumb and finger, the chain catching the reflected light.

David was so engrossed by Melik that he didn't notice the movement at first. Celia's eyes were open!

He shouted, "Get the nurse!"

Madeira bolted out the door. "I'll get the professor, too,"

she called over her shoulder.

The nurse arrived and removed the feeding tube. It happened so fast, David didn't gag or get grossed out. She lifted Celia's head and offered her water, which Celia sipped, and then choked on a little.

"Where am I?" Celia's voice sounded like the cough of a rusty engine.

The nurse stepped away and David took her place next to the top of the bed. He touched Celia's cheek, glad for the coolness he felt there. "You're in the home of the American ambassador. There was an earthquake."

She closed her eyes just when Professor Delaney burst in, wearing blue pajama bottoms and no shirt. He skidded to a stop in front of Melik, noticed the coins balanced in the kid's palm, and then he fell to his knees next to Celia's bed.

"Celia," he said. "Honey."

She looked at the professor, the corners of her mouth turned up into a little smile. Her left arm lifted slowly, as if tied down by a rope, and then fell back to the bed. It seemed she was too weak to reach out. The professor laid his head on top of her arm and started crying. David wanted to find a polite way to leave and give them privacy.

"I knew you'd be okay," the professor sobbed, his tears falling on Celia's arm. "I knew it."

CHAPTER 14

The American ambassador's house, Ankara, Turkey,
May 26, 2032

The spacious hallway of the ambassador's home felt cramped as the seven of them waited for the professor to leave Celia's room. David stood awkwardly next to the nurses, Melik, Madeira, as well as the ambassador and his wife.

Finally, the ambassador said, "We'll go make some food."

Once he and his wife left, David turned to Melik, "Can I have the coins back?"

He reached for them, but Madeira put a warm hand on his wrist. "Hold on a minute, David."

"What?"

"I believe one of those coins belongs to Melik now."

He looked at Melik. Years ago, David had been at a racetrack with his father when one of the horses broke its leg. He remembered the wide-open expanse of the frightened animal's eyes, and the way the breath huffed from his nostrils. Melik had the same pained and terrified look on his face right now.

David asked, "Are you sure?"

"Yes," she said.

Melik stepped back, started speaking in a language David didn't recognize, and waved his hands frantically in the air. As his panic escalated, he covered his mouth and then his ears from time to time, while continuing to speak rapidly and erratically.

The nurses backed away from Melik and stumbled onto the stairs, scuttling up slightly as he continued his tirade.

"Calm down!" David braced himself. Geez, the guy was acting possessed or something. Then he wondered, is he? For real?

He turned to Madeira, "Do I need to do the thing?"

She looked at him like he was crazy.

"Is he possessed?" David asked.

This shut Melik up. Completely stunned, he stood, immobile, looking at them like they had just slapped him.

Madeira said, "He's not possessed, for crying out loud. He's speaking in tongues."

David pulled on the sleeve of Madeira's blouse, as they stepped into the ambassador's living room with Melik and the professor. "Can I talk to you?"

"Not now."

"But…"

"Not now, David. We can discuss it later," she said, shrugging off his grip.

The professor escorted Melik by the arm. Poor kid was shell-shocked. As he lowered onto the plush cushions of the sofa, he reminded David of a kid being dragged to the doctor's office for some unwanted procedure.

Madeira must have noticed it, too, because she said, "Nothing bad is going to happen to you, Melik."

To him? Who the heck cares if anything happens to him? If Melik has the gift of tongues, then he can find Debiaxo, their cave in Mexico. Should the coin make him unstable like his father, he'd be more dangerous to them, and the whole world, than he is to himself.

David sighed and plopped down on the cushion next to Madeira. So the kid was freaked out – he was, too, at first. It wasn't Madeira's job to babysit everybody, was it?

She glanced his way as if reading his thoughts, rolled her eyes, and said to Melik, "Whatever weakness your father had, Melik, it doesn't need to be yours, too. You're in good company here, and you have the ability to change your fate."

"I don't want it," he said.

"Then why did you come?" Madeira stood, crossed over to Melik and dropped to her knees in front of him. David started to stand, but the professor shook his head to stop him.

He hovered, his ass half in the seat, half out of it.

Madeira took Melik's hands in hers and repeated, "Why are you here?"

Melik started to shake. "I heard," he said, his voice unsteady. "I heard how she had saved everyone."

"Celia?"

He nodded, and after a moment said, "She saved my cousin and almost died! Everybody is talking about it. I needed to see. For myself."

Madeira stood.

David settled back onto the sofa.

"To see what?" the professor asked.

"If she really saved them. If the world is ending, like my father said." He looked at each of them in turn, his hands clenching and unclenching.

The professor said, "I know you're confused by this recent turn of events. It's not easy when a gift from God comes to you."

Melik said, "I don't believe in any of this."

Professor Delaney smiled. "Corinthians says, 'Tongues are a sign, not for believers but for unbelievers; prophecy, however, is for believers, not for unbelievers. So if the whole church comes together and everyone speaks in tongues, and some who do not understand – or some unbelievers come in, will they not say that you are out of your mind?'"

"What are you saying?" Melik sat back, putting distance between him and Madeira. She stood up.

"I'm saying," the professor leaned in, "That it's ok not to believe if you need to, to stay sane."

"How do I get out of this?" Melik asked.

"You can't," David said.

"Honestly, Melik, we don't know how the coin chooses people," the professor said. "The understanding is, that bonding with and hoarding more than one coin is what causes the mental instability and illness.We believe it's dangerous and mentally and physically overwhelming for one person to bond with too many coins and absorb too much power. We think that's what happened to your father."

After a long pause, Melik let's out an indescribable sound - part moan, part sob - and said, "They cut him open."

David knew he should feel bad for the guy, but for some reason he was having trouble empathizing with Melik. Maybe it was a trust thing. After all, he just met the kid. Maybe it was because Madeira seemed to have enough empathy for all of them when it concerned Melik. In any case, he just wasn't in the mood to be delicate. "Don't eat your coin, then," he said. "Learn from your father's mistakes. Be the bigger man."

If Madeira's glare were words, it would have said, "Stop being an asshole!"

Melik studied him a moment. "What can I possibly do to help?"

Professor Delaney said, "you can guide us to the seven churches of the apocalypse."

Melik frowned. "I can't. I don't know anything about them."

Before anyone could comment, they were interrupted by the ambassador. "Lunch is ready."

"Thank you," the professor said, standing up.

David wanted to make sure Madeira wasn't overly influenced by Melik's suffering. If she wasn't seeing him clearly, then David would make damn sure she did.

On the way to the kitchen, he grabbed her arm, almost knocking her off-balance when she tried to leave the room. "Whoa," she said.

"Sorry," he said, not sorry at all. "But we need to talk. Now!"

She sat down on the couch. "Go ahead."

He planted himself next to her, leaning in real close so he could speak quietly and smell her cologne. "I need to know what you see when you look at Melik."

She looked away a moment, checking the doorway to be sure no one could overhear. Then she sighed, "It's not pass/fail. Melik is hard to read."

She had straightened up in her seat, so he pulled her close to him by the sleeve of her shirt. "What do you mean he's hard to read? Tell me how you do it. What do you see?"

She smirked. "It's hard to explain."

"Try."

"I see colors."

"Colors? What does that mean?"

"Well, emotions and intentions have a color. So when you asked me back when we first met if I could read your mind, I answered, 'no'. But, I can see the colors of you." She paused, making a smug face. "For instance, back there with Melik a few minutes ago, you were jealous. Insecure."

He put his hands on his thighs. "Colors, like green-with-envy colors?"

"Exactly," she said. "Where do you think they got that from? Anger is red. The purest color is white, or light blue."

This was too full of hippie influences for David's liking. "You see an aura?"

She shrugged. "Kind of."

"How can you tell when someone has a coin?"

"I see purple," she answered. "Nobody else has that color purple."

"Not purple with passion?" He was only half-serious.

She answered, "No," in a matter-of-fact tone. "Passion is yellow. As is love, but only brighter, more pure – closer to white."

"So how do you know someone won't be white one minute and a bad color the next?"

"Certain colors that relate to innate aspects of the soul don't change. Other colors can be present, but the main colors are consistent. And white, light blue, black, and dark blue are absolute, if they're your primary color."

"Am I white?"

"No, but you have some white. Typical people display several colors. You have a lot of turmoil, envy, and anger blended with your good colors. But you don't have too many deep tones – and no black. The deeper the tones, the less room for pure light. Evil men, like the men who shot as us, have a lot of dark hues - no yellow, no white, or light blue." She said, "It's complicated because I can read more than just the colors, but I don't know how to describe the rest to you."

"So what's the deal with Melik?"

She frowned, and then chewed her lip a little. God, she was the most beautiful thing he had ever seen. He bet she was all white and yellow.

Madeira said, "Melik is the first person I've met with white and black. His pure colors outweigh the others, but there's innate conflict."

"Do you think his father was like that?"

"I don't know."

"We need to be very careful, Madeira. We can't jeopardize the safety of our other teams," he said.

"I know. I think his negative colors account for his extreme fear. He's very fearful by nature."

"But you can't be sure," David said, treading carefully. "We'll need to keep him nearby – to watch him closely. You need to monitor him closely."

"I know," she said.

"Until he's a known entity, we guard what we know, understood? Melik continues with us on a need-to-know basis. We can't let him out of our sight."

She nodded her head, "I agree."

"You sure, cause you seemed to be giving him the benefit of the doubt back there?"

She smiled, wide and mischievous. "I'm not foolish. I'm trying to gauge him, but mostly I liked watching you get greener and greener."

He didn't smile back.

The American ambassador's house, Ankara, Turkey, May 27, 2034

The bright white ceiling was a menace. Even opening her eyes a mere slit caused intense pain at the back of Celia's head. The room dipped and swirled with dizziness and vertigo. If she forced herself to look, she could sustain a view for a few moments, no more, before the sensations overwhelmed her. She found she could talk to them with her eyes closed, hoping they understood her through the medicated slur of her speech.

David was saying, "She can't hear us."

"I can," she said, warding off the fatigue that pulled her back to sleep every few minutes. "My eyes hurt, but I'm listening."

She felt a hand on her cheek, but didn't know whose it was.

Then Ryan said, "Celia."

"I'm listening," she repeated.

"Ok, honey. We just want to tell you what we're doing, okay?" Ryan said, and the hand moved from her face to her arm.

His hand was so cool and she wondered if she had a fever again. "Okay."

He told her about a trip to Patmos. She managed a noise or two, a word here and there to let him know she was with him. He said, "We're following St. John's steps to the seven churches, starting with the ruins at Ephesus. In order to be back in the evenings, we're traveling by helicopter, courtesy of the US Embassy and ferry. The ambassador will notify us if you need us here."

She wanted to tell him to go on, but she was too weak. She didn't know why she was still alive. Before she woke, she was in a place of peace, free of pain, and Jeff was there. Many people were there. She had wanted to stay, but they sent her back. She told Ryan, "I saw you."

"I'm right here," he said, misunderstanding.

She tried to shake her head, but the effort was too much. "It's okay. Go. I'll look for you to come again."

She didn't know if they understood her, but the fatigue

won. She dropped back to the space where it was quiet and peaceful, hiding from the pain. Come to me in your white robes, Ryan. I'm waiting for you.

Basilica of Saint John, Ephesus, Turkey, May 27, 2032

As they pulled up to the ruins of the Basilica of St. John, David couldn't help but say, "My life in Ruins. Wasn't that an old movie?"

"Yup," the professor said as Melik parked the rental car they drove from the nearby airstrip. "It was situated in Greece."

"You saw it?" Madeira asked.

"No. You?"

Melik gave them all a look of indignation. Clearly he wasn't expecting mundane conversation on this excursion. Kid needed to lighten up.

David changed the subject. "What do you think, Melik? Was St. John buried here? There's a lot of controversy over it."

Melik stepped out of the car, puffs of dirt rising from his feet as he tread on the unpaved road. He said, "My father studied religion. I studied science."

"I thought your father studied science, too?" the professor said, as they neared the crumbled archways.

Melik looked away. He said, "Religious study was his hobby." Then he turned back. "Science was his job."

"What's your hobby?" David asked.

"I don't have one," Melik turned his back to him, and stepped between two pillars of the basilica walls.

"Evasive," David said under his breath as he and Madeira

stepped through. She elbowed him in the ribs.

They wandered around for a few minutes before Melik said, "What are we looking for?"

Melik turned to him, he turned to Madeira, and Madeira turned to the professor. The professor shrugged. "I don't know."

Melik stood with his hands on his hips and raised his eyebrows. "Very scientific."

David smiled. "We aim to please."

Melik pursed his lips, clearly unimpressed with David's wit. He turned to the professor and asked, "What about the book you got from Father Alexander?"

"It's being translated, we'll have it shortly." The professor avoided looking at Melik, David noticed. Quite a conundrum. Until they were sure Melik could be trusted, they couldn't use him to decipher the codex even though his gift of tongues would be useful, assuming he could interpret language like Cardinal Margrave.

"Well," David said, interjecting. "Let's check out the marker of St. John's supposed tomb."

Melik shrugged and lead the way. For someone who claimed not to know much about this place, he seems to know right where to go.

In an attempt to annoy Melik, because he liked doing it so much, David sidled up next to him and asked, "What kind of science did you study at the university?"

Melik looked sideways at him, and answered, "Physics."

David stepped around a tourist taking pictures. "I studied psychology." He expected a reaction, but they arrived at the marker and Melik said, "Here it is."

David looked at the unremarkable marker, like an over-sized stone scrabble piece. "This is it? Not much, is it?" It occurred to him that someone who had studied physics may have an idea about his theory. "Melik, what do you think about the theory of cyclical time or fourth dimensions?"

Melik strolled around them, looking about. Finally, he said, "I think they're probable."

This surprised David. He was certain Melik would have baulked at his suggestion. Could it be they had more in common than he first guessed?

"Why do you ask?" Melik said. Although his expression was bored, he was interested. David could tell by his body language.

The professor said, "David has speculated that the new beginning, or the apocalypse, may be tied into those scientific probabilities. The new world could possibly be one where science and faith unite and those open to the truth could experience living in an expanded reality, existing in all dimensions and navigating cyclical time."

After blinking several times, Melik muttered, "And they thought my father was crazy," before kicking his toe against the stone marker.

"You don't think it's possible?" David asked.

"You do?"

"I wouldn't have thought so four weeks ago," David conceded. "But I've seen things and felt things that have made me question all my beliefs. Every one."

Melik nodded.

"Like just now," he said, smugly. "I spoke to you in French and you understood every word."

Melik looked mortified, but now David knew his gift was like Cardinal Margraves. Melik could decipher language.

"Be cynical all you want, Melik," David said. "If you're going to hang with us, you'll need to throw your fears, your doubts, and your skepticism out the door. Don't you think?" He smiled wide and bent down to the marker. "What do you say, St. John?"

He could see Melik's shadow on the marble floor. His silhouette was shaking its head. "Is everything a joke to you?" Melik asked him.

He looked up with a sharp reply on his tongue, but as he did, the sun created a halo around Melik. David saw the shape of a white bird over Melik's left shoulder and a black bird over his right. David stepped back in surprise, lost his footing, and fell backwards onto the dirt.

Madeira bent and grabbed him under the arms. "Are you all right?"

She helped him to his feet and the illusion dissolved.

"Yeah," he said. "I thought I saw something."

Melik looked around. "What?"

"A bug," he lied.

The professor and Madeira were both staring at him while Melik snorted with distaste.

"Where to, Professor?" he asked, brushing the dirt off his pants as casually as possible. "You're the prophet - what's the prediction?"

"Legend has it that John wrote his Gospel here in Ephesus, but that would have been before the basilica was erected. I've read that he wrote on Ayasolik hill, right here below the fortress," Professor Delaney said.

"Let's check it out," Madeira suggested.

Melik led the way through the ruins to the hillside. David fell behind and motioned to Madeira to walk with him. Whispering in the lowest voice he could manage, he asked her, "Did you see anything back there? Any animals or birds?"

She turned back to look.

"No, I mean like your colors?"

She stopped, but he grabbed her sleeve and made her keep walking. He didn't want to arouse Melik's suspicions until he knew what he saw.

"No," she said. "Did you?"

They caught up to Melik and the professor, so he couldn't answer her, but he nodded his head to indicate, yes, he had seen something.

"This is interesting," the professor said, stopping at a section of ruins where a block of stone stood turned on its side. It appeared to be a section of the basilica, a relief that was propped up. A large crack marred its surface, but otherwise the fresco was intact. He asked, "Does anyone know what this means?"

The rectangular stone surface was engraved with a large circle in the center connected to two smaller circles, like Mickey Mouse ears. Each of the three circles had a different design. The largest looked like a flower with sixteen petals. The smaller circle to the upper left had another flower, more star-like, with six pointed petals. The upper right circle sported another possible floral motif that looked like a fan of some sort. The three circles were connected, and along the bottom there was a wavy double line ending – at both ends - in large, symmetrical crosses. Two smaller, more traditional crosses were positioned, as if buried, under the hill of the wavy double lines. At the four corners of the rectangle were arrows pointing inward from an organic floral leaf edging.

The professor tilted his head and said, "I think this smaller symbol is the lost symbol of Christ."

David looked closely at the stonework. "Arrows can symbolize martyrdom. And these smaller crosses on the bottom look like they're buried underground. Could the left side represent Christ and the right represent the second coming?"

Professor Delaney reached for the crack in the stone. When his finger met with the ancient rock, he slipped to his knees.

"Oh no, not again." David blocked Melik when he reached for the professor. "Don't touch him. It's catchy."

Melik laughed, and then pulled away from him and tried to help the professor up. Just as they witnessed at St. John's cave, Melik went down.

David said, "I told you so."

Madeira frowned at him.

"Well, I did."

After a few seconds, they both sat on the sacred ground to wait it out. Whatever was happening to the professor, he hoped it provided them with some answers. After the last episode at St. John's cave, the professor told him his visions were becoming clearer and that he had some sort of spiritual epiphany or something.

David, on the other hand, walked away from that experience feeling confused, embarrassed, and another feeling he didn't care to have – humbled. He tried to avoid being humble if at all possible. Which reminded him.

"You didn't see anything back there? You didn't see any birds around Melik?" He asked Madeira.

"No."

He frowned. "When I looked up at Melik, I saw a white bird over one of his shoulders and a black bird over the other."

She pondered this a moment, but David was impatient. "Have you ever seen animals? You know, as an aura or something like that?"

"No, David, but I think it's significant that you did."

Just then, Melik began to stir, so David stood up.

"Have a nice nap?" He asked Melik.

He wanted to roar with laughter at the look on Melik's face. David remembered how he felt after learning he had a part in this spiritual treasure hunt, or whatever else this was. It amazed him that he had become so accustomed to these mystical experiences that, instead of fear, now he felt – what was it he felt? He wasn't sure how to label it, but if he were to put a word to it, it would be "hope".

"What just happened?" Melik asked.

Madeira stepped up to Melik. "You need to calm down, Melik. Take a deep breath."

David was concerned. Madeira had never tried to calm him, even when he threw up on her. What did she see? "What's wrong?"

She glanced at David and said, "He's lit up like a Christmas tree. Fear. Distrust. Anger."

"That's ridiculous," Melik said, taking a step back from them.

Madeira said, "You don't need to be afraid here with us, we're the good guys." She took a step closer to him.

David hesitated, not sure what to do.

Melik's mouth was agape as he clenched his hands a few times. It was no fun being accused of being afraid by a girl. Sure that he was going to deny it and bolt, David said, "She can read minds, Melik, so don't even bother debating or running. You have a coin. I can't let you go."

At this, the professor stood and gave David a harsh look. Then, in a calm manner, he said, "Melik. You've just witnessed my being overcome with a vision. It happens sometimes like that, that's all." He stepped closer and put a hand on Melik's shoulder. "As a scientist, I'm sure you can understand that energy and time are mysterious things. Whatever occurred just now, whether you attribute it to science - or to faith - it is not for us to understand right away. I don't know if we'll ever understand it. You won't lose your mind by simply witnessing. I know you're haunted by what happened to your father. Any person would be."

"You don't understand anything," Melik said, stepping out from under the professor's hand, and away from David and Madeira. "And you don't know what happened to my father. You have no guarantees and no answers. You don't even know what we're doing here!"

You didn't have to be a mind-reader, or to read auras like Madeira, to see that Melik was furious, insulted, and conflicted – all at once.

Madeira shuffled her feet, and the professor looked away. The truth was, they'd never know what Melik's father intended or what happened. All they know is that there were a group of people killing for these coins, people who had become obsessed with the coin's powers and who would stop at nothing to gather all thirty pieces. What would become of the world if that happened was unknown. All they did know is that if they gathered the thirty coins the right way, based on the ancient Roman documents buried with coins in Italy and England, based on the Mayan writings in Mexico, based on notes concealed inside the cross at sea and shipwrecked in Texas, and based on information hidden in texts in the library at the Monastery of St. John, "Heaven on Earth," would be realized. Whatever the heck that meant.

David looked at Melik, understanding the confusion he faced, the pain he was suffering, and he could empathize, he could. David had a hard time believing, trusting, even after having seen Celia's stigmata, which was freaky enough. If he had not personally experienced every bizarre and intense milestone from that day until this one, he wouldn't have believed at all. Hell, he would probably be dead - one of the many people who were killed in the tsunami.

For some reason, fate had brought him here. He wasn't at school when the tsunami hit. He wasn't killed in the earthquake, or the hurricane, or by flying bullets back at the hospital. Who would even have imagined those possibilities? Who would ever have imagined, instead, they would be in Turkey with some guy whose father was disemboweled by a maniac over an ancient Roman coin. Not David.

And, apparently, not Melik either.

Melik drove the car back to the airstrip. They had persuaded him to calm down, had talked him off the ledge momentarily. Having him drive was a way to keep him occupied.

The professor, exhausted from his vision, reclined in the passenger seat and slept. In the back seat, next to Madeira, David pretended to be looking up information about the next church on their list, St. Polycarp Church, but instead he was on his mobile device searching the web for the significance of white birds and black birds in Christianity.

He sent a text to Madeira, even though she was sitting right next to him. It was killing him not to be able to talk to her, but with Melik's paranoia and mixed colors, they had to be careful what they said. His text read, "Black ravens are a symbol of sin."

Her phone bleeped and she read the message. She smiled and turned away from him so it appeared she was looking out her window, but she was using her mobile. After a while, she texted him a message, "The Norse God Odin had a pair of ravens, one on each shoulder. Maybe Melik's not a sinner, but a Norse God."

She threw him a look over her shoulder as he read. He could tell the play had begun. This was a fun game, so he went back to his device and searched some more, then messaged her, "To European Christians, the black raven is the antithesis of the innocent white dove."

She sent back, "Ravens are messengers of the Gods. In the bible they are mentioned. I have sent the ravens to provide for you."

She was good. He smiled and typed, "you'd make a great research assistant."

She sent back, "U 2."

It was his turn, so he went back to his results page and found, "In Native American folklore, the raven is a hero, messenger, creator of the world, thief, and trickster." He copied it and sent it to her.

She replied, "Damn, I was just going to say that."

He laughed and Melik looked at him in the rear view mirror.

"Sorry," he said.

Another message came though from Madeira. "Among the Celts, the white crow was the emblem of the heroine."

He sent back a reply, "two blackbirds sitting together is a symbol of peace – a good omen."

"But you didn't see two blackbirds," she answered, her fingers tapping the device with expert precision.

"True," he responded.

"Was the white bird a dove?" she asked in a text.

He sent, "I think so," anticipating that she knew something. Her dark eyes sparkled before she turned her back to him again to search for the relevance of the white dove.

In a spontaneous moment, he texted her, "I can't stop thinking about that kiss on the boat."

Her shoulders tensed a moment when she read it. Clearly, not the text she expected. Her body relaxed and she manipulated the mobile before a text appeared on his screen. "So do I."

He reached over and touched her back, but she continued to face away from him in the back seat of the car. Her body was tense and she was still maneuvering her mobile device, typing on the screen. His mobile vibrated and he read, "The song of the blackbird is a symbol of sexual temptation." Then another message came through that read, "To pagans, the dove is a symbol of conjugal affection and fidelity."

He smiled and sent back, "I think I want to keep Melik away from you in any case."

As they drove, he stared at her turned back in anticipation. After long moments, he put his device down, just as it came alive. The message read, "I am safe with Melik as long as you're here with me."

He looked up to find her staring at him. She reached out and took his hand. He allowed her to intertwine their fingers while he imagined their bodies wrapped around each other. For now, he simply let the energy move through her palm, her fingers, and her pulse, while he stared straight ahead at the road they travelled, past Melik, past the professor, and out to the unseen horizon.

The American ambassador's house, Ankara, Turkey, May 27, 2032

The ambassador's house had become command central. David and Melik were staying in one of the spare rooms. Madeira had her own room, and Celia remained downstairs in the "hospital" room, which was previously a sitting room off the main entrance. The nurses shared the largest guest room at the end of the hall and took turns monitoring Celia and providing her care.

Due to the long commute, they had missed the evening meal. Madeira warmed up some lentil soup while the professor pulled together sandwiches from leftovers in the fridge.

Melik walked in from the hallway. He had been speaking

to the nurses about Celia. He looked more surly than usual, if that was possible. David didn't think he'd ever seen that kid without a puss on his face.

"How's she doing?" The professor asked, stopping halfway through spreading hummus on a sandwich. He must have noticed Melik's expression, too.

Melik nodded but didn't answer.

David poured a glass of wine and said, "Spit it out, Melik, what's on your mind?"

Madeira turned to look at Melik just as he took a robotic step towards her and Professor Delaney.

"She sat up today and called his name," Melik said, gesturing toward the professor. "She called out, 'Ryan.' Right around two o'clock this afternoon."

"So?" David asked, not understanding why Melik sounded so angry. He always sounded so fucking angry. David thought he cornered the market on broody, but this kid was so wound up you could breathe on him wrong and he would unravel.

Melik said, "Don't you think it's a strange coincidence?"

David wasn't following, and he could tell that Madeira and the professor were just as confused as he was.

Melik stepped closer to Professor Delaney. His nose was only a fist away from the professor's. He said, "The nurses saw you in her room. They saw you, like a ghost, when she sat up and reached for you."

The professor took a deep breath in and out. "The nurses think they saw my ghost?"

"Were they drinking?" David asked.

Melik, the professor, and Madeira all frowned at him

in unison before Melik turned and thrust his hand under Madeira's nose. "Look at my watch."

David stood up.

"My watch stopped," Melik said in a loud voice, but not quite shouting. "When I blacked out at the Basilica."

"I'm sorry," Madeira said. "We can get you a new one."

Melik blew out two lungs worth of air and said, "No, you don't understand." He dropped his hand and turned around to face David as if pleading with him to catch on. "My watch stopped at 2:12pm, the exact time logged by the nurses on Celia's chart. The exact moment they all saw his ghost." He thrust a hand out in the professor's direction.

"You were looking at Celia's chart?" The professor asked in a quiet tone.

They were all quiet for a moment. David was seeing phantom birds, the nurses were seeing ghosts, and the professor kept going into trances - what was next?

"Could they have seen your spirit, Professor?" Madeira said, as if wondering aloud and not really asking the question.

Stepping around the table, David asked the professor, "What happens when you have a vision? When you go into these trances of yours?"

The professor said, "I'm not sure. It feels like sleep. Sleep with vivid dreams and sensations - only, not restful."

Madeira said, "The last time it happened, when you blacked out during the day, Celia's fever broke."

"What's your point?" David could tell by her tone that she was on to something.

"Maybe the professor's visions, or slips of consciousness,

are helping to heal her."

"I don't think that's possible," the professor said. "Besides, she came out of her coma when Melik arrived, not during one of my black-outs."

Melik said, "How long do you think it will be until she's well?"

"I don't know," The professor replied. "Why?"

Melik shivered and said, "I saw her."

A long pause followed. It was clear he had something on his mind, but he was holding back. This kid was a royal pain in the ass.

David sighed and tossed his hands up. "For God's sake, Melik, what's your point?"

Melik rubbed his eyes, his hands working their way to his temples as if he was trying to massage out his words. "I lied before. When we blacked out at the ruins. She did heal me. An old soccer injury – it's bothered me since middle school. I have pins in my ankle. I can't feel them for the first time in years."

His choice of words confused David. Not I was healed, but she healed me. "What do you mean, 'she'?" he asked.

Melik said, "Celia. She healed me," his voice had that same void tone he had when he mentioned his father the first time they spoke with him.

"How can she have healed you?" Madeira asked. "She wasn't there."

"No," Melik said. "But, I was here - in that room, with the professor." He stabbed his finger into the air for emphasis and they all looked toward the room where Celia was recovering.

David looked at the professor. "Do you know what he's talking about?"

The professor moved to the table and dropped into a chair as if his body was too heavy for him all of a sudden. "No."

David asked, "Are you, or your spirit, or something, here with Celia when you're in your trance?"

The professor looked stricken. He shook his head. "If I am, I have no memory of it."

Madeira must have ben making the same assumption, because she joined the professor at the table. "Could Celia have healed Melik through you, as a conduit?"

David asked, "Is that what happened at St. John's cave?"

"Anything's possible, I guess," the professor said. He looked both smaller and bigger at the same time. The professor seemed completely baffled by the possibility of having done something that magnanimous without even knowing he had done it.

Madeira pursed her lips in that seductive way she had when she was deep in thought.   "This isn't logical," she said. "She would start bleeding again, wouldn't she?"

No one answered.

"Do you think the episodes could make her weaker?" he said, reaching across the table and picking up a bite of cheese to have something to do with his hands.

The professor looked drained. "I need to eat. To sleep." He rubbed his head, which had begun to sprout hair since he hadn't shaved it in over a week. David didn't like the militant look on the professor any better than he liked him bald.

"Okay," Professor Delaney said, after a moment. "Let's talk to Celia tomorrow, before we head out to Izmar. Maybe she can shed some light on this."

He wanted to point out that Celia was barely coherent at the moment, but the professor looked so overwhelmed that he let it go. What the hell, it was just one more mystery to unravel on this lunatic joy ride.

Melik's easy breathing grated on David's nerves. How could he sleep? David tossed and turned while his restless pulse kept him as far from slumber as humanly possible. Giving up, he got out of bed and threw on a pair of jeans. In stocking feet, he stole downstairs and peeked in on Celia. She looked peaceful despite her pale coloring. All of her tubes and machines had been removed. Her bleeding had stopped and, although her hands were still bandaged, her head wrap had been removed and the marks there were fading quickly. All evidence said she was on the mend, but his stomach held a sinking feeling he couldn't shake.

If he were home in America, he'd head to a bar right now for a drink - or, to see a girl, or two. Nothing better to soothe a restless mind than a warm body and foolish conversation, but there wasn't any foolish conversation to be had here - conversation with the occupants in this house was anything but foolish. Maybe that was the problem. David could use some foolishness.

He sat for a moment in the chair next to Celia's bed, drumming his fingers on his thighs to a tune in his head.

He jumped up and snuck back up the stairs, checking his room to be sure Melik was still sleeping, and then he approached the door across the hall. The knob turned silently in his hand. Madeira's thick brown hair was spread luxuriously across her pillow. Her mouth was open in sleep. He closed the door behind him, and then prowled across the room, lowering himself next to the bed where Madeira rested.

He didn't want to scare her.

As gently as possible, he touched his lips to her face and kissed her cheek. She stirred. He did it again. In the twilight, the smallest hint of a smile appeared on her features before she opened her eyes. He wasn't sure what to expect. He didn't know Madeira very well, and didn't have her power of perception.

Tentatively, she reached out and moved her hand over his chest in a way that charged his whole body with desire. Her warm palms encircled his sides, moved toward his back, and pulled him closer to her so their lips met in a heated kiss, picking up from where they left off on the boat. He was half on the bed and half off it. Every part of him ached for her.

She ended their kiss and shifted over, lifting the covers for him to join her.

"Are you sure?" he whispered, before she grabbed his arm and pulled him in.

The American ambassador's house, Ankara, Turkey, May 28, 2032

They stood there like four posts, each at a corner of Celia's bed. Ryan's eyes were red and tired. David looked anxious as he gulped his morning coffee. Madeira stood by her left foot, her focus on all three men in the room. And Melik, awkward and fidgety, stood by her right foot.

"Good morning," she managed to say, despite the drugs and the pain.

Ryan pulled up a chair and sat by her right shoulder. "How are you doing?"

"I'm okay," she told him, wondering if she was slurring her words.

Ryan and David exchanged a look, then David said, "We have something to ask you."

She closed her eyes for a second or two. The pain seemed a little worse this morning.

As if reading her thoughts, Madeira said, "Celia, tell us if it gets really bad. We needed you to be lucid, so we asked the nurses to reduce your pain medication a little."

She opened her eyes a moment, squinted and nodded her head. "That explains it."

"Honey, this won't take long," Ryan said, and she wondered when he started calling her honey? She closed her eyes again. He used to call her honey, back in school, back when they were inseparable.

"Is she asleep?" Melik asked.

"No," she said, opening her eyes. "I'm ok. Just hurts."

Ryan winced. "Let's make this fast then. Did you see me yesterday, in this room?"

After a moment, she said. "I saw you. Not in this room."

She could tell she wasn't making sense by Ryan's confused expression and how he ran his hand over his head.

"I told you I would wait for you," she said.

"When we were young?" Ryan asked.

"No. When I was sleeping. Since I've been here."

"Did you see me when you were sleeping?"

"I wait for you to meet me in the place where the others are," she said, forcing her eyes to stay open, despite the pain.

"Honey, the nurses say they saw me here yesterday, but I was at Ephesus," Ryan said.

"They saw you, too?" she asked.

"Yeah, I guess so." He touched her shoulder. "When you saw me, did you see Melik, too?

She had to think a moment - and to think, she needed to close her eyes. She remembered the room and Ryan in his flowing robes. There were many people. "Yes, I think he was." She said. "His father was there, too."

Melik gasped and he stepped back away from the bed. "That's not funny."

"Forgive your father," Celia told Melik. "He wants to help you now."

Madeira reached out a hand to Melik, but not in time. He backed away and bolted out of the room.

David raced after him, and Madeira followed, leaving only Ryan.

"I don't understand," Ryan said.

Her mind was aching from the pain. There was so much to say to him, but she had to heal first. "Keep coming to me," she said.

He nodded and held her hand. "Nurse!" he called out. "She needs her meds, please." Then he laid his head on her breast and said, "Hang in there, Celia. No matter where you are, I promise, I will keep coming to you."

"I know," she said. "I've always known."

David was young and fast, but Melik had an advantage over him: He lived in this town.

No sooner were they on the street, running at full-speed, Melik ducked into a shop and after a hastened search: David lost him.

"Damn it!" he yelled, backtracking and looking for him around cars and corners. He was gone.

Several yards from the ambassador's home, he found Madeira looking for them.

"You lose him?" she asked.

"He's gone."

"He'll be back," she said.

"What, are you a prophet too, now?" The sharp retort left his lips before he could stop it. He was angry he lost Melik.

Madeira ignored him as they walked back to the house.

The professor and the ambassador stood in the doorway wearing anxious expressions. "Where is he?" the professor asked.

"I don't know," he said. "I lost him."

When he saw the professor's stricken expression, a knife twisted in his gut.

The ambassador said, "I'll call the authorities."

Professor Delaney held his mobile out. "Use my phone. It's secure."

The ambassador nodded. "We'll need to relocate. My home isn't safe for you now."

"Neither is our location in Mexico," David said. "And

Melik knows we're heading to the other churches, too."

"I don't think he's dangerous," Madeira stepped up behind him on the stoop.

"Maybe not," he said. "But others may be, and we don't know what he'll do now that he has a coin."

She nodded.

"Let's get inside and make some arrangements," Professor Delaney said.

The ambassador walked to the kitchen with the phone and pulled aside one of the nurses. "Is Celia well enough to travel?"

"Yes," the nurse said.

He dialed the phone and started issuing orders to someone on the other end. David could not be more jittery if there were red ants crawling all over him. It took all his effort not to stomp around the house in a fit, swearing his ass off, he was so angry. How could he have lost him?

He exhaled and started pacing while Madeira skirted around the edges of his tantrum, trying to give him time and space to work through it. The professor stood at Celia's door, deep in thought.

When the ambassador tried to hand Professor Delaney his phone, it took several attempts.

"Sorry," the professor said, finally taking it.

"It was vibrating while I was on it. Someone's trying to reach you."

The professor checked his phone. "It's a text," he said. "The cardinal has translated Father Alexander's codex and sent us the translation."

Madeira asked, "Has he arrived safely in Mexico?"

"Yes, he's there."

"Ambassador," David said. "Is there someplace else we can set up a home base for Celia? Someplace safe?"

"I'm working on it," he answered.

"Let's pack our things." The professor headed toward the doorway. "I have an idea. I know where we'll be safe." He took the steps two at a time. David followed, climbing normally, watching Professor Delaney as he started texting on his phone like a teenager.

At the landing, he stepped aside to press send, and David noticed the confirmation, "Your message to Father Alexander has been sent."

The professor pocketed the mobile. "Meet me downstairs in twenty minutes."

David nodded, watched Madeira disappear into her room, and then turned to his door and entered.

This morning, in his daze after an inspiring night of lovemaking unlike any he could have ever imagined, he had not noticed the subtle changes in the room from the day before. But now, after this traumatic change in the game, it was so obvious, he wanted to scream. His heart stopped beating for a second while shame and fear gripped him so tightly his breath was forced out. The secure phone was gone; the computer was gone; Melik was fucking gone with them.

"Professor!" He yelled at the top of his lungs, right before a slew of curses erupted and he started overturning furniture, hoping to find his precious belongings. At least he had the Private Key safely in his pocket. It would be nearly impossible to break their encryption without it.

The professor, Madeira, and the ambassador appeared

so fast you'd think they had been standing right outside his door.

"Call the cardinal. We're in deep shit," David said.

Ferry, Aegean Sea, approaching Patmos, Greece, May 31, 2032

David agreed that it made sense to set up their home base near the seven churches of Revelations, but the ferry ride was tiresome and long. The Monastery on Patmos had a secret dormitory. Father Alexander shared that bit of information with them at their last visit. He also disclosed that a coin originally accompanied each of the seven letters sent to the churches in St. John's time. Where that coin may be now is unknown. This was big news for them. Up until now, they had planned to visit the churches on a whim of the professor's. Now, at least, they knew that St. John had some of the Judas coins when he made his pilgrimage here. Based on the documents Celia got from Renata at the beginning of their journey, they also knew that the Roman soldier who was with Jesus when he was betrayed had instructed the apostles to separate the thirty coins after Jesus's death. Apparently, John took his seven and distributed them to the churches with his letters.

According to Father Alexander, information about the coins' whereabouts and St. John's letters were recorded in the codex he gave to the professor, passed down from monk to monk over the years. He had no idea if Melik was technically savvy, but if he has their electronics long enough, he may be able to break their encryption and decipher information about the coins before them. The team back in Mexico was working getting them copies of the translation via the encrypted mobile devices. Of course, Melik has one of those as well, thanks to David.

There was no describing the shame he felt knowing that his actions could actually, in fact, result in the end of the world. If the coins got into the wrong hands because of his stupidity, he didn't think he could live with himself. How does anyone look into the face of that possibility and not jump right off the rail of this ferry? He couldn't even look at the professor. And every time Madeira came near him, he wanted scream at her, knowing full well none of this was her fault, but wanting to blame her anyway. He should never have gone to her room and taken his eyes off Melik. Madeira knew better than to approach him right now, and he knew better than to let her.

He couldn't get far enough away from them on this boat. As he pressed himself against the railing, he tried to think, but was too overcome with regret and time was wasting.

How quickly could they set up Celia in the secret dormitory under The Monastery of St. John so they could go back to Ephesus, and to the other churches, to find these coins before Melik did?

As he leaned over the edge of the railing and stared into the sea below, he felt like his heart was shrinking in his chest. Something in him snapped and he started bawling. Completely overwhelmed by the enormity of their predicament, he came apart, sorrow wracking him from skull to toe. What the fuck had he done?

Tears soaked his sleeve as he rocked back and forth, holding the rail of the ferry, his knuckles white. Passengers moved away, afraid of his pain. While his spirit broke, Celia slept below-deck, in the back of the ambassador's van, with the aid of heavy medication. She had sacrificed so much, and David had failed her. He had failed everyone.

"David," he heard in between sobs.

A firm hand rested on his back. He did not look up, instead pounded the railing with his fists in anger.

The professor squeezed his shoulder. "David," he said again.

"I'm so sorry," he wailed. "I'm so sorry, please forgive me."

"Shhh," Professor Delaney said. "It's not your failure, David, it's Melik's. He's the one who did this, not you."

"I let you down," he said, unable to stop blubbering. "I let everybody down." He felt the weight of all the incidents with his father, all the times he was told he was a disappointment, and that he would never amount to anything. Had his father been right?

Professor Delaney said, in a firm voice, "We wouldn't have made it this far if not for you. This was all meant to happen, David. It's God's plan. You're human, Son. Love is never a mistake."

The professor stood beside him, like a rock, his hand firmly planted on David's shoulder, his presence reassuring. Nobody had ever done anything like this for him since his mother died. God knows his father would never have stooped to comfort anyone. Hell, if he had cried like this in front of his old man, the jerk would have laughed or walked away. The professor repeated, "Love is never a mistake." His strong grip pulled David together. He said, "Fear is the only mistake. Melik's fear is why this has happened."

David looked at his teacher, his friend, with burning eyes.

"I let this happen. I let that asshole out of my sight."

For the first time, the professor looked at him with disapproval. He thought he was going to ream him out, but Professor Delaney pulled his priestliness out as a weapon instead and said, "You aren't listening to me. You're making the same mistake as Melik, the same mistake that so many people made when Christ was alive. You're following your fear, and dismissing the value of love."

The professor should know this stuff doesn't sit well with David, but his words had managed to wrestle his mania away for the time being.

He said, in a very gentle, fatherly, priestly voice, "Do you know the passage in Corinthians about love? It's often used at weddings, but if you listen to the actual words - it talks about gifts, after all that has happened – you may feel like your hearing it for the first time. I've memorized it because it mentions tongues and prophecy.

"If I speak in the tongues of men and of angels, but have not love, I am only a resounding gong or a clanging symbol. If I have the gift of prophecy and can fathom all mysteries and all knowledge, and I have a faith that can move mountains, but have not love, I am nothing. If I give all I possess to the poor and surrender my body to the flames, but have not love, I gain nothing."

David had never heard that part before. It was so poignant with relevance to them. He shuddered at the mention of tongues, which Melik now has, of prophecy, which is the professor's gift, and of flames, thinking of the predicted fire from heaven, and he wondered how bible readings could hold so many mysteries and interpretations.

The professor was reciting a part he had heard before,

"Love is patient, love is kind. It does not boast…it keeps no record of wrongs…always perseveres. Love never fails."

Then, he started another part David hadn't ever heard, "But where there are prophecies, they will cease; where there are tongues, they will be stilled; where there is knowledge, it will pass away. For we know in part and we prophesy in part, but when perfection comes, the imperfect disappears."

David repeated, "When perfection comes, the imperfect disappears. That's what we're doing this for, right? Supposedly, if we get this right, if we unite the coins before the bad guys do, we're supposed to experience perfection. Heaven, right? Heaven on earth."

"I hope so, David. I really do."

CHAPTER 15

The Monastery of St. John the Divine, Patmos, Greece,
June 1, 2032

The monastery seemed different to David on this their
second visit. The monks were helpful, but they didn't seem
happy that their undisclosed spaces and secrets had been
disclosed. As several monks helped them smuggle Celia
down into the underground dormitories, David got his first
glimpse into the hidden chambers.

The subterranean structure was very old.

He asked, "When was the Monastery built?"

"It was built in the 11th century," said a short, red-faced

monk who spoke English. "Over the ruins of the ancient temple of Goddess Diane."

"Were these rooms built then, too, or do they predate the monastery?" They stepped into a low, narrow hallway that went on for some time. Several similar hallways branched out in each direction, lacing the hillside under the main fortress.

The monk said, "These rooms predate the monastery. We spent considerable money bringing modern amenities, like running water, to most sections twenty years ago. There's no television in the sub level. Electricity is used to illuminate rooms and for the newly built kitchen and infirmary, where it's needed."

He said, "Probably no cell phone signal down here either?"

"That is correct," the monk answered. He had about as much personality as a brick.

Another monk said, "You have permission to use Father Alexander's office to conduct any business. However, we must ask that you use care and caution when moving between the main building and the dormitories below as not to be seen. I'll show you the passages you're allowed to take. Not all the residents know about these rooms. And, of course, the public is unaware."

Professor Delaney said, "Of course."

"When are you going to make the public aware?" David asked.

"What do you mean?" The serious monk stopped walking.

"I mean, when the time comes and the sky rains fire as

predicted, how will you inform the public that there's a safe haven here?"

They reached an area at the end of one hallway where several larger rooms were grouped and joined together. David assumed this was the infirmary. As with the rest of the smaller, single rooms, the walls were stone - there were no decorations, no windows, no paintings or tapestries. Throw rugs softened their footsteps and twin beds, made with crisp blue sheets and comforters, sat next to side tables with a bible and lamp. David already missed the ambassador's lavish house. Even the giant, open cavern in Mexico had a welcoming, mystical, archeological feeling to it - like being thrown back in time. This place felt sterile in comparison, more like they slipped into the seminary or something.

Madeira said, "Surely you have a plan to bring people to this sanctuary when the time comes?"

The monk said, "We were led to believe that the elect would bring the chosen here to us."

The professor said, "We aren't the ones deciding who will enter."

They started transporting Celia from her wheelchair to the bed. Ayla and Ceyda, her nurses, had insisted on coming with them. David didn't think they would ever leave Celia's side now since she had saved their lives in the earthquake.

The monk said, "From what we've read, the elect will guide the chosen."

Madeira, the professor, Celia, and David exchanged looks. This was news to them. They had come to believe they were the elect, but they didn't know for sure.

Professor Delaney asked, "Can you show me where it's

written?"

The monk nodded.

Professor Delaney looked at him, and David said, "I'll stay with her and get us settled."

He acknowledged this with a slight movement of his head, and then a glance at Celia.

She said, "Go. I'm feeling better every day."

She didn't look better, but she was more lucid with each conversation.

As the professor was lead away, David wondered how on earth they were going to locate the final coins and guide the chosen, whatever that meant.

He looked around the sparse room and said, "Celia, babe, you need to get well now. There's no TV here. Too many long days staring at these walls and I may need to cast demons out of you."

She laughed - a soft, feminine laugh. "You just may, David."

"Or," he said, with a laugh of his own. "You can sneak on down to the cave with the professor, have him stick his hand in that hole again, and see if you can cure yourself."

"Wouldn't that be great," she said.

Madeira sat on the edge of Celia's bed. "You would love the beautiful artifacts and paintings in the cave." She put a hand on Celia's leg.

Celia closed her eyes, clearly exhausted from the trip and the conversation. "I bet I would," she said, as David watched her body relax, and they left her in the nurse's capable hands to go and move their things into adjacent rooms.

The Monastery of St. John the Divine, Patmos, Greece, June 2, 2032

Now that they were staying at the Monastery of St. John, all the locations they planned to hit were within driving distance of the ferry. Of course, this meant they were subject to keeping to the ferry schedule in order to get anywhere. That morning, everybody was edgy as they sat around a large wooden table in the newly renovated kitchen below the main monastery. David would die for some fresh air, a window, and simply to get his ass out of this place.

He said, "You know, I've been thinking about what we learned yesterday: The part about having to choose the people to bring to the shelters. If the earth is already reacting to the joining of the coins with these natural disasters and extreme storms, we can expect some bad events if we don't do this the right way, or worse, if we fail. Will underground caverns be enough? And, if so, who gets to be sheltered and who doesn't?"

The professor said, "I had the same concern, David. The monks here predicted we would come, and that we would be bringing the chosen with us. They were expecting us, but not expecting we would be so-"

"Clueless," he said, finishing the sentence.

The professor smirked. "If we're supposed to anoint chosen peoples to go underground, I don't know how to do that."

"We don't have any criteria," Madeira agreed. "Do we?" She fiddled with a napkin on the table. "I mean, do I gauge by purity of color? Are we supposed to pass judgment? I'm not comfortable with that."

"It's probably written somewhere, but none of us have found it," the professor said. "Or maybe God will provide guidance, I don't know. I've seen nothing in my visions. Father Alexander has the same gift as you, Madeira: discernment. One would think he should have been choosing people for this sanctuary, but he didn't. Like us, he believed that job wasn't his."

"So, what does that mean?" David asked. "Do we just guess, or leave everything to chance?"

The professor said, "I asked Cardinal Margrave to look over the markings in the cavern again and see if he missed any reference to the chosen."

"I feel like Noah and his ark." David sighed. "We really are acting on pure faith."

"Something else the cardinal told me when we spoke yesterday made sense to me," the professor said. "We may need to plan for the possibility of a total blackout. If the fire from heaven turns out to be some kind of massive solar flare or something like that, the electromagnetic and atmospheric changes could mess with telecommunications, power grids, satellites, and God knows what else. Or the fire from heaven could represent comets or something falling from space. We have to be prepared for all scenarios. We can't count on anything.

"That means," the professor got up to toss out his trash and patted David on the back, "that all that hard work you're compiling digitally might be lost in the end."

As much as this horrified him, Professor Delaney was right. He didn't know why he hadn't thought of that himself. David took a few nibbles of his breakfast, thinking it over. "I should see if any of the monks will copy our data onto paper.

It never hurts to have printed back-up, just in case."

"That's a good idea," Madeira said.

"At some point," he added. "We need to make the call about moving Celia to Debiaxo in Mexico if she's not well enough to travel with us and look for coins."

The professor nodded, looking at the door as if he could summon her, but she was not there. She was down the hall, like a sack of laundry, taking up space on the bed. It hadn't been the same since she got hurt. And now, with Melik on the loose, David was beginning to doubt he would ever see heaven on earth. And he wondered, as they sat there, if the world would ever know the sacrifice she had made in an attempt to save the world?

He said, "We definitely need to talk to the monks and ask one of them to record our journey." He didn't say the following aloud, in order to spare Madeira and the professor his pessimism: but if they failed, and if God gave others a chance to save the world - whether a year from now or two-thousand more – and they were the pavers, as Celia once suggested, they needed to make sure their efforts helped the next chosen messengers.

Because the ferry schedule was so strict, David had to copy their backup files in record time once they arrived at the Monastery, and then print out the translated codex in Father Alexander's office, and then rush off at lightening speed with documents in hand. They missed saying good-bye to Celia as she lay in a semi-medicated slumber in the sterile, windowless infirmary.

Sitting together on a wide bench, they sifted through the printed pages. "Look at that," he said, pointing to a drawing included with the translation.

Madeira leaned over. "It's the rock from the Basilica."

The professor smiled. "We start there."

"All the best ruins need to be visited twice," David said, as they picked their way over the rocks and valleys of the ruins at the Basilica of St. John again. "It worked for us in Palenque."

The professor and Madeira picked up the pace and David saw why. The giant stone tablet had been overturned.

He almost fell on his ass when his mentor started to swear like a trucker. He had never heard the professor use profanity and it was really unsettling.

Professor Delaney tumbled to his knees and put his hands on the broken pieces of stone.

Madeira stepped a fraction closer to him, hesitated, and then stepped back again.

Ryan said, "We're too late. Melik, or whoever has been here, has the coin."

"Could Melik have broken our encryption so quickly?" Madeira asked as they started back to the car.

The professor seemed calmer as he said, "We just received the translation today. It's unlikely. Unless he's having visions of his own, or someone else knows about it, he must have just guessed."

They reached the car. Madeira grasped the door handle and said, "You're assuming Melik is the one who took the coin. We don't know that."

"True," the professor said, "but-." He was about to say more when his phone rang. "It's Celia," he said, and took the call.

He hung up. "Change of plans," he said, tossing the keys to David over the car. "You drive; I have some calls to make."

He came over to the passenger side and David asked, "What's up?"

"All hell has broken loose, that's what," he explained. "Vandals already hit Saint Polycarp Church in Izmar."

"Which was our next stop," Madeira said, as she buckled in.

"Exactly," the professor slammed his door. "The ambassador is sending a police escort for us. They're meeting us at the Monastery." He tossed the ferry map onto the dashboard. "The monastery is in complete chaos, David, and it's all your fault."

David felt his testicles jump up into his stomach like he'd been kicked. "My fault?"

"Yeah, you really lit a fire under those monks this morning!" The professor laughed, sounding hysterical, to the point where he started choking and needed to take a sip of water from the bottle in the cup holder.

"What? How?" David didn't know what the hell the professor was talking about.

"The monk, this morning, did you give him some notes and explain to him why we wanted a copy of our data? You told them that electricity, Internet, and other technology might be compromised when the coins are reunited?"

"Yeah. So?"

"Well, I think it occurred to them after we left that reno-vating and modernizing the dormitories may not have been such a good idea after all. Celia says they have crews digging out sections right now. They hadn't anticipated that there may not be running water and electricity when the chosen arrive and the coins are united. I guess the original latrine and fire pit were perfectly engineered for just that possibility before they were reworked in the 1980's!"

David had a visual of the monks digging shit holes and reopening old ventilation pipes and started laughing.

Madeira laughed, too. She said, "I hope they're stocking up on candles."

The professor snorted when he said, "And can openers that work by hand!"

It really wasn't all that funny, but David was so relieved that it was nothing worse than a houseful of hectic monks that he could cry, and he'd done quite enough of that already, thank you.

The Infirmary, Monastery of St John, Patmos Greece, June 2, 2032

David's banter swirled in Celia's head as the monks, who stole about the place like Oompa Loompas, worked around her in her room, down the hall, and up above in the hallways of the monastery. What was it David had said in jest? Sneak down to the cave with the professor, have him stick his hand in that hole again, and see if you can cure yourself.

She wondered…

"Are you sure you're up to this?" Ryan asked, as he heaved Celia into the wheelchair.

"It's worth a try," she said, feeling shaky and nauseous. She waffled between concern over her health to worrying about how she must look without any make-up. Her hair was a matted mess.

"What I wouldn't do for a long, hot shower," she said, as he wheeled her down the corridor.

Ryan kissed her cheek and said, with his face next to hers, "That can be arranged. I'd be happy to help."

"Excuse me?" she said, turning to look at him as best as she could without suffering from dizziness.

"Remember those showers in the frat house, and the time we got caught by Glen Saverhill?"

She did remember, but didn't comment. She felt a million years older and a lifetime less attractive than she was back then.

She was certain Ryan mistook her silence. He changed the subject, and said, "Tell me again why we're sneaking around?"

"I don't want the ridicule from David if this turns out to be a mistake."

"And, if it doesn't?"

"Then he'll have earned the right to gloat."

Ryan snickered as they reached the top of the ramp and passed quietly through one of the seven permitted passageways to the upper floors where Father Cornelius waited. He was expecting them.

"Is everything clear?" Ryan asked.

"Yes," he led them through the monastery. "Our guards are on alert and the cave has been evacuated. We're closed to outsiders for the evening; you're free to take as long as you need. I'll accompany you, too, if that's permitted."

"Yes, thank you," she said, fighting off the weariness.

Celia wished she had been able to see this place in the light of day. When they arrived on Monday, she was hidden in the rear of the van. Now, as they traversed the path from the monastery to St. John's cave, it was too dark to see much of anything. She could hear the call of the wind and smell the exotic blooms by the side of the road. The air was warm and no storms threatened. She took that as a good sign.

Celia dozed off a few times, awaking only when her chin bounced off her chest.

Finally, she saw lights flickering up ahead.

Ryan said, "It's a good thing you haven't had much of an appetite lately."

"Why's that?"

In one fluid movement, Ryan scooped her up out of the chair into his arms and whispered, hot against her ear, "Cause there's no wheelchair access here, and you're lighter now."

He kissed her neck and then with surprising agility, started to descend the stairs holding her as if she were a small child. Like a child, she rested her head in the welcoming curve between his shoulder and his chin.

Candles lined the walkway and soft flickering light vibrated against the stucco walls. She twisted slightly to gaze at a sky full of stars before they ducked under an archway and she sensed Ryan's arms were getting tired.

"Getting me back up might prove difficult."

"Not if you walk out," he groaned, straining against her weight now. "I'm not sure I can carry you up all these stairs."

He practically dropped her down onto the stone floor of the cave, and then he squatted down next to her. "Sorry."

"It's ok," she told him.

"Do you want to look around, or should we try straight-away?"

"I'm afraid I may pass out if we wait too long. The dizzi-ness and nausea are intense from the way you jiggled me coming down those stairs — "

He smiled. "Well, David says, 'All the best ruins need to be visited twice.'"

"He would know," she struggled against a migraine build-ing.

Ryan touched her face and said, "Give me a few seconds."

"Then what?"

"Then make physical contact with me."

She winked at him. He smiled, and then sat down, lowered his head, and reached into the hole in the wall. She could hear him trying to slow his breathing, but the exertion of carrying her was probably making it difficult. She looked around briefly at her surroundings when, all of a sudden, she lost sensation in her legs. Maybe this wasn't such a good idea. The room started to swim and she tipped sideways, forcing her body against Ryan's. All at once, she felt nothing and everything, much like when she performed a healing. Instead of heat, and in place of pain, she felt vibrant nothing-ness and, unexpectedly, blessed ecstasy. The most exquisite sensations engulfed her - filling her, almost to the point of consuming her. She grabbed onto Ryan's shirt and groaned while the energy surged through her, orgasmic and intense. She rode the rapture as long as she could until she felt her consciousness slip away, her grip on Ryan loosened, and she slid down to the floor of the cave.

"Celia, honey," Ryan's voice purred against her ear. "Wake up."

With his strong arms surrounding her, she smelled his clean aftershave and laundry soap. They were curled against each other on the floor, sitting. Her face was resting against his shirt and she could hear the pounding of his heart, a steady, soothing repetition.

She let out a long exhalation and opened her eyes. Her skin was tingling all over, almost as if her nerve endings were just born. All her senses were on speed. She felt like she had been transported into some sci-fi video game – the colors were so bright and the sounds amplified. But, when she squinted against the onslaught, she realized the pain was gone. She sat up and looked around.

Ryan jumped at her sudden movement and watched her with concern.

"I'm ok," she said, as she felt hot tears develop out of nothing. It felt so good to feel good. There was no explaining it, and she knew she was frightening Ryan a little sitting there in this bizarre funk, crying, but she couldn't contain the joy. She hadn't even realized herself how much pain she had been in until just now as she moved about, feeling young and vibrant and reborn.

Celia explored the cave with new eyes, touch the rough and ancient walls with new hands, and smelled the stone, the metal polish, and the floral and sea air. She breathed, filling her lungs again and again with the joy of each breath, each inhalation of blessed oxygen. If she closed her eyes, she could almost feel the nourishment the breath brought to her brain and blood. She investigated the circumference of the room, touching, smelling, and experiencing everything, until she was back by Ryan. He was standing now, watching her with fascination and a wide, wide grin.

"We did it," he said.

She pulled him to her and hugged him, letting herself feel the love and the health, and most blessedly, the lack of pain. "Thank you," she said, and she pulled him tighter before releasing him. Celia planted small kisses all over Ryan's face, just enjoying the sensation of her new lips against his rough skin.

She yelled, she actually yelled, "This is incredible!"

The monks and guards in the doorway twitched in surprise and Ryan laughed. He laughed, and pulled her to him around her waist, picked her up by her middle and spun her around and around. Their laughter carried out into the night like the hoot of an owl or the call of a coyote – primal and instinctual reactions to their elation.

David's room, the Monastery of St. John, June 3, 2032

He had taken some of Celia's pills to help him sleep last night. Between the reconstruction going on outside his room, thinking of Madeira in the next room, and knowing someone was one step ahead of them vandalizing the churches they planned to visit before they got there, David couldn't even calm himself enough to lie down, never-the-less sleep. It was the professor's suggestion, actually, after several hours of listening to David hash out plans, revise them, swear, and start over, he pressed the sleeping pill into David's hand. The armed guards on patrol only served to make David crazier.

Now, as he awoke groggy and confused, his tongue felt like a well-worn floor mat, and his eyeballs felt like they'd grown hair, he wondered if taking the pills had been such a good idea.

He stretched his stiff and sluggish body until it was limber enough to contort into some clothes and shuffled to the kitchen. He wondered if he was still high, or dreaming, because he saw Celia and the professor sitting at the table eating toast and eggs and laughing like children.

He froze, then slapped his cheeks a few times. They were still there.

"Good Morning, David," Celia said.

"What the hell?" He broke from his stupor and went over to hug her.

She leapt from her chair and said, "You are the most brilliant boy!"

"Man," the professor said.

"The most brilliant man," she corrected herself, hugging him close.

"What are you talking about?" He held her at arm's length. She looked wonderful. "How?" he stammered, having a hard time clearing his head.

Madeira walked in, stopped short, blinking her eyes in confusion. "You're well!" She jumped up and down, hugging each of them like a schoolgirl.

"I am," Celia said, hugging her back. "Thanks to David."

"Huh?" He must be more stoned than he thought.

The professor said, "Hey!"

"And, thanks to Ryan," Celia added.

Professor Delaney smiled and Madeira asked, "How did you do it? What happened?" She sat down at the table. David was still standing with his bed-head and bare feet, staring at Celia like she was a phantom.

"Ryan and I went to the Cave of the Apocalypse like David suggested." Celia said with a shit-eating smile on her face.

"Get out!" he shouted, moving to sit next to her. "You healed yourself. Damn, I am brilliant."

"Told you he'd gloat," she said to the professor, but stopped when she saw his face. He couldn't help himself, he was so blown away to see her well that he was getting choked up. When did he become a such a wuss?

"Oh, David." Celia pulled him into her arms.

He was really embarrassed, but he couldn't pull himself together. He joked, "Who knew miracles could unman me?" as he pulled away from her embrace and went to the fridge for some cold air to chill him out and orange juice to give him something to do with his hands.

To fill the silence, he added, "Not for nothing, but I'll be glad if this is the last miracle I see, you know? All this constant drama is exhausting. Hey, how bout we blow off chasing coins and psychopaths today and go see a movie instead?"

He sat down with his glass and stole a piece of toast off of Celia's plate.

"I'm game," Madeira replied, without conviction. Still, he appreciated her effort to keep things light so he could compose himself.

Celia wasn't helping his mood when she said, "You guys could use the chance for a real date."

Madeira laughed. "David's got no intrigue if he's not puking all over me, dodging bullets, or encrypting messages from the president and the pope."

"Don't forget from God," he said. "His messages upstage those other guys."

"Except, you can't seem to decipher those as easily," Madeira teased, getting up and going to the counter to peel a grapefruit over the trash can.

He threw his crust at her.

"Hey!"

"Seriously, David, thank you," the professor said.

He didn't want to get emotional again, so he said, "Movie?"

The professor shook his head. "I'm afraid we have other things to see today."

"Kill joy." David attempted to steal a piece of the professor's toast, too.

He slapped his hand away, and said, "Go make your own breakfast, will ya?"

David moved to the far counter, and then started to open the bag of bread. "So," he said to Celia over his shoulder, "I guess this means you're coming with us? Are you completely recovered?"

"Better than recovered," she said.

He raised his eyebrows, turned his head to her as he popped two slices into the toaster, and repeated, "Better than recovered?"

She smiled, stood, and stretched. "I'll tell you about it on the ferry. Right now, I'm taking a long shower, then I'm going to dry my hair, brush it until it's untangled, and put on mascara."

Suddenly, with Celia back in the game, their chances were looking better and better. It wasn't logical, and they'd done okay without her, but to David, Celia was like God's conduit. She was superwoman in a very un-super-woman body, with more awesome powers and a lot of other benefits. He felt shielded, stronger, better, when she was around. If he was honest with himself, it felt like having a mother again.

"The world is falling apart, and you're worried about your hair?" He teased her, not wanting her to know his thoughts. It was bad enough that Madeira perceived every stinking feeling he had as she used her radar on him.

"I'm alive!" Celia said. "And I really, really want to feel clean and new. I want to breathe the air, feel the water under my feet on the boat, and touch the sacred places with my own two hands." Her hands lifted to her face and she looked at them as if she had never seen them.

Was everyone else wondering the same thing as David? How many more times could Celia heal or perform miracles before the act killed her? Those beautiful hands held powers, potential, and peril all at once.

"Go shower," David said. "I can't stand the smell of you."

Then he winked at her as his toast popped up.

Executive Suite, Movenpick Hotel, Izmar, Turkey, June 3, 2032

Cardinal Everett Jusipini paced next to the king-sized bed in the lavish hotel suite. He drummed his fingers on his thigh. How had she done it?

Eduardo, one of his followers, had just left the room. The smartest of the three disciples working with the cardinal, Eduardo's gift was prophesy and, like Professor Ryan Delaney, he had visions. The other two worthless souls working with him had gifts as well. Delzel's was ministry and Selim's was faith. Useless gifts, easily manipulated. But Eduardo had skills. He was a military and religious extremist. It hadn't taken much for the cardinal to convince Eduardo that Celia and the others were false messiahs and needed to be stopped at all costs.

A woman could never be the one to bring enlightenment to the world. That would be preposterous. The cardinal was clearly designated as God's messenger and was better equipped to fulfill Christ's destiny than any woman or fallen priest. He had used that argument as leverage to gain Eduardo's trust. Once Eduardo bonded with the coin taken from the dead Bishop in Texas, he started to have visions, and that had sealed the deal. There had been other followers, other thugs with power, the two involved in the shooting at the hospital in Ankara, but now their coins were with the cardinal's enemies, and the two imbeciles were dead or incapacitated. This Celia and her followers had been one step ahead of him until now. When she was out of commission, the professor and his brat sidekicks should have been easy prey.

How had the woman healed herself? She had been near dead, Eduardo had prophesied that she would die, then something had happened to change fate. Celia was now healed and traveling with the others. How? Even when that Italian whore Renata came to Turkey, she was unable to heal her cohort. What had changed? And how could the cardinal get ahold of that solution?

If he could heal himself or be healed after using his gifts, as she had clearly done, he would be invincible. He had to find out how, then he could rid himself of Eduardo and the others. He had been healing Eduardo every time a vision put him out of commission, but the effort of doing so put strain on the Cardinal. He would bleed, be weak, hurt in all the places the stigmata appeared. He needed Eduardo's prophetic skills, and he needed Eduardo to be well to do his bidding. It was becoming troublesome.

Eduardo's visions were growing clearer and more frequent since the boy Melik broke from the group. They were going to the seven churches. The cardinal's associates had already beat them to two of the churches, amassing coins from each. They had yet to discover where the gathering place Debiaxo was. Eduardo's visions revealed only a cavern, the name, and a few of those hiding in refuge there. That was where they would gather the coins, but first they had to discover where the hideout was. Maybe, if they could reunite Melik with the others, they would learn more.

He stood over the table by his hotel room window, looking at the bouquet of fresh flowers and remembering when he first learned he could use his healing gift in reverse to make something healthy, unwell. It was harder than healing and more detrimental to him physically. He had discovered the skill via an accidental experiment on a potted fern at the Vatican. Now, he lifted his hand and passed it over some fresh flowers in the vase, watching them instantly wilt and curl. It had been much harder to do the first time he tried it, but he was stronger now. It had become easier to perform such feats at the blink of an eye.

He sat down on the bed, weary. The after-effects however, were still problematic. The bigger the miracle, the more disabled he was immediately following, and if he used the power in reverse to cause harm, the physical after effects were multiplied. He licked the blood from his wrist, his stigmata and pain not the blessing he once thought it was. He had not killed anyone with his power since Tomas at the Letňany Exhibition Center almost twenty years earlier. He was severely ill for over a year following that episode. It was too stiff a price to pay. Now, others did his dirty work and he kept his hands clean. But if he could heal himself, anything was possible. How had Celia surmounted that obstacle?

It was time to set a trap for Melik, unsuspecting mouse that he was, and get some answers.

Ferry, Aegean Sea, approaching Patmos, Greece, June 4, 2032

The ferry rode on calm waters as Celia watched the sea gulls chase them as if it were a party game they played. She watched them dip and swoop and call. She listened with her new ears as David tried to digest what she had just said.

"So," he played with his chin, then dropped his hands to the rail. "You're not just 'recovered,' you feel 'reborn'?"

"Yes," she said. She felt renewed in a way she had never

experienced before. "I keep using the word, 'reborn,' because it's the only word I can find that comes close to describing how fresh everything looks and feels - how alive I am."

"You're not tired?" he asked.

She could see Ryan grinning over David's shoulder. Ryan felt it, too. They both had this extra energy and insight since their episode in the cave together. "I'm not tired!" She shouted, throwing her arms up into the air in praise. "Everything smells wonderful, feels wonderful, and tastes wonderful. Life is wonderful."

Madeira said, "I wish you could see it, David. All around her, pure white and piercing yellow. She's glowing, like an angel."

"Maybe she is one," David said.

Celia breathed deeply, feeling the salt air fill her with its healing power. "Maybe I am," she agreed.

Göçmen St., approaching the Pergamon Ruins in Turkey, June 4, 2032

Professor Delaney was driving, but he wasn't paying attention and it was making David crazy. The professor and Celia kept exchanging glances across the front seat. They were acting so strange that he felt like he did that day on the plane when he first set out with them, an intruder in their personal space. Besides, they were acting like kids who just snuck their first taste of beer. It was really irritating.

Madeira, sitting next to him in the back seat, nudged him with her foot.

"What?"

"Stop biting your nails," she said.

He looked down at his hands, and then out the window where their armed escort rode in the neighboring lane. The hairs on his arms kept standing on end as if they knew something he didn't. "I don't like this," he said.

When he glanced over at Madeira again, he caught a glimpse of the ruins of Pergamon out the window over her shoulder. They didn't look like much, just some random rock piles and a few columns supporting broken sections of a roof. The amphitheater stairs were visible from this distance and he wondered if he could pull a Rocky and run up all of them without stopping. Celia probably could, now that she was "reborn".

The professor took a right turn putting the ruins directly ahead. David leaned forward and said, "You know-" when a section of columns blew sky high in front of them and the professor stomped on the breaks.

"Jesus!" he yelled, as Madeira's face slammed into the headrest in front of her. His outstretched hands braced him from the sudden stop.

The police escort raced ahead.

"They beat us here," the professor said, the surprise in his voice made David want to shake him. Some prophet, David knew something was wrong before he did. The professor stomped on the gas and David was thrown back in his seat.

Several heart-stopping moments later, they arrived at the location of the explosion.

They got out of the car and worked their way toward the ruins, staying alert and on guard. It looked like some tourists had been injured, and David spotted the police racing on foot up the hillside after somebody. Another group of police stood with their backs against each side of an archway that may have been the old aqueducts. Gunfire erupted from inside one tunnel. David ducked behind a stone and heard Madeira say, "Melik!"

"Where?" He spun around, anger building in his chest, making his whole upper body tense.

Madeira crawled forward toward a figure on the ground. David had assumed it was one of the injured tourists, but now he could see it was Melik, and he was hurt.

"Mother fucker." He darted forward. "Madeira! Get away from him!"

He was shocked when she yelled back, "Shut up, David!" and kept going.

Dust was still falling all around them from the explosion and, as he scrambled forward, rubbing the dust from his eyes, he saw the two birds again, hovering over Melik and Madeira like phantom creatures. The sight of them only delayed him a moment. Without thinking, he dove into Madeira, pushing her aside and then grabbed Melik by the shirt, pulling him up. From this angle, he could see Melik was bleeding heavily from a wound in his side.

"You bastard!" He shouted. "What have you done?"

Melik said, "I didn't do this."

Madeira, recovered from the blow, stumbled back to them and said, "Get undercover!"

She grabbed David's arm and pulled at him with little affect.

"She's right," Melik said. "Get us behind that rock!"

David wanted to strangle him, but he'd never know where his computer was and what Melik had done if he were dead.

He wrapped his arms around Melik's chest and dragged him backward by the armpits, his legs and bottom dragging, until the three of them were behind a very unstable-looking rock wall.

David heard more shooting and looked around for the professor and Celia. He could see them crouched across the way against some pillars.

"How were you hurt?" Madeira asked.

He turned back. "Who cares?" He shook Melik. "Where's our data and who the hell is shooting at us?"

Melik didn't struggle or resist. He looked pale, probably from loss of blood, and his voice was weak and raspy. "The data is safe," he said. "I wanted to find out if what you said about my father was true. I knew you were keeping things from me, and I wanted to know."

"You had no right to run off with our property!" David snapped. "There's more at stake here than your curiosity!"

"I know that now," Melik said. "You left the ambassador's house. I went back there, but you were gone."

David could hear people shouting up on the hill. The sound of gunfire was coming from far away now. Whoever had done this was escaping.

"Who are those men?" David asked.

"They're associated with Cardinal Jusipini. I heard them talking. They were already here when I arrived. I came looking for you. When I saw they were up to no good, I hid over there and watched them, listening to their conversation," Melik nodded to one of the many openings. "Then, I saw them plant the explosives and ran out to warn the tourists."

"What were the men saying?" Madeira asked.

Melik cringed and said, "They knew you were coming. I heard them use your names. Eduardos, the leader, has visions. He was bragging all the while." The imaginary birds around Melik circled and David swatted at them, but it was like smacking air. "They have coins, but from what I heard, they're only hired hands. They killed some bishop in Texas and stole his coin. They probably killed my father, too."

David must have looked like he was going to explode because Madeira said, "It's okay, he's telling the truth."

David didn't care what she said, he placed his hands on Melik's chest, pushed, and shouted, "I cast you out!" Summoning his power. The birds collided and dissipated like exhaled cigarette smoke. David fell backwards and hit his head on a stone on the ground.

Like a giant yawn, the air around him seemed to whoosh. The previous noise of gunfire and panic vanished, and David's nostrils flared like a vortex of air was pulling them laterally. His skull started to hurt. Then the vacuum reversed and his senses reeled, making him shiver and tremble. Every hair on his body stood on end and then fell flat again. The dust that had been falling blew upward and dissolved.

Madeira said, "David."

He tried to sit up, but the altered air pressure from using his gift was holding him fast, like when you're on a carnival ride that's spinning.

Then, just as quickly as it started, it stopped. His body released from the odd gravitation and he raised his head to find Madeira staring at Melik, and Melik sitting up, looking down at his body as if it were estranged. He was still bleeding, though, and pressed his hands over the gash in his side.

The gunfire had stopped and one of the officers jogged over to them. He spoke Turkish and Melik answered, then explained, "They got away."

Celia and the professor came running over. Celia said, "Lay down, Melik." And he did what she asked.

"I tried to stop them," he said, looking at David. "What did you do to me?"

David had no idea what he had done.

Celia laid her hands on Melik.

David panicked. "Don't!"

The professor held him back, grabbing him in a surprisingly strong body-lock. "Let her," he said in David's ear.

He had no choice but to watch on as Celia healed Melik. When she pulled away, he searched her head, sides, and hands for signs. Nothing. The professor released him.

"No stigmata?"

"It's over," the professor said. "Celia's done suffering."

"How?" He moved aside and sat on the dusty ground, rubbing the back of his head where he had bumped it.

"Something to do with our experiment last night," Professor Delaney said, looking at Melik, clearly nervous about saying more about the Cave of the Apocalypse and the miracle of Celia's recovery.

"We need to get to the next church," Melik's eyes were as big as saucers as he lifted his shirt and inspected his body where the wound just was. "They stabbed me with my own knife and stole my coin. They'll stop at nothing. After they recover the last coin, they'll hunt us all down, me included. They won't stop until we're dead."

David said, "They left you alive. It doesn't add up. The

coin is useless to them if you're alive. They can't use its powers until you're dead."

"They plan to kill all of us," Melik said. "But not until they find the location of the temple where the others are hiding."

"I see," the professor said.

David stood up on unsteady feet. "I don't trust you, you lying, stealing shit," he said to Melik.

Madeira stepped up to David and supported him as he stumbled. She said, "His colors have changed, David. You did it. Melik's no longer a threat to us."

"I don't care what color he is," David said. "If he changed once, he can change again."

"What do you mean, colors?" the professor asked.

David waved him away.

"That's not how it works, David," Madeira said. "You've mastered your gift. Melik's demons are gone."

"I'll believe it when I see it," he grabbed Melik by the sleeve and hoisted him up. "You're never leaving my sight again." He dragged Melik to the car. "Where's my phone and my fucking computer?"

As they drove the thirty-five miles southeast to Akhisar, to the ruins at the worldly church: Thyatira, Celia listened as Madeira and David bickered over colors and birds in the back seat with Melik sandwiched like a tortured teen between two demanding parents.

They were all stunned by the destruction they just

witnessed at Pergamon. Even if what Cardinal Margrave had said was true, and bonding with multiple coins would cause mental degradation, delusions of grandeur, mental illness and instability, how bad it gets and what one might do in this state was hard to imagine. That these assailants would go out in broad daylight and blow up a portion of sacred ruins to get their hands on coins was disturbing. That they had disemboweled Melik's father for his coin, unthinkable. Why had they left Melik alive?

David was behaving like an irrational mass of energy, fueled by having had to use his powers for the first time, not knowing what he's doing, and being unsure what to feel about any of it, no doubt. It had been like that for Celia at first, too.

Then there was Ryan, who seemed to have utter clarity all of a sudden. He had spoken to the police at length, and it was on his recommendation that they were rushing, head first, to Thyatira right now.

In the back seat, David was having a heated argument with Madeira about Melik. No matter how much she assured David that Melik's colors were all positive now and that David's "exorcism" had cured Melik of any harmful tendencies or evil energy, David was full of disbelief, and Madeira was quick to recognize this and point it out.

Celia trusted Madeira, but what did they know for sure? David's powers were hard to comprehend. What, exactly, happened to someone who had been touched by him, been "cured", if that's what you call it? Madeira believed that David had the ability to "exorcise" demons by dissolving all inclinations towards sin. She argued that David could cure a soul of greed, jealousy, hate, and fear. If she was right, then perhaps David possessed the strongest and most valuable gift of all of them.

She was about to say this to David when he shocked her into silence by yelling, "And what the hell is your deal?"

"What?" She turned in her seat to look at him.

"Not you," he replied, throwing his hand into the air. "The professor! He's so distracted by you, he let a psychopath prophet beat us to three coins. Now they have Melik's, too."

Celia and Ryan said nothing. It would be so easy for them to point out to David that he was distracted by Madeira once and Melik got away, but neither of them did.

Madeira said, "Cast your own demons out, David. I think when you helped Melik, you may have ingested some of his anger and fear yourself. Your dark colors are swirling like crazy."

"Get serious," David said, crossing his arms over his body.

"I am serious," she snapped back, crossing her arms over her body and turning away from him.

Great. Celia was in a car full of hot-heads.

Ryan looked at her, sighed, and then focused his attention back on road.

"David," she said, turning around as best she could in the front seat. "We all need to calm down and get our act together before we arrive at Thyatira." She knew if she could just lay her hands on him, she could calm him enough to get him out of his funk - if he'd let her.

"We can't just show up; these guys have guns," Melik pointed out.

"And your knife," David spat. "Don't forget that."

Melik rolled his eyes and turned to stare out of Madeira's window.

"We have a plan," Celia said "But, David," she reached back and touched his knee. "We need your help."

She was surprised, at the first touch, by the energy radiating out from David's body. Madeira may have been right to some extent - David's physiology had been altered in some way. She decided to talk to him, and to see if she could perform some gentle healing at the same time. But first, she needed to take care of Melik. He may be trustworthy, now, she didn't know, but it was too risky to include him fully until they were sure. She had used a technique once on her father when he had been really agitated at his nursing home. Back then, when she performed mild acts, she still suffered from negative after-effects and bleeding. That was not the case now. She was going to experiment and see what she could do.

She unbuckled her seat belt and turned around in her seat, kneeling on it, one hand on each side of the low headrest. "Melik, how are you feeling?"

He looked down at his body and said, "Okay. You did a good job, There's no pain or soreness where I was stabbed."

"Come here," she said, beckoning with her fingers. "Let me feel your head for fever."

He leaned forward, claiming, "I don't have a fever," when Celia used her gift to put him to sleep. It worked faster than she remembered, but of course when she had tried it on her father he was in the midst of a complete Alzheimer's meltdown and was struggling. Like some hypnotist's trick, or those evangelist healers who knock people unconscious with a touch, Melik slumped forward, out cold.

"Whoa," David said, "What was that?"

She didn't answer as she tried to figure out how to get David to let her calm him next. Celia had a renewed confidence in her gift. And she no longer had fear of any kind. Even when the gunfire was happening moments ago, back at Pergamon, she wasn't afraid. Whatever happened, she had no doubt now that it was God's plan. Maybe, if she tried, she could share that revelation with David.

After reclining her seat some to bring her closer to David, completely turned around now, kneeling backwards in the passenger seat, and hunched over a bit to keep her head from bumping the roof, she said, "I had to put him to sleep so we could speak freely. Ryan and I have worked out a plan, but, David, we need you for it to work." She grabbed him by the forearms, and summoned up the energy to heal, while she delivered the speech she worked out a few moments ago.

"Melik was right. We can't go up against these guys when they have guns and knives. We need to position ourselves somewhere we can trap them when they flee, catch them off guard, so you can step in and do your thing."

She had him, right up until that last bit.

"You're nuts," he said, pulling back, lifting his arms up by his head. "The both of you are completely crazy. Hell, for all I know, you're all nuts, just like Melik's dad, and just like those assholes who blew up Pergamon. Fucking lunatics."

She grabbed for him again, and said, "That's enough, David," as she snatched his wrists and pulled them toward her. She held them as tight as she could, trying not to let the effort show on her face while she struggled to heal and speak at the same time. She could feel his illness in her hands. The repercussion to David expending his power differed from Ryan's exhaustion as a consequence of a vision, or her bleeding as a consequence of healing. As far as she could tell, David was super-charged. It was like the energy was bouncing through him at an incredible rate, almost as if he were on speed. She needed to mellow him, but how?

She glanced at Madeira, who had propped Melik up in his seat and was looking on with interest. Should Celia play her trump card, even though she and Ryan had agreed to wait? She knew when David heard this news it would change everything.

She said, continuing to hold tight to his wrists and feeling every pulse beat, "You need to pull it together, David. For me, for Ryan, for Madeira, and for the world."

He took in a deep breath, and before he could respond, she said what she withheld. "You need to pull it together for your unborn child. The child you and Madeira conceived when I was in a coma."

"My what?" David felt the car sway under the professor's hand.

Celia continued to hold his wrists. Her grip was hot, almost searing hot, but he lacked the ability to pull away.

He saw movement to his left as Madeira looked at him.

Celia said, "She's pregnant. I knew it the moment I touched her, even though she doesn't know it yet." She looked at Madeira. "Sorry, I had planned to let you find out the normal way, but nothing here is normal, is it?"

Madeira looked completely stunned.

"Also, there's more," Celia said. "It's not my child that Ryan professed would keep the commandments of God, and have the testimony of Jesus Christ. Remember, in Palenque, the prediction he made in the restaurant?" Her eyes bore into David's.

"Mine?" he asked, remembering the professor's haunting words back in Palenque, and how he had so easily assumed the words referred to Celia. David recalled how he poked fun at her denial. It wasn't so funny now.

"Yours and Madeira's child," Celia said, releasing his hands at last.

He knew she had used her gift on him because he felt that same bizarre Valium calm that came over him in the Cave of the Apocalypse.

Madeira started to cry. She looked more thrown than he was. He supposed it was one thing to take on the world, to complete this spiritual quest, in the first place, but quite another to do it carrying a child.

"You're sure?" he said to no one and to everyone.

The professor said in a firm, fatherly voice, "Your child will fulfill the prophecy, David. He will deliver peace after the apocalypse. I've seen it.

"He'll be a great prophet who'll have all the coins' powers when Eden returns, and will act as a reminder to all to stay free of sin and rejoice in God's gifts. He's the second coming, if we succeed in reuniting the coins before his birth."

It was too much to take in. David looked at the back of the professor's head as he drove the car and said, "He? It's no bigger than a raisin and you're already calling it 'he'?"

David had a frightening thought. What happened if they failed? Heaven would be lost, they knew that much from the prophesies. But what does that mean?

The joining of the coins would produce physical effects to the earth, and to the universe, David imagined. Look at what happened in Turkey when Celia had two coins on her person. Imagine what may happen if all thirty come together in one person's (the wrong person's) hands. If this cardinal and his thugs got the coins, all would be lost. The opposite of salvation and heaven. That could mean cataclysmic weather events and mental depravity, fire and destruction instead of rebirth. And what becomes of his son if that happens? The question was paralyzing.

He was going to be a father. That's a big discovery on its own, but to learn he may be the father of a savior, a gifted child, that was unthinkable. Could it be? He knew one thing for sure, he'd be damned if he'd be as half-assed at being a father as his old man had been.

He reached across Melik's sleeping form and took Madeira's hand. She was still weeping. For the first time in his life, David didn't feel embarrassed or afraid of his feelings. He said, without hesitation, and with a wholeheartedness he'd not felt since his mother was alive, "I love you, Madeira."

She nodded, wiped a tear with her free hand, and said, "I know."

David pulled her to him and gave her an awkward hug obstructed by seat belts and Melik. When he released her, he admitted, "This isn't the way I envisioned this. Ever."

He decided that whatever happened, no matter what God's

plan, he'd move mountains to ensure this child grew up with both parents in a world where heaven on earth was possible, and where lunatics would not destroy the fabric of humanity. Celia wasn't fooling anyone if she thought he didn't know that's exactly why she dropped that bombshell on him. It was time to stop fucking around and save the world. The ball was in his court.

"If I get shot, you'll heal me, right?" David said, as he and Celia hid in the back of the bandit's getaway van at Thyatira - a van they broke into with help from the local police, a van they expect will be filling up with lunatics escaping a crime scene at any moment. Goose bumps rose along David's neck in anticipation. They learned from the Vatican that Cardinal Jusipini was here in Turkey. This plan of the professor's better work.

Celia smiled, but didn't justify his question with an answer.

Despite knowing the police were staked-out not twenty yards away, he was trying not to give in to doubts. What if Madeira was wrong about Melik and he double-crosses them? What if their plan sucked and they both got killed? What if he couldn't do what they all expected of him, including the ambassador and Prime Minister who set up this covert operation, the president and the pope who provided aide to them, too, and God who had his own expectations? What about his unborn baby? Would he be leaving him fatherless so soon?

Celia's phone vibrated. David jumped like a moron, thinking she accidentally set off the stun gun she was carrying. She looked at the text. "They're headed this way."

It took all his concentration to remember to breathe.

Thanks to Melik and the cops, they now had a better understanding of who these guys were.

Of the three, Eduardo was the most dangerous. A rogue member of the Italian armed forces, Eduardo was convinced he had been chosen by God to defeat those who would proclaim to be the next messiah. How he got this idea into his head, David would never understand. Shortly after hooking up with Cardinal Jusipini, the Vatican librarian, he murdered Bishop Reilly in Texas and got his hands on one of the coins. He had been traveling with the Cardinal and two others. They fully expected David to use his powers to neutralize them with help from the authorities.

David glanced at his own stun gun, turned on the safety, and slipped it into his pocket. He couldn't believe he was trusting God to handle this for him, but there it was. He hoped his hands would be all the Tasers he would need.

From what they'd learned, Eduardo's two accomplices, Delzel and Salim, were recruited with stolen coins and one acquired by killing a man in a cab on his way to the airport. The local authorities were very motivated to capture these guys. It took some talking to convince the authorities to let them be involved. Now, if someone could just convince David.

"Here they come," Celia said. "Duck down."

He took a deep breath, let it out, and then contorted himself so he was hidden behind the front passenger seat of the van they had parked for a getaway. David's favorite part of this so far was when the police picked the locks to get them inside. This was made-for-TV stuff, and kind of cool.

Celia, aka Rambo, gave him the "get ready" nod from behind the driver's seat. Who would ever have guessed this woman was comatose ten days ago?

The driver's door opened and a guy landed in the seat, the gun in his right hand reflecting the grey overcast skies. David couldn't see the guy's face clearly since he was wearing a hat, but he thought it was Salim from the pictures the cops had shown them. The guy dropped the gun onto the center console at the same time the passenger door opened, and he yelled, "Get in."

David fought to control his breathing and stay hidden. He was terrified and trying not to tremble or breathe too hard. The more he thought about his fear and his breath, the harder it was to control it.

The driver was focused straight ahead from where they had come. He didn't notice David and Celia hidden in the back and had no reason to think anyone was stowing away in their van. That was their advantage.

As bad-guy-number-one jammed his right hand into the pocket of his sweatshirt for keys, Celia reached up with her left hand and zapped him on the side of his neck with her stun gun. He twitched and jerked in sync with bad-guy-number-two dropping into the passenger seat. The man's dark skin was marred with acne scars. He had a long nose and a thin face. It was Delzel.

David reached around before Delzel noticed his friend had been stunned, and he slammed his hands on the man's shoulders from behind and said, "I cast you out!"

He forgot about the repercussions from using his gift, about the gravitational pull and vacuum that resulted, until he found himself sprawled against the floor of the van, twitching like he'd been zapped with a stun gun.

Much to his horror, Celia panicked when Delzel spun in his seat, his gun still in hand, and she zapped him on the wrist. This sent the gun flying onto the floor next to David's head, but he was unable to move and get it.

Where's Eduardo? David's eyes begged Celia to be careful when the back doors opened and Eduardo's foot was about to stomp on his head. It took only seconds for the newcomer to react. Eduardo stepped back at seeing them and took aim at Celia.

Somehow, David managed to move his arm enough against the pull of gravity, and he grabbed the loose gun and flung it at Eduardo with all his might. The butt of the gun smacked the enemy in the eye just as he fired a shot, and then he turned and ran down the alley where the police were waiting.

David swiveled his head to find Celia sprawled on the floor at his feet. Before he could let out a primal yell, she sat up, unharmed. It was then he realized the bullet was deflected when he pitched the loose gun at Eduardo. Instead of hitting Celia, Eduardo blew the jaw off of Delzel's face.

Celia turned and grabbed Salim's gun off the console and aimed it at Delzel. "You're not going to give me any trouble are you?"

Who is she? And, man, when did she grow balls?

Delzel was grabbing at the bloody mass that was once his

chin and shaking from shock.

Celia said, "I didn't think so."

She put the gun down next to David, still watching Delzel, and said under her breath, "Damn, I can't heal that right."

She put her hands on David. "You first."

He felt the weight of the vacuum lift, the gravity released itself, and his body returned to normal.

"Take care of Salim," she said, then she moved forward with caution. "Delzel, I'm going to help you, but you have to trust me."

Delzel's eyes were open so wide it looked like his eyeballs might drop out. Between the shock of being shot and whatever he felt from what David had done to him, his mind must have been as close to mush as yesterday's steamed vegetables.

David couldn't look at Delzel any longer. He crossed over to Salim, put his hands on the unconscious, stunned man's shoulders, and shouted to his sorry tasered ass, "I cast you out!"

The guy's body convulsed and, once again, David was thrown back onto the floor. The cycle started all over.

Celia ignored him as the after-effects worked him over. He felt the energy coming from her as she healed Delzel's wounds. From this perspective, all David could see was the back of her as she laid hands on him. It was a much better view that what was happening on the flip side, he was sure. He closed his eyes and let himself experience the energy of God, to feel the power spinning in his body, and in this van. He let go of his worries about Eduardo. That was up to the police, and God. He just hoped, no, he prayed, that Eduardo was not the one who had the coins on his person. Please God, let the coins be in this van.

Executive Suite, Movenpick Hotel, Izmar, Turkey, June 4, 2032

Eduardo entered the cardinal's hotel room with trepidation. He'd been ambushed by their enemies in the van, and he didn't know how they pulled it off. He had not seen this coming. Although he still had his coin, he was certain the others had lost theirs by now. He had failed. Not only that, but he thought he may have accidentally killed Delzel.

Eduardo was bleeding from a head wound and the pain was blocking his ability to engage with his visions. His head was full of noise and confusion.

The cardinal stood at the window and turned at his approach.

Eduardo struggled to gather his thoughts and words. "I was taken by surprise by Celia and the others at Thyatira. They captured Selim and Delzel somehow. I escaped the police, but just barely. A shot missed me, but loosed a wooden sign that struck me hard on the head as I ran by. Delzel is injured, possibly dead."

The cardinal's face was cold and cruel. "Why didn't you detect the trap?"

"I'm not sure," Eduardo admitted.

"Where are they going next?" the cardinal asked.

"I don't know." Eduardo faltered.

"What do you know?" The Cardinal's voice was hard, his expression angry and full of venom. Eduardo had never seen this side of the holy man. He stiffened and when the Cardinal noticed, his expression softened.

"Are you critically injured?" Cardinal Jusipini stepped forward.

"No," Eduardo said, "but I may have a concussion." He walked to the bed and sat on the edge, knowing that the Cardinal would heal him, as he had done many times after the visions weakened him. He would heal him, and together they would plan their next move.

Backlit by the window and the setting sun, the cardinal stepped forward and came to the bed. "Let me assess the damage." He reached out to touch Eduardo with his healing hands, but Eduardo was assaulted by a vision and recoiled. For the first time, Eduardo feared this man of God. It became clear to him suddenly. He was expendable. The cardinal had no intention of healing him this time. If the head injury wasn't critical, it soon would be, and the power of prophesy would be passed on.

Eduardo's military instincts took over. He kicked out with his feet, propelling the cardinal away from him. With rapid speed, he pulled out his gun, aimed, and fired a killing shot before the good cardinal could utter a sound.

He'd seen the cardinal bleed many many times, but never from his heart. He looked on as the red stain spread over the cardinal's robes a few feet below the holy man's vacant stare. "If you had prophesy, Cardinal, you would have seen that coming."

The Cardinal's eyes widened slightly before he expelled his last breath.

Eduardo stripped the man of his belt, including the coins nestled there in the secret pocket. When he strapped the belt around his waist, his whole body vibrated with a supernatu-ral, electric energy, assaulting every one of Eduardo's senses. He felt sensations he did not know he could feel. Staggering from the room, he knew he had to find a place to lay low, to heal, and to acclimate to this onslaught of phenomenal power.

Father Alexander's office, Monastery of St. John, Patmos, Greece, June 5, 2032

David felt the muscles in his neck soften at the thought of returning to Mexico. Celia booked their flight while the professor wrote a vision in his notebook, which was quite full by now.

Despite his heavy heart over only finding two coins on tweedle-dee and tweedle-dum in the van yesterday, David was ready to go back to Palenque. Madeira would be safe there, even though she scoffed every time he said that.

If Salim and Delzel were to be believed, Eduardo had two coins, one of them Melik's. The cardinal had ten coins. David tried to imagine what it must feel like to have all that power. Even with all the gifts the cardinal had, Selim had explained, he didn't have visions and relied on Eduardo to guide him. Getting Melik's coin had been part of the plan. They surmised the coin would act as a conduit, a connec-tion to Melik, and perhaps intensify the clarity of Eduardo's visions. They left Melik alive to attempt to track Celia and discover the location of the hidden cavern and the rest of the coins.

The monks were guarding Melik, Selim, and Delzel right now in the infirmary while Celia booked their flights.

David said, "I'm still not comfortable with the plan."

Professor Delaney looked up from his work.

David raised his hand to stave off any protest. "I know we all agreed last night to do this, but I worry you're putting too much stock in my powers. Plus, we've been flying by the seat of our pants. When you let your pants do the flying, you're bound to get your ass kicked."

"My visions are very clear, now, David. You can stop worrying and trust me. It's true, we've been fumbling around for months, piecing together hunches and clues and getting lucky. I know what God is asking now, I do, and I'm asking you to have faith in it."

Celia said, "There are no more bad-guys to fight, save for Eduardo now. You saw the news report of the cardinal's death yourself. It's time to get our hands on the last coins and that has to be done in Palenque. Just as Eduardo planned to use Melik as bait to capture us, we'll use Melik as bait to capture Eduardo. Better to have this battle where friends can help us."

"Except that he's crazy," David said. "Unpredictable. He has military training and visions. What do we have but a bunch of misfits and misguided monks?"

"Hey," the professor said. "Us misfits and monks have done pretty well so far."

"All the coins are accounted for," Celia said. "There's no more to find and no place left to go but where all the documents and clues have lead us, back to Mexico."

David sat in one of Father Alexander's cozy chairs. "We'll need to keep Melik in the dark as long as we can. We don't want to alert Eduardo to where we are prematurely. And any tricks or plans you two have will need to be kept from him, too."

"I can put Melik to sleep at will if we need to keep things from him," Celia said.

"That's a handy skill," David said. "We might need that as a secret weapon."

CHAPTER 16

Debiaxo Cavern, Palenque, Mexico, June 7, 2032

Ryan sat down at the Flintstone table in the cavern beneath the Palenque ruins, safely back in Mexico. They had recalled the other teams and regrouped here in Debiaxo. Melik, Selim, and Delzel were at the hotel, guarded by Hector's brother and Father Alexander.

The remaining thirteen in their group were talking about Eduardo, trying to figure out how they were going to stop him when he came for their coins to complete the set of thirty.

"Look," Cardinal Margrave said. "If Eduardo is as dangerous as you say, and as determined as we think, we need to be prepared for war. I wouldn't put it past him to drop a bomb on Palenque and sift through the ruins later. You said he blew up a portion of Pergamon?"

"That's right," David said. "And this guy has a military background. And, he's fucking nuts, too, demented by the coins and God knows in what state of mind."

Madeira had been quiet up until now, but she commented in a thoughtful voice, "Eduardo will need to gather up new forces now that you've disabled Delzel and Salim, David. He won't come alone and he won't risk getting close to you now. You have the ability to ruin all he has sought to achieve with the touch of your hands and a few words. Your power, your gift, could change everything and he knows it. Evil knows the power of God and is adept at evading its touch.

"I would have liked to get a read on Eduardo, to see if he's like Melik at all." She sighed and looked away. "Maybe he has some good in him somewhere…" She let the thought trail off.

The air was heavy with nerves and worry. Ryan wished he could think of the right words to calm everyone, to give them a taste of the spiritual strength he received from his two episodes at the Cave of the Apocalypse.

"Eduardo knows we're in Mexico, but he doesn't know how to find this cave and, if he does drop a bomb on Palenque, those in refuge here will be safe." All of a sudden, Ryan remembered his first vision of Palenque upon arriving here the first time, his premonition of the hotel in flames. At the time, he had assumed the devastation would be a result of the predicted fires from heaven, but now he wasn't so sure. It's possible the damage he foresaw might be caused by Eduardo.

He shared his concern with the group.

"We should bring everyone to the cave," Madeira suggested.

David said, "We don't know if we can trust Melik, Selim, and Delzel. What if they aren't meant to be chosen?"

She argued, "Who are you to decide who's saved? Besides, you've cured them. Don't you trust me or trust your own gift?"

David said, "Trust doesn't come easily to me, Madeira. It's a hard habit to break."

Ryan said, "The monks at St. Johns are scouring the library there to see if they missed some reference to the chosen. We should do the same here. There has to be some clue we've missed to understand how this discernment works. Madeira's right. At some point we need to trust our gifts."

"Well," David said. "Maybe if I pour over our notes and documents again, I can find something."

Hector said, "The system at the hotel is completely updated with all our data, including the recent information you transmitted two days ago, as well as some documents uncovered in India by team three." He stood, laughed, and said, "Oh, man, are you gonna be loving me when you see this!"

"What?" David smiled. "What'd you do?"

"I'll be right back and show you," he answered, like an excited teenager before the prom. He dashed off down one of the many extensions of the intricate labyrinth.

"What is it?" Ryan asked.

Cardinal Margrave said, "I'm not spoiling it. He's been dying to show you and David."

Hector skipped back into the room holding a giant, leather

bound book.

David jumped up and moved closer. "What is this?"

"My cousin, he collects old printers. He's an artist, you know. Anyway, he showed me how to use this old hand-cranked press and how to make plates."

He extended the book to them with great pride on his face.

Ryan couldn't help smiling at him. "Christmas in June in Mexico." He had grown so fond of everyone here.

"Ho ho ho, dude, open it," Hector said, putting the book in Ryan's hands. "The leather cover was made by my uncle who has a cattle ranch not far from here."

"Get out!" David said, running his hand over the thick leather, stamped with the words, "Thirty Pieces," in several languages.

"The cardinal, he told me how to translate the cover. The rest is in English, though," Hector said. "I have the press here in the cavern, want to see it?"

"You brought the press here?" David opened the book.

Despite the hand-made exterior, the inside had a three-ring binder. Each page, printed on very thick paper, has small wafer-stickers around the holes.

"Yeah, I brought it here. We'll need something to do if we're stuck down here later and the world has ended," Hector said, so matter-of-factly that Ryan wasn't sure he had heard him correctly. "Especially if there's no electricity, or satellites. You should see the area we've constructed for the animals."

"Animals?" Celia asked.

"Well, we can't save all of them," Hector said. "But most of them, the ones that aren't dangerous-"

His voice trailed off when he saw the astonished looks on their faces.

Celia put a hand on Hector's shoulder. "Wow."

Ryan hadn't thought of the animals. "Hector's ark," he said.

"Uh, Hector," Celia made a face. "Do you plan to have howler monkeys down here?"

Ryan tried not to laugh at her pained expression.

"Of course," Hector said. "Wouldn't be Palenque without howler monkeys."

"No, I guess it wouldn't," she agreed with a grin.

Ryan returned his attention to the artful book. "Hector," he said, running his fingers appreciatively over the pages. "This is truly amazing."

Hector stood a bit taller, puffing out his chest.

"Can you do this with my journal?"

"Sure can," Hector said. "May take a while, but it can be done."

Ryan nodded. "New age scrolls. This book may be read for ages and ages if we succeed and record all we've learned."

They were quiet a moment, each contemplating the severity of what was to come. Will this be remembered as their last supper? The question was, who was the sacrificial lamb?

David followed Hector into the hidden office in a utility closet at the back of the hotel.

"Pablo and I've made sure to record every message transmitted from all the teams, including phone messages and texts."

"Texts?" David asked.

"Yeah, that's what's so great about these devices. Well," he said, turning and shutting the door, "I don't need to tell you. You set them up."

He sure did. That meant all the personal texts between Madeira and David were on Hector's computer somewhere and recorded in the book he put together. He could imagine a few thousand years from now, some poor schmuck reading The Gospels of David the lovelorn. Was this why the Catholic Church edited and approved all materials deemed "credible" for the public? Probably not.

He was trying to think of how to delete the texts when Pablo knocked, walked in, and said, "Hector, your cousin is here to see you."

Hector lifted his chin. "Which one?" He put down the mail he was reading.

"The loco one," Pablo said, laughing.

Hector smiled at David and said, "That don't narrow it down much, amigo."

He may pretend to be just any ordinary Mexican guy whose family owned and ran the villa here in Palenque, but David knew better. Hector had many layers. He's the kind of onion David would pick at any market, anywhere. "Go ahead, Hector, I'll be fine here," he told him, bending his head to scour the data they had amassed.

It took him only a moment to get lost in page after page of information that Hector had accumulated in the weeks since they left Mexico. He could sit here all day reading this stuff; it was fascinating. Each and every team met with their own adventures, obstacles, and experienced their own divine miracles as they went out gathering coins, just like they did. David scrolled through, wondering what the hell they were going to do with all this? Somehow, somewhere, with some rhyme or reason, all these events fit together - there had to be a pattern, an answer, a solution to the puzzle. There couldn't just be more clues and random mishaps. His scientific brain said that wasn't the case, but he couldn't help but wonder, when would the burning bush appear and the voice say, "Here's the point!"

He rubbed his eyes and laughed as he remembered that he had signed on to this quest as research assistant to the professor. Served him right.

He stepped out into the hallway when he heard several heated voices coming from the main office. They were speaking Spanish, but something in the tone and the manner of the talk made him pause.

Creeping up to the doorway, he caught a glimpse of Hector being held at gunpoint by some crazy Mexican guy in an orange shirt. Ducking out of sight, David retreated down a secondary hall to the resort's lobby, waving his arms frantically to signal to Pablo who was on the phone.

After a moment, Pablo jogged over to David.

"The cousin's got a gun," David said. "Pointed right at Hector."

Pablo froze. He hadn't been mixed up with all the shit David had seen and done lately, so he had no experience with lunatics. He was about to get a crash course.

David grabbed him by the shirt collar. "I need you to distract him, make sure his back stays to me, so I can manage him."

"Manage him? Man, what are you talking about?" Pablo said.

"Just trust me," he grunted, releasing Pablo's collar, grabbing him by the sleeve, and dragging him down the hall. "Get him to turn his back to the door," he insisted, as they got closer. "Distract him." He ducked behind a trash barrel and tried to breathe as quietly as possible.

From where he was hiding, he could see the room through the crack between the wall and the trash can.

"Que pasa?" Pablo shouted as he walked right in. Not how David would have chosen to make an entrance, but it worked.

The armed man turned and, after catching sight of Pablo, directed him to stand next to Hector with the tip of his gun.

"Hector," Pablo said, "What is this about?"

"You've been holding out on me, Hector," the gunman taunted in English. "You planning to give your friend here a cut, too?"

"I already told you, Carmine," Hector said. "There's no hidden treasure."

Carmine went on a rampage in Spanish which David couldn't follow, and then said, "Then why is some gringo asshole gathering every able-bodied Mexican to find it, eh?" He laughed. "I don't need any stupid Italian to lead us to treasure when my cousin owns a hotel right here, right? Nothing happens in Palenque without you knowing, Hector."

Pablo said, "What Italian?"

David started to crawl into the room on his hands and knees as soon at Carmine, the gunman, was facing the other way.

Hector explained to Pablo, "Some guy named Eduardo's looking for a demolition crew to help him unearth hidden treasure."

David froze when he heard Eduardo's name. He was here already? That wasn't good. They weren't even remotely prepared.

Hector said, "If I had a nickel for every Indiana Jones wannabe who came here looking for treasure, I'd be rich, eh?"

"Yeah, well," Carmine said. "He knows about that coin you have on your keychain. And he says there are thousands of others, plus gold and fortune, buried under one of the temples."

Eduardo may be coin-crazed, he may be a possessed lunatic on a killing spree blowing up ancient temples, but it was clear to David now as he tried to figure out how to get to Carmine without being caught, that they may have underestimated their adversary considerably. By enlisting a bunch of hungry, poor, undereducated Mexican troops, Eduardo could easily build himself a dispensable army of treasure-crazed demolition experts and trained killers without even having to come near them himself. Not as crazy as one may think.

Hector spotted David and continued to engage Carmine. "Really," Hector said. "Which temple?"

"Exactly why I'm here," Carmine answered him, lowering his gun a fraction. "To ask you."

Taking a slight step forward, Hector moved just a hair, drawing Carmine's attention straight ahead and not behind him where David was creeping closer. Hector said, "If there

"Ok, then," David said. "We'll need to try this out on his men first, before we'll know if it'll work on Eduardo."

Temple of Inscriptions, Palenque, Mexico, June 8, 2032

Wedged into the corner of the small room inside the temple of inscriptions next to Celia, they were so close together David could smell her soap and the faint hint of toothpaste on her breath.

"The professor's gonna be jealous," he teased.

"Hardly," she peered around him, glancing up the stair-way.

"What, I'm not good enough to be a threat?"

"You're fine," she moved back and pressed against the wall again.

"Fine?" he said. "That's insulting."

"No," she nudged him with her shoulder. "That's not what I meant."

"Yeah, yeah," he smiled. "Just admit it, I'm not your type."

"You're exactly my type." She swatted at a bug and said, "If I had a son, I'd want him to be just like you."

"Would you?" He gave a short laugh. "I'm not so sure about that."

She looked him dead in the eye without blinking and said, "I'm sure about that."

This moved him deeply, but he wasn't about to admit it. "So you're saying I'm too young for you."

"Not too young," she bumped him with her shoulder again. "Too cocky. Now, be quiet, or they'll hear us."

He changed his voice to a whisper. She was right. They

should be quiet. It was just easier for him to talk when he was nervous. "I hope he doesn't bring more than five guys. If he brings too many, we'll be like sardines in here. Plus, this may not work."

"It'll work," she whispered back.

"How do you know?"

"Because even though you're cocky, and too young, you're clever and, so far, you've been right on target."

"Flattery? See, you're flirting with me," he moved back closer to her when he thought he heard footsteps. "Careful, or I'll tell the professor."

"Shush," she said.

They were coming. "Don't forget, hold onto me. We need to be touching."

She grabbed his shoulders and mumbled against his sleeve, "Now who's flirting?"

He heard, rather than saw, the first of the soldier's footfalls. Inhaling for all he was worth, he braced himself for action.

Did he need to say it? Or, could he just think it? Did he really need to speak the words, "I cast you out?"

As an armed and uniformed man stepped into view, he saw them right away.

"Hey!" David said, with his hands in the air. "Whoa, what's going on? Somebody rob a tomb or something?"

The soldier ordered, "All civilians upstairs. This is a military matter." He gripped his gun in front of him and jerked it toward the steps.

But as David remembered from their earlier visit to this room, it was difficult to pass up the stairway when people were coming down. That was what he had counted on.

He remained standing where he was with his hands up. Celia pretended to cower behind him, her hands on his shoulders as they skirted around the new arrivals. Thank God, there were five, just as they'd planned, with Carmine taking up the rear, followed by Madeira, their supposed hostage. He heard Carmine shout, "What's the hold up?"

The man up front turned and shouted in Spanish.

Madeira said, "Well, move over and let them pass." Talking about David and Celia.

One man said, "Shut up, Bitch," and it took every effort not to jump him and beat him to a pulp.

They were counting on the men not knowing what Celia and David looked like. If Eduardo had pictures, their plan would fail. The idea was for David to try his powers on a group with Celia touching him to stem the after-effects of his gift. The close quarters assured a better opportunity to get everybody within touching distance for the gift to carry across multiple persons. It was a long shot. The thinking was, if David couldn't change their behavior by removing fear, greed, and hatred, then Celia might have a shot at putting the armed ones to sleep with her gift.

As they predicted, the men grouped together at the end of the steps. Carmine, now working in cahoots with them, stopped on the second-to-last stair and said to Madeira, "Get in."

That was her cue. In an Oscar-worthy performance, she fake stumbled in her short skirt and heels down the last three steps, falling breast-first into the throng of unsuspecting soldiers. Like clockwork, they lowered their weapons to catch her and, as they did, David reached in to help, touched the closest soldier, focused with every molecule in his mind and silently screamed, "I cast you out."

Unlike all previous times, the only sensation he had when the energy and gravity hit him was the scalding touch of Celia's hot hands on his body. Her energy burned through his energy, which burned through the man next to him, through him to Madeira as a conduit, and to each of the four other soldiers holding her. He could almost see the strands reaching out, like you could see water evaporate on a hot sidewalk. He had no idea what the soldiers were feeling as they froze, like someone startled, their muscles tense, their hearts beating loudly, adrenaline rushing. David watched the shock dissipate as fear, hatred, greed, and other demons evacuated the room; replaced with calm, peace, and solemn vagueness – like newborn babies.

A forest clearing, near the ruins of Palenque, Mexico, June 8, 2032

"Remember," Celia said to the small army in front of her. "We just need to get David close enough to Eduardo without him suspecting."

She couldn't believe she was standing there, in a remote area of the forest, addressing a small Mexican army, and giving advice about how to capture a crazed lunatic. When she reflected on her life, it seemed impossible that she was doing this. Everything from the moment Jeff got sick, until now, was a blur. And her life felt twisted, like taffy on a pull - the past, present, and future all mixing up into something that she hoped would taste sweet in the end.

Celia had a hunch. It seemed they had been most successful when they joined together, their coins and gifts working in harmony, no power play, no hoarding of power. The term "communion of saints" popped in her head, although none of them, certainly, were saints.

Ryan placed his hand on the small of her back. "Let's review the steps again," he said. "I want to make sure no one will get hurt when the explosives go off."

Celia stared at him as if seeing him for the first time again. He had changed. Not just the small career and life changes she saw in him when she found him on campus in April. This change was monumental. When they were young, and dating, he was still striving, going somewhere he couldn't define, looking for something he couldn't comprehend - but knew was out there waiting. That drive, that longing, was something Celia couldn't fulfill. No one could - no earthly person, at least. She understood that now, but hadn't then.

She remembered how abandoned she felt, how small and passed over. Who could have known that the priesthood would not be where Ryan found his place? Rather, he had realized his purpose, under God, right here in Mexico, beside her. Go figure.

Ryan said to the confused soldiers recently altered by David in the cave, "You've been given a gift from God, freed from all the things that lead you away from grace. This state is a blessing, and is only a taste of the promise of heaven to come. Join with us and you'll have riches beyond anything promised to you by Eduardo or anybody else, I promise you that."

Celia said, "You all need to keep your minds clear. If Eduardo suspects treachery, we're in trouble and heaven will be lost. There'll be chaos and suffering, natural disasters, and more. We can't even imagine the consequences of failure."

One of the men in front says, "If Eduardo has visions, as you have said, how can we prevent him from seeing what we're planning."

"I can help," she told them. "If any of you are unsure whether you can clear your minds, step over here."

All fourteen soldiers stepped over. She laughed. "Okay then, one at a time."

Ryan rubbed her back and said, "Good luck. I'm going to walk through some logistics with Hector."

"Go ahead," she said.

When Ryan stepped away, she called the first soldier forward. "C'mon, I won't bite."

He was an older man with craggy skin weathered by the sun. His brown eyes twinkled when he stepped near. "You can bite, if you want. I can take it."

She snapped her teeth at him playfully and the other soldiers relaxed and laughed. They could look down the nose of a rifle and duck from enemy fire without pause, but tell them God's going to heal them, and loves them, and they quiver with doubt. Her calming would clear their heads, yoga for the brain. Eduardo would not discern or visualize anything from these men's thoughts when she was done with them.

White Skin House, Palenque, Mexico, June 10, 2032

"We have to stop meeting like this," David said, as he stretched out on the ground of one of the smaller temple ruins in the Palace at Palenque, and Celia settled on top of him.

"Shut up," she replied, moving her shoulders to the side so she could rest her head on her hand, her elbow planted in the dirt. "This was Ryan's idea."

"Professor Delaney's twisted."

She laughed. "Let's hope not. Let's hope his vision is right."

"If it is, God definitely has a sense of humor." He tried to ignore the warmth of her thighs resting on his. "If I die today, this is the way to go."

"You're incorrigible." She said, shaking her head.

He smiled.

"Seriously, are you ready?"

"I was born ready," he said.

"Can you stop being flippant?"

He shook his head no. "What fun is that? Besides, I trust you, Celia. I followed you here and you've saved my ass before. You can do this. You have to. Do you think Eduardo will take the bait?"

"I think so. You were very convincing when talking to Melik about the underground passageways here," she said. "You even had me believing there was a secret cavern beneath the Palace."

"There may be."

"I hope we're doing the right thing," she said.

"No worries." He smiled. "God is with us, I can feel it."

She looked at him long and hard, then said, "I was thinking yesterday about how much Ryan's changed these past weeks, but I think you've changed most of all."

"Change is over-rated. I prefer, 'evolved'."

She rolled her eyes. The phone in her pocket vibrated and made him tense up underneath her. That was the signal: four minutes until blastoff.

He winked. "It's never dull around you, is it?"

She laughed. "Five years ago, if you looked up 'dull' in the dictionary, you would have found my picture there."

He said, "I doubt it."

She said, "Oh, you're right. I lay on top of guys every weekend waiting for someone to blow up a temple on top of us, then I order pizza and vacuum the house."

He looked at his watch. "I'm counting on you to be very un-dull in about 3.2 minutes."

She nodded.

"Good luck." David closed his eyes. He prayed with a genuineness he would never have imagined two months ago. Celia was right, he had changed. And even if he died today, he thanked God for this adventure; He had never felt more alive, useful, and needed. No one had ever needed him before. No one had ever, in his whole life, expected anything from him before now. It felt good.

Celia lowered her cheek onto his left shoulder and planted her elbows on either side of his head so her hands formed a teepee over David's face protectively. As she breathed, her soft exhalations relaxed him. His prayers fell into the rhythm of her breathing, her head rising and falling with his chest as he also took in air and let it out.

This was a crazy plan. The soldiers were going to detonate a small explosion on a select portion of the temple, supposedly uncovering a passageway to the hidden cavern. David and Celia were going to play possum, Celia intending to protect them from harm with her healing and then fooling Eduardo by altering their pulse so he would think they were dead. All they needed was to convince him long enough to make physical contact so David could exorcise his demons or maybe Celia could knock him out with her sleeping spell or whatever she did. It was just crazy enough, maybe, to catch an insane person possessed, wielding God's mighty gifts, and, hopefully, carrying a handful of coins that would save the world.

She closed her eyes. David's chest rose and fell, soothing her into a deep trance. She sensed God all around them in the ancient structure, in the ground, in the air, and in her. She tried not to think about what would happen if they succeeded. She tried not to think of what would happen if they failed.

Whatever happened, she welcomed it. She embraced it.

Summoning her gift, she channeled energy from all around her and used it to protect herself and David. When the blast hit, it felt as though it was far away, outside the protective bubble of force surrounding them. She didn't feel pain, fear, nor did she feel the rocks as they landed all around them. All she felt was the electric sizzle of her exertion, a jolting charge all over her body, and the heat of David's body underneath her.

David's breath was stolen from him when Celia ignited

her power. She sucked all the air from around them, creating a black hole, right here, in the temple in Mexico.

He panicked when he couldn't inhale. The force of her efforts was strangling him.

The stones pummeled her body. He felt the impact shake her. He was slipping away, blacking out for lack of air. He couldn't! He needed to be conscious when Eduardo and the others dug them out.

FIGHT! Breathe, damn-it!

From far away, he could hear the detonation reverberating over the hills from the explosion. The ground trembled as the structure fell. In the echo of the noise, around the drumming of his thoughts, there came a voice. It wasn't Celia's. It wasn't his mother's. It wasn't God's. It was Madeira's. He could see her in his mind's eye, back in the cave when they first found it weeks ago, washing off his puke and telling him, "Fear is our enemy," as she squeezed the water from her hair. "Choose the path of fear, and you choose wrongly."

If he died today, here in Palenque, among the Mayan ruins where the end of the world was predicted on the very day he was born, it would be a good death. He would do it to save the world. He would do it for his son. He would do it for his God.

David stopped fighting and let go of his fear.

C'mon, David, come around.

Celia heard the men picking through the rubble, talking in Spanish, and Italian, and English.

One of them shouted, "Mira!" Look.

They had found a coin, one of the decoys they planted to throw off Eduardo. Would he notice it was ordinary? Would he see through the farce?

She moved her fingers around to David's throat and felt for a pulse. He was alive, but out cold.

C'mon!

She was afraid to heal him with Eduardo this close, not wanting to tip him off.

She heard Carmine say, "The passage should be towards the back."

The soldiers were very convincing, and Carmine, as ring-leader, most of all. David cured them of their demons, freed them from their doubts, fears, and disbelief when he used his gift in the temple two days ago. Then, Ryan shared their plan, and she taught them how to pull off the deception, how to heal their minds from unwanted thoughts. She was impressed by their ability to pull this off, as much as she was counting on it.

Selim, Delzel, and Melik had been escorted with blind-folds to the real cavern the night before so they would not know how to get there, and so that Eduardo could not tap into their knowledge. All they knew was that they were somewhere in Palenque at the Mayan ruins underground.

One of the soldiers, just as planned, uncovered Celia's leg. They had done an amazing job setting the explosion so that the temple crumbled away, not landing entirely on her and David. Or maybe she had done that, as she had in Turkey during the earthquake, she wasn't sure. "Someone's here!" the soldier shouted in English as they uncovered her and

David's bodies.

Good. Keep up the ruse.

C'mon, David.

Nothing.

Then, as several men shouted, "Coins!" noticing additional decoys they planted around themselves, the skies rumbled. She tried not to move, and couldn't figure out what was happening.

One man shouted, "El Chichón!"

She had no idea what that meant, but before she could think further, the sky darkened and the soldiers stepped away, shouting.

She took the opportunity to act. With her face still pressed against David's chest, she summoned restorative energy.

The ground shook. Was this another earthquake?

As the energy surrounded her, she heard Eduardo's name called out and someone said, "Forget the Volcano! Grab the coins, you idiots!"

"Don't move," the voice murmured.

Where was he? And why were hands covering his eyes?

"Be still," Celia whispered. Then he remembered.

David breathed in and started choking.

Shit.

A man's voice said, "Someone's alive in there."

Another voice said, "Get out of the way!"

David felt Celia's body shift as someone pulled stones off

of her and then moved her over to his left, uncovering him.

This was all planned, but something was wrong.

Rather than the calm and methodical search for an entrance to a fictional underground cavern, all David could hear was bedlam.

"We need to act quickly before the ash covers everything!" someone shouted.

Ash? What the hell?

"Get her off him," another voice said.

Celia's body was jerked aside, but he could feel her hand lying next to his. He had already ruined their cover by coughing, so he opened his eyes. No use pretending to be dead now.

In the sky, he could see a giant mushroom of black forming. A volcano! Oh shit, is this the fire that was coming? He coughed again as the dust from the temple assaulted his lungs.

In silhouette, standing a distance away, he saw a figure. Above each shoulder, a bird, one black and one white. The figure spoke. "It's you, from the van. You have nine lives."

Eduardo.

David didn't respond.

Carmine said, "The entrance is under him."

"Get him up!" Eduardo shouted to the men, keeping his distance. He was smart enough to stay out of reach.

David and Carmine locked eyes.

The earth rumbled again as the volcano spit more ash into the sky.

David put his elbows under him. "The coins," he said, trying to reason with Eduardo, to gain his trust. If he couldn't get close enough to use his gift, maybe he could use psychology, put his college education to work in his favor. "Their powers are too much for one person, Eduardo. You must know that. I can see that they are tormenting you."

Eduardo moved cautiously, pulling his gun out and pointing it at David. The sun broke through the ash for a brief moment and shone on him. David saw the man's wrists were bleeding.

David said, "If you want to save the world, Eduardo, you can do it. You can fulfill the prophecy. But not by killing. God doesn't reward murder, Eduardo. Murder is a sin."

Eduardo seemed confused. He shook his head several times and mumbled to himself, although the gun remained steady in his hands. David wished he could hear what the man was saying, but the noise coming from the mountain, the soldiers, and the forest was interfering.

He sat up, and Eduardo yelled, "Stay where you are!"

Carmine continued to pick up the decoy coins, working his way closer to Eduardo. "I'm getting the coins before the ash does."

Several of the soldiers that Eduardo brought with him were ones that David had purified with his gifts in the temple. They were now fearless, freed from hate, freed from greed, empowered with God's love. Celia had trained them to clear their minds so Eduardo would not know their plan. David noticed they were slowly surrounding Eduardo, their guns aimed at David, a disguise of solidarity with their deranged leader.

Eduardo kicked at the ground, connecting with Carmine's hand. "These coins are useless, you moron. The real treasure is underneath!"

David moved closer to Celia so that his leg touched hers. She was still pretending to be dead. If David hadn't known better, he would've believed she was. He didn't know what to do now that their plan was ruined. He had to be near Celia, touching her. He had to be ready.

Eduardo pointed his gun at Carmine. "Stop what you're doing." He glanced at David. "Forget the coins. Restrain the boy."

Carmine stepped back, positioning himself between Eduardo and David.

The soldiers took their opportunity to act and moved forward, forcing Eduardo closer.

"Back away from me you idiots!" Eduardo shouted as he tried to resist the wall of his own army, moving him ever closer to his adversary. Just like when Celia used her powers earlier, David felt the air around him shift, but Celia wasn't using her powers now, Eduardo was. He put his arms wide and the men around him began to tremble and falter. Blood started forth from Eduardo's head, dripping into his eyes as stigmata kicked in.

Who is he healing? David was confused, until he realized that Eduardo wasn't healing, he was inflicting damage.

Celia stirred, responding to Eduardo's surge of power. She sat up and grabbed David's hand, just as Carmine lunged at Eduardo.

Eduardo's arms came together in one swift motion, despite the power he had been expending, and his military instincts took over. He shot Carmine in the head while the other soldiers converged, still moving him forward.

Eduardo swiped with his arm, trying to get the blood out of his eyes, and shot blindly at David, missing, stumbling over Carmine's fallen body. The earth trembled as the volcano coughed and spat. The soldiers shoved him forward, the blood flowing from his wrist weakening his grip on the pistol. The pistol slipped to the ground and Eduardo fell onto David, driving him into the earth as El Chichón spewed blackness toward the heavens.

David's breath was knocked from him, but he pulled forth his skills, embraced God's power, and said, "I cast you out!" as the volcano echoed with a mighty roar.

Eduardo was convulsing slightly, like someone who just finished electric shock treatment. Celia sat up, still rebounding from David's act, from healing him, and trying to orient herself with all that was happening. She looked at Eduardo, suffering, sweating, and recovering from whatever David had done to him. He was covered in blood, both from the stigmata and from shooting Carmine.

Celia acted quickly, not waiting to see if he was "cured" or still dangerous. She knocked him out with her gift, and then grabbed the satchel tied to his belt loop and pulled it hard. The ten coins in it burned her palm. The volcano burped and bellowed and then erupted with intense energy.

Celia looked up to see a ball of fire falling a hundred yards or so from them.

"Christ," she said.

Her body began to pulsate, the combined energy of the

coins expanding her lungs and making her feel like she was swelling. Her muscles ached and her head started pounding.

A craggy old soldier held Carmine's lifeless body. "Heal him," he implored.

"I can't," she said, standing, putting the coins in her pocket with a trembling hand. "There are some things I can't do."

"Try," he pleaded.

She knew it was impossible. She couldn't resurrect anyone. Saving the baby had been a fluke. She had been moved by all the pain of having lost her own child. Still, she could feel the power of the coins emanating from her, and wondered, if she grabbed them all, could she heal Carmine? It was compelling to try.

"He was my nephew," the old soldier said.

Her skin was on fire and her nerves felt exposed. The temptation to use the combined power of the coins was intense. It was the rumbling of the volcano and the sight of another ball of fire soaring across the sky that brought her to her senses. She yelled to David, "Quick, let's get to the cave," then she ordered the soldiers, "grab Carmine's body and Eduardo and follow me."

They struggled under the weight of Carmine's dead body and Eduardo's unconscious one. It was only a fifteen-minute walk to Debiaxo under normal circumstances, but these were not normal circumstances.

Celia and David led the way with their recently converted army, and at least a dozen others who came with Eduardo and were panicked and confused by the turn of events. Most were local folks, poor farmers promised money, now scrambling for the promise of shelter from the erupting volcano.

The multitude struggled to keep pace with Celia, and she had to slow and pause several times while they maneuvered the rocks and pathways carrying bodies.

"You're covered in sweat," David said.

Celia nodded, unable to explain the physiological turmoil happening in her body as the coins in her pocket throbbed, confused, weakened, and invigorated all at once. Twice, giant flaming boulders came dangerously close, fire from heaven, creating panic and haste.

Not only was she sweating, she hadn't stopped trembling since she placed Eduardo's coins in her pocket. This was momentous. Thirty coins paid to betray Christ, scattered over two-thousand years ago, would shortly be reunited, by her, amid chaos and an erupting volcano. The power of the coins surrounded her, fueled by adrenaline and exertion. She fought to keep her wits about her as another flaming boulder landed to her left, igniting a dead tree and starting a fire a dozen yards away.

Several times, sparks or smaller projectiles from the volcano landed on someone and Celia healed them, trying to quench the urge to touch the coins, to bond with them, to make them hers.

Beyond a flaming tree, she saw Madeira, Ryan, Cardinal Margrave, Father Alexander, and Renata standing at the entrance to Debiaxo.

"We have the coins," she said.

Catching Madeira's confused expression, Celia turned and took a good look at the melee following her up the hill, including the two bloodied bodies being carried, one dead, and the other their sworn enemy. Who should come inside with them?

"Madeira," she said. "Can you and Father Alexander discern these people?"

Madeira nodded, but Celia noticed all the color drain from the young girl's face.

David stepped up and made a suggestion. "Good colors to the left, others to the right."

Madeira nodded again, and she and Father Alexander went to work.

Almost everybody passed their inspection, with only two of the pack on the right. Madeira said, "This one's dead," with tears in her eyes.

"I know," Celia said. "He comes."

"What about Eduardo?" David asked.

Madeira shook her head. "Too many colors, I can't tell. And Celia," she said. "You're lit up like a Christmas tree."

"It's the coins." Celia's heart was beating double-time. She wasn't sure what to do with the ones who didn't pass. Maybe David could fix them? Was there time for that?

In answer, several more flaming boulders shot across the sky. She made a rash decision. "Everybody inside," she said.

David threw her a panicked look.

"Everybody. It'll be okay." She turned without further argument and pushed her way past Ryan, Madeira and Renata to the entry to Debiaxo.

CHAPTER 17

Debiaxo, cavern under the Palenque Ruins, Mexico,
June 10, 2032

A knot of anticipation wrapped itself around Ryan's upper intestines as he followed Celia down the stairs to the cavern below Palenque.

El Chichón was erupting, whether in jubilation or rage, he didn't know.

He smelled sulphur. Warm air blew through the ruins – hot breath from the mountain. The ash covered Palenque in the 1980's. Would it do the same again? What kind of world would they find when they emerged?

For a group of almost fifty, they were eerily quiet as they marched in solemn unison, like ants, their many feet brushing the cavern floor. Celia took the lead, as she had done since he first met her. She looked pale and sick. Sweat covered her, and he was concerned by her body tremors and ticks. He followed protectively, making sure the soldiers stayed in step, thinking about what Celia said to David a few days ago when they prepared to return to Mexico. "There are no more bad guys to fight. No more coins to unearth."

That may be true, but this wasn't the end of the adventure. He felt it in each hair standing on end on the back of his neck. This was the beginning. But of what?

One of Celia's hands was wrapped around the satchel of coins in her pocket, the other rubbed the coin hanging around her neck. "Madeira," she said. "Gather ten people with the brightest colors who don't have coins. Everyone else with a coin, make a circle."

They were standing in the largest area of the open cavern. Celia could hear the animals Hector and the others had brought down here, their howls and bleats echoing down the long corridors fanning out through the labyrinth of tunnels and caverns.

She dumped the coins from the satchel onto the ground in order not to touch them. She asked each of the ten people Madeira and Father Alexander identified as the purest souls to take one. She smiled when one of them turned out to be Salvatore.

"Hector," she said, "Help me put Carmine's body in the middle, next to Eduardo. Everybody else stand back, please."

He looked skeptical, but did what she asked. The ones not "chosen" obliged and moved to the far wall, glad to be safe here below ground, no doubt.

She looked around the circle. Twenty-nine, including her.

With a shaky hand, she searched Eduardo for his coin, worried for a moment he may have swallowed it, an obstacle she had not considered until this very moment, but she found the coin in his pant's pocket and exhaled with relief.

The unconscious man lay on his back next to the man he had killed, Carmine. She placed the coin in Eduardo's hand and then joined his hand with Carmine's, already cold and slightly stiff.

Then she stepped back into the circle and nodded to Ryan, who had foreseen this moment in a vision. She was still trembling even though she no longer had all the coins in her pocket. Their combined power pulsed through the room. Could they all feel it, she wondered?

"Join hands," she said, taking David's hand in her left, and Ryan's in her right. When the circle was complete, she said to Cardinal Margrave, who was standing nearest to Eduardo, "Make contact with Eduardo, if you please."

He kicked off his right shoe and placed a stockinged foot on Eduardo's leg, uniting the coins with that simple contact.

A blast of wind hit Celia – as if the air curled up its fist and punched her full force under the chin. She was propelled several yards, all of them shoved by an unseen force, their hands unlinking, the circle broken.

She heard shouts from others as they hit the walls of the

cavern or the ground. A noise, like the sound of a whale crooning, filled the room.

Her ears hurt for a moment as the air pressure shifted. One minute she felt like she was deep underwater, being compressed on all sides. The next, she felt like a balloon, expanding, afraid she would burst into placid, useless fragments.

The air weaved and wobbled in front of her eyes, like she was looking through one of those shower doors with tear-shaped waves on the surface.

She shook her head to clear her view, but it was useless. She squinted.

"Jeff." Her eyes burned as tears built up, further impairing her vision.

"Jeff," she said again, reaching out, knowing that her physical hand was not adequate to touch him, but he was there. And he was holding their child. This place she was glimpsing looked like where she had been in her coma. Was this heaven?

"Ryan?" she said, looking around, wanting to show him. "Ryan, it's Jeff." But she couldn't see Ryan right now. He wasn't there in his white robes like he'd been before. Perhaps he's seeing his own glimpse of heaven, of loved-ones.

Celia felt the pull of time, dimension, and an opening drawing her between. She never knew there was a place in between. But, there was, and she was there, on earth and not – all at once. David had been right, it was possible to see time and dimension in another way, and she was doing it now. She may have been doing it before, in her sleep, when she was in a coma, and times when she allowed herself to let go of what she thought she knew, what she could physically touch, and just was, like when she meditated. It was that rare occurrence when one gave in to that sixth sense, the energy that passes between people and that lingers when people are gone. It was that energy you feel is trapped in crevices of old buildings, that sensation that you have been somewhere before, know someone you only just met, or the flash of a presence of someone who has died.

To say she felt Jeff's warmth and love was wrong. "Feel" was an inadequate word. Words were inadequate. How do you describe the indescribable, the unimagined, or the perfection of this? God said to Moses, "I am." She never understood that, until now. Now, it all made sense to her.

Life was not linear. All that will be, all that ever was, is now and forever, world without end - a circle, complete and connected to everything, to everyone. They had been blessed with a glimpse of heaven, an understanding of cyclical time, knowing for certain, not just guessing, that earthly life is only one part of a spirit's journey. This earthly life was but a blip in time, an experience to be human, one form of an everlasting spiritual adventure.

EPILOGUE

When they recovered from the episode in the cavern, Celia was surprised to find the rumblings of El Chignon had ceased. Ryan dared to emerge and investigate, reporting that the volcano was quiet, but there were several fires ignited by the flaming boulders and ash. In any case, it was safe to emerge.

They had all been altered, renewed, much like Ryan and Celia had in the Cave of the Apocalypse. Including Eduardo, who Madeira defined as having colors as pure as everyone else. "No doubt," she had said, "this was a sign of God's forgiveness in its truest form, a lesson for them to heed and follow example."

Carmine did not come back from the dead as Celia had hoped he would. But after this experience, Celia now knew moving on to the next phase of this spiritual journey was not something to mourn, but to rejoice.

Hours later, after reaching out to other shelters around the world, they understood that the gathering together and joining of hands and coins in the cavern Debiaxo had not just transformed them, it had created a universal enlightenment and produced a mass healing. Their uniting had erased sickness everywhere, of mind and body. This worldwide exorcism cleansed the earth and its people of fear, jealousy, greed, anger, hatred, prejudice and other maladies. All their sources confirmed, from president to pope, that a global phenomenon had occurred. Volcanoes erupted worldwide, all at once. Several hundred people had been killed. Hector's hotel, as Ryan had seen in his vision, had burned to the ground, but

Hector was not concerned with that. He had a new calling now. He had a new life to lead, they all did.

Everybody across the globe had experienced the rapture, had insights into the fourth dimension, had a new enlightened understanding of time. "World without end" was understood. All those loved and gone before were seen, as Jesus was seen after his death, with the understanding that their spirits resided with them, as they would some day reside with others in spiritual form. Eternal life was not something you won, it was something that existed now. Be not afraid. Love one another. Forgive and sin no more. The thirty, and every soul living on the planet when the coins were joined, suddenly understood what Jesus was trying to teach when he walked the earth. All you need, all you'll ever need, has been given you.

Two days later, they stood on the hill by the entrance to Debiaxo where Cardinal Margrave was marrying David and Madeira.

When Celia started out on this quest, she had felt alone. Now she understood that it was through the uninhibited and loving connection to others that one finds God. No one was ever alone. The Divine was within each person, and when people gathered in a united manner, miracles happened, and you connected with the divine in one another. Celia had a bigger family than she could ever have dreamed, a family of humanity with a heavenly father.

The Lord's prayer came to her. These were the words Jesus gave them to say, and all of a sudden they had new meaning. She understood why, even in her darkest hours, even when she was a lapsed person of faith, she still prayed those words before she fell asleep. She must have intuited, all along, deep in her soul, her divine spirit, that the words were not meant as a request to God, but of each other. Feed your neighbor, forgive your brother, clothe those without clothing, shelter those without shelter, forgive mistakes, even your own, choose love over fear, love unconditionally. It was so simple. It had been said before. But it hadn't resonated with her then.

They were all part of each other. That's what she missed. That's what God tried to remind them of when he sent Jesus. Whatever you do unto me. Humans had hurt themselves too long.

The cardinal said, "Do you, David, take Madeira, to be your lawful wife…"

David placed his hand on Madeira's belly, touching the small bulge of life that grew within, as Cardinal Margrave spoke the words Ryan asked him to say on this special day.

"If I give all I possess to the poor and surrender my body to the flames, but have not love, I gain nothing."

Celia smiled at David, at Madeira, at Ryan, and all those who surrounded her now as the cardinal continued, "Love is patient. Love is kind. It does not boast…it keeps no record of wrongs…always perseveres. Love never fails."

They had been given a new start, reborn, free of illness, sin and demons. Each living person was enlightened, had glimpsed the mysteries of the universe, had seen heaven. Eden was here and now. Let's hope no one ate the apple this time around.

THE END

About the Author

G Horgan is an artist and writer. Currently working on her fourth novel, she also writes poetry, short stories, and has written and illustrated a children's book about her son. She loves storytelling and connecting to other people through her words and her art. Her paying career as a Creative Director allows her the opportunity to travel around the country on photo shoots, to write marketing copy, and to design ads and materials that help "sell stuff". When she's not with her family, working, or devoting her energy to raising awareness about Autism, she is usually writing, reading, playing the harp, doing yoga, or thinking about writing, reading, playing the harp, and doing yoga. She lives in Massachusetts with her two children.

words4autism
getcreativesense.com

Made in the USA
Middletown, DE
21 January 2019